THE MAYAN TILES

by
Lauren Zimmerman

Book Two of
OTHER WORLDS: The Series

A story given to the author during a series of dreams
and visitations
from those who live beyond Earth's borders.

Definition:
Maya:
The transitory, manifold appearance of the sensible
world, which obscures the undifferentiated spiritual
reality from which it originates; the illusory appearance
of the sensible world.

AUTHOR'S NOTE

THE MAYAN TILES was written during the 1980's. Now, here we are in 2012, with the energy of great change and a plethora of opportunities for Humanity.

In the years following my promise to follow through, to the end, the creation of OTHER WORLDS: The Series, I've become unmovable in my Knowing that Earth's reality is changing and is going to continue to change. We are not alone. Not by a long-shot. Even if I had not experienced all that I have, I would remain firm in my Knowing that we are sharing this universe with others.

I had no idea what it would take to get here, to 2012 and to this edition of TILES. Had I known there is a good possibility that this book would have vanished into the world of 'we will pretend it never happened.' As I sit here now though, pondering the enormity and significance of this path I've walked, and these books I've written, I cannot regret a moment ... or understate how important to my own infinity that walk has been.

What has taken place and what I've learned, and come to understand, about the 'story' within these books would fill another book entirely. Possibly two. Let me boil it down into a couple of sentences. Long ago, during the Mayan times, an extraterrestrial society brought wisdom from their world to Earth in an attempt to show how to create a world that was in harmonic balance with the rest of the Universe. That wisdom was not acted upon, the receivers of the wisdom died, a new plan for reaching Earth's society had to be created.

2

For centuries those from other worlds have attempted, in various ways to teach Humankind by interacting with them in a variety of ways. This time the plan has changed. The bottom line is that each individual has the ability, and the responsibility, to learn how to live a conscious and aware life with a 100% awareness of not only themselves but all others. 'All' meaning … every person and every thing is an aspect of a Divine and Infinite Existence and therefore matters. Matters greatly. That being said, after intervening repeatedly and yet still seeing the results we see here on the planet today, it became obvious that doing the same old thing was getting the same old results. Meaning, no results at all. Earth's society continues on a self-destruct path unlike anything that could ever take place in a more responsible and caring planetary system.

So what is the new plan? Teach from afar. Bringing their own members of their own society down into this chaos had little to no impact. Not to mention, why risk your own lives and well-being when the reality is that every person has within them the ability to do better, as far as learning to be an aware and responsible being.

Now, here in 2012, the 'energetic doorways' into higher dimensional realms are open, with more opening constantly. Messages and messengers speak to this world daily, in countless ways. From a safe distance, wisdom-keepers offer ancient knowledge and caring, praying that, one by one, people of this society awaken and then turn to help awaken another.

Those from other-world societies are here, without

doubt. But they, as far as I know, do not plan a physical, en-masse' intervention. And why should they? Why should they come to 'our home' to clean up our mess when we are perfectly capable of cleaning up our own mess? There may come a time when they show up en-masse' but if and when they do, it will be because events here threaten the well-being of the rest of the Universe. Personally, I think we are already harming the rest of the Universe. But, those who are wiser stand by and loudly say ... 'You broke it, you fix it. We're giving you that chance.'

On a personal note, as time has passed and I've peeled off enough energy layers to allow myself to get to the answer of why I am writing these books and why I have been approached and had this task asked of me, there is a powerful memory of having been involved with the first attempt to get this wisdom to the people. I was involved before. I am involved again. And existence continues on, allowing the possibility of change and the energy of hope.

ISBN: 9781520742557
Imprint: Independently published

Library of Congress Cataloging-in-Publication Data

Zimmerman, Lauren
The Mayan Tiles/Lauren Zimmerman
p. cm. ---- (Other Worlds: v. 1)

Human-alien encounters—Fiction. 2. Life on other planets—Fiction. 3. Spiritual Fiction

Cover Design, Book Design: Lauren Zimmerman

Published by nLight Press

To Discover Other Books By Lauren Zimmerman
   http://www.nlightpress.com/

Though this book was written in fiction form, many of the events described are actual events. The concept, storyline, and cover art were presented in dream-form to the author. All of the metaphysical aspects of this book are actual experiences and occurrences within the author's personal life.

ACKNOWLEDGMENTS

Through the years and efforts to bring OTHER WORLDS to the world, the list of those I need to thank has grown beyond measure. This work has turned into almost a communal effort of people around the planet, as well as souls from all dimensions. Words fail me. 'Thank you' doesn't seem like enough. To those who have helped me along the way, keeping me going when I didn't think it was possible, my soul says thank you .. thank you. You know who are.

Professional endorsements for

CALLED
The first volume of
OTHER WORLDS: The Series

"This is the novel for which thousands of 'Star
People' all over the world have been waiting -- only they
will know from their personal experiences with the
'Others' that Lauren Zimmerman's provocative work is
fact, not fiction!"
Brad Steiger, author of 'Starborn' and 'UFO Odyssey'

"This is a very important piece of work, coming as it
does during a time of great change in our world and our
acceleration towards the heavens of other worlds. Many
of us have not overlooked the significance of events
occurring on Earth itself, which includes the thousands
of UFO reports from all parts of the globe. We have had
to wait until now for the first cracks to appear in our
government's secrecy surrounding the subject. As we
move into the 21st century, the French and British
governments admit that there are objects in our skies
suggesting something or someone has 'Called'."
As I read through this book, it became apparent that
there was such resonance to the story that it did more
than cement the story into place but registered an eerie
kind of message to us.

"Current scientific findings and technological
advances bring us to a place where we should be
thinking constructively about our wider future in the

universe. Visions cast today will undoubtedly become reality sometime in our tomorrows. CALLED is a book to be enjoyed, but it shouldn't be taken too lightly either.

"A great read, this book will deeply touch people who have had unexplained experiences and who continue to suffer in silence, rather than chance rejection by friends and colleagues. All thinking people will feel the timing of the material. CALLED did not arrive on our bookshelves a day too soon."
Colin Andrews, author of "Circular Evidence" and President of Circles Phenomenon Research International

THE MAYAN TILES

CHAPTER ONE

THE DREAM THAT WAS NOT a dream stands out in Paul's mind as though it was only yesterday. The giant mothership hovered above, calling him silently. The alien beings aboard the craft greeted him like a brother. By the time he returned to Earth, he understood why. He is their brother. He is from elsewhere.

Only weeks before he'd been living in a small apartment in a large city and existing pretty much the same as everyone else. Now he is standing in a remote forest in central Arizona watching an alien craft depart with the man he has called Grandfather. It isn't the first craft he's seen since leaving his life in Sacramento. It is the third. The first had been the reason for the dramatic changes that have occurred in his life during the last few weeks.

Paul shook his head in disbelief as he watched the huge alien craft lift silently away from Earth. It had arrived silently and swiftly, taking over the night sky so completely that it seemed that the night was never there at all. The ship's mass blocked out the sight of the moon and most of the stars that have been lighting the night. Now it is departing in the same way, silently and swiftly, taking Grandfather with it, leaving Paul with the knowledge that, once again, his life was going to change dramatically.

11

The mountain air at four a.m. was cold and slightly damp. An involuntary sigh of weariness escaped him. He was only twenty-nine but at the moment he felt much older. Running his hand through his sandy-colored hair he absentmindedly noted that he needed a haircut. His thoughts flashed from the mundane to the otherworldly events that had just occurred and back again, dashing rather frantically through the events of the last weeks. He struggled to accept the enormity of the series of events that had changed his life, changed him, so dramatically, and brought him to this moment that had him watching this huge craft departing with a man he knew and loved.

He turned to study Jessica. Standing next to him, her head barely reached his shoulder. She seemed small and vulnerable but in the brief time they'd known each other, he had come to realize that the aura of fragility was a myth. Her strength was monumental. He was glad of that. They were probably going to need it in the days to come. The message they'd just received from the craft included her in a big way. She was going to be a larger part of his life than he'd originally thought.

Though there was little light to see by, Paul could see the unchecked tears on her cheeks as she stared at the now-empty sky above. For a minute he fancied that she was ethereal, a spirit manifesting from another world, a deeper world that held mysteries that he would never know. In the darkness, her eyes seemed more deep-set than usual, emphasizing her high cheekbones. The gloom of the night caused the green of her eyes to appear black.

He hesitated, suddenly in awe of her. He had no idea how he was going to deal with her and his sense that she was far wiser and stronger than he. Combined with his unspoken intimidation was the reality of what they'd just been asked to do. In the jungles of Belize a set of tiles awaited them. Brought to Earth by an alien society many years ago, the time was now for the tiles to be revealed. And the success or failure of the mission to retrieve them could affect the entire planet.

Suddenly and unexpectedly, the dream of several weeks ago, the one that had changed his life and caused him to come to this present moment, rushed into his thoughts. In the dream that he now knew wasn't a dream at all, he'd been taken aboard a giant mothership. Had it been the same one that just took Grandfather? The craft had been instantly familiar, as had its crew.

Korton, the imposing Commander with enigmatic eyes and a look that seared through Paul's soul like a hot knife, exploring him in ways that no one else ever had. Zo, the small one who captured Paul's heart the minute their fingers had touched in greeting. And Eia. Soft in ways the others were not, she brought the hint of a lifetime from his past. They all seemed as familiar to him as if they were his family, long unseen but always loved, somewhere in the region of his subconscious.

Within weeks of this meeting, Jessica had appeared in his life. The fact that he felt like he'd known her as well, in some other place and time wasn't lost on him. She wasn't familiar in the way that the crew of the huge craft had been, but still a vague memory was there, unreachable but nagging. He had decided that they had

13

more than likely shared a past life together and that the timing of the dream, her sudden arrival in his life, and his compulsion to know who he really was all tied together somehow. But what it all meant, he still wasn't sure. As with the hidden memories of Eia, his thoughts about Jessica were the same. A nagging feeling that he'd left something undone somewhere in his past,. Some words that hadn't been spoken. Or some emotion that hadn't expressed. He couldn't pinpoint his vague suspicions about his past but he was fairly certain that if he continued on the path that seemed to have been chosen for him, he would figure it all out eventually.

With his thoughts darting chaotically, like frightened butterflies afraid to light anywhere, the power and unspoken purpose of the aliens and their mission pressured his thoughts back into focus on the events that had just passed. The aura of the powerful craft still hovered in the air around him. It seemed that the small mountain meadow had memorialized the arrival and disappearance of both the alien craft and Grandfather by holding the energy of change in the air. To breathe deeply meant to return to the first breathtaking sight of the craft, as if the craft had literally changed the air he breathed. Brenda and Bill, asleep in their tent, had managed to sleep through the entire event. Marlen, Grandfather's nephew, had silently disappeared into the forest after watching Grandfather's departure with wide eyes and heartbreak. Paul and Jessica were now alone with the message from the alien craft standing between them as though it were tangible.

Jessica, reading his thoughts, turned to him as he opened his mouth to speak. "Belize," she said softly,

14

shaking her head. "I can hardly believe we're going to Belize." At 5'1", she had to tilt her head to meet his gaze.

"Then you're certain that you want to do this?" he asked hesitantly. He was surprised by what appeared to be her immediate acquiescence to the alien request. "We've only known each other for a week. How comfortable are you with going all the way to Belize with someone who's almost a stranger?"

Jessica laughed softly. The sound was like a musical note hovering in the still mountain air. "Maybe we're strangers in this lifetime but we've known each other before. I think we'll manage."

Still not used to her casual attitude about everything mysterious to him, Paul blinked in vague surprise. Why he thought that he was the only one who would readily remember their connection was a mystery to him. After all he had seen and experienced during the last few weeks, he readily accepted the theory of life after death and reincarnation. But it was still an effort for him to control his knee-jerk reaction of questioning everything. "Okay," he agreed noncommittally, not ready to talk about his own thoughts. "You might be right."

He knew it would be easy for him to get lost in the effort of trying to retrieve the memories of the past because he found her wonderfully attractive. But if they were going to make this trek to Belize there were more important things to think about. "Anyway," he continued, "I'm going to state the obvious and say that I think what they're asking us to do isn't going to be easy."

15

"I don't imagine it will be," she said tartly. "It's a foreign country. Neither one of us know the language. We'll have to sort out visas and all that stuff. Then we're going to have to somehow find and bring back ancient tiles that no one knows about. Not to mention how we're going to get them through airport security. No," she continued, her tone exaggerated, "I would venture to say that it won't be a cakewalk. But then, they didn't say it would be, did they?"

Choosing to ignore her flippancy, Paul's mind suddenly filled with images of what could go wrong. He hoped he was up to the task that was being asked of them. He chased his fears away with a change of subject. "Why do you suppose the tiles are so important? I mean, what do you think they're all about?"

Jessica was quick to respond. "What I know so far is that an alien society brought them to Earth during the Mayan times in an effort to share knowledge with Earth. I've been shown, in visions and dreams, that much about them. The rest is as much a mystery to me as it is to you. I know I'm too tired to try to figure it out right now. We were chosen to go get them and I guess that's what we're going to do. Maybe we're not supposed to know any more than that." She yawned widely and stretched her arms. "I'm going to try to get an hour's sleep before the sun comes up. How about you?"

"You can sleep after all of this?" Paul asked, surprised.

Jessica chuckled lightly. "If I lost sleep over every metaphysical or other-world event that I've seen I'd be

16

dead by now." Still chuckling, she turned on her heel and was gone before Paul could react.

Now there was only the silent mountain air to keep him company. Paul pulled his jacket closer to his ears and headed toward the small campfire, hoping that it would warm him. Tossing several logs onto the fire, he sank to the ground, leaned his back against the log that had recently been vacated by Grandfather, and dropped into a reverie that soon turned into something that felt like a memory.

He was walking, flat-footed, along the shore of a distant land. The air was warm and tropical. The smell of the salty sea dominated his senses and he breathed deeply, a sense of joy and peace stirring his solar plexus. Across a small expanse of sea he could see another island. His instincts told him that there was someone there who he loved deeply. He missed her. But he was on a mission and there would be time for love after he returned. He turned away from the view of the island and knelt beside the small leather pouch that he had emptied of its treasures. The crystals sparkled in the sun. The day was warm and filled with the tropical scent of orchids, palm trees, and the fresh, unpicked dates that hung heavy and limp from the branches.

Kneeling beside the crystal treasures, he chose a deep purple amethyst point. Setting it gently into the palm of his left hand, he held it to the light, allowing it to absorb the sun's rays. When he felt the temperature of the stone change, he took it between his thumb and index finger and pointed it toward the distant place of light that had been his home before coming to this planet. Because it was daylight, he could only faintly see the crystalline-pink hued outline of the energetic communication grid that he used to communicate with those at home. Though the connection was weak, he knew it was there as surely as he knew that he had two hands. He had left home to come to this planet in order to assist in forming the energetic grid that would soon be established around this world. Verona, his love, had come with him. The grid would make this world habitable for life, balancing the planet within it solar system so that its formerly erratic existence would calm in a way that could, and would, sustain the form of life that was being planned for it.

He felt his mental connection with the council members at his home click into place. The amethyst had helped to establish the necessary link between the two worlds. Setting it down carefully, he chose the next tool, a slim wand of pure crystal, so clear that it appeared to be glass. Using the wand as a beacon, he set his thoughts into it and then mentally projected them through the crystal, across space, and into the minds of those who were listening.

In his mind's eye he could see the council members gathered, calm and pleased with the progress that had occurred so far.

"We'll call this land 'Lemuria'," Paul heard Jasperia say.

"Indeed," Solomon agreed.

At the sound of Solomon's voice, Paul felt the tug of a smile around his lips. Though he could only sense the other council members, in his mind's eye he could see Solomon clearly. They had walked together for eons. Through thousands of years the single word he had just spoken had been like a talisman between them. A single word that echoed agreement with decisions that Paul had made through the centuries. Decisions that had affected his soul throughout time.

"Indeed," Paul whispered to himself, savoring the word and its implications.

"The main goal, as you will recall," Jasperia continued, "is to create an energetic field that will make this area of existence more accessible to those who desire a third dimensional experience. Therefore, the planting of the crystals and the threads of knowledge and energy that they contain is crucial. They will assist in holding the energy of the sacred grids that will be laid. You have the map in your energy field, Paul. Don't be concerned that you will make a mistake."

Paul nodded. He wasn't concerned. Certainly he felt slightly alienated, having left his natural world to come to this foreign place. But he liked the planet and its energy. It was beautiful. He smiled. Obviously a tropical environment agreed with him.

The home he had left to come to Earth was beautiful beyond description. He had existed there for many years, living a simple life of peace. As a council member he had carried responsibilities that would undoubtedly

19

burden him beyond endurance if he had lived in a lower vibrational energy. But Questar supported the high level of intensity by its own high level of clear energy.

This new land, this land that would be called Lemuria, though beautiful, was still third dimensional, as opposed to Questar. The energy here was soft, nurturing, soothing. He knew without being told that the energy of this place could lull him into forgetting his mission. The thought of lying on the warm sand with Verona by his side, tasting the sweetness of the low-hanging fruits on the nearby trees was powerful, seductive. On Questar everyone was serious, intense, and goal-oriented. Their tasks were many, their responsibilities enormous. It would not occur to him, on Questar, to spend his days resting and lolling about.

He shook his head once again, tossing aside the temptation of his thoughts. Scanning his energy field with his mind, he accessed the energies of the map that had been placed there. Once again the enormity of his mission settled around him. The largest crystal, the single point that weighed twelve pounds, needed to be taken to the farthest side of this island. With a small nod he reached out to touch the leather case that held it, reassuring himself of its safety. He had a long walk ahead of him. The small cart that carried the larger crystals had sunk its wheels into the sand. It would not be an easy journey.

He felt the air around him move. Coming out of his reverie slowly, he looked in time to see Marlen sit down heavily on the log next to him. He watched as, with a dull kick, Marlen used his foot to pop a small stick of kindling into the fire. For a second, the fire snatching at the new wood lit the darkness.

Eerie shadows of ancient history seemed to be written on Marlen's round, tanned face. His American-Indian features seemed more pronounced as the firelight cast shadows across the crevices and wrinkles that the native sun had etched into his skin. His shoulder-length black hair was tucked behind his ears. His mouth was grim and his eyes, which were normally twinkling with secret humor and unspoken thoughts, looked tired beyond description.

"Hey," Paul said quietly, not sure how to greet this stranger who was his friend.

"Hey," Marlen muttered.

"How you doing?"

Marlen shook his head slowly, staring at his hands, which were methodically breaking a twig into tiny pieces.

Marlen glanced up at him once, quickly, a flick of a glance, before looking back at his twig. "It's a bitch," he muttered. "Grandfather was the best friend I've ever had."

Paul nodded in sympathy, silently looking for adequate words. "I'm sorry," he finally said, knowing that the words weren't enough.

Marlen lifted his heavy shoulders in a shrug. "Guess it is what it is," he said dismissively, as if the casual words

21

could make the pain less than it was.

"Who knows," Paul said. "Maybe they'll bring him back."

Marlen shook his head, still staring at the rapidly dwindling twig. "Nope. You and I both know better than to believe that."

"You're right, I suppose." Paul stretched his legs toward the fire, realized he was still cold, and stood. Selecting a stick from the nearby stack, he stirred the fire until the flames rose high. For a brief, confusing minute he found himself in the future, on the day when the fire would go out. It had been burning for weeks, a constant warmth for those who sought it. A fanciful thought hit him. When the fire died ... what would die with it?

Out of the corner of his eye he caught a movement. Startled, he reflexively moved closer to the fire, suspecting something menacing. But whatever it was simply sat in the air, hovering like a small phantom. He stared at, totally bewildered. Before he could speak to get Marlen's attention, the thing drifted closer. He stared in bafflement. It was a piece of paper, appearing out of nowhere, drifting toward him like a letter from heaven.

He grabbed for it as it headed for the fire. Catching it, he turned toward Marlen, his mouth gaping open with astonishment.

Marlen was staring at him in surprise. "What the heck is that?"

Paul turned the papyrus-like paper, trying to see it in the dim light of the fire.

Marlen impatiently got to his feet and reached for the paper. "Well, what is it?"

"It's a piece of paper."

"That's obvious," Marlen said gruffly, "but what's it say?" He reached for the thing again and managed to wrest it from Paul's grasp. Moving closer to the fire, he peered at it closely. "What the hell is it?" he muttered.

"What's it say?" Paul asked, attempting to look over his shoulder.

"It looks like a map." Marlen's voice was soft with astonishment.

Paul resisted the urge to snatch the paper back and instead tried moving to get a better view. "A map of what?"

"I don't have a clue," Marlen muttered, turning the paper around in his hands.

"I think I know," Paul said abruptly. His knees were suddenly and inexplicably weak. Blindly, he sank back down to his log. His instinct was telling him that it was a map of Belize and the location of the hidden tiles. An astonishing belief was consuming him. The belief that this had materialized from another world, that it had been given to him as a gift from another dimension, that it would show him the way. In addition to that, the full

23

realization of what they'd been asked to do, the fact that they would do it, and the impact it might have upon Earth's civilization were falling on him like ice-cold raindrops. Goosebumps chased each other over the surface of his skin, making him shake involuntarily.

Marlen turned to stare at him curiously. "What?" he asked roughly.

"It's a map of the area around Belize. Where the tiles are."

"What?" The single word carried several tones of question and doubt.

"Belize," Paul echoed dully, shaking his head in disbelief. "Where Jessica and I are supposed to go to retrieve the tiles."

Marlen stepped closer, blocking the light of the fire so that Paul was instantly, unexpectedly dropped into darkness. He shook the paper. "You're telling me that they materialized this? That they're giving you a map?" His tone was incredulous. He sighed and rubbed his forehead as though he had a headache.

Paul knew that his irritation was based on his shock over Grandfather's disappearance. He opened his mouth to comment but stopped as he heard a sound behind him. He jumped, startled, as Jessica appeared out of the darkness. He hadn't heard her footsteps.

"Let me see the paper," she said quietly, reaching for it with an air of authority.

24

Without hesitation, Marlen handed it to her. Paul looked at him quizzically. It wasn't like Marlen to do as someone asked without first questioning or protesting. It was just his nature to be a take-charge kind of guy. After staring at Marlen for a second, Paul turned back to Jessica to watch her reaction.

She stepped closer to the fire, turned the paper to see it better, and nodded as if satisfied.

"What?" Paul asked a trifle sarcastically. "You were expecting this?"

She glanced at him but didn't answer directly. "This is the map of where the tiles are. If it's all right with you, I'll hold onto it." She started to fold it.

"Wait a minute," Paul protested. "I haven't had a chance to even look at it."

"You wouldn't be able to read it anyway. We don't know the area. It will be meaningless to us until we get there." She glanced at the paper. "Actually, it probably won't even be necessary. I think we'll be totally guided. Besides, I think I'll be able to remember most of it."

Paul looked at her suspiciously. "Remember it how? How can you know the area? Have you been there?"

Jessica shook her head. Paul thought he saw a sudden, deep sadness appear on her face before she deliberately changed her expression and smiled at him. "Not in this lifetime," she answered mysteriously.

25

"Anyway, I've been remote viewing the area since I learned about the tiles."

Paul looked confused. "What the heck is remote viewing?" He looked at her quizzically. "And are you talking about that lifetime? The lifetime the tiles were brought here?" His voice was rising in volume with each question. "And you're telling us that you already knew about the tiles?"

She caught a loose strand of hair and tucked it behind her ear before answering him. Her expression was thoughtful and distant. "Remote viewing is exactly that. You travel with your spirit and view a place or person with your spirit instead of your eyes." She shrugged lightly, as though she were speaking of a commonplace thing. "And," she paused, studying him before continuing, "Yes, I am talking about that lifetime. It might have been. I'm not absolutely certain yet." She chewed on her lip lightly, lost in wondering.

"I didn't know that was even a possibility," Paul said quietly. He wanted to think of something else to say. It was clear that beneath her casual attitude, there was concern. He changed his tone. "You didn't say anything about knowing you were going after the tiles," he accused good-humoredly, hoping to lighten her mood. "You knew you were going and that's why you were doing the remote viewing. Is that right? Why didn't you tell me?"

She smiled slightly. "Why would I? I didn't know they were going to include you."

Behind him he heard Marlen stifle a small snigger.

26

"Maybe they figured she needed you as an escort," he said.

Paul shook his head and reached for the paper. "Anyway, if it's all right with you, I'd like to study this thing."

Jessica shrugged lightly. "Fine." She handed him the paper. "Just don't drop it in the fire or anything."

Paul glared at her. "You don't have an ounce of faith in me, do you?"

She studied him for a silent second, a tiny smile threatening to escape. "Not yet I don't." She chuckled lightly to show that she was teasing. "You're going to have to show me what you're made of before I trust you."

"What the heck is that supposed to mean?"

Her chuckle turned to laughter as she strolled calmly away from them, heading back to her tent.

Paul looked at Marlen for support. Marlen was shaking his head, a grin like a small boy watching a circus clown spread across his face.

Paul shook his head in disappointment. There wasn't going to be any commiseration from Marlen. He obviously agreed with her. "Between the two of you," he muttered, "it's a wonder that I have any ego left at all."

Marlen gave a quick spurt of laughter, like the last burp of water out of a rusty faucet. "Maybe that's the point," he said. "Maybe we're in your life to challenge you."

"Well," Paul sighed, "you're both doing a splendid job of it."

"Thanks." The smile fell off of his face abruptly as he glanced up at the sky and the memory of Grandfather's leaving once again came to sit on his shoulders. "I think I'm gonna catch a nap before the sun comes up. I'll help you fix breakfast for everyone if you'll wake me up in an hour or two."

"Sure," Paul agreed quietly. The momentary distraction of the map and the brief levity had left as quickly as it had arrived. The pain of Marlen's loss came back to rest on them both.

They studied each other silently for several seconds before Marlen nodded slowly, acknowledging Paul's sympathy. He turned and headed for his tent.

Listening to the sound of Marlen's retreat, Paul was once again alone with his thoughts. The significance of everything that had happened came again to enshroud him, wrapping him in its reality like a heavy woolen blanket on a hot summer's day.

CHAPTER TWO

ONLY AN HOUR LATER the morning sun began to dominate the sky. The soft, rose-colored sunrise tapped Paul and promised a warm day. Bill emerged from his tent with Fric and Frac, his two Irish setters, tripping along behind him. After a hard shake, a high-backed stretch, and a yawn, the two dogs galloped off for their daily exploration of the forest surrounding the small camp. Paul watched them with a smile for several seconds before turning to Bill.

Bill's spiky, uncombed hair made him look vulnerable and child-like, even though his jaw was dark and unshaven. The now-familiar sight of his burly chest, his perpetual smile, and his compassionate eyes was a welcome sight after the last, silent hour of worry that Paul had endured. "Coffee?" he asked, reaching for the pot that was sitting on a boulder next to the fire.

"Sure." Bill accepted the cup with a yawn. Zipping up his thick denim jacket against the morning chill, he sank down to a log. "Thanks." He looked at Paul speculatively. "You look tired. You didn't sleep well?"

"I didn't sleep at all," Paul said shortly. "You missed one hell of a night."

Bill was instantly alert. "What did I miss?"

Paul's shoulders drooped with the weight of his news. "Grandfather's gone," he said quietly.

Bill scoured the campsite quickly, his eyes taking in the absence of Grandfather. "What do you mean gone?"

Paul knew even before he spoke that his words were going to be unbelievable. "A craft showed up and when they left, they took him with them."

Bill's mouth dropped open. He stared at Paul, a stunned look in his eyes. "A craft showed up? Are you kidding me? You saw a craft and you didn't wake me up? And they actually took him?" He stared at Paul with wide eyes, attempting to assimilate the information.

Paul nodded. If he hadn't seen it for himself he might have been as stunned as Bill. Even after all of the interaction with those from elsewhere that he'd had recently, it had never occurred to him that they were capable of simply lifting someone away from the planet as easily as plucking a grape off a vine.

"Why didn't you wake us up?" Bill complained.

"They came and went too quickly to even think about it. "I'm sorry," he apologized.

"I don't believe this," Bill muttered. "It was only a couple of weeks ago that we were leading a fairly normal life." He looked up and smiled abruptly. "If you can call living with a psychic author a normal life, that is."

"I can only imagine."

"It's been interesting ... but nothing compared to what's happened since you arrived on the scene."

30

"Should I apologize?" Paul asked, only half-serious.

Bill chuckled but abruptly fell serious again. "No, don't apologize. I never expected to see this much or learn this much in my entire life. It's been interesting." He paused. "And entertaining as well. Payson, Arizona isn't exactly a metropolis, you know. All that's happened recently has given me more entertainment than I've had in my entire lifetime."

"Something else happened too," Paul told him, changing the subject abruptly.

Bill looked at him sideways, suddenly wary. "What? I hope it's not something even more outrageous. Speaking of which," he added, glancing around, "how is Marlen taking all of this. Or does he know yet?"

Paul nodded. "He knows. He was here when it happened."

"Is he doing all right?"

"As well as can be expected. I imagine he's in shock. Grandfather was a great friend to him. I hope he manages to deal with it all right." Paul looked around at the forested mountain scene that had emerged with the morning light. "I don't know what he's going to do. Whether he's going to stay up here or go to Flagstaff or what."

"I imagine he's going to want to spend some time alone," Bill speculated.

31

Paul hung his head; as if his thoughts were suddenly too heavy to hold it up any longer. He recalled vividly his unexpected turmoil following his most significant craft sighting. The craft had hovered above him for almost forty-five minutes. He had shocked himself to the core with his all-consuming need to be taken aboard and transported to a place that he remembered with his heart more than with his mind. He imagined that Marlen was feeling not only the loss of Grandfather but the soul-question of why he hadn't been taken as well. He stared unseeingly at Bill before realizing that Bill was watching him curiously. He shook his head, struggling to remember Bill's last sentence. "I don't know," he finally muttered. "I don't know what he's going to want to do. But whatever he decides I imagine he's got some tough times ahead."

Bill reached across the small space between them and tapped him lightly on the knee in an attempt to offer comfort. He took a sip of coffee and cleared his throat, letting his gaze wander around the innocent mountain scene that surrounded them. "Well, do you want to tell me what else happened? What did I miss?"

A bemused smile came over Paul's face. "Well, Zere came down before they took Grandfather. He was here just long enough to tell us that there was another thing that needed to be done." He shook his head slowly, absorbing the information all over again. "They want us to go to Belize to retrieve some ancient tiles that his society brought here a long time ago."

"You're kidding!" Bill gaped at him with an open

mouth and wide eyes.

"Nope." Paul took a sip of coffee and watched Bill's reaction with mixed emotions. "It's not going to be as easy as the first thing they asked me to do, which was hard enough in itself."

"Well, yeah. Coming to Arizona from California isn't anything compared to going to Belize." Bill's forehead wrinkled in thought. He turned to Paul suddenly. "Who was Zere talking about? All of us? Or just you?"

"Jessica and I. At least that's how I understand it."

"And what are these tiles about?"

"As near as I can figure, they contain information that needs to be revealed to the world. The tiles were brought here by Zere's society. They were given to a small band of Mayan people. Something happened and the Mayans died before they had a chance to reveal them." He glanced at Bill quickly. "Apparently Jessica was shown the tiles in a dream a while ago. She mentioned it briefly before she took off to get some sleep."

Bill stared at him, attempting to absorb the news. "No kidding?" Obviously at a loss as to what to think, he took his hand out of his pocket to scratch his head, stared at his other hand and the cup of coffee that it held, and finally looked back at Paul. "This is a lot to absorb." He sighed, scrubbed his strong hand over his face, and stared across the small meadow.

33

Paul nodded in agreement. "But at least you managed to sleep through them picking Grandfather up. This way you're getting it secondhand. Maybe it's easier to handle that way."

Bill shook his head in negation. "I don't know. It's still an awful lot." He peered at Paul, a dozen unasked and unanswered questions parading behind his eyes, anxious to be let out. "So what are you going to do? Are you going to go to Belize? Has Jessica agreed to go? That's a foreign country, for Pete's sake!"" His words tumbled over each other as the enormity of the task sank in. "How are you going to manage this? This could be huge!" he exclaimed as it all began to sink in.

"Indeed," Paul said, nodding with a small, slightly ironic smile. For some inexplicable reason, the single word seemed to instantly instill a tangible calmness in the morning air. Bill took a deep breath and stared at him silently for several seconds before shaking his head in bemusement.

They talked quietly until the rest of the members of their group roused to face the day. As if called, Marlen strolled out of the forest the minute everyone had a cup of coffee warming their hands. He poured himself a cup and settled down next to Paul, his back leaning up against a log. Brenda responded to the news differently than her husband. She nodded slowly, listening as Paul filled her in on the details of the night. "Grandfather was able to reach the point where he could transform," she stated simply.

As the others stared at her, waiting for an

34

explanation, she proceeded. "As I understand it, our physical bodies are drawing light into them. Some of the beings traveling our skies right now are assisting certain people to bi-locate, meaning they're energizing the physical body so that it can be transported to other realities in order to access knowledge that is not available on Earth. And, as far as I know, The Esartania, which is the craft we've all been interacting with, is a Lightship. The shape of it, the bipyramids and tripyramids, is a representation of sacred geometry, the sacred shapes that created this Universe. It enters galaxies when a galaxy is preparing for a new state of evolution. Which we are," she added, gazing at them all with clear-eyed satisfaction. She grinned. "I, for one, think all of this is way beyond exciting. We're tremendously lucky to be living at such a time in history."

Paul felt the truth of her words and knew she was stating facts. How she knew all this, he didn't know. But her words resonated as truth in his mind. They awakened in him a new vision of himself. He had been interacting in dream state with these alien beings most of his life. He had recently come to accept that he was actually one of them. Following that line of thinking, he had no choice but to accept that he was on Earth to complete a mission far larger than he had imagined. It was both exciting and agonizing at the same time. Was he going to be able to set aside the human beliefs and emotions that had been ingrained in him to the degree that he could call upon the knowledge he would need? He hoped so. Obviously Brenda had learned how to do it.

35

He looked at each person in the small group. He certainly had the friendship and support he needed to pull it off. He gave silent thanks for the events that had brought them all together.

Jessica took a sip of coffee and met his eyes with an unspoken message. As he looked at her curiously, unable to read her thoughts, she dropped her gaze. "Um, I hate to be the one to make the suggestion, but it seems like it might be a good idea for us to head back to Payson and get ready to make this trip."

Paul glanced at Marlen. The last thing he wanted to do was leave him alone. "Do you know what your plans are?" he asked.

"I think I need to spend some alone," Marlen said. He waved his hand at the forest. "I'd like to just stay up here a while."

"You're going to be all right?" Paul questioned worriedly.

"Don't be a mother," Marlen scolded lightly, glancing at Paul with a small smile. "I'm fine. I've been livin' this way all my life."

"But not alone," Paul countered.

"I have an entire family down at the cave if I want company," Marlen reminded him.

Paul glanced in the direction of the cave. "That's right. I'd forgotten."

36

Marlen reached out and slugged him lightly on the knee. "You've got things to do. Go do them," he ordered.

Still reluctant, trying to deal with his conflicting emotions, but admitting that Marlen was right, Paul rose and headed toward the tents to begin breaking camp. The rest of the group followed suit and within an hour the Bronco was packed and ready to go. Fric and Frac bounded into the back of the Bronco with tails wagging while Bill, Brenda, and Jessica said fond farewells to Marlen and climbed into their places.

Accepting that everyone but himself was ready to leave, Paul turned to Marlen. "Are you sure you're all right with this?"

Marlen nodded, his round face solemn with thought. "I need some time alone. I'll be fine." He grabbed Paul's hand and shook it quickly. "And you take care down there. I don't know much about Belize, but it's a foreign country. Anything can happen."

"We'll be fine," Paul assured him. "Maybe we'll see you when we get back?"

"I've got Bill's number. I'll keep in touch."

Paul nodded and turned to leave. On impulse, he turned back and pulled Marlen into a quick, awkward hug. "Take care of yourself," he muttered.

He was quiet on the drive back to Payson, though the others chatted and planned and speculated about the

37

upcoming adventure. With relief he pulled into Bill's driveway and shut off the engine. Though he had only lived in their small guesthouse a short time, it looked like home to him and he was anxious to retreat into its silence.

After helping the others unpack the Bronco, he walked the short distance across the patio and stepped into the cool interior of the place he now called home. When Bill and Brenda had offered it to him, he had hesitated. He had always had a tough time letting other people get close to him. This living situation wouldn't allow him to keep his normal distance. Their generosity and obvious desire to take him into their family finally forced his decision. And he had been happy with that decision.

The small guesthouse was tastefully decorated in pastels, with two deep, comfortable chairs and a loveseat in the small living room. The kitchenette made it handy for him to fix himself a snack when he wanted to eat meals alone. Right outside the door sat the covered patio of the main house and the pool that he was free to use anytime he chose. He was content. The peace of the small valley that sat on the outskirts of Payson was the perfect place for him to think and absorb the sudden and dramatic shifts that his life had taken.

Shrugging off the jeans and T-shirt that he'd been wearing since yesterday, he stepped into the shower and allowed the weekend to wash away from him. A nap seemed in order, since he'd had little sleep. He was awakened some time later by the sound of voices on the patio. Hearing his name, Paul smiled slightly, slipped into a fresh pair of jeans and a T-shirt and, barefoot, walked outside to join the others.

The nearby mountain range reflected the heat of the day onto the pastures that spread across the land on the other side of the chain link fence. Fric and Frac, worn out from their weekend adventure, lay sleeping on the cool stone near the patio door. Brenda was carrying a pitcher filled with iced lemonade out through the patio door. Fric opened one eye and stared at her until deciding that she didn't have any food. Closing his eye, he fell promptly back to sleep.

Watching him, Jessica let out a small chuckle.

Paul, turning to her, blinked at the screaming lime green shirt she'd chosen. She certainly is noticeable, he thought. "You're cheerful," he commented aloud.

"I was just thinking about you and I trekking off to a foreign country and how the heck we're going to pull this off successfully."

"And why would that make you so cheerful?" Paul asked dryly.

Jessica studied his face and chuckled again. "Life is just mysterious, that's all," she said enigmatically.

"You have a tendency to talk in riddles," Paul told her. "Has anyone ever told you that?"

She nodded without replying, a small smile on her full lips.

39

"So how are you going to go about doing this?" Brenda asked, looking from one to the other.

Jessica turned to her. "I know I haven't mentioned it to you but I've suspected for a while that something like this might happen. I needed time to get my thoughts together and make sense of it all before I talked to you about it. I've been having dreams and visions of some kind of ancient tiles since I was a child. I was pretty sure they were Mayan. I became so sure, in fact, that I studied the area on the Internet. I've been bi-locating there for quite a while now, kind of scouting out the lay of the land, so to speak. I didn't know that I would be one of the ones asked to retrieve these tiles. I just thought I was being informed about them for some reason. Maybe so that, when they were revealed, I would know that I was hearing the truth. Anyway, now that I know I'm going to help get them into the United States, I'm beginning to feel that this is only the beginning." She glanced at Paul. "I think this is part of our original mission, our purpose for this lifetime," she stated flatly. "And I feel certain we'll be successful."

Brenda looked at her thoughtfully. "That's a good way to look at it. It kind of overrides any human doubts that you may have, thinking of it as already successful, even before you begin."

"Not everything works that way," Bill advised quietly.

Brenda reached over and patted his cheek lightly, her face aglow with affection. "My steadying influence here. My resident skeptic."

Bill captured her hand, brought it to his lips, and kissed it lightly. "You know better than that. I've come to believe in almost everything since I met you. Even more so since the events of the last few weeks. But thinking that this is going to be a walk in the park because it was something you planned on doing before you incarnated might just be tempting fate a little too much."

"Agreed," Jessica said. "The visions have shown me some potential problems. Besides, obviously the plan to reveal them when they first arrived a millennium or two ago, or however long ago it was, failed and I imagine that wasn't expected to happen. We won't have the same problems they had at that time, of course, but I can foresee some other things. Not the least of which is the fact that we're going to be followed. We're not the only ones who know about these tiles," she added.

Paul felt a sense of foreboding creep into his chest. "Who else knows about them?" he asked, forcing himself to speak lightly. "And how do they know?"

"I don't know exactly who this is I'm seeing," she answered, closing her eyes briefly. She was mentally envisioning the strangers. "I can't get a clear enough vision of them. They seem to be masked or something."

Paul's lips curled involuntarily as he rejected her words. "What? Masked as in Zorro or something?"

"No," she said tartly, throwing the word at him as though it were a gauntlet. "Masked as in cloaked.

41

Psychic energy cloaking them so that I can't see them. They don't want to be known. They don't want us to know they're aware of the tiles. They're hoping that we'll be caught off guard."

A rush of fear charged through Paul's stomach. "Are you serious?" Images of bullets ripping through his flesh flashed through his mind. He didn't want to die alone on a jungle floor.

"You won't be alone," Jessica said quietly.

Startled, Paul stared at her. There it was. The first evidence that she could read his mind. He knew that she was a practicing psychic in Sacramento but he hadn't been absolutely certain that she could read thoughts. There had been hints ... but no certainties. He sighed inwardly. This wasn't going to be an easy journey.

"When do you think you'll leave?" Bill asked, unaware of their silent exchange.

"Today's Sunday," Jessica said quietly. "I'll call my assistant tomorrow and tell her not to make any appointments for me for the rest of the month." She glanced at Paul. "And then, I guess if you're ready, we can leave on Tuesday. Or Wednesday?" She paused, thinking. "You do have your passport and visa already?"

Paul nodded absentmindedly. His thoughts were elsewhere, thinking about the ending, rather than the beginning, of this journey. "Yeah. I have all that. I was planning a summer vacation to Spain," he added thoughtfully. What a huge directional change his life had taken since he'd made those innocent plans.

Brenda grinned. "This is exciting. I wish I was going with you."

Paul turned to study her. As usual he was struck by the sense of comfort that overcame him every time he looked at her. She was petite and pretty. An unexplainable aura of peace and compassion seemed to radiate from her, affecting those around her. Her auburn-colored hair lay softly on her shoulders. Her violet-blue eyes, when they looked at someone, seemed to view the person with unconditional acceptance. Right now, they sparkled with enthusiasm and the desire to be a part of the adventure. She would be a welcome addition to the journey, Paul thought.

"Why don't you two come with us?" he asked impulsively. He glanced at Jessica without registering her reaction and then looked at Bill to see how his suggestion was received.

Bill's look was doubtful. He shook his head. "I don't think so. As tempting as the thought is," he added quickly. He glanced around. "There's no one to take care of the house and dogs."

Fric lifted his head, sensing that he was being talked about. Realizing that there still no food being offered, he dropped back to sleep.

"And," Bill continued, "the newspaper is going to be doing a big weekend special for next weekend. I'll be editing every day, maybe even working overtime."

43

Paul nodded in acceptance. "You're right. You have too much going on here to be taking off."

"Still, it sounds dangerous but exciting," Brenda said longingly. She took a sip of her lemonade and set the glass down, wiping her hand on her shorts. She looked at Jessica. "Are you okay with all of this? I've known you, what, fifteen years? I haven't known you to be this much of an adventurer."

Jessica flipped her hand negligently on the arm of the chair. "I'm okay with it. It wouldn't be my first choice of how to spend the next week or two but, in the long run, I think the rewards will far outweigh the dangers. I'm not looking forward to it, to be quite honest. But just think ...." She hesitated, her eyes suddenly shining, displaying her thoughts. "Think about the significance of these tiles. They contain information from another world. Think what they could mean to our civilization. It will be dangerous but worth it," she repeated. She glanced at Paul before continuing, her eyes now serious. "Equally dangerous will be the fact that the military may still be watching you. If they are, they're going to follow us to find out what we're up to."

"What?" Paul cried, his voice rising in dismay. He jerked and pushed himself to the edge of his chair to stare at her intently. "What are you talking about? They've dropped the subject, I'm sure. And they can't be watching me. How would they do that out here in the middle of nowhere?" He looked around at the placid countryside suspiciously.

44

The low range of mountains lay innocently beyond the small pasture. Small ranches dotted the little valley. Only straight, white fences paraded across the blank expanse of fields. There was nowhere to hide.

Jessica shrugged lightly, as if indifferent. "They can watch anyone, anywhere, from what I understand. You don't think those satellites they have can spot a flea on a horse's ass? Don't be naive" She shook her head at him in disgust. "Besides that, they know about remote viewing too. There are people hired by our government, by other governments too, to do just that." She glanced at Brenda quickly. "I call them 'watchers.'"

Brenda nodded in agreement.

Paul shook his head, refusing her concerns. "I don't think they'll be involved. They got everything from that crash except the aliens Marlen and I rescued. And they had no proof that there were more aboard than just the two who died and were left aboard to be found. Plus," he added forcefully, attempting to convince himself as much as the others, "if they were watching then they saw the mothership pick up the survivors. They would have no more interest in me once the aliens were gone."

Jessica looked doubtful but she shrugged slightly. "You may be right. I guess we'll find out." She glanced at Brenda with a small smirk and a shake of her head. She would humor him, her expression said, but she herself didn't believe a word of it.

Bill spoke up. "No matter what happens I bet you have one hell of a trip."

45

Jessica grinned broadly. Paul scowled darkly, suddenly suspecting that she was actually looking forward to being chased across the globe, even though she denied it. "Yep. I suspect it will be," she agreed.

Ignoring her good humor, holding onto his fear, Paul voiced his concern. "If we're in the middle of a freakin' jungle, faced with a bunch of determined thugs who are hell-bent on getting the tiles away from us, how are we expected to get away?" he demanded.

Jessica looked up at the sky, perhaps seeing something there that he didn't. "I imagine that the details will be worked out by our invisible support system," she told him serenely.

Paul followed her eyes to the cloudless sky. He supposed that she was talking about their combined army of spirit guides. Or maybe the ETs who had originally brought the tiles to Earth? "I sure as heck hope so," he mumbled, talking to them as much as to her.

Off and on he had been given the gift of communicating with Solomon, who was acting as one of his spirit guides. But Solomon had been strangely absent for the last several days. Paul missed him more than he wanted to admit. It had been easy to get used to the presence of this invisible friend. He missed the comfort it had brought him. And with Solomon's silence came the question ... would he be there if Paul got in trouble?

"Well," Brenda said, interrupting his thoughts, "one way or the other, I know you're not going to turn the assignment down. So, what do we need to get you ready?"

A minute later the two women were headed toward the computer, chattering gaily about on-line reservations and plans. Paul rolled his eyes at Bill, who only smiled benignly.

Thursday's sky was cloudless as Paul tossed Jessica's suitcase into the Bronco with his. It was almost four o'clock and the heat was oppressive and thick. The flight they were taking to Belize, from Phoenix, would leave early tomorrow morning. Deciding that it would be easier to stay in a motel one night and get an early start to the airport, they'd chosen to spend most of the day resting by the pool. That choice now had them standing in the hottest part of the afternoon saying their good-byes.

After a quick hug from Brenda and a handshake from Bill, Paul gingerly set himself on the hot leather seat of the Bronco and closed the door. Doing his best to ignore the concern he was seeing in the look that was exchanged between Bill and Brenda, he smiled and waved as he pulled out of the driveway.

Beside him, dressed in her hot pink T-shirt and blue jeans, Jessica looked over her shoulder, waved one last time, and turned to settle in. "Whew," she sighed. "I never really thought this day would come. I've been dreaming about these tiles off and on for years. Maybe I just kind of subconsciously believed the tiles were just in my imagination."

47

Paul glanced at her. "You're not having second thoughts are you?"

She grinned. "No. Not a chance. This is something I'm going to try to enjoy. I haven't had much adventure in this lifetime." She chuckled. "I think I covered a lot of that ground in other lifetimes."

Paul stared at her skeptically. "There's got to be other kinds of adventure that you'd enjoy a lot more." He turned right onto the highway leading to Phoenix and settled in for the long drive by taking a deep breath.

Jessica looked at him sideways. "It's not the chase and the danger that I'm excited about. I'm excited about the chance to be a part of something that's so significant to our planet. I mean, think about it. This is information that was supposed to be released at least a millennium ago." Her eyes were shining with mystery and hope. "Think about all of the possibilities that might be revealed. Not to mention the fact that even having these tiles in our possession will be bringing us closer to another society. Just think about what this will mean. Ancient tiles. Alien, at that. Bringing wisdom from other worlds." She waved her hand at the countryside. "Imagine. I mean, just imagine." Her voice reverberated with barely suppressed excitement.

Paul heard the hope in her voice. He thought about her words for a minute, absorbing the vastness of the idea. "I wonder how this group of Mayans died. Why were the tiles brought to them in the first place? How did they die before they got the chance to reveal them?"

48

"I've spent a lot of time meditating on this. Trying to uncover those answers." She glanced out at the passing countryside and then turned back to him. "From what I've been shown, there was a small group of Mayans who didn't go along with the program set up by all the others. They didn't agree with the belief systems and things such as that. You know, there were sacrifices back then," she added with a slight shiver. "For the sake of religion or the good of all, or some such crap." She shivered again and rubbed her arms vigorously. "Anyway, not many people are aware of the whole story. This group broke away and set up a camp by themselves. They were practicing a different religion, following different rules."

"And the aliens noticed them and decided to bring them the tiles?" Paul interrupted.

Jessica shook her head. "No. The rebels were highly spiritual and psychic. They had always been. Most, if not all, of them had already been having contact with higher dimensions long before they broke away. The strength of that contact, I think, was what gave them the strength to go against the beliefs of the majority. Anyway, as far as I can tell, they began to communicate even more with this one group of aliens. I think they must have been told about a possible physical contact. Possibly even told about the tiles. And so they broke away from the rest of the group and went into the jungle to wait."

Paul glanced randomly at the sky and then at Jessica. "That would make sense. Based upon how clear their messages to me were before the crash and that first visitation."

49

"Yeah. It could have been pretty much the same kind of thing. Anyway," she said, getting back to her story, "the rebels and the aliens made an agreement that the tiles would be brought and that the rebels would reveal them to the others. I think it was believed that the information given would wake up the others. Kind of make them come to their senses and change their ways. If it had all gone as planned, the entire reality of life on Earth might have evolved differently," she added.

A new tone of speculation and deep thought had entered her voice. Paul took his eyes off the road long enough to study her for a minute. It might have been his imagination but it seemed to him that she almost glowed with a sense of purpose. The thought occurred to him again. Could she really have been one of the Mayans who had died before getting a chance to reveal the tiles? Could that be why she had been assigned this task? The huge trail of possibilities that ran through his mind caused him to shake his head in confusion. "Life can get confusing," he said out loud.

Jessica glanced at him. "You're referring to our participation in this project during that lifetime?"

"Our?" Paul asked, surprised.

Jessica raised her eyebrows at him. "You don't think I'm the only one who was involved, do you? Why do you think they chose you, out of all the people down here? Obviously you were involved as well."

Paul wrinkled his brow in confusion. Thoughts and

50

possibilities rushed at him like vaporous ghosts, pushing through veils of reality.

Jessica shrugged lightly. "It will all be revealed, I imagine. But right now we have to keep our perspective in the here and now. What failed before cannot fail again," she stated flatly.

What she failed to vocalize was that apparently everyone who had been involved the first time had probably believed it would succeed then as well. With an effort, Paul pulled his thoughts away from the present day danger and asked about the past again. "So what happened to cause the tiles to be lost? Why didn't the Mayans reveal them? You said they broke away from their group and went to live somewhere else with the tiles?"

"No. They didn't have the tiles when they left. They just all believed that there was a different, a better, way to live and so they left the tribe. Maybe they received the message that the tiles were going to be brought to them. That's pure speculation on my part. Anyway, the original group of Mayans were really pissed off that the small group broke away. They thought that the small group was trying to tell them that they were wrong in their beliefs and practices, which, as you know, no one likes to hear. Especially those who are seeking power." She rolled her eyes dramatically.

"Anyway, the rebels came under fire, so to speak. The leaders of the civilization sent out the troops to destroy them, since they wouldn't change their ways and come back to the tribe and follow all of the rules that

51

were being set out for them. The rebels had been living in the jungle. They had found an underground cave and were living there. The aliens had been communicating with them. You see, the rebel group had raised their vibrations enough to make it even easier for them to communicate with the higher dimensions. I think that the friendship and trust built to the point where the alien society believed that the Mayans would use the information in the tiles wisely. And so they brought the tiles to Earth. Not long after the tiles were given to them, the society members that they'd escaped from found the group. The rebels were all slaughtered." She shivered, chilled at the thought. "Sacrificed, was what they called it. The leaders told the people that the deaths were a sacrifice to the gods, that the gods had demanded the deaths. They said that, with the deaths of the rebels, everyone else would all be granted longer lives."

Paul forced his thoughts away from the mental image of the slaughter. "And so the tiles were left behind. The leaders didn't know about them and so didn't go looking for them?" he asked quietly.

Her voice seemed to come from a distance, perhaps from the past, the history of what had been. "My sense is that the tiles aren't in the cave. They seem to be somewhere nearby."

Paul glanced at her curiously but she continued before he had the opportunity to comment.

"The others searched the cave, of course. But nothing else around the area. I suppose the leaders didn't figure that the rebels had anything worth looking for,"

Jessica said, her tone quiet and sad.

Paul's sigh was deep and filled with a desire to change the past. Though fruitless, changing the past history of Earth was something he often thought about. "It's hard to think about a lot of the things that have happened down here," he commented.

Jessica looked over at him sadly. "It's difficult, yes. But we're all playing out the roles we need to play out in order to learn the things we need to learn, I guess. It's a fine line to walk. Being in the here and now and handling everyday situations but still seeing life from a higher perspective, trying to live the truth of the soul. But I think the more we know about the soul and why the soul chooses to physically incarnate, the more we can learn to monitor our behavior and, hopefully, change things for the better."

He could sense a subtle change happening within her. Possibly the drive through the quiet countryside was relaxing her. He allowed himself to relax too. He let go of some of his stress by rolling his shoulders and cleared his throat. "There's something we haven't talked about yet. This is going to be a long trip. How do you want to handle the motel situation?"

She glanced at him, recognizing his reluctance to bring up the subject. "Don't worry. It will work itself out. I'm not one to stand on ceremony. If we have to room together, that's what we'll do. I have a feeling we're going to get pretty close in the next couple of days." She cleared her throat with a slightly nervous sound and glanced at him again before dropping her gaze. "Um,

53

Brenda and I made an arbitrary decision and booked just one room down in Belize. It has two twin beds," she added quickly. "The cost was cut in half, you know," she explained, her voice drifting into nervous silence.

Paul did his best not to show his surprise. "That's fine," he assured her. "I'm sure it will work out just fine." He changed the subject abruptly. "While we were up at the campsite, after Grandfather was taken, you went back to your tent and I was alone for a while. I fell into what I think was a memory. I was in a place called Lemuria. Or 'on' Lemuria, however you want to phrase that. Anyway, I knew that a woman had come with me. I called her Verona. I didn't see her. But I sensed her. I knew she was there." He cleared his throat, deciding to just plunge into the question that was on his mind. "Was that you?"

She turned to face him squarely, resting on one hip. "Yes," she said without hesitation. "I remember it clearly," she added.

He glanced at her. "I thought you might," he said, nodding to himself at the validation she'd just given him.

She tucked a wisp of hair behind her ear. "We were lovers on Lemuria. Our home was Questar and we traveled from there to here in order to help establish energies and create a grid."

His mouth opened with unspoken surprise. He was amazed that she had such clear recall of the time, place, and circumstances. In addition, her matter-of-fact attitude and her lack of artifice struck him. There was no flirtation in her voice. "That was a hell of a long time ago," he finally said. "I'm surprised that you remember, number one, and that we're meeting again, number two."

She smiled at him calmly and settled herself more comfortably in her seat. "First of all, I have a good memory." She laughed gaily at her small joke. "And I also know about soul groups. That's a group of souls who work together throughout time to accomplish certain things," she explained. "It's an overall agreement between souls who have similar energies and similar goals. A group of souls who were created together, in the moment, for a specific reason. Various lifetimes serve to help us accomplish our goals. We're all commonly suited for certain missions due to the energies that we carry. And so it stands to reason that, due to similarities, we come together time and time again. Like attracts like and all that," she concluded.

Paul nodded. "Okay. That makes sense to me." He glanced at her. "Do we have similar relationships each time?" he asked with a grin, teasing her.

She chuckled lightly, instantly reading his thoughts. "Not always, no. For instance, we weren't lovers on Questar. We only went into that type of relationship after we came into this 3-D vibrational energy." She reached out and touched him gently on the arm, as though she was trying to reassure him about something as yet unspoken. She cleared her throat, the first sign that Paul had ever seen of any nervousness in her. "Paul, I don't know yet if we're going to be lovers again this time. It will be a matter of the choices we make. Relationships don't always go the same way each lifetime.

55

As a matter of fact, I remember a time when you and I were mortal enemies. I ended up killing you."

It felt like a dozen spiders were suddenly walking on Paul's skin. An involuntary shiver of fear raced through him, making the hair on his arms stand up. He could feel the memory attempt to come to the surface of his mind. He pushed it back down with a shudder. He knew by his reaction that she was telling him the truth. "That's not going to happen this time, is it?" he asked only half-joking.

"I'll do my best not to kill you," she chuckled. "Or get you killed," she added, changing her tone and raising her eyebrows.

Hearing the tone in her voice, he asked, "This is serious then, these guys who are going to try to get the tiles away from us?"

"Serious enough."

"But they won't succeed?" he asked, looking for an assurance that he suspected she couldn't give him.

She shook her head and once again tucked her hair behind her ears. "No. I don't think so."

"You don't think so?"

She looked at him without humor. "It's not in the plan. This is big. What we have to do is going to impact a lot of people. Not only those who live in this dimension but this entire universe." She turned on her hip to face

56

him again, exhibiting an intensity that he'd only seen in her once before. "You see, our world is on the verge of merging with worlds beyond. We're on the cusp of evolving beyond what we've been for millennia." She tapped the seat between them with excitement, emphasizing her words. "This, this very point in time, has the potential to spiral us into a reality that heals the separation between truth and illusion. It can usher in energies and truths that would assist us in creating a reality that matches our souls, not our wounded personalities and fears. The whole scenario that is planned for this Universe, including Earth of course, could provide us with the opportunity to heal this world."

Her voice was strained with suppressed ecstasy. It was obvious to Paul that she had found her mission and was dedicated to contributing all that she had to the goal, to the possibilities that sat in the invisible world surrounding them.

"I can't imagine that it will be allowed to fail," she whispered.

Paul wanted, with all his heart, to tell her that it wouldn't, that it couldn't. But he remembered, deep in the caverns of memories that traced his soul's evolution through time, that failure was as real as success. "I'd love to see it happen," he said carefully. He glanced up as he thought of those who lived in the dimensions beyond. "And let's hope everyone out there agrees with us," he added dryly.

Jessica's mood changed abruptly. "I guess we'll find out, huh?" Beneath her words was a hint of bitterness.

"Sorry," Paul said. "I don't mean to burst your bubble. I'm just trying to keep a grip on reality, that's all. I love the possibility of what you're talking about." He reached for her hand but she pulled it away. He regretted dashing her exuberance but he felt it was imperative to deal with reality as well as hope. "This is a huge, incredible thing you're talking about," he said reasonably. "You're talking about changing the entire planet in one single flash." He shook his head. "I'd like to believe it but it's difficult."

"It's not one single flash," she flared. "It's going to take a thousand years. And the planning and grid work has been in transition for almost fifty years already." She glared at him. "If Humankind can't evolve to a more spiritual way of being after being given a thousand years, and assistance from every dimension in existence, then you're right. It's hopeless."

"Hey!" Paul cried, wanting to defend himself. "I'm not saying it's not going to happen. I'm only trying to deal with the fact that opportunities like this have been given before. And look where we're at. We're nowhere. We're no closer to being evolved than we were thousands of years ago."

Her voice sizzled with anger. "And never before have all the dimensions participated, have the grids been redesigned and re-calibrated, have so many from higher dimensions taken incarnations down here in order to spread the higher energies and vibrations and open portals and channels." She paused, breathing deeply. "You're no neophyte, Paul. You know that thoughts of negativity and failure contribute to this reality staying

58

the way it is. How can you justify thinking the way you're thinking?"

He wanted to respond with anger, to rise to his own defense. But he knew she was right. He thought about his words carefully before he spoke. "Because," he said quietly, "we've tried so many times before. And we've never succeeded."

Recognizing his efforts to keep the conversation calm, Jessica responded in kind. "You're right," she agreed quietly. "But we can't say we've seen nothing but failure in our efforts. Maybe evolutionary change didn't happen in the time-frame we thought it would but we made a difference. Every society that has been encouraged to evolve, and assisted in the effort, has made some kind of progress. Who are we to judge how valid and valuable that progress is?"

"I never thought about it that way."

"I know. I didn't used to either. But then I went through an excruciating lesson about judgment and expectation. It changed my way of thinking forever."

"It sounds like that was painful."

"It was, believe me." She turned her face away to gaze out the window. For several minutes she silently watched the surrounding countryside fly by. Paul studied it as well. He used to think of Arizona as mostly desert. That had turned out not to be the case. The highway ran by a small stream, several small glades of trees, and small farms and ranches. A range of mountains bordered the road, shading it. It was a charming scene, one that might entice viewers to move away from the big city into a small community.

Her comment, when she spoke again, startled Paul, both by the sudden breaking of silence and by the subject matter.

"I really loved that lifetime," she said.

"The one where you killed me or the one where you loved me?" Paul asked quickly.

Caught by surprise, she laughed aloud. It was an infectious laugh, one filled with simple joy. "Loved you," she said simply.

He watched her, surprised, but she didn't turn to him again, didn't attempt to turn the comment into sentiment or flirtation. To her it was a simple statement of fact. To him it opened up a world of possibilities. He immediately struggled to tame his thoughts and hopes. Rather than tempt fate by jumping to conclusions again, he made up his mind to allow Jessica to take the lead. When night came, when it was time to book a motel to have this relationship unfold.

He nodded to himself, agreeing with his decision as if someone other than himself had made it. "What was it about that lifetime that you enjoyed so much?" he asked tentatively.

She stared out the window in silence for several seconds, thinking. "I think it was the simplicity, the

60

serenity, the newness, the absence of complexity."

"Meaning?" Paul asked, intrigued by her answer.

"It was a pure time," she said quietly. "We knew our souls. We knew our mission. There was no huge gulf of separation between soul and soul-wisdom and the fact that we were in a physical incarnation." She flopped her hand on the seat between them. "I mean, like now. Having a physical incarnation now, there is a huge gap between the reality we know as truth and the reality that we're living. Life on Earth has become such a hodgepodge of emotions that it takes a super-monumental effort to live your truth and put into practice the truth of your soul. The energy grids are so clogged and bogged down with crap that it's almost impossible to see the hope of light." She looked at him seriously. "I'm blessed. I have a profession that allows me to interact with my soul on a daily basis. I seldom lose sight of who and what I am. But my clients, it's different for them. The dichotomy between what they experience on a daily basis and what they feel they should be experiencing is overwhelming."

Paul chewed on the inside of his lip for a second as he thought. "I can relate to that. Take me, for example. I've been given the memory and awareness that I'm from another place but I still have to work on reminding myself of that all the time. It's hard to keep things in perspective."

"Exactly," Jessica agreed. She nodded thoughtfully but didn't share what she was thinking. "But getting back to Lemuria," she said thoughtfully. "We used the knowledge, and the wisdom, and the gifts of our soul. We lived our soul, if you want to put it that way. We did the work we came to do. We had a huge job to do but we did it easily and well. And the Earth was pure. It was unpolluted by everything that has occurred throughout its history since then. The grid was fresh and clean and the energies flowed purely. Communication with the other dimensions was pure. There was no deception." She sighed. "I don't know. It was just a pure time," she finished.

Paul agreed. He had sensed the same thing about Lemuria during his brief memory of it. He could feel something inside himself reaching for it, wishing he could return. With the yearning for that easier time in history came the yearning for the love they'd known. He changed the subject abruptly. "So what do you think is going to happen after we get the tiles?" he asked. "Providing we get them away safely."

"First of all, let's think positively. Like we talked about, to a large degree, we create reality with our thoughts. So, let's just envision getting away from this safely." She sighed lightly. "Anyway," she continued, "I haven't been shown the entire thing yet but from what I've been shown, I think we're going to have to take some time to interpret the material in the tiles. It's not just going to be spelled out for us in plain English. And then we're going to have to find a way to pass the information along. Maybe through a set of books or a web site or something. I don't know yet." Her voice drifted off as her thoughts spiraled through possibilities.

Paul stared at her. "Books as in more than one?"

Jessica looked at him with obvious consternation. "I thought you already knew most of this. It surprises me that you don't."

Paul shook his head. "No. No. I didn't know," he told her, still shaking his head in negation. "Writing a book has been mentioned a few times but I don't think the idea has ever really settled on me as something that would really happen. I know I've agreed to it and am working on myself to get into the right space to do it but...."

She shrugged lightly, dismissively. "We'll have plenty of help."

Paul rolled his eyes without humor. "That's what Brenda said. I hope you two know what you're talking about."

Jessica nodded sagely. "Oh, we do," she assured him. She yawned hugely. "Do you mind if I take a quick nap? I didn't sleep well last night."

"No. Not at all. Go ahead," Paul said, noting the tired lines that had suddenly appeared around her eyes. He hadn't noticed them earlier. He blinked. He was usually extremely observant. How had he missed the weariness that seemed to have suddenly consumed her?

Watching her anxiously, wondering if she might be coming down with the flu or something, he told her once again to rest. When she was lightly snoring, he turned his mind to his driving and his miscellaneous thoughts.

63

CHAPTER THREE

THEY REACHED PHOENIX early in the evening. The motel she had booked online looked clean and quiet. Across the street was a nondescript restaurant with interesting smells wafting from it. With a silent, tired nod, Paul pulled the Bronco into an empty parking space and turned off the engine.

"Looks like a good enough place to spend the night," Paul said, getting out of the Bronco and stretching hugely. He looked over the hood of the car at Jessica, who was doing the same thing.

She ended her stretch, tugged on the hem of her vivid pink sweater, and glanced around noncommittally. "It'll do. Let's check out the restaurant. I'm starving."

"Why don't we check in first? Get that done so we can relax."

"Sure," she agreed. She glanced toward the motel office but didn't make any move toward it.

Paul started to walk toward the office door. When he sensed that she wasn't following, he turned back. "You're not coming?"

She was standing, watching him with silent speculation. "Why don't you check in while I check out the menu," she said casually. "I need to use their restroom anyway."

Paul raised his eyebrows at her in surprise. "Okay." He hesitated. "All right," he drawled slowly, staring at her. "You want to stick to the room arrangement you made?"

She smiled mischievously. "Why don't you surprise me?" She turned and headed across the street without looking back.

Still staring at her, Paul shook his head in consternation. She was, he decided, a complicated woman. Still shaking his head, half in amusement and half in exasperation, he stepped into the office and paid for a single room with twin beds. After signing in, he joined her in the small, rustic restaurant. He waited for her to ask about his decision but she didn't. Instead she chattered cheerfully about mundane items of interest and threw her attention enthusiastically into her meal when it arrived. Paul followed her lead, closing his eyes with delight at his first taste of shrimp scampi.

"That was utterly delicious!" Jessica cried, rolling her eyes in mock ecstasy after she'd taken her last bite of a tequila-lime prawn. "This chef should be working at some fancy New York restaurant instead of down here where no one can find him."

"If he was in New York," Paul told her reasonably, "we wouldn't have found him."

"That's true," she agreed with a sigh of satisfaction and a grin. She picked up her napkin and wiped her lips. "So," she asked, peering at him with amusement, "what did you do about the room?"

66

Paul smiled enigmatically. "I thought you wanted to be surprised."

She wadded up her napkin and tossed it at him playfully. "You're a cad," she laughed.

"That's right," Paul agreed with a laugh. He looked at her empty plate. A starving man could not have cleaned it more thoroughly. "So, are you finished?"

She moaned softly as she stretched and patted her stomach. "I couldn't eat another bite. It was wonderful. Fabulous even."

"I'm glad you enjoyed it," Paul said. He pushed his chair back and stood, dropping his napkin next to his plate. He reached for the check but she snatched it out from under his fingers before he could blink.

"We'll have to share expenses and you'll have to learn not to argue with me about it," she told him tartly. "By the way, how much do I owe you for the room?"

Paul couldn't resist the temptation to watch her reaction. "Rooms," he corrected quickly.

Whatever reaction she had to his comment was gone before he could read it, sliding across her face like quicksilver. "Okay," she said mildly. "Rooms. How much do I owe you for mine?"

Caught in his own web, he ruefully admitted to his lie. "Sorry. It's just the one room. But two beds, like you

67

said" he added hastily.

She stared at him. "Why did you say it was two rooms?" she asked in surprise.

Paul felt himself blush. "I wanted to see your reaction," he admitted.

"And ...?" Jessica asked, studying him. "What reaction did you see?"

Paul tilted his head to look at her. "None, to be perfectly honest."

"Okay," she said in a quiet, clipped tone. "Well, let's not play that game again, okay? If you want to know something, just ask me. If you want to know what I'm thinking or feeling, ask and I'll tell you anything you want to know."

Paul nodded, abashed. "All right," he said quietly.

Her eyes studied his for several seconds. As if satisfied by what she had intuited about him, she nodded. With her free hand she reached out and touched him gently on the cheek. "I don't know if I'm ready for anything more serious than friendship. I don't crave a relationship in the way you do. I know it sounds cliché but I want to know if we can be friends. And let me just say one other thing, okay? Just because we've had other lifetimes together doesn't mean that everything will automatically be perfect and that we'd make a great couple. We were different people then. Each time we've come together we've been different. This time is the

68

same only in the fact that we know each other's soul. But we don't know each other's personalities yet. Sometimes the soul shines and lives and makes us who we are. Sometimes it gets overthrown by the personality and the ego and all of the things we've experienced. Let's take it one step at a time. Get to know each other again without expectations. And then what we both get out of it will be perfect for what it is." She studied him quietly. "Okay with you?"

He considered her for a minute, thinking about what she'd said and drawing his own conclusions. "Yes," he said quietly, "it's okay with me. But keep in mind that I have every reason to keep myself safe as well."

"It's not about keeping yourself safe, Paul. I wasn't saying any of that because I was making sure I wouldn't be hurt." Her tone was soft and puzzled. "It's about making the right choices for who you are and where you need to go with your life. Coming together to walk for a while or coming together to walk for a long time. Either way, if it's appropriate for your personal path and growth, then it's perfect. Whether it lasts for a week or a lifetime, it's perfect because something was gained. If we stay safe, we don't grow. I didn't say what I said because I fear what will happen between us. I said it because I want us both to be in this with total awareness, not rush forward in ignorance."

Paul looked at her without comment. He realized that his reaction to her words had cost him some of the spontaneity that he would have liked. She wasn't trying to create a distance, a safeguard, between them. She was trying, in her own way, to tell him to value what they

69

would share, no matter what it was or how long it lasted. With a rueful smile, he tilted his head toward the door. "Come on. Let's go for a walk."

He was instantly rewarded with her infectious grin.

"Let's," she agreed, allowing herself to be pulled toward the door. Laughing, she dropped the check and a wad of bills into the hands of the cashier, who had been watching them curiously, and followed Paul out the door.

Once outside they looked this way and that and then finally at each other. In the fading light of day, it looked like they hadn't chosen a motel in the safest neighborhood in town. The gloom of the falling night cast brooding shadows across the sidewalk. Closed doorways seemed to hide danger behind them. Several characters, their cigarette smoke curling in the air above them, leaned in the shadows, silently watching the night.

Jessica tugged on his hand, forcing his attention to her whispered words. "I have a better idea," she said. "Why don't we go to the room and see if there's a good movie on."

Paul nodded in quick agreement. In his mind it seemed that the danger that awaited them in Belize was more than enough to warrant taking the safe path here in Phoenix. His gaze traveled the narrow street as he wondered if any of the characters that lurked there had already singled them out as possible targets.

No one seemed particularly interested in them.

There was no one staring, no one pretending not to stare. As he scanned the street he noticed a faded and rusty blue pickup in the parking lot of the liquor store. Had he seen it on the highway coming down from Payson? If he had, it would be one hell of a coincidence. Or was his fear playing tricks on him?

He glanced at Jessica. She seemed unconcerned. Well, he decided, since she's psychic she would know whether the guys in the truck were the danger they'd been anticipating. She hadn't said anything. Shrugging to himself, he dismissed the truck from his mind. He tugged playfully on Jessica's arm, grinned, and nodded at the motel with his chin. Reading his intentions, she glanced back and forth at the street, noting the lack of traffic. She let challenge leap into her eyes and, without a word, started across the street at a dead run. Laughing, Paul broke into a run as well. He passed her just as they reached the opposite curb.

Stopping in the parking lot, he turned and grinned at her. "You're too darn fast for me," he laughed, gasping for breath. Running, even a short distance, after a heavy meal hadn't been his best idea of the day.

She was bent over at the waist, gasping for breath as well. "Hey!" she puffed. "No fair making me race after a big meal."

Still laughing, Paul turned the lock of the room he'd rented and pushed the door open. He blinked once, taking in the shabbiness, and instantly wished that he'd chosen another motel, another part of town. He turned to offer his apologies to Jessica.

71

She touched him lightly on the arm as she passed him, stepping into the room. "Don't worry about it," she said, reading his thoughts. "Neither one of us have ever been here. We don't know the area and we don't know if there's a better place down the road or not. Why chance it and end up driving on, looking for a better place, and find ourselves out of road and possibilities in the middle of the night?" She turned to him with a gentle smile. "Don't worry about it," she repeated. "Everything doesn't always have to be perfect in order to be right."

The simple statement caught him unaware. It rang through him like the toll of a bell, calling him to attention. That's something, he told himself, that I'd like to remember.

He smiled at her. "Thanks for reminding me of that," he said quietly. "You just alerted me to the fact that I get too intense about things sometimes."

"You always have," she told him, looking him straight in the eye.

"You mean other lifetimes, too?" he asked, staring at her. "I've been this way all along?"

Jessica stroked her forehead absently. "We have certain tendencies that kind of get ingrained in our energy fields. I guess that's the best way to phrase it. We kind of carry them along with us wherever we go. Don't worry about it," she said easily.

Paul pursed his lips and nodded. "Okay, I won't. At

least not much." He smiled at her and tucked the knowledge away to think about later.

Jessica chuckled and looked around. The two beds were haphazardly draped with faded, limp bedspreads. Pillows as flat as airless balloons lay beneath the covers. A white, coffee-stained shelf was bolted to the wall between the two beds and a small television was bolted onto the wall at eye level on the opposite side of the room. A chipped-paint, cream-colored door led into the bathroom.

She turned back to Paul and grimaced slightly. "Well, if you were planning on pushing the beds together you're out of luck."

Surprised, Paul opened his mouth to deny the allegation. He stopped when he saw the laughter in her eyes. "Damn," he joked, snapping his fingers in pretended frustration.

Jessica laughed. She tilted her head and studied him. "You don't think I sounded prudish back there, do you?" she asked, waving in the direction of the restaurant. "I mean, saying that I only wanted to be friends?"

Paul shook his head. "No. You were right." He perched on the edge of one of the beds. "Getting these tiles out is more important than anything else." He picked at a loose thread on the bedspread. "There's no point in complicating things."

Besides, it might just be interesting to have a female roommate. It was something he'd never tried before -

73

friends without intimacy. He stood and gave her a quick, awkward hug. Stepping back, he studied her face. She had the deepest green eyes he'd ever seen.

"I'm fine with this," he said. "Whatever it's going to take to make certain that we stay in each other's lives is fine with me. I think," he said slowly, "that our friendship during this mission is going to end up being more important than anything else."

She smiled slightly. "I'm glad you can see that. We have a long way to go. I'd like us to go as gently and peacefully together as we can. The tiles have to take priority over everything else." She smiled wryly.

Paul nodded. "That's true," he agreed. He turned away to look for the TV remote. "Actually, truer words were probably never spoken."

They chose a movie that they both thought they would enjoy and flopped down on separate beds to watch it. Before long, Jessica was snoring lightly. Amused, Paul turned the volume down, finished watching the movie, and quietly drifted into sleep himself.

In the morning there was a flurry of activity while they decided who would shower first, who wanted to be the one to run across the street for coffee, and who wanted to drive to the airport. Finally they were on the road, with Jessica in the driver's seat

As Paul settled himself, struggling not to spill his coffee while adjusting his jacket around him, he noticed Jessica's eyes flick to the rear view mirror several times.

74

"What?" he asked, feeling a sudden, unexpected tension drop onto his shoulders. He fought to keep himself from flipping around in the seat to look out the back window.

"It's probably nothing," she said quietly. But her eyes flicked back to the mirror again.

"Is it an old blue pick-up truck?" Paul asked, his voice low with tension.

She turned toward him quickly, as though responding to a sudden threat. "Why? How'd you know?"

"I noticed it last night. I thought it was my imagination." He turned and looked quickly over his shoulder. It was the truck he'd seen last night.

She slapped the palm of her hand on the steering wheel in sudden anger. "You can help matters by not dismissing your intuition, dammit! If I'm not paying attention, you should. Don't depend entirely on me. We're in this together. If you thought he was suspicious, you should have said something." She snapped a glare at him and turned her eyes back to the road. "Now we've got him on our tail and he knows what direction we're heading. He's bound to be smart enough to figure out we're headed to the airport, even if we managed to lose him right now."

"Not necessarily," Paul said, defending himself. "There's probably a thousand places we could go between here and there. It's a big city," he stated flatly, attempting

75

to defend himself. He glared across the small space between them. "Besides which, you're the professional psychic here. Why didn't you pick up on him last night?"

"Maybe I was thinking about other things," she snapped. "Maybe I don't want to be 'on duty' twenty-four-seven. Maybe I was counting on you to help me." She glared at him once again. "Maybe that was my mistake."

He waved his hand at her in an attempt to calm the air between them. "Okay. Okay. We're both getting off track here. The important thing isn't who's to blame but what the hell we're going to do about it." He watched her closely, trying to ascertain if her anger was dissipating with his words. He couldn't tell.

"Okay," he repeated. "Let's think. What can we do?"

She took a deep, steadying breath and looked at him quickly. "Sorry," she said contritely. "I guess I get mad when I get scared."

Paul dismissed her anger instantly. "Don't worry about it. I'm not so good at this either." He turned again, scanning the road behind them, doing his best to make it look natural.

Jessica heard him snort in surprise. She slid her eyes to the rear view mirror and studied it intently. "What ...? Where the hell is he? He was there a second ago." She looked at Paul quickly. "You saw him. He was there ... right? I didn't make this up?"

Paul shook his head. "No. You didn't make it up. I saw him. But where in the hell did he go?"

"That's my question!" She stared at him, her mouth slightly open in surprise.

"Humph," Paul coughed slightly. He studied the road behind them again. "I guess it was just a coincidence. He must have been headed in the same direction but turned off."

"I don't believe in coincidences," Jessica muttered.

"Well, I admit that I'm beginning to question them myself but...."

Jessica interrupted her own thought. "Well, it is whatever it is." She shivered slightly, an involuntary reaction to the release of tension that she was experiencing. "I just want to get these tiles safely away, that's all."

A sudden thought occurred to Paul. "And then what? Will they be safe just because we got them out of Belize and into the United States?"

Jessica snapped another glare at him. But this one wasn't as threatening as the last. "Don't even start with me!" she threatened lightly. "One crisis at a time is all I can handle."

Paul held up his hands in mock surrender. "All right. I won't bring up reality if you don't."

A laugh of surprise burst from her like a sudden, unexpected bark of a dog. "You've got one hell of a sense of humor, you know that?"

Smiling, Paul settled back against his seat.

They passed through the checkpoints at the airport without incident. Strangely quiet, both of them were suddenly captured by the enormity of the task before them. The flight to Miami was tedious, plunging both into their own private thoughts and apprehensions. By the time the plane landed, they were exhausted from the silent stress of their own thoughts and the steady, inescapable drone of the plane's engines. Having neglected to plan a hotel stay, they passed the hours before the next leg of their flight wandering lethargically between the snack bar, the restrooms, and the hard, plastic seats of the waiting area. It was with relief that they both sank into the seats of the next flight that would land them in Belize City.

With a wry grin, Jessica shared her thoughts. "I can tell you're as relieved as I am to be getting on this plane."

She chuckled. "You would think we'd be more stressed, instead of less stressed. We're at a point where we can't turn back, you know."

Paul smiled and lifted one shoulder in a wry gesture. "Yeah. You're right. We should probably be terrified by now. I don't know about you but I'm too tired to be terrified." He gave a small laugh.

Jessica rolled her head against the back of the seat

and yawned largely. "I'm not terrified of anything," she said lethargically. "But I am tired. Travel like this doesn't appeal to me. It takes too much out of me."

"Maybe we can take a day or two off to enjoy ourselves before we head off into the wilderness looking for these things."

Jessica pursed her lips in thought. "I doubt it. Seems to me we ought to get in and get back out as quick as we can."

"They've been there for a hell of a long time without our help," Paul argued. "Seems they'd be ok for another day or two."

The wheels running on the tarmac and the rushing sound of the engines gathering speed drowned out Jessica's response. Paul smiled at her tiredly, shrugged, and nodded. They'd talk about it later. He wasn't in the mood for an argument about anything. He glanced at the man coming down the aisle toward them. He looked vaguely familiar, like someone who had played a role in a movie Paul had seen recently. A sinister role. A dark, surly man with eyebrows that crawled across his forehead like a giant caterpillar. Why wasn't he in his seat with his seat belt fastened? Caught off-guard by the scowl the man gave him, Paul turned away. He glanced at Jessica, wanting to share his sudden sense of uneasiness, but she'd turned to the window and was staring out at the land of Florida as it disappeared from beneath them.

A few minutes later, lulled by Jessica's continued silence and the drone of the engines, he fell into a fitful doze. Danger seemed to surround him like an invisible shroud. The air itself seemed to hold secrets that were menacing. Figures lurked behind every building and tree. Somewhere a cat was hissing. The sound ran along Paul's spine like the grate of a steel blade. Just before he tore himself from sleep, the face of the familiar-looking man on the plane with them peered at him with thoughts that Paul knew spelled danger. He woke with perspiration dripping from his armpits. He was, for some irrational reason, glad to see the clouds parting as the plane began its descent. It was better, he silently reasoned, to face whatever awaited them, rather than fantasize about what might happen.

As the plane circled, waiting for a small twin-engine prop plane to land, Paul thought back to the last time he'd felt a deep lurking sense of danger. He'd forgotten to pick up razor blades on the way home from work. He hated using dull blades. He could have used one anyway. Or he could have gone without shaving for a day. But that stubborn streak of his, that everyone told him was there but that he continuously chose to ignore, worked on him until it had gotten him to ignore his intuition, which was telling him to stay inside.

It had been dark out and the city seemed to be telling him something as he stepped out into the still, night air. He chose not to listen. Instead of taking the Bronco, he'd decided to walk the few blocks to the store. The potential mugger was waiting in the shadows of a darkened doorway about a block away from Paul's destination. His voice had been low and demanding. Paul's feet had instantly felt as if they were nailed to the ground. He stopped in mid-stride. A cold chill swept

80

over him, along with a mad desire to tear the kid to shreds to teach him a lesson.

Though the night was so dark that the kid was only a shadow, Paul could tell he was small and lean. He knew he could take the kid down in a flash. He'd trained in the martial arts for almost two years, though it had been several years since he'd seen the inside of the training facility. But did the kid have a weapon?

Waiting for the next second to show him his future and help him make his choice about what to do, Paul caught a glimpse of the kid's eyes. With a shock, he realized that there was fear there. The rage he was feeling left him as suddenly as it appeared. His instinct told him that there was no weapon. Ignoring the icy touch of his sweat-soaked shirt against his fear-heated skin, he began walking again. Ignoring the kid's hiss of rage, he kept on walking. It wasn't until he'd reached the safety of the store lights that he allowed himself to breathe again.

His sense of danger at this moment was ten times what it had been that night. He didn't want to ignore his intuition and walk himself and Jessica into what was obviously going to be a dangerous situation. But what choice did he have?

He instinctively gripped the armrest as the plane bounced along the rough asphalt as the plane touched down. Silently unbuckling his seat belt, he picked up Jessica's carry-on and his own and walked behind her down the aisle into the humid, distinctly scented air of Belize.

The Jeep they'd rented was waiting for them. As they got on the road, they realized that, though it looked the worse for wear, it was one of the nicer vehicles on the road. As they drove around a bend and spotted Belize City, they both breathed a sigh of relief. It was a lot bigger, and more modern, than Paul had expected.

A short time later Jessica's tension was gone. "This is gorgeous!" she exclaimed, dropping onto a pillow-strewn wicker chair.

The chair sat on the small, wooden-railed deck of a rustic bungalow. She and Brenda had discovered the quaint motel with tiny bungalows when they'd browsed the Internet. The on-line brochure had been accurate. The pristine-looking beach sat only steps away from their door. The wooden shingles that dressed the small cottages were weathered and white-edged with sea salt. The interior of the room they'd been given was dim but a window gave them a view of the sea. Paul considered the place to be the highlight of his day, even if the residence was slightly less than what he had hoped for. But, as Jessica reminded him, they weren't here for a vacation.

Sweaty and exhausted from the tension, the humidity, and the drive, he dropped into the chair next to her and stared at the tropical-blue of the ocean. The waves were gentle, the day warm, the air kissed with the smell of the tropics. The jungle that lurked nearby seemed to emanate an almost-visible steam as it absorbed the sun and gave it back to the atmosphere in the form of humidity.

Jessica rolled her head against the high-backed chair to look at him. "This is really, really beautiful." She pushed several limp tangles of hair away from her face. Her face was pink from the heat. The shirt she had put on that morning, glowing purple swirls with brilliant, royal blue flowers, hung on her thin frame like a rag that had been dunked in dishwater.

Instead of being repelled, Paul found her all the more charming for her dilapidated appearance. "There's a part of me that wishes we were here under different circumstances." He studied her without speaking, letting his eyes talk for him.

A self-conscious blush made the pink of her cheeks become pinker. "Stop," she protested. "Friends. You promised."

"I did no such thing," Paul protested with a grin.

"You did!" Jessica teased.

"Did not!"

"Did!"

"Children! Really! Stop bickering."

The voice stopped them both instantly. Paul's heart leapt to his throat, shocked at the intrusion. He struggled to sit up, looking around for the person who had been eavesdropping. He coughed, choking on the sudden fear that gripped his throat.

"Oh. I apologize. I didn't mean to frighten you."

The voice showed itself as a small, rotund man emerged from the shadows between the bungalows. Paul studied him intently. He fit every typical description of a monk that he'd ever heard or read about. He wore a full-length, dirt-brown robe, tied at the waist with a worn hemp rope. A cowl draped limply down his back. His pudgy feet were adorned with thick leather sandals. He was clean-shaven and almost bald, except for a fringe of dark hair encircling his scalp. He had a wide nose and full cheeks and a large stomach. He reminded Paul of Santa Claus except for the darkness of his complexion. He appeared to be about sixty years of age.

"It's good to see you both," he said, his voice laced with a thick Spanish accent. "By way of introduction, my name is Louis. Louis Ramirez. And you're Paul," he added, nodding at Paul. "And you are Jessica?" he asked, peering at Jessica with admiring eyes.

"I'm impressed," Jessica said immediately. "You must be extremely psychic to know our names already."

Paul couldn't tell if she was being droll or not. He himself was shocked that the man knew who they were. He thought she was being extremely casual in the face of things. He flashed her a warning message with his eyes but she ignored him.

"Perhaps," Louis replied, with twinkling eyes and a small nod.

84

"Really?" Paul asked drolly, raising his eyebrows in question. He stared at the man with challenge in his eyes.

A small laugh exploded from Louis as he noted and then dismissed Paul's unspoken challenge. "Your names were given to me in the message."

"What message?" Paul asked suspiciously. "Who gave you a message?"

Jessica tapped his arm lightly. "You're being impolite," she told him quietly.

She turned back to Louis with interest. Paul was surprised but before he could react, she had spoken again.

"Won't you sit?" she asked, gesturing at the two narrow steps that led to the small deck.

Without hesitation Louis perched on the top step and leaned his back against the baluster. "Are you both prepared for your journey?" he asked brightly. Humor beamed from his eyes.

"I think we should talk about how you know us before we talk about anything else," Paul muttered, tossing another cautionary glance at Jessica, who continued to ignore him.

Louis bobbed his head agreeably. "All right. I was given a message. Much the same as the message that was

85

passed to your friend in Flagstaff."

Shocked, Paul found himself pulling back involuntarily. His back straightened. His neck arched. "How could you know that?" he snapped. He had met Marlen in Flagstaff, after Marlen had received a psychic message that he was supposed to meet and accompany Paul on his mission to rescue the survivors of the fallen alien craft. Out of the corner of his eye he could see Jessica shaking her head in aggravation.

"You would think that after all you've seen in the last couple of weeks, you would be more accepting by now," she stated.

The look she gave him made Paul feel flat inside. She was right. Part of him was ready to accept everything that he was experiencing but another part of him wondered if he wasn't lodged in a dream world that didn't resemble reality at all. "Sorry," he apologized quietly. "You're right." He forced himself to embrace the seeming impossibility and looked squarely at Louis. "Okay," do you know who passed you the message?"

"It was those on the mothership." Louis glanced up at the cloudless sky as if looking for the great craft.

"And what did they say? What's your role in this?" Paul asked.

"I am here to lead you to where they are. To the things you seek." Louis answered evasively. His eyes darted here and there, alert for anyone who might be listening.

Following his eyes, Paul glanced around as well. The small beach was empty except for a flock of tiny sandpipers that were scurrying this way and that, leaving thread-like tracks behind them. The day was clear, the air peaceful and quiet. If they were being followed, the people who were following them were invisible. "Do you think there are others looking as well?" he asked curiously.

"I don't think, I know," Louis said quietly but emphatically. "I haven't seen them yet. But I've sensed them. They're here somewhere. In due time they'll show themselves."

The face of the man Paul had seen on the plane flashed quickly before his eyes. He felt a sense of dread clutch his throat.

"They'll wait until we've recovered them," Jessica said flatly. "They don't know exactly where they are. They'll let us do the work of recovering them. And then they'll move in to take over."

Paul noted the lack of the word 'tiles' by both of them. Obviously they were both nervous about the unseen followers. "But you know where they are?" Paul asked, studying Louis.

He nodded without speaking, studying Paul in turn. He bobbed his head, as if he'd made an unspoken decision.

A sudden thought occurred to Paul. "Why haven't

87

you retrieved them if you know where they are?"

Louis studied him before answering. "It was not my task or my right," he finally answered.

After tossing a quick glare at Paul, Jessica interrupted their silent challenge of each other. "I don't want to seem anxious or anything," Jessica said, "but when do we start?" She glanced around quickly. "As beautiful as it is here, I'd like to be on our way back as soon as possible."

"We can start tomorrow morning, if that's all right with you," Louis answered. His eyes looked kindly on Jessica. "Perhaps we can meet for breakfast. Early. And then do what we must. I think we should be back in a day or two. We'll camp there one night." He looked at Paul. "I suggest you pay for the room for a week so that it's here when you return. Reservations are hard to come by and rooms fill up unexpectedly."

Paul nodded without answering. He'd already paid a week in advance.

"We were given a map," Jessica interrupted.

"Yes, I understand." Louis nodded enthusiastically. "I was told that it would be given. More as a confirmation than a direction, I believe."

Paul's brow wrinkled in puzzlement. "Excuse me?"

Louis waved his pudgy hand through the air. "They wanted you to know that they will be with you, leading

88

you, protecting you. I know where the things are. I will lead you. Your map won't be necessary."

A sense of suspicion returned to Paul. He glanced at Jessica covertly.

Louis caught the glance. "No," he protested quietly. He waved his hand again, cutting through the air in an attempt to erase Paul's suspicion. "It is all right," he insisted. "I won't mislead you."

Jessica glared at Paul once again. She turned back to Louis. "There has to be a doubting Thomas in every group, I suppose," she said, smiling at him apologetically.

"I wish you would accept," Louis said, leaning toward Paul insistently. "It will make it much easier."

"We'll see," Paul said noncommittally. His hesitation and doubt stood like invisible sentinels beside him. He had been warned of possible danger on this trip. He was in a foreign country. He felt responsible for Jessica's safety as well as his own. Letting down his guard could get them both killed. He wasn't about to let that happen. This man could well have gotten the information about them by tapping into the psychic energy of the experience, rather than directly from the mothership. He had no way of knowing for certain who this man was and what his intentions were. He would have to wait and see. But there wasn't much time for that if they were going to leave in the morning.

He stood, stretching tall and doing his best to appear casual. "Why don't we meet tomorrow morning?"

He took a step toward the bungalow door and glanced at Louis and Jessica with unspoken meaning. He used his chin to point in the direction of the tiny outdoor cafe that sat next door to the motel office. Brightly colored umbrellas shaded the chipped white enamel tables that sat in front of the cafe doorway. "We can meet over there. About six o'clock," he added.

Louis stood and studied Paul with eyes that were suddenly shielded. Gone was the sparkle and humor that had been there a minute earlier. He nodded once, deferring to Paul. "As you say," he agreed quietly. He stepped off of the porch and took one step backward.

Paul caught an unspoken exchange between Jessica and Louis before he was gone, as quickly as he'd appeared.

"What was that about?" Paul asked. He studied Jessica, taking in the angry flush on her cheeks. He wasn't going to back down though. He was responsible for keeping them safe. Or at least he thought he was.

Jessica stood, tugged on her shirt, and turned toward the door. Her attitude dismissed him like he wasn't there. "I don't want to discuss it," she snapped. She tugged open the screen door, pushed the wooden door open so hard that it slammed into the wall behind it, and stomped inside.

Not knowing what else to do, Paul followed her. She was standing at the window looking out. Her arms were crossed against her chest, a clear indication that she was furious. Doing his best to ignore her unwillingness to talk to him, Paul stepped to her side. "I just want to make sure that we're dealing with the good guys here. Not the bad guys," he said reasonably.

Her voice was laden with anger. "Don't you think I have the ability to know a good guy from a bad one?"

"I trust your abilities," Paul told her solemnly. "But I also know that people can camouflage themselves. You know that too." He touched her arm lightly and was relieved when she didn't pull away. "How can you be sure that he's not just really good at using psychic energy to convince you that he's a good guy?"

Jessica turned to him urgently. "I don't just read a person's energy as they are right here and now. I go way beyond that. I look at the line of energy that extends down from their soul. The connection between soul and spirit. You can't lie about that," she informed him.

Paul hadn't realized that it was possible to read so much about a person. The idea of seeing so much inter-dimensionally while still carrying on a conversation boggled his mind. "How can you sit and have a conversation with someone and still be tracking them through existence at the same time?" he asked.

Having calmed herself, Jessica smiled slightly. Paul breathed an internal sigh of relief. The last thing they needed was to be at war with each other.

"It's easy really. Once you get practiced at it."

91

"You'll teach me that trick?" Paul asked. He smiled, resisted his urge to reach for her, and turned away in order to stifle his sudden need. When they'd arrived he'd tossed both suitcases on one of the small, serape-draped beds. The serapes, though worn and faded, still brightened up the room with their flagrant coloring. Now he pulled his suitcase toward him and began rifling through it, looking for a clean shirt. "Why don't we change and get some dinner? Maybe go to bed early? It's going to be a big day tomorrow if we're going to do this."

He glanced over his shoulder at Jessica. She was still standing where he'd left her, her eyes closed in contemplation. His voice dropped instinctively to a whisper. "What?" he asked.

"I'm just passing a message to Louis," she answered immediately. Her eyes popped open and she peered at him brightly. "It's all right. He understands. He'll meet us tomorrow morning."

Paul blinked at her in surprise. "You can communicate with him that easily?"

Jessica nodded her head, smiling. "You have the ability too," she told him. "Once you get into the swing of being who you really are, it will all fall into place and make sense."

Paul stared at her, slightly bent out of shape about her cavalier attitude. Deciding not to pursue another argument, he turned back to his suitcase, and chose a pale blue T-shirt.

92

Opening her own suitcase, Jessica pulled out an eye-popping, glowing-red shirt, grinned at him, and skipped lightly into the tiny bathroom to change.

CHAPTER FOUR

THE NEXT MORNING, after a breakfast so large that Paul couldn't stop an occasional moan of discomfort, Louis bustled them into the Jeep, rustling around them like a mother hen with chicks. Paul had, during the night, decided that it was safe to trust him and, as though he intuited this, Louis behaved as if the doubt of the day before had never happened.

Smiling indulgently at Louis' herding, Paul allowed himself to be ushered into the driver's seat. Satisfying himself that they were comfortable, Louis hurried off and came back almost immediately with a large picnic basket. He settled in comfortably in the back seat beside him and, with the smell of fresh, warm tortillas filling the air, they headed toward the jungle.

"We'll head toward Belmopan," Louis instructed. "There's an open market there where we can get everything we need.

Paul nodded. "I tried to think of everything." He reached into the pocket of the jacket he'd laid beside him and pulled out a sheet of paper. "I have a list I made up last night. If you want to, check it out and see if I've forgotten anything."

"Do you have lanterns on the list?" Louis asked.

Paul shook his head, frowning. "I didn't think of that. Why will we need lanterns?"

"Well, we'll stop and get at least one. This cave is underground, you know."

Paul glanced back at him. "That never occurred to me." He gave Jessica a small, apologetic smile. "This isn't something I do every day."

Louis reached across the seat and patted Paul's shoulder. "I do not do this every day either, believe me. It's ok. I probably would not have thought of it either if I had not lived here all my life. But between the three of us, I think we will be all right." He turned and glanced backward again.

Paul watched him in the rear view mirror. "You looking for someone following us?"

Louis flipped him a quick glance. "Very astute. I'm looking for cars, yes."

"You see anything?" Paul asked.

Louis shook his head. "I don't see anyone." He looked at Jessica. "Do you sense anyone?"

Jessica tossed a glance at Paul before answering, as though she hoped to gauge his reaction before it happened. "I'm sorry to say that I do, yes."

Paul felt his heart thud dully against his ribcage. He closed his eyes for a brief, indulgent second of wishing that she hadn't said what she'd said. They had moved away from the populous area and were traveling along an increasingly rough road. They were passing through a

95

dense jungle of ceiba and tikal trees that were heavy and burdened by vines of undetermined origin. It was exotic, mystical, and threatening by its very nature of strangeness and murk. Adding anything else to the already tense situation would be almost unbearable.

Not bothering to stifle a heavy sigh, he took his eyes off the road long enough to glance at Jessica. "What now?"

She shook her head slightly. "We go forward. We can't back down now." She turned in her seat and studied Louis' face. "Did you bring a weapon?"

Paul swallowed hard, forcing down the shock he felt at her words. The reality of weapons hadn't occurred to him. He didn't believe in being a victim but he also didn't want to believe that violence would become necessary. As much as he hated to think about it they might have no choice but to defend themselves. Behind him, he could sense Louis nodding.

"Two," Louis said quietly.

"Good," Jessica said. The single word vibrated significantly through the air. She turned to face forward again, crossed her arms over her chest, and fell into silent thought. Heavy silence and anticipation permeated the car until the sight of Belmopan and the market place came into view.

At Louis' direction Paul stopped the Jeep across the road from a wide, open field. A cracked and rickety wooden bench served as a bus terminal. A rusted, glaucous-green, bus sat empty and waiting, the glass of its windows gone. The bus driver and passengers were nowhere in sight but then, judging by its appearance, they could have abandoned it ten years earlier.

An old man and woman were sitting stoically beneath the market's thatched roof. Wooden slats made up the walls. Four by fours held up the roof. There was no front to the tiny building and the two old people stared openly and curiously at the three strangers who had driven into their solitude.

"Belmopan is Belize's inland capital," Louis informed them as they all exited the Jeep. "On the other side of that hill over there," he said, pointing, "is the actual town. It's a neighborhood actually. Not a very large place."

"Are they going to have a lantern here?" Paul asked skeptically, studying the tiny, open-air market and the two proprietors who still stared unblinkingly at them.

Louis nodded enthusiastically. "Oh, most certainly." He started toward the market, his bulk bouncing slightly under his robe, his feet shuffling and kicking up a minor dust storm. "We will ask. A carbide lamp," he said over his shoulder. "That's what we'll need."

Paul walked around the car to stand next to Jessica.

She was standing, arms crossed, holding her elbows. Tension radiated from her. She muttered under her breath. "Going underground doesn't appeal to me at all."

97

It was the first time that Paul had seen her totally unnerved. "You'll be all right," he assured her, touching her arm sympathetically. He resisted the urge to draw her into a comforting embrace. "We'll go in and you can wait outside," he added, standing close. He hoped his presence and his words would help her to overcome her fear.

Jessica shook her head strongly. "Absolutely not. I need to be a part of this. I can handle it."

Paul stared at her, a serious expression dominating his face. "I think we need to know now. Were you one of the Mayan people who received the tiles?" he asked. He knew that it wasn't an appropriate time or place but it felt like it was imperative for him to know. If she reacted to her situation based upon her past life experience, he would need to be informed so that he could help her if she needed help.

She avoided looking at him directly, her eyes flitting around the landscape like anxious butterflies. She ducked her head quickly and made a half-turn away from him, re-crossing her arms over her chest as she did. "I'm pretty sure that I was, yes." She rubbed her arms with her hands as if warming herself. "Now that I'm here and can see and smell this place, I'm almost one hundred percent certain." She glanced at him quickly and away again, dropping her gaze to the ground. "I have a memory of being there. It's not crystal clear though. I'm probably avoiding it because it's too painful."

"You weren't responsible for the tiles not being revealed," Paul said softly, instinctively following her line

98

of thinking. He tucked his finger beneath her chin and lifted it, forcing her to meet his eyes. "You weren't responsible," he repeated, emphasizing his words while his eyes attempted to drill the truth into her.

"I know," she said tensely, jerking her head away.

"You wouldn't be reacting this way if you didn't feel somehow that you were responsible," Paul insisted. "Look at you. You're as tense as a trapped rabbit."

She spun toward him abruptly and glared at his face. "I died here," she stated flatly. "And it was a horrible death. Do me the honor of allowing me to react to that."

"I'm not telling you to deny your emotions," Paul said quietly. "I'm trying to get you to address them before we get there. Better now than down inside that cave."

Involuntary tears sprang into her eyes. She rubbed her hands harshly over her arms. Behind him, Paul heard a spurt of loud Spanish from Louis as he exchanged conversation with the old couple.

"You're right," Jessica admitted begrudgingly. "Absolutely right." She waved her hand toward Louis. "Why don't you go help him and leave me alone for a few minutes? Let me deal with this in my own way."

Paul considered her and then, understanding her need to be alone, he nodded and reluctantly turned away. But even as he walked toward the market, his senses stayed with her. He could feel her struggling against the tears and the horror of her memories.

Louis greeted him with a big smile. "Look," he said happily, pointing at the narrow wooden boxes that made up several narrow aisles in the small market. "Papayas, aguacates, you name it! We have everything. Look," he said again, pointing at something that looked like fish bones. "Those are petrified fish. And here, these are fossilized turtle shells," he told Paul, shuffling his bulk sideways down the narrow aisle. "Very valuable. Very sacred to some."

"They're heavy," Paul said as he lifted one. "How old are they?"

Louis lifted one shoulder in a shrug. "Who knows? Many, many years. It takes thousands, sometimes millions of years to fossilize some things."

"Where do you find them? I mean, originally?"

"Oh, here and there. Throughout the region." Louis waved his arm randomly. "There are many ruins, many sacred places, many things to find in this land."

"I can imagine," Paul said, raising his head and sniffing the air, attempting to breathe in the antiquity of the land. "It's a really beautiful place."

Louis nodded agreeably. "Yes. Most beautiful."

The two men raised their heads simultaneously at a sound that seemed to be roaring toward them at a high rate of speed.

100

Paul looked at Louis with a puzzled glance. "Trouble?" he asked.

Louis nodded. "Trouble," he verified.

Before Paul could react, Louis was headed toward the Jeep, kicking his robe away from his ankles with every step. Paul quickly followed, not knowing what to expect.

Into sight came a rusted, faded-orange truck. Two men, both with hats pulled tightly over their foreheads, stared intently at Paul as the truck raced past. The passenger yelled something indecipherable. The truck screeched to a halt several hundred yards away. The two men proceeded to yell harshly at each other in Spanish, waving their arms at each other with threat.

Paul, standing next to Louis by now, pointed at the men with his chin. "That's them," he said tensely.

Louis nodded. The angry look on his face seemed out of place with his monk outfit. He pulled the door of the Jeep open. Paul realized that he was planning to get the weapons that he'd mentioned earlier.

He reached for Louis' arm, stopping his action. "No. Don't start anything here." He glanced toward the old couple who were now standing and staring, open-mouthed, at the truck and its occupants.

"Senor," Louis insisted, "they will follow if we don't stop them."

101

"We won't get what we came for if we end up in jail," Paul told him, his tone dripping with significance as he nodded at the couple. "You don't think that, if we start something here, we're going to be allowed to leave, do you?"

Louis dropped his head in acquiescence. In doing so, he noticed that he had several pieces of fruit in his hand that he hadn't paid for. He shook his head in aggravation. "Pretend that we do not know," he said quietly, commanding Paul's attention with his eyes. "I will pay for the fruit and get the lantern. I will walk like I have not noticed them." He glanced surreptitiously at the truck, where the two men had stopped waving their arms and were settling back into their seats. "They are leaving. I'm sure they have decided the same thing we have. They will wait until we lead them to the hiding place."

At the sound of the grinding gears of the truck, Paul risked another glance at the two men. "Looks like you're right." He shrugged his shoulders in an attempt to loosen the tension that had leapt on him at the sight of the truck.

Louis tapped him lightly on the arm and then tapped himself on the temple. "Think. You do not have the treasures yet. They will wait until you do. That is why I wanted to stop them here. Before they know where the treasure is. But you are right. They would not find the treasures if we did not lead them. Perhaps by then we will think of something to eliminate them."

Paul shook his head, disagreeing again. "If you're

thinking about what I think you are, forget it. We can't risk going to jail."

"You did not think you would get away with the treasures without some casualties, did you?" Louis said tightly. "They can't be allowed to succeed. We will have to do whatever it takes." He turned abruptly and walked slowly back to the market, his head bent in thought.

Half an hour later, at Louis' direction, they pulled off the rutted road onto an almost invisible track. Paul winced as branches scraped the sides of the Jeep.

"We're going to be ending up paying for a paint job," he muttered to no one in particular.

"This is a good thing," Louis offered.

"Paying for a new paint job is a good thing?" Paul grumbled.

Louis shook his head innocently. "No. It is a good thing that we pull off here. We stop for a while and give them a chance to wonder where we are. Maybe they will backtrack. Maybe we will lose them." He smiled complacently. "Make the men wonder where we are since they went ahead of us. I am sure that they are waiting somewhere nearby for us to pass. Now we don't pass. And they wonder why. Maybe they will double back," he said again.

Jessica chuckled unexpectedly. "I'm surprised at

103

myself but I'm not really worried about all of this any more."

Paul studied her, suddenly concerned about her. "You're not?" he asked, raising his eyebrows at her in question.

"No. I don't know why." She shrugged lightly. "I'm just not."

To Paul she seemed almost euphoric. He wondered if she was all right. He was going to ask when the track ended abruptly. Startled, he slammed on the brakes. With a shaking hand, he pointed into the distance. "What is all this?" he asked.

In front of them lay a wide-open field of soft violet flowers, delicately bathing the landscape in serenity.

"An orchid field," Louis said placidly. "We have many. The climate is perfect for them."

"They're awesome," Jessica breathed. She shoved on her door and stepped out of the Jeep to inhale the soft smell of wonder.

On a nearby tree a parrot released a heart-stopping screech and took flight.

"I guess we stop here for a short while," Louis commented, following Jessica out of the Jeep.

"We don't have much choice since the road ended," Paul protested feebly, following them as they headed toward the sweet-smelling field.

Louis turned back to him. "We will have a piece of fruit. Relax. Not worry." He patted Paul's arm as Paul caught up with him. "Not worry," he repeated.

Paul rolled his eyes with an exaggerated show of patience and allowed himself to enjoy the sight in front of him. Rolling waves of fragile violet mixed with vivid threads of velvet green grass. A distant, low-lying range of forest green mountains sheltered the meadow. It was a scene that inspired peace, even for the most resistant person.

After enjoying the serenity and several pieces of fruit, they all agreed that it was time to continue on. They hadn't heard the sound of the truck. The men, apparently, had decided not to backtrack and look for them but instead to lie in wait somewhere back on the main road.

Once back on the road, Paul asked, "Where exactly are we headed?"

"We will camp overnight near the edge of the Usumacinta River," Louis answered. "We can bathe there. Tomorrow morning we will hike into where the cenote lies."

"What's a cenote?" Jessica asked.

"It is a crater," Louis told her. "Normally there is a pool of water at the bottom but this one is dry. It is a sinkhole, I believe you might call it. This one is perhaps one hundred feet deep. Along the walls are hidden shelves where the Mayans hid treasures. Unknown to anyone, their cave led into this cenote. We can enter the cave and travel through its tunnels until we reach the pit. That way we do not have to rappel down with ropes. Once we get to the cenote, we will search the walls until we find the treasures."

"One hundred feet below the surface?" Jessica asked weakly.

From where he sat, Paul could hear her gulp back her panic.

"Will this be a problem for you?" Louis asked, laying a hand on her shoulder.

Jessica took a deep, steadying breath. "I don't know. I'll try. We'll see how it goes." She took another deep breath. "I'll do my best." She smiled weakly at Paul, who was watching her carefully.

He reached out to touch her arm. "You don't have to do this," he told her once again. "We can go down alone."

Louis shook his head. "I do not know. The other option will be to leave her above while we go down. That would be dangerous." He glanced at the empty road behind them. "If the men show up again, she will be alone."

"That's true," Paul agreed, nodding. He grimaced in thought. "Well, we'll just have to see how things feel once we get there, I guess." He reached across the seat and squeezed Jessica's hand lightly. "It will be all right," he assured her.

She attempted to smile at him, her lips trembling. "Let's take it one step at a time," she said. "Now let's drop the subject for the moment. You're making me nervous by talking about it."

It wasn't long before they reached Louis' chosen destination. They hadn't seen any sign of the orange truck. Jessica had lost her sense of them. Perhaps they had given up after all. More relaxed than before, Paul gaped at the sight in front of him and leapt from the Jeep, stretching vigorously. "This is perfect," he cried. Taking off his sneakers and socks, he ran across the brief sand shore and walked into the gentle river, instantly soaking his pant legs.

"I don't believe this," Jessica cried happily. She pulled off her sandals and followed Paul into the water. Her face was alight with pleasure. "This is beautiful," she cried.

Together they stood on the shallow edge of the water and gazed around in wonder. The jungle pressed against the thin, winding river. Vines reached across the water, stretching from tree limb to tree limb, lacing an umbrella over the water. Sunrays touched the water here and there, making the river bottom appear diamond-strewn. Two tropical red-breasted birds with iridescent plumage watched curiously, unafraid. Toads and river frogs talked amongst themselves hoarsely. Wildlife tracks paraded back and forth from both shores.

107

"Oh, look!" Jessica whispered, pointing cautiously.

A wild turkey paced on the opposite shore, watchng them nervously.

After setting up camp, the serenity of the place took them all into its embrace. For the moment, thoughts of the men who were following them, the dangers that waited, the perilous hike through the cave to the cenote, all were put aside. After choosing to forgo lunch and make the picnic basket full of food their dinner, Paul stretched out beneath a canopy of heavy foliage. Jessica and Louis sat nearby. Their voices low, as if fearful of disturbing the tranquility, Jessica and Paul filled Louis in on the events that had led them to this place.

"I have only seen the craft in my visions," Louis told them as they finished the telling of their story, "though those visions are crystal clear." He peered up through the foliage at the calm expanse of space above them. "It would be such a joy to see one physically appear." He sighed lightly. "But I have a feeling that I would be depressed as well. I would want to leave with them." He looked significantly at Paul. "As you did," he added quietly.

Paul glanced at Jessica. "We both wanted to leave with them." He studied his hands, thinking. "This is not our home. We both know that." He looked up quickly, surprise at his own thought etched on his face. "I wonder if it's anyone's home," he speculated. "I never thought of that!"

108

Jessica spoke up. "I have. Because we're all originally in soul form, not physical at all but rather a light form that lives everywhere and nowhere at once, I imagine that this is really home to no one." She spread her hands the way one might if offering a gift to another. "It makes sense to think that we choose to become physical on this planet in order to accomplish something for the good of our soul. Why else would we do it? So, if we are not originally physical, how could this be home to anyone?"

Louis pursed his lips in thought and rubbed his chin, a habit that Paul was noticing more and more often. "Perhaps those who feel like Earth is truly their home have simply had more incarnations here than the two of you. Or me, for that matter." He gave them a smile that resembled the grin of a shy child.

"My first and only metaphysical teacher gave us some food for thought once," Jessica told them. "She suggested that it might be possible that we are living on other dimensions simultaneously. That we believe we are only here and not elsewhere due to the fact that our entire focus is here." She smoothed her intensely purple blouse over her frame, hoping to avoid wrinkles, before she stretched out on her side with her head propped on her hand.

Surveying them with shining eyes full of curiosity, she continued. "I mean, that could make a lot of sense. Think of this ... if we are limitless souls and we exist out there someplace, then obviously we exist in at least two places at once. Right?" She peered at them brightly, waiting for a response.

109

When the two men only nodded thoughtfully, she went on, speaking her own thoughts aloud. "So, does it make sense to think that our soul, as limitless as it is, would settle for expressing itself in only one way at one time? I mean, physically down here but nowhere else? Do you see what I mean?" She pulled delicately on a thread of grass.

To Paul it was obvious that she was struggling to contain a bushel full of speculations and wonderings. He could read in her eyes a lifetime full of far-reaching thoughts as she pondered the mysteries of the universe. Until a few weeks ago, he had encountered other worlds only in his dreams. But Jessica had been psychic, 'sensitive' as she called it, since birth. Similar to his own life, most of her life, he decided, must have been spent trying to figure out how she had landed on Earth in such a limited form as a physical body when there was a vast existence out there that was hers to explore.

He left his thoughts to address her question. "It makes sense, I suppose," he said thoughtfully. "Obviously there is more to existence than just this." He waved his hand for emphasis and then glanced at Louis. "I mean, this is extremely beautiful but, well, you know what I mean."

Louis nodded enthusiastically. When he got excited his accent was as thick as molasses. He was excited about this subject. Paul struggled to follow his words.

"I know what you mean," Louis said, shifting himself and using his body to emphasize his words. "Beautiful but limited. Yes. But is not all of life here on Earth limited?

By the very nature of its solid form? But what we have to remember is that there is a reason for it. As brilliant as we are, our soul is what I mean, we would not limit ourselves for no reason. You understand?"

Paul got the gist of what he was saying. He nodded his head in agreement. He opened his mouth to comment but shut it abruptly as Louis' thoughts continued to tumble out.

"That is what we do, no? We spend our time trying to understand why we are here. Why we are on Earth. Perhaps our souls have the answer? Perhaps it would help if our souls would tell us?"

Jessica laughed, the sound erupting from her like a suddenly activated fountain. "I wish!" she exclaimed. "If it was only that simple." She laughed again.

Obviously she was charmed by the very idea of things being that simple.

"Wouldn't that be the answer to a prayer?" Louis said. His pleasure at Jessica's amusement was evident.

"Well, I, for one, am putting out a call to my soul," Paul told them, only half-joking. "I'm open for any answer at all."

Jessica clapped him on the knee with her hand. The suddenness of her touch made Paul jump.

"Don't say that," she warned him soberly. "Be careful what you ask for. Be specific. Otherwise, you will get

111

exactly that. You'll get any old answer. The universe will supply you. But you have to ask for exactly what you want. Otherwise, you'll get the answer from the garbage heap of thought forms out there. Ask for the answer to come directly from the source of your own soul and be specific about what you want to know. That way you'll hear Truth."

"That makes sense." He grinned. "You would make a great teacher for me. I'm new to all of this you know."

Jessica snorted in denial. "New, my foot. You've been at this incarnation thing as long as I have. You just don't remember as well as I do."

"And why is that, do you suppose?"

She lifted her shoulders in a quick shrug. "You made different choices. You had a different game plan than I did. Your soul wants to accomplish different things with this lifetime than mine does. It's not deep," she added with a smile. She studied him briefly, her head tilted like a dog that was only mildly curious about something. "We plan the way we're going to live our lives before we come here. Not the activity of every day, of course," she added quickly, "but the way we're going to present ourselves. The knowledge that we'll remember. What we'll need from our soul connection in order to achieve what we hope to achieve."

"I should have planned differently," Paul grumbled good-naturedly.

Jessica chuckled. "Maybe next time you'll be more

careful." She sobered. "But I think we can also change things for ourselves. If we grow more than we supposed that we would we can expand our awareness more than we originally planned to."

Paul smiled at the comment. "I, for one, would like to see that happen for myself." He peered at her curiously as a thought occurred to him. "Are you one of those who believe that we live all lifetimes simultaneously?"

Jessica shook her head. "I haven't been able to wrap my brain around that concept yet. I've thought about it but I just can't quite grasp it." She shrugged. "Maybe it's true. Maybe it's not. I don't know yet."

"Yet?" Paul smiled.

Jessica smiled. "Yet," she asserted. "If I really want to understand something all I have to do is tell the Universe to explain it to me. Eventually, if I pay attention, the answer will come."

Paul pursed his lips and nodded thoughtfully. "Sounds like something I ought to try."

Another laugh exploded from her. "Maybe!" she exclaimed joyfully, shaking her head. "You're such an entertainment to me," she added, still chuckling.

Paul shook his head in mock reprimand. "I can never tell if you're teasing me or making fun of me."

"I love you," she said lightly. "You know that."

113

The glance she tossed him was almost a tangible form, fraught with meaning. At least that's the way Paul chose to see it. He struggled to think of something to toss back at her, could come up with nothing appropriate, and decided to let the comment stand alone. He glanced at Louis, who raised his eyebrows in silent question but said nothing.

A sudden exhaustion gripped Paul. He was unsuccessful at stifling a yawn. "I think I need to take a nap," he said. "For some reason I can't seem to keep my eyes open."

Jessica looked at him significantly. "That's because you're being sent a message. They can't get to you while you're awake because you're not listening. So they'll put you to sleep and talk to you in dream state."

"Why don't they just give you the message and you can give it to me?"

Jessica shook her head. "Not my job." She chuckled once again.

Dusting his jeans off as he stood, Paul left them to their conversation and laid down on top of his sleeping bag, his hands tucked under his head, staring at the canopy of trees as though they could show him what it was that he wanted to know. The future, he told himself. I want to know the future. He fell asleep with the thought.

Solomon, his spirit guide, waited for him on the other side of the veil. His appearance, as usual, was comforting to Paul. The now-familiar salt and pepper hair that blended down his jawbone to his short, blunt beard. The deep, wisdom-filled blue eyes that looked at Paul with knowing and acceptance. The thin but strong shoulders that sat beneath the robes he wore.

Paul greeted him affably.

"Greetings," Solomon replied. "You are well?"

Paul found himself nodding. "Yes. I'm well. And you?"

Solomon's smile was small. "Always well. Indeed."

Paul grinned. Just the knowing that Solomon walked beside him filled him with pleasure. He recalled the time when the veil that cloaked his memories of their time together had been lifted. He had been given the memory of their lives together. He and Solomon had walked together for centuries, through time and experience, joy and hardship. It was a friendship that had stood throughout history. When one walked in spirit, the other walked in flesh, and vice versa.

"You are prepared for this leg of your journey?" Solomon asked quietly.

"I think so, yes." He looked around. They were standing together in space, nothing surrounding them but air. It was vast and somehow unnerving. Paul realized that he had grown used to having physical

115

evidence of his existence, even while he fought against the limitations it presented.

"You will succeed," Solomon told him confidently.

Paul eyed him doubtfully. "You seem very certain. You know there are men following us?"

"Of course I know," Solomon assured him. He cast his hand through space with a nonchalance that Paul wished he himself could feel. "They are of no concern." He paused. "But there are others who might be of concern."

Paul stared at him. "Well, the men concern me," Paul said, not understanding what he was alluding to but knowing that it would be revealed. "Louis has a couple of guns. I don't think either he or Jessica will hesitate to use them. I don't want this. And now you're telling me there are others I should be worried about too?"

Solomon simply nodded without giving him more specifics. "Hopefully it won't come to the point of having to use your weapons. I would hate to see that too," he said ruefully.

Paul stared at him. "Hopefully? You mean you don't have the answers? I thought up here you could see all of the results of everything."

Solomon shrugged slightly. "Everything is based upon people's choices. Every person's choices affect all things and all people around them." His age-wise eyes peered at Paul intently. "Some things are knowable. Others are

116

not. The only thing that is certain in this universe is that all events affect all other events. All things being energy, you know."

Paul knew. He'd been told time and time again that all things were made up of energy and were not solid. Therefore, all energy was capable of affecting all other energy, since energy has no boundaries. "And this is or isn't knowable?" he asked, going back to the original topic in search of more reassurance than he'd received thus far.

"It is time for the tiles to be revealed," Solomon told him, his tone matter-of-fact and confident. "It is your task to reveal them. I remain confident that you'll do exactly as you set out to do."

"I wish I had the confidence in myself that you seem to," Paul muttered.

Solomon held up one commanding index finger. "Aha! And therein lies the difference between you and I. A difference you should address, I might add."

"And what is that supposed to mean?" Paul asked with irritation. He shook his head. "It would be so much easier if everyone didn't speak in mysteries and just said, point blank, what they had to say."

"All right," Solomon said instantly, surprising Paul with his acquiescence. "I will put it to you this way." He pointed to a marble bench that had mysteriously appeared, suggesting that they sit. "My friend," he began, after they were seated, "every time that you have created

117

a physical expression of yourself you have fallen into doubt. The problem is, of course, the dichotomy between the reality of physical expression and the reality of soul expression. However," he held up an admonishing index finger, "that isn't a good enough excuse to set aside your truth and your personal power. This will be your final lifetime in this universe. It is the perfect opportunity to heal that dichotomy. That is why your soul has chosen the challenges that it has chosen. To deal with this final issue before you move on to other experiences.

"Healing the dichotomy is the last great lesson for you in this universe. You have a mind that accepts and understands energy quite easily. You also understand the tremendous impact of one energy upon another. But what you fail to understand is how to put the energy of your soul into an energy such as an Earth life."

Paul easily accepted the truth of what Solomon was saying. But why was it necessary to do as he was suggesting? It was a question Paul had asked himself more than once. Now he asked it of Solomon. "Why is it necessary? Why did I have to come from a place where I know absolute peace and place myself into chaos? That doesn't make sense to me. It never has."

"How else would you learn your strengths?" Solomon asked gently. "How else would you come to understand the limitations that you've placed upon yourself if you don't create a situation wherein you can address those self-imposed limitations? And how else would you learn to be a creator if you do not come to understand the darkness and the light, the positive and the negative?" He waved his hand at the supreme emptiness that

118

surrounded them. "There are no limitations in existence. None whatsoever," he emphasized. He tapped Paul on the chest gently. "And there are no limitations to the soul. But because the physical body is a limited form of expression, you have allowed it to limit your spirit as well. The point of taking a physical incarnation can be lost when one allows this to happen."

"And what is the solution?"

"The solution is simple. Allow your soul to guide your spirit and allow your spirit to guide your body."

"That sounds simple enough," Paul told him, "but it's easier said than done."

"Why?" Solomon's eyes were cool and direct as he challenged Paul.

Paul fell silent as he struggled to put his answer into words.

"You see?" Solomon said, interrupting Paul's thoughts. "By the very fact that you have to struggle to name your limitations, you are alerting yourself to the fact that you have created those limitations. In your mind you are fighting with your limitations, trying to name them. They are the children of your creation and you are struggling to defend them, to speak out loud their right to exist. You are in the process of defending your creation." He tapped Paul on the knee lightly. "Apply that same struggle, that same passion, to defending your soul's right to express through your physical body, and you'll have a great work of art.

119

Something to be proud of when you pass through the veil on your final journey away from Earth."

To Paul, it seemed as if a veil had been lifted with the words. It seemed so simple. Why, he wondered, do I hesitate to express my soul and the truth of who I am on Earth? Is it fear? He immediately knew that the answer was yes.

"Why do I fear so much down there?" he asked out loud.

"You have had lifetimes during which you have suffered greatly. You resist more suffering and so you hide yourself. You fear to expose your truth, for if people know your truth they may choose to attack you or try to change you. It's happened before."

Solomon laid a gentle hand on Paul's shoulder. "You are not alone. Many people on Earth have experienced similar things and are in fear as well. They have been persecuted for who and what they are and the pain was so great that it is lodged in their energy fields even now. And so they hesitate to speak. Or they hesitate to love. Or they hesitate to live. Do you see?"

"I see," Paul said soberly. He felt a surge of energy rush through his chest like a brush fire, sudden and all consuming. He smiled as he wondered if this might be the first sign of his real purpose on Earth. He vocalized what he was thinking. "I want to make it my purpose to heal myself so that I can achieve a freedom for my soul."

Solomon gave a brief, satisfied nod. "You have found

what you were looking for during this meeting, my dear friend. I will meet with you again soon."

Before Paul could react, he was waking up near the Usumacinta River beneath the overhang of leaves and vines.

Jessica glanced over at him and smiled. "You have good timing. Dinner's ready."

In the jungle the night comes early and fast. The heavy foliage draped the jungle floor with a cool, murky darkness. After a full meal, some light conversation, and a quick rinse in the chilly water of the river, they were all ready to call it a night.

The early light of morning woke Paul before the others. He sat up quietly, pulling his sleeping bag over his shoulders for warmth, and surveyed his surroundings. It felt like he'd stepped into another world, both physically and emotionally. He was anxious to tackle the problems of the day. Get the thing over with and get on his way back to relative safety. He glanced impatiently over at Louis, who still slept. Looking for an avenue for his pent-up apprehension, he tossed the sleeping bag aside and strolled to the river where he scrubbed his face with the cold morning water. Feeling a stir in the air around him, he turned to find Jessica next to him.

The sweat suit she'd slept in was bright red and as wrinkled as a wadded-up Kleenex. Her hair looked golden as the early rays of light tangled in it. Her cheeks were pink, her eyes tired and swollen.

"How'd you sleep?" she asked.

"Fine," Paul answered. He studied her. "You look exhausted. You didn't sleep well?"

She shook her head. "No. I had bad dreams." She pulled her fingers through her sleep-tangled hair in an attempt to straighten it.

"Want to tell me about them?" He could sense her dreams sitting upon her shoulders like invisible shadows. Instinctively, he wanted to brush them away for her.

She shook her shoulders and tossed her head, making an effort to toss off the memories. "Just being here. Living here. The whole experience," she said shortly.

"And the dying?" Paul asked quietly.

"That too." She waved her hand, waving away his sympathy. "We all die. It happens."
Paul nodded in agreement. "Yes. But we all aren't massacred. At least, I don't think we are."

Jessica tilted her head slightly, thinking. "I don't know. I often think that maybe every one of us has to experience every single thing there is in order to know it, to truly understand it."

"Really?" Paul asked with interest. "I hadn't thought of that but it makes sense."

122

"Yes. I think we're experiencing all things so that we can become creators. And if we're going to create something, we have to know the good and bad of it all. Don't you think?" She peered at him quizzically.

Paul nodded in thoughtful agreement. Her words sounded much the same as Solomon's. He studied her silently, again wondering who she really was. Each time they came together to talk, the stirring of recognition within him became deeper and stronger. At a movement behind her, he glanced over her shoulder to see Louis stirring. "We ought to get going pretty soon," he said. "The sooner we have the tiles and are on our way back, the better I'm going to feel."

"I know what you mean." She grimaced slightly and looked around the serene setting. "I can sense those guys. I think they're watching."

Suddenly as tense as a cat next to a bathtub full of water, Paul rolled his shoulders in aggravation. "Damn," he muttered. "Come on," he ordered, heading back to the sleeping bags. "Let's get this over with."

Jessica followed him without protest, as anxious as he was to get the journey successfully completed.

After a change of clothes and a quick snack of cheese wrapped in tortillas, Louis led them along a thin, tree-shaded path that seemed to be threading them back through history. All three were silent, listening for followers, listening to their own fears. When the path ended they were standing before a nature-sculpted

123

outcropping of clay. The clay was weather-worn in such a way that it looked like a sentry guarding the cave entrance. The outcropping towered over them about twenty feet. Where the earth met the foot of the giant cliff, the earth simply disappeared, seeming to spiral downward into a vortex of empty space. The light in the cave was an unearthly green-gray that turned to black as it went deeper into the earth. Looking like dragon's teeth, stalactites grinned down at them from the ceiling.

"Be careful here," Louis said, going forward without hesitation. He held up a carbide lamp, lighting the way. Paul carried one as well, in case they were unlucky enough to get separated.

Paul hesitated, watching Jessica for signs of nervousness. She gestured him forward with a commanding sweep of her hand. "Go," she snapped. "I'm fine. Let's just do it." She locked her jaw around her tension and urged him forward.

With tentative steps, they made their way deeper into the cave. As the darkness swallowed them, Paul felt his skin crawl. He fought with himself as he felt a weird, unexplainable sensation crawl through his heart. It felt like the cave and its history were claiming victory over them now that the draw of the tiles had compelled them to return. For several heart-stopping seconds he imagined that history had created this ploy to lure them back to the original failure in order to re-play their deaths again and again. He reprimanded himself silently. This is bizarre. Get a grip!

But as they threaded their way deeper into the cave

124

the sensation of death gripped his throat with the intensity of a furious lion. He could only imagine what Jessica was going through. He could sense her behind him, agonizing with her own ghosts. He deeply admired her courage.

"Look," Louis said. His voice was a whisper. He nodded at the walls of the cave.

Paul held his lamp high, shining the light on the wall. A cluster of hieroglyphs decorated the wall.

"Kanul," Jessica whispered hoarsely. With a trembling hand she touched one of the etched pictures. "A supernatural guardian."

Paul felt chills race along his spine.

Beside him, Louis nodded. "Right," he agreed. "Ancient. Very ancient."

They continued on, each of them warring with their own memories and ghosts. When Louis veered to the left and entered another hallway, Paul and Jessica followed without question.

Paul stopped as he noticed a shiny blackness on the floor. "What is it?" he whispered.

"Water," Louis answered. "An underground stream. The water is rancid. Don't even think of drinking it."

"I had no intention of it," Paul assured him hoarsely. Suddenly the air around them began to hiss.

125

Instinctively, Paul ducked and dropped to a crouch. Behind him, he felt Jessica do the same.

"What the hell is it?" Paul gulped, staring at Louis through the dim light.

"Bats," Louis said calmly. "Don't worry. They're more afraid of us than we are of them."

"I wouldn't bet on that," Jessica said quickly.

Paul bit back a bark of laughter that bordered on hysteria. He wanted, with every fiber of his being, to be out of this place.

"We're disturbing them with our light," Louis advised.

"Well, by all means, let's leave them alone," Paul muttered. Still hunched over, hyper-anxious and vividly alert, he followed Louis as he continued on.

Minutes later he felt his heart stop once again. Before him loomed a forest of bones. It was a macabre garden of death, propped beneath the world as if in its own hideous rejection of reality. Behind him, Jessica gave a small shriek of anguish. He stood still and bowed his head in agony as he felt her come close and rest her head against his back. Turning, he gathered her into his arms with silent, heartbreaking compassion.

"What is it?" Louis asked, turning to stare at them curiously, not bothering to acknowledge the graveyard they stood beside.

"These bones!" Paul hissed, abhorring the man's callousness.

Louis smiled patiently. "Those aren't bones. Those are plants. They grow from the seeds that pass through the bat's intestines. They have a name but I can't recall it right now."

"Oh, geez," Jessica moaned. "Dear God, get me out of here."

Paul felt an almost unbearable clutch of empathy for her. He kissed her forehead lightly and released her from his hug. "It will be all right." He brushed her cheek lightly.

She swiped her hand across her forehead, leaving a streak of dust. "I'll be fine," she said tiredly.

Her attempt to gather herself was evident to Paul. He gently wiped her forehead with his sleeve. "Come on," he said, taking her hand. "Let's get this over with."

They hadn't gone far before Paul noticed a change of light. "Wait," he whispered. "There's light. Someone else is here." His heart thundered in his chest. It sounded like it belonged in the heart of a train engine rather than in his chest.

In front of him, Louis shook his head. "No. This is the sinkhole I told you about. The light comes from outside. Even though we're about a hundred feet down, some of the light still manages to penetrate."

127

Paul's heart fluttered in relief. He followed Louis into the small, circular space. Blue-gray, lichen-covered walls towered above them. The sky appeared to be a hundred miles away. Beneath his feet the ground was littered with thousands of tiny xute snail shells. He shivered with revulsion. "This is just too weird feeling," he muttered.

"Let's just get the tiles and get the hell out of here," Jessica said, her voice shivering with stress and exhaustion.

Paul looked at Louis. "You know where they are?"

Louis shook his head. "We'll have to search the walls for the cubby holes. They can't be too far up, I wouldn't think. The people would have had to be able to reach them easily."

"No," Jessica interrupted suddenly.

Paul turned to stare at her. Her voice was distant and lost in time. Her eyes were unfocused, staring rigidly at something he couldn't see.

Her voice wrapped around them like solidified history. "We placed them high up ... just in case. We used the nooks as a ladder to climb to them. Here, I'll show you."

Paul studied her with concern. She seemed almost hypnotized. Trance-like, she placed her hands on the walls, glanced down at her feet, and slowly but steadily began to climb. Mouth open, he watched her as she

128

lifted herself, hand over hand, up the seemingly flat wall.

Not as dumbstruck as Paul, Louis began to follow her. "I'll hand them down to you," he said gruffly, turning back to Paul. "Stay where you are. I'll hand them down," he repeated.

His nervousness penetrated Paul, causing his hands to shake even more. He merely nodded in confused agreement and watched the two of them climb slowly. When Jessica stopped, every nerve in Paul's body leapt into high gear. He shivered violently. Beside him he sensed an energy. He identified it as Solomon but didn't turn to acknowledge him.

"Stay calm," Solomon whispered easily. "It's going to be all right."

Solomon's words felt like a breath against Paul's cheek. He wasn't certain if he'd heard the words out loud or somewhere inside his mind. But he was grateful for them either way. "Thank you," he muttered. "I needed to hear that."

He felt the weight of Solomon's invisible hand on his shoulder and forced himself to draw in a deep, steadying breath. Shaking his head, he tossed away the memory that was struggling to return. He was holding a tile, solemnly passing it to a dark-haired woman who was nodding in acceptance. He shook his head again. Now was not the time to allow his thoughts to drift back into history.

Jessica's hand entered the wall and drew back.

129

Clutched in her fingers was a small clay tile. It was a faded curry color and appeared to be brittle with age. From where he stood, Paul thought that he could see symbols etched into the clay.

Odd, Paul thought. I remember them being larger. He shook his head again, bringing himself back to the present moment once again. It never occurred to him to question how he could remember them at all. Obviously he had been a participant in the long ago past of the ancient symbols. Obviously the speculation he and Jessica had been doing was fact, not fiction.

As he watched, Jessica handed the tile to Louis, who promptly passed it down to Paul.

As his hand wrapped around it, Paul was stunned to find involuntary tears springing to his eyes. He clutched the tile tightly and brought it to his chest, holding it with an urgent and unnamable emotion that caught him in its grip as surely as a vise. His eyes closed without volition. He found himself rocking mindlessly, held in the arms of unexplainable emotions.

One by one, the tiles were passed to his hands until he held five. Still ensnared in his own world of mystery, he didn't notice as the others came back down the wall and stood next to him, watching him curiously.

"Paul?" Jessica said, touching his arm tentatively.

Opening his eyes, he saw her as she once was. The dark-haired woman. The woman of his dreams. He thought she might be the answer to his prayers. He could

130

do nothing more than stare at her, unwilling tears falling unchecked.

Studying him, Jessica smiled softly and nodded with sudden understanding. "Come on," she whispered. "We have to go." Her hand rested on his sleeve. She intended to lead him, to draw him from the past into the present and from the present into the future.

He nodded without thinking. All at once the air around them moved. Reality seemed to be splitting in two. Another dimension opened before them. They were joined by three alien beings. Paul recognized them instantly. Zere. Galin. Elan. The three friends he had helped to rescue from the fallen craft in Arizona, just weeks ago.

"Are you here?" he asked unsteadily, not certain if he was imagining things.

"No," Zere said. "We are casting holographic impressions of ourselves to you. We want to assist you to safety."

Paul stared down at the five small tiles in his hands. "Yes," he muttered hypnotically. He looked up at Louis. "The bag. Where's the bag we were going to put them in?"

Louis was staring, open-mouthed and stunned, at the three holographic aliens. Without taking his eyes from them, he shrugged off his backpack and dipped his hand into it, drawing out a leather pouch with a drawstring. He held it out to Paul without speaking.

131

As Paul placed the tiles, one by one, gently into the bag, he questioned Zere. "I remember these differently. What's happened to them?"

"Time and vibrational energy have altered them slightly. But the information is within them. Their exterior appearance is not important,"

Paul could actually feel Zere's smile as he added, "Similar to the way it is with humans, you know?"

Then Zere went on with his explanation. "They are smaller, yes. This is a good way to disguise them."

"Of course," Paul said, nodding. "That makes sense."

Jessica interrupted. "Can we get out of here?" she asked tensely. She ducked her head quickly and glanced at the three aliens. "It's not that I'm not thrilled to see you. I just don't think I can stand it down here another minute."

Zere looked at her kindly. "That's understandable. It's good to see you, my friend." He nodded in the direction of the mouth of the cave. "Let us proceed."

Jessica smiled suddenly, the light of her eyes and her obvious joy at seeing him shining through the dim light, as Zere's presence penetrated her nervousness. She reached her hand out tentatively, obviously wanting to touch him with her caring. "I apologize. I'm so pleased to see you. Thanks for showing up," she said quietly. She took a deep breath and turned toward the exit. Stopping

132

suddenly, she turned back to Zere. "So, when do I get to come home?" she asked with a small, quavering grin.

Zere gave her a fleeting smile. "You know the answer to that." He turned serious again and nodded toward the exit. "Let's go." He turned to Paul. "You need to know that there are men above. They wait for you. We'll accompany you and do what we can. But let's get this over with as quickly as possible."

Snapped out of his reverie by the frightening words, Paul turned to Louis. "You want to lead the way out of here?"

Looking from one to the other, Louis nodded. "Let's do it," he said gruffly. He turned on his heel and walked deliberately in the direction they'd come. As he walked he struggled with his backpack, scrambling inside it to find his weapon.

Paul caught his breath and steadied himself as the light of the carbide lamp glinted off the pistol that Louis shoved into his hand.

It seemed to take no time at all to reach the circular-shaped room that led to the mouth of the cave. Louis stopped abruptly near the entrance, causing Paul to collide with him.

"Stop!" Louis hissed. With his gun, he gestured angrily at the entrance.

A slovenly man with a sinister face waited calmly, his back resting against the wall of the entry. His lips curled

133

with disdain as he glared a challenge at them. He was bearded, unclean, and had long, straggly hair. His filthy jeans were torn and hung low on his hips. His stomach protruded from beneath a ragged, too-small T-shirt. Dusty boots completed his distasteful outfit. Picking at his fingernails with a toothpick, he looked them over calmly. "Now that you've done all the work, I'll take those off your hands," he said, nodding at the bag in Paul's hand.

His evil laugh crawled over Paul's skin like cold slime. He shuddered. "Like hell," he muttered, glaring at the man.

Louis snarled. With the gun pointed directly at the man's heart, he stepped out of the shadows so that the man could see the weapon.

The man didn't flinch or even blink. He gazed at them calmly. "You won't use that thing. It's a toy in your hands. You don't have what it takes."

His look warned Paul. He spun around just in time to see the familiar-looking man from the plane appear out of the tunnel behind Jessica. Before Paul could warn her, the man had his arm around her throat and was pulling her backwards.

"Thought you were psychic, huh, girl?" the stranger snarled, leaning over toward Jessica's ear. "Guess your gifts failed you this time."

Paul stared at the man, as much surprised by his appearance as by how suddenly he had appeared. He was dressed neatly. He wore leather hiking boots that looked relatively new. His shirt was pinstriped, short-sleeved, and the collar buttons were neatly fastened. He wore gray corduroy trousers and a dusk-gray belt. His hair was dark almost to the point of being black and was cut short and neat around his ears. If it hadn't been for the thick rope that was looped over his shoulders and the streak of dirt on his cheek, he would have looked like a businessman going out for lunch.

Why hadn't the man been stopped by the alien holograms, his thoughts hissed. If other worlds were going to intervene and help, now would be the time.

Louis interrupted his thoughts. "They don't have the tiles," he said, his accent so thick that Paul had trouble understanding him. "I have them. What I gave them was fake." He gave an evil smile to the group and calmly tucked his gun inside his rope belt. Still grinning, he stepped closer to the man at the mouth of the cave.

"What the hell are you talking about?" the dark man snapped. "Why would you do something like that? Drag them all the way out here just to give them fakes?"

"I knew of the real tiles and knew that these two were coming to retrieve them. If I threw them off by giving them fake ones, they would leave. And you would follow them. Then I would be free to take them away without anyone following me, you see? Everyone would believe that the fake ones were the real ones, no? And then I would be free? You see?"

His fake smirk nauseated Paul, who stared at him in

135

stunned silence.

"That doesn't make a damn bit of sense." growled the man. But his expression made it obvious that he was listening, hesitating.

Louis lifted his heavy shoulders with an exaggerated shrug and flopped his arms helplessly. "I am not as smart as you, no? You see I cannot fool any of you. It was a stupid plan, no?" He thrust his lower lip out, clearly annoyed with himself. He peered at the man anxiously. "Now you will kill me in order to get the real tiles, no?"

His chin quivered with fear. His eyes darted here and there with his acceptance of his fate. But suddenly his eyes lit up with an idea. "But ... you won't kill me until I show you where the tiles are hidden!" he proclaimed.

He turned and gave Paul an evil grin. "It seems that I will live a while longer than you, my friend."

Paul's thoughts raced. Had he been right to distrust this man in the first place? Was Jessica wrong? Were the tiles fakes? They didn't look the way he remembered them. Maybe he'd been right about Louis all along. But then, why did the ETs go to the trouble to cast holographic images of themselves in order to oversee the taking of these tiles? Why had Solomon seemed so calm? Who was who? his thoughts screamed.

While he was rapidly going insane with his own confusion, the men were staring at Louis skeptically, considering his words. The business-like one, obviously the decision-maker, broke the silence. "I don't believe a

136

word you're sayin', old man." He pulled Jessica even closer to his chest and stared at Louis calmly. "If you're telling the truth then tell me where you've hidden the real ones. She goes with me. We go get them. If they're there, she walks. If not, she dies. It's that simple." He validated his threat by tightening his grip on Jessica's neck.

Jessica's eyes were blank, as though she'd abandoned her body for a better life and hadn't told anyone that she was leaving.

"I buried them," Louis said quickly. "The map is back at our camp."

"Take us there," the man ordered. "Show us."

With Jessica still very much in harm's way, Paul decided not to risk a confrontation. Meekly following orders, he handed over the gun that was still in his hand, though he'd completely forgotten about it, and he and Louis stumbled along the vine-laden path with Jessica walking blindly behind them, still clutched firmly in the thin man's grip.

Paul was completely consumed by confusion and fear, his thoughts racing in a way that made him think he'd gone mad. If these were the real tiles, where were the aliens? What was the plan? What were Zere and the others going to do to keep everything on track so that the tiles would be safe? Why had they allowed this to turn into such a dangerous situation? But if the tiles were fake, it made sense that they'd just taken themselves out of the situation. Paul was instantly plunged into a feeling

137

of abandonment and loss. But, his thoughts raced on, if they were gone, if he had no help at all, how was he going to go up against not only these two strangers, but Louis? How was he going to save Jessica?

His nerves jangled under his skin like tautly stretched violin strings. He was ready to snap. And he was ready for some answers from the invisible ones that he hoped, against all odds, were still around him. Come on, he muttered silently. Make something happen!

As they approached the campsite Paul could see that the thieves had already been there. Jessica's clothes were draped over the sleeping bags, looking like widows weeping on graves. The air itself felt ravaged. Paul felt the rage rising higher in his chest. He fought with himself to stay calm, to think of a rational plan.

"Game's over," the man from the airplane snapped. "Where's the map?"

Louis' eyes were innocent as he stepped with dignity to Jessica's duffel bag. The map peeked out from under the bag, apparently tossed there by the men when they'd searched the camp. Louis pointed at it. "It is here, sirs," he said meekly.

Shocked, Paul watched him leaned down and moved the bag, and pointed at the map that had been materialized after Grandfather had been taken aboard the mother craft. The man stepped forward, shoved Jessica into his partner's arms, and pushed Louis aside.

"We already saw this, nitwit. This is a map of where

138

we are right now," he snarled, glaring at Louis. "What the hell are you pulling?"

"The tiles are near here," Louis whispered, glancing furtively at Paul, wanting him not to hear his words of betrayal.

With a movement as swift and unseen as a bullet, the man's hand shot out and grabbed Louis by the throat. His tone was low and menacing. "You know better than to mess with me, right?"

Louis nodded wordlessly, struggling to breathe, his arms flapping helplessly.

The man released him with a snap, causing Louis to stumble backwards.

"I respect you, Senor," Louis coughed, clutching his throat. "I will not lie to you." He waved his hand at the map. "Take it. Study it. You will see."

The man studied the map again, looking for possible clues. His eyes darted from the map to Louis' face and back again.

Suddenly, shocked beyond words, Paul watched as the entire campsite blew into action. With eyes as big as silver dollars, he saw the map burst into flames. He saw the thin, violent flames scorch the man's eyebrows. He saw the man throw the map away from him, screaming in shock. He blinked in amazement as Jessica came suddenly to life. She exploded out of the fat man's arms, leaping into the air, spinning, landing a kick directly into

139

the man's paunch.

At the same time, Louis leapt into action, flying through the air like a ballerina, and landing squarely against the thin man's chest. They both went down with a thud; Louis planted firmly on top of the man. Jessica adroitly twisted the fat man's arms behind him in a way that made Paul wonder if she hadn't done the same thing a hundred times before.

While all of this was happening, he was seeing Solomon, Zere, Galin, and Elan appearing, hovering in the air, calmly watching the frenzy of activity below them.

Stunned beyond understanding, he stared at them in astonishment until the full awareness hit him that they were really there. He gestured at them wildly to do something. When he realized that they weren't going to intervene, he looked wildly around at the chaos, trying to decide who to throw himself at first. Just as he moved toward Jessica, he felt a strong, insistent hand on his arm, stopping him. He turned to see Solomon shaking his head 'no.' "What am I supposed to do?" he asked angrily, trying to pull his arm away. "Stand here and do nothing?"

"Keep the tiles safe," Solomon instructed calmly. "That's why you're here."

Feeling totally inadequate, he watched as Jessica and Louis manhandled the two thugs into sitting positions with their backs against a tree. They used the rappel rope to firmly tether the two thieves together, using the tree

140

to keep them separate from each other. When the flurry of activity died, and the air fell silent, they all stood looking at each other and the mess that was strewn around them.

"Well," Jessica said, matter-of-factly, rolling up the sleeves of her shirt, "guess there's nothing to do but clean up this mess."

Paul stared at her, blinking. He glanced only once at Solomon, who was slowly dissolving his energy, before wordlessly joining her efforts. When he looked up again the air was clear and silent, making it seem like the holograms had never been there at all. He wondered dully if perhaps he had fallen into an alternate reality. Nothing seemed real. Robot-like, he returned to the cleanup of the camp. An hour later, the campsite was broken down, the supplies stowed in the back of the Jeep, and the three of them stood staring down at their prisoners.

"Now what?" Paul wondered aloud.

"We toss them into the back of their truck," Louis said with authority. "I'll follow you. We'll drive them into town. Turn them over to the police."

Not so calmly, Jessica offered her suggestion. "No. We tie them to the hood of the car ... like dead antelope. Then we drive them to the police."

Paul gave a quick, nervous laugh. "Antelope?"

Louis, thinking about his comment, broke into a

141

broad grin. "One dead duck, or antelope, is the same as the next, no?" His chuckle rang with malice. "Either way, these two won't be bothering us again."

Paul studied the two men. Though captive and apparently subdued, the businessman's eyes did not speak of defeat. Quite the opposite. He looked at Paul with challenge and threat, though he didn't speak.

He crouched down in front of the man, an arm's length away. "What I want to know is why they want the tiles?" Paul said quietly. "What the hell do you want?" he asked the man directly, hoping for an answer.

The man simply glared at him.

"I think they've been sent," Jessica said, walking up behind Paul and resting her hand on his shoulder.

"Sent by who?" Paul asked tightly. His jaw felt sore with unexpressed tension.

"I don't know. But it's someone serious." She squatted down next to Paul and stared at the man intently. "Isn't it?" she asked. "Someone very serious, I would imagine. Am I right?"

After waiting several seconds for an answer that didn't come, Jessica pushed herself up and stood next to Paul. "Come on," she said, setting her hand on his shoulder again. "We're wasting time. It's going to be dark by the time we get back anyway. Let's not get caught out here for another night with these two characters."

142

Paul reluctantly gave up his quest for answers and helped Louis re-rope the two thieves. After shoving them into the back of the truck, with Louis driving, Paul turned the Jeep back toward Belize City.

CHAPTER FIVE

IT WAS PITCH DARK WHEN THEY hit the edge of town. Paul followed Louis as he guided them to the small building that served as the police station. As they pulled up, the door popped open as if someone inside had been waiting for them. The cop strolled nonchalantly to the top of the stairs leading down to the street and propped himself against a post, staring at them openly. His skin was tanned to the look of a dark leather hide. His black hair was long and tucked behind his ears. His faded uniform was sweat-blotched, as though he'd had a rough day. Even with his hat pulled down over his eyes, the heavy, dark bags around them were visible. Paul couldn't read his expression.

"You say they did what?" the man asked laconically, spitting on the sidewalk next to Paul's shoe. After listening expressionlessly to the story, he'd finally stepped off the porch and sauntered to where the truck was parked.

"They broke into our campsite," Paul said for the second time. His patience was wearing thin. "They threw everything every which way. Looking for valuables, I guess." He shrugged for emphasis. "Then they followed us into the cave we were exploring. They pulled guns on us. Threatened to kill us."

"Why would they want to do that?" the man asked, shaking his head in ostensible confusion.

He peered at Paul stupidly but Paul could tell it was

144

an act. The man wasn't stupid. But lazy about putting up two men and having to feed them ... probably.

The cop scratched his chin slowly and looked from Paul to the truck and back again. "You must have somethin' they want," he said slyly. "What do you suppose that might be?"

Paul took a step away from him, struggling to contain his temper. "Are you going to do something with them or not?" he snapped. "If not, just say so and I'll take them on down the road to someone who will."

"Well, now. You can't take them anywhere. That would be breaking the law, you know," the man drawled. He took a step closer to the truck and peered inside at the two men. "Appears to me that they're being held against their will," the man said. "You sure you're not the one in the wrong here?" He studied Paul casually and slid his toothpick to the other side of his mouth with his tongue.

Paul sighed in exasperation. "I've told you the story two times already," he said tiredly.

"Can't hold 'em without just cause."

"I don't believe this," Paul muttered under his breath. "Look," he said out loud. "The guys have guns. They threatened us. Isn't that enough? What has to happen here to get your notice? Do we have to be shot or killed?"

The man shrugged nonchalantly. "Well," he drawled,

145

"I wouldn't want to see that happen but still...."

Paul looked toward the Jeep, hoping Jessica would pop out with a brilliant suggestion. She and Louis, who was leaning casually against the side of the Jeep beside her, seemed to be deep in conversation. He was on his own. "How about I just leave them with you and we get on our way then?" he asked, trying to think of a compromise that the cop might be willing to accept. Leaving the men might at least buy them enough time to get to the airport.

"You steal this truck from them?" The cop glared at Paul with suspicion.

This was doing Paul no good at all. He could feel his nerves beginning to chew on his muscles like they were hors d'oeuvres. He dropped his head, took a deep, steadying breath, and tried again. "Look, let's say I leave them here with you. You can hold them or not. Whatever you choose. We'll be on our way and everything can be forgotten. How's that?" Paul asked, staring at the man with what he hoped passed for a look of rational thought.

"I still got to wonder what you got that they want," the man said shrewdly. "If you're so willin' to give up on prosecutin' 'em, maybe I'm right in thinkin' they didn't do anything."

For the first time, Paul felt a small chase of fear through his stomach. Would the man insist on searching them and the Jeep? Would he confiscate the tiles, claiming that they were artifacts, which, in truth, they were? Would the aliens be capable of casting another hologram and saving them again?

Paul made up a story on the spot and silently asked forgiveness for his lie. "Well," he said hesitantly, pretending to struggle with his coming confession, "the truth is that my girlfriend, there in the Jeep," he added, nodding at Jessica, "she just inherited some really valuable jewelry from her grandmother. I guess, these guys read about it in the paper. It was all over the news at home," he added quietly. "I guess because her grandmother was so well known. Anyway, we decided on this vacation and I guess these guys figured she brought the jewelry with her. They followed us from home." He coughed uncomfortably. "I didn't want to tell you. We figured that the fewer people who knew we had the stuff, the better."

"Then ya have the jewelry with ya?"

Paul couldn't read his tone or intentions. "Well, yeah. Kind of." he said slowly.

The man jerked his chin at the car. "'K. Get 'em out of there. I'll take it from here."

"Excuse me?"

He stared at Paul as though he thought he was dull. "I said, get 'em out of the car. I'll take them over."

Paul blinked in astonishment. If he'd known that it would be that simple, he would have lied half an hour ago. Sometimes, he thought, the means must justify the

147

end. "Okay," he agreed. "Um, thanks."

"No problem." The man shifted his toothpick to the other side of his mouth again.

Curiosity consumed Paul. Why had the cop changed his mind so abruptly? He didn't want to risk spending any more time hanging around. Deciding that it wasn't important enough to waste time on, he turned toward the rear of the truck, intending to do as the man had said.

"Scum broke into my house not long ago."

Paul turned back to listen.

The cop was standing, legs spread and arms wrapped solidly across his chest. "Can you imagine? My house. I'm the police, for Pete's sake!" He coughed and spat on the ground beside him. "My wife is still havin' a fit and givin' me hell about it. I won't give up lookin' for those ones. But these guys will do until I find the others." His smile was clear and innocent.

With a small nod of understanding, Paul turned away. Smiling with satisfaction, he opened the door of the Jeep and handed the two men over to the cop.

But the businessman wasn't done with them. "The others will be along shortly," he snarled, glaring at them over his shoulder as the cop tugged on his arm, dragging him toward the small jail.

"So, now what?" Louis asked as he stood in the

148

doorway of the small motel room and watched Jessica and Paul toss the rest of their belongings into their duffel bags. "It's late. It's dark already. You won't stay one night?" He looked at the bag of tiles with longing as it sat on the bed ... a bag of secrets and mysteries waiting to be revealed.

Paul followed his gaze. "I'm sorry, Louis," he said sincerely. "I really am. I know you would like some time with them. But we simply have to leave. I don't know what's going to happen with those guys. That cop might decide to let them go." He shrugged heavily. "He may not. But the fact is that we still don't know who they are or why they want the tiles ... or even how they found out about them. I just don't think we should risk staying." He glanced at Jessica for confirmation.

Louis' normally jovial expression was gone. "I understand," he said, his voice low with disappointment.

"Getting them to safety is more important."

Jessica stepped to his side and rested her hand on his arm. "Don't say that," she urged. "You're important. You played a vital part. But the tiles need to go to everyone." She swept her arm around the room gracefully. "None of us really count, in the long run. The tiles are what are important. We're just the instruments."

"It is understood," Louis said sadly. He made an attempt to smile at them. "But we had some fun, did we not?"

Paul gave a small brief chuckle. "There were some

149

good moments, yes. And there's more appreciation than I can voice for the help you've given us." He hesitated and then gave Louis an awkward hug. "I would say that we'll keep in touch but I don't want to make any promises I can't keep. I don't know for certain what's going to happen next."

A spurt of laughter escaped Jessica. "So, what else is new? Your life has been anything but predictable lately."

"Right," Paul agreed. "Which is why I'm not promising anything."

Jessica glanced around the room one final time. "I think we've got everything," she stated quietly. She studied Louis with sympathy. "Thank you again," she said, giving him a quick hug. "Your help was invaluable."

Watching from the small bungalow porch, Louis waved good-bye as they got into the Jeep, turned on the engine and lights, and headed off into the night, heading toward the airport and, hopefully, a clear understanding of what they were supposed to do next.

Paul glanced across the front seat toward Jessica and turned his eyes back to the unfamiliar road. "Well, he had a good question. What now?"

Jessica chortled slightly. "Your guess is as good as mine." She looked at the bag of tiles that lay on the seat between them. Her hand hovered over them, hesitant, perhaps fearful that they might be too fragile for the touch of a human hand. She studied Paul for a brief instant, countless thoughts parading across her face.

150

"Sorry," she finally told him. "I guess I don't mean that. I need to get serious. Let me contact my guides and see what they have to tell me."

Paul looked over at her but her eyes were already closed in silent communion with her spirit guides. He waited in silence. When her voice came again, it was the voice of a Master, a being of great wisdom. The hair on his arms rose abruptly, like he was standing in the midst of a field in an electrical storm. He shivered and forced himself to concentrate on the words, rather than on his reaction.

"What we have is a piece of history as well as a piece of the future. The presentation of the messages will cause great fear in some and great joy in others. The messages come from beyond this reality but not from beyond the realm of understanding. Most people will understand, for in the deepest recesses of Earth's history the interactions between those on Earth and those from beyond still exist. The memories are buried but the energy of the relationship still lives." She glanced at Paul before continuing. "We are responsible for making certain that the message is given but we must keep in mind that we are not responsible for the reactions it will cause. If we allow ourselves to be swayed by the emotions of others, we will fail."

Paul's reaction was so strong that he was compelled to pull to the side of the road. He began to slow the Jeep but a wave of her hand let him know that it was the wrong thing to do. He pressed the accelerator again and risked taking his eyes from the road to stare at her. Her eyes were closed but, sensing his gaze, she opened them and stared at him. He felt like he was in the car with someone he didn't know. Swallowing hard, he opened his mouth to speak. Before he had a chance, she spoke again.

"We can't afford to think about the failure of the past," she told him quietly. "It was a combination of many things that caused the mission to fail. But this time, if the message is not delivered, it will be solely our failure."

Paul felt his heart lurch at the tremendous sense of fear and responsibility that gripped him instantly. He struggled to keep his attention on the road while fighting with his personal feeling of impending doom. Beneath her words he sensed a warning that spanned the age of his soul, from beginning to end. The words reached across infinity and held him up for an examination of his personal reason for existing. They scoured him, looking for flaws and failures. He wanted to weep. He wanted to rage. He wanted to be rid of the frightful responsibility that had come to ride next to him as they tumbled blindly through the night.

"Why?" he whispered, his voice as rough as a stone against a grinder. "Why us? Why did we put ourselves in this position?"

"If not us, who?" Jessica asked. "Are we less than anyone else? Is there someone else greater who could do a better job? Is any one soul greater than another?"

Paul stifled his urge to scream at her that she was greatly overestimating him, if not herself. "Yes," he stated

152

flatly. "There are probably hundreds who are more suited for this."

"Why?" she asked, her voice as sharp as a blade.

Paul flapped his hands feebly, looking for words to put to his feeling of inadequacy. "We are just two simple people, living simple lives. Why not give these things," he waved his hand at the bag, "to the government or something. Or to someone like Oprah," he cried, suddenly inspired. "She has a voice," he said excitedly. "She has an audience. She would reach millions." He looked at Jessica with something bordering on hysteria. "That's it!" he stated. "We'll contact her. We'll tell her all about this. And she can tell the people. They'll believe her."

"And they won't believe us?" Jessica asked flatly. Her words fell on the seat between them like a broken-winged bird.

Her disappointment in him was almost as tangible as the vehicle they were riding in. Paul felt it as deeply as a knife wound. He swallowed, grabbed onto his tirade, and bridled himself in. Blowing out a great sigh of stress, he struggled to calm himself. "Okay. Okay. I can see what you're saying." He peered at her through the darkness. "You're telling me to believe in myself. You're telling me to live the truth of my soul. Believe in my soul and let it override my little human fears."

When she didn't answer, he continued dropping his words into the empty space between them. He felt alone. It was as if she had found him so lacking that she had

153

removed herself. He realized that he was arguing with himself, having a debate with his own inadequacies and fears, but he couldn't seem to stop himself.

"Look," he reasoned, "I think it's a good plan. She could reach six million people in a minute. It could take us years." He glanced at her to see if she was listening but he couldn't tell. "If we give them to her we would have accomplished the mission, which is to give the message to the people. You said yourself that that is the only thing that matters. How we accomplish it shouldn't be the issue here. You see?"

Jessica shifted onto her hip to face him directly. "Look," she said softly. "These are your own fears you're confronting. You're arguing with yourself, not me. I know what part I need to play in order to satisfy the needs of my soul. I don't want to let myself down. I don't want to finish this lifetime and be disappointed in myself. And," she said slowly, "you and I discussed this mission before we took this incarnation. We discussed the drawbacks and the fears and everything else. We covered this ground already. Just because it was before we incarnated doesn't make it any less valid." She paused. A sigh as small as a wisp of vapor left her lips.

"Maybe it will help if I tell you this," she continued. "You had a past life where you spoke up against hundreds of people. You stood up for what you believed and you were executed for it. You were stoned to death," she added flatly.

Paul felt as though he had taken his own truth, flattened it with an iron, and then placed in on a distant

154

shelf. His soul, his truth, didn't seem available to him. It was as though he'd placed a wall between himself on Earth and the rest of himself that lived in other worlds and other realities. He hated the separation. He wanted the wisdom, the power, the memories, and the knowing. But he wasn't certain how to access them.

"The memory is still with you," she continued. "Of course, you buried it deep. That's understandable. But because your memory is so deep, your fears are deep as well. The deeper we bury things, the more difficult it is to heal them."

Out of the corner of his eye, Paul saw her drop her head. Her hands touched each other in agitation. He took a deep breath, bracing himself for her next words. He had a sense that he wasn't going to like them.

"I was one of those who killed you," she said softly. She didn't look at him, instead focusing her eyes on her lap and her hands that now laid as still as dropped stones.

Paul's reactions were totally involuntary. His gaze went to the roof of the Jeep, seeking solace from above. He pressed himself back into his seat, asking the solid comfort of the seat against his back to comfort him. Letting go of the steering wheel for a brief instant, he scrubbed his face with his hands. He didn't speak. He simply allowed himself to absorb the truth of her quiet statement. He tried to avoid the tugs of his imagination as he relived the feel of stones hitting him again and again and again -- until he could feel no more.

155

"Now I need to repay you by helping to give you your voice back," she said. Her voice was a whisper. "I not only need to ... I want to," she added softly. Her hand fluttered on the seat beside her, struggling with the decision of whether to touch him or not.

Her words were a gift. Paul could feel her offering them like precious gifts of gold. A gift from one soul as old as existence to another soul as old as existence. They had walked through history together. They had played all of the roles, lived all of the scenes. Injured each other. Loved each other. Killed each other. And now they were in this place and time to heal each other.

"You're here to help me gain the strength and courage to live my truth," he said, voicing it in the only way he knew how. He could sense her nodding in agreement, though he didn't glance her way. He kept his eyes on the road, searching the landscape, sightlessly searching for his future.

"In the only way I know how," she told him quietly. "And I can accomplish that only if I can stay strong in the truth of my own soul. If I begin to doubt, I will be doing you a disservice. I will be harming you all over again."

Paul could feel her eyes studying him. He waited.

"And I don't want to do that," she whispered.

Her words wrapped around him like loving arms. Paul allowed himself to feel the comfort she was offering him.

156

"It's wonderful that you're both coming to these understandings."

Paul's heart leapt like a frightened deer at the sound of the unexpected voice. He jerked the steering wheel in fright, struggled to keep the Jeep on the road, and, after succeeding in righting it, looked over his shoulder at the man in the back seat. "You scared the hell out of me," he snapped, still attempting to calm his heartbeat.

"To have the hell scared out of you, as you so succinctly put it, would not be a bad thing," Solomon said with good humor.

"Solomon," Jessica said warmly, greeting him.

Paul stared at her in stupefaction for several seconds before realizing that he should be watching the road. "You know him?" he croaked, yanking the Jeep back into the lane once again.

Jessica stared at him in surprise. "Of course I know him. Why wouldn't I?"

"But ...," Paul said. Her gifts still continued to amaze him. He didn't fully understand how she did what she did and how she knew what she knew. He shook his head, struggling to make sense of his thoughts.

"Look," Jessica said soothingly, reading Paul's confusion. She set her hand on his sleeve, calming him. "They're only in another dimension. Their energy just vibrates at a higher rate than physical forms, that's all.

157

And I've trained myself to see other energy vibrations, other dimensions. It's that simple. No big deal," she concluded, removing her hand. She shifted and draped her arm over the back of the seat to talk with their sudden guest. "So, what's caused you to make this appearance? And how'd you pull it off?" she asked quizzically.

Solomon smiled at her, clearly pleased at being in her presence. "Several things, actually," he told her, addressing her first question. "First of all, the tiles are going to take you places you never dreamed of and I wanted to forewarn you. Secondly, it seemed appropriate for me to put in an appearance, due to the fact that I'm going to be playing such a large part in the events that will follow. And as to how I pulled this off, the tiles, in case you haven't noticed yet, have altered the energies around you. It makes it easier for the higher dimensions to interact with you."

"You're saying we were too dense for you before?" Paul asked, slightly irritated.

Solomon lifted his shoulder in a half-shrug. "Through no particular fault of your own," he stated. "The mere state of being in this section of the third dimension can be off-putting, to say the least. For us to lower our energy to accommodate it is extremely uncomfortable." He paused. "But on the other hand, you actually have to live in it. Either scenario can be unpleasant ... or pleasant ... depending upon how one looks at it." He peered over the seat at the leather pouch. "However, the higher vibration of the tiles have made things easier for us to connect. At least for the moment."

158

"Yeah," Jessica interjected. "Once we get back into the reality of having to hide them until we reveal them, and everything that will go along with that, we'll sink right back down, I imagine."

Solomon shrugged again. "Perhaps," he said without concern. "But don't worry about it," he added, patting her arm gently.

Jessica beamed at him, clearly enjoying his presence. "So, what can we expect?" she asked. She hesitated when Solomon didn't instantly reply. "You are allowed to tell us, aren't you? I mean, isn't that why you showed up?"

"Oh, yes," he assured her. "I was just thinking of how I was going to say this."

The hint that things were going to get difficult was in Solomon's words, as far as Paul was concerned. For several seconds, his imagination ran wild, thinking of all that could be wrong.

Reading his thoughts, Solomon addressed them. "I just want to do my best not to confuse you with things. It's important for you to be clear when you explain your experiences to others. You'll just have to keep in mind the bottom line, which is that reality is only a perception and when you change your perception, the energy of your experience changes as well. In this case, the needs of the tiles come before your needs, my friends. And so it is that you will be plunged into confusion for a short while."

159

Paul blinked, wondering what on earth he was talking about. "Explain. What do we have to look forward to?"

"Realities must merge so that this one may heal," Solomon said gravely.

Before Paul could blink again or ask another question, he realized that the landscape surrounding them was changing dramatically. The sultry, tropical sky had become cloudless. Dust no longer clouded his vision as the Jeep sped along the dirt road. The smell of salt air and heated jungle was being replacing by a faint, indefinable perfume. As he opened his mouth to comment, the structure of a tall, obviously ancient structure came into view. With a tap on Paul's shoulder, Solomon indicated that he should pull over and stop. Thoroughly bewildered, Paul did as he was instructed. When the Jeep was stopped, he pushed the car door open and stepped out, leaning his arms on the top of the car door and staring in astonishment at the ancient building.

The building was made of what appeared to be marble. Massive pillars stood tall, bracing the imposing overhang that sheltered the veranda and the steps that led to the massive oak doors. Thick veins of ivy clung to the two outer pillars, while the two pillars that stood directly beneath the overhang stood bare and white with faint veins of ebony running through them. Eight steps led up to the wide veranda. Looming above the veranda were dark, narrow, curtained windows.

Paul felt a chill run through him as he sensed hidden

160

eyes watching him. He turned to Jessica, who had stepped out and was staring as well. "I don't remember seeing this on our way from the airport."

"That's because it wasn't here," she said quietly. She turned to Solomon, who had exited the Jeep and was standing beside her. "This is one of the Council buildings. Am I right?"

Solomon nodded, studying her with a pleased expression. "That's right."

"What Council?" Paul asked. He glanced around suspiciously. "Where are we?"

Jessica was flushed with quiet excitement. Her eyes sparkled across the roof of the Jeep at him. "Don't you remember this? We're in the eighth dimension!"

"That's not possible," Paul said flatly. He looked back at the road like it might somehow confirm his statement. The road was no longer there. In its place was a forest of burgundy-veined leaves that cascaded from the thick trees like liquid. Bewildered? That wasn't a strong enough word to describe how he felt. He turned to Solomon, looking for some kind of explanation.

Solomon smiled at him kindly and glided smoothly around the Jeep, stopping beside Paul. "Jessica's right. We left the third dimensional energies and are now in the eighth. You've been here a million times before. You know you have nothing to fear."

"I'm not afraid," Paul asserted. "But I am curious. I

161

want to know how we did this."

"That's exactly where we're going to begin," Solomon assured him. He dropped his hand on Paul's shoulder and gently steered him toward the great doors.

CHAPTER SIX

THE ROOM WAS CAVERNOUS. The walls were paneled with rich, dark wood laced throughout with thin veins of emerald-green. Tall, thin windows rose from three feet above the floor to three feet below the ceiling, which rose almost twenty feet high. The thin windows cast strips of light into the dark room, highlighting an intricately woven rug that covered most of the floor. Ornate fretwork was etched into the framework of the ceiling and the columns that marched along the length of the room.

The room seemed so solid and so filled with an intangible sense of power and age that Paul could only stand and stare, breathless and filled with wonder. He turned at a small sound behind him.

"Greetings." The man who had entered the room stood about six feet tall, was as thin as a fence post, and had a thin, braided, white beard that lay against his chest like a talisman. His head was bald, his eyes deep set and studious. He wore a hemp-like robe that touched the ground and hid his feet.

Paul moved forward to greet the man. He looked familiar but Paul had a sense that everyone and everything he was going to encounter in the future was probably going to feel familiar.

"This is Fedor," Solomon told him. "He's a member of the United Federation of Creation and Creatorship."

163

Paul stepped aside as Jessica stepped forward to greet Fedor warmly. Obviously she recognized him.

The only indication that Paul had that someone else was entering the room was his sense that the air had whispered. There was no sound or movement, other than the sudden appearance of a small, slender figure. His eyes scanned the being as he searched his memory for a hint of having met her before.

"And this is Slindah," Solomon said quietly.

Slindah was of the ivory clan. Five feet tall, her ivory skin spread smoothly over her small frame. Her head was bare and slightly elongated. Her almond-shaped eyes bored into Paul's, stripping his soul of its secrets. Paul barely registered her three-fingered hand as she extended it to touch his arm lightly.

Fedor's gaze went to the bag of tiles that was firmly clutched in Jessica's grip. His eyes moved to Solomon's in silent communication.

Solomon gently pried the bag from Jessica's fingers. "Come," he said, gesturing at a table that had mysteriously appeared nearby. He unwound the cord from the bag and carefully spilled the tiles onto the table. Paul caught his breath at the sense of mystery that seemed to spill out with them.

Fedor reached out and lightly lifted one of the tiles. It was dwarfed by the largeness of his hand. "This is the tile that has the wisdom of the various dimensional experiences hidden within," he said quietly, meeting

164

Paul's gaze with his own. "This is the one we'll begin with since this is the experience you're currently having. Meaning, you have crossed several different dimensional experiences just in the last few minutes." His eyes twinkled mischievously. "Just in case you hadn't noticed." His gaze became serious once again. "You understand," he continued softly, "that the tiles will not be read like one might read a book. Rather, they will reveal the wisdom they contain. As one merges one's energy and intention to learn with the tiles, the knowledge merges and becomes one with the seeker. Similar, I would suggest, to adapting, learning, and accepting the energy of a new person into one's life. One learns about the other person as one allows oneself to know and understand that other person. So it will be with the tiles."

His hand brushed one of the tiles gently. "As well, the tiles will take those who desire the knowledge on journeys to other dimensions of wisdom, traveling through and beyond the limitations of time and space, as the seeker allows his or her limitations to dissolve."

Paul nodded with understanding. "Thank you for that. It will make it easier not to be impatient with the process of unraveling the mysteries." He glanced around the room, wanting to voice a question out loud but uncertain whether it was appropriate to do so. He glanced at Solomon who encouraged him with a nod. Paul turned back to Fedor. "I'd like to understand how we so easily switched dimensions. How can we be driving along in third and then just drive right into eighth?"

Fedor glanced at Solomon before moving his intense

165

gaze back to Paul. "You had a rather exceptional set of circumstances." He waved his long hand slowly through the air. "You had the vibrational energy of the tiles and you had Solomon with you as well as the tiles. The energy that was created made it easy for you to transcend." He peered at Paul more closely. "You're aware, of course, that dimensions are energetic experiences, compiled of circumstances that are dominated by the vibrational energy of the dimension?"

Paul nodded. "I understand the theory. I can't really say that I know how to apply the theory in a way that could cause me to easily slip from one reality to another though. I mean, consciously creating a dimensional exchange."

"There are some key things for you to think about. Resistance is one. And focus. Detachment. Resistance manifests resistance due to the fact that one is not surrendering to the natural flow of the Universe. Resistance also creates a friction between two things. Friction creates an energy of its own. One of the things that separates third dimension from the next is the energetic veil that resistance to other realities has created." He waved his hand nonchalantly. "That's not the only thing, of course, but it plays a big part." He stared at Paul. "You do understand how two things with different vibrations would create a wall of energy between them?"

Paul nodded.

"And focus and detachment?" Jessica asked. "What part do they play?"

166

Fedor turned his tall frame toward her. "What do you focus on when you're in the third dimension?"

"Oh, my! There's a million things, I imagine."

"And how many of the things that you focus on are real?'

"Real?"

Fedor nodded matter-of-factly. "Yes. Real. As in ... real to your soul. Important to your soul and your existence within the entirety of existence."

Jessica blinked rapidly, thinking about her response. "I don't know. Not many of them are crucial, I don't imagine." She leaned forward intently, her hands braced on the table. "But I've questioned things like that all my life. How much is real? How much is critical to my soul and my personal relationship with existence? You can boil it down to a point where nothing at all is really critical to your soul's existence."

"You could," Fedor agreed slowly, drawing out his words. "But that would not be the truth. If your third dimensional experience was not critical to your soul you would not be in it."

Jessica opened her mouth to offer another opinion but closed it again, a puzzled look on her face.

Paul took the opportunity to speak. "Let me toss out an idea. Is it possible that we must all have a third

167

dimensional experience but that, due to the fact that it's malleable energy, we can live it, manifest it, play it out, if you will, in a different way than we have up until now?" His eyes brightened with the possibility. "Could it be that Humankind can create an entire reality, which is exactly what they're doing already, albeit subconsciously, but that they can create it in a way that is entirely different than what's here now?"

Paul sensed Solomon's piercing gaze on him. He turned. "What?"

"Earth isn't the only third dimensional experience. You remember that, don't you?"

The words caused several visions to flash across Paul's thoughts. Another planet with rivers running wide and deep. The land that bordered them was rich with reds and golds. The sight of two moons hovering in a velvety violet sky. Brothers and sisters sharing the world around them but looking much different than humans. He nodded without speaking, musing on the vision.

Solomon gave him a small smile. "I thought it was time to remind you," he said quietly.

Paul's thoughts leapt to another possibility. "Ok. If there's more than one third dimensional experience, why does a person choose the one that's happening on Earth? And ... can you change from one to the other? As a matter of fact, like we've done right here. We're sitting here in eighth right now. Can you shift from one to the other at will?" He cast his gaze to the tall ceiling, thinking. "Well, obviously you can, because we're doing it!"

The possibility of consciously choosing a different dimensional experience filled him with intrigue. He had always dreamed of visiting other worlds and other realities at will. He'd seen dozens of other worlds in dream state. But if he could voluntarily shift his reality to another ... well, the possibilities were endless. What if it were possible? What if one of the other dimensions held answers for some of Earth's seemingly unsolvable problems?

Slindah interrupted his thoughts. "You, as a soul, have the ability to exist in all dimensions. Your focus, where you place your thoughts, your energy, and your spiritual essence is what determines where you "exist" for the majority of your time. When your body sleeps, your spirit is free to explore all of the other realities that are available. As you sit here, you appear to be in the eighth dimension. But you are on other dimensions as well. Your focus is here. This is where your soul needs you to be focused at this moment and so here you are."

"And detachment?" Jessica asked eagerly. "Where does that fit in?"

Solomon explained. "When you become so firmly attached to the reality of a dimensional experience that you forget the truth of who you are, detachment is the way to break free from the illusionary trap. That is, if you desire to overcome your limitations and live more fully in the truth of your soul, you detach yourself from the belief that what you are living is all there is."

169

"And so you have to detach from what you believe to be real?" Paul offered.

"Something like that, yes," Solomon agreed, nodding affably. "Everything is real and yet nothing is real. Everything is real because you are creating reality as you live your experience. But until you create it and live it, nothing is real, in the true sense of the word."

Paul blinked in surprise. "That's a pretty huge statement."

Solomon nodded in pleasant agreement, smiling calmly as he watched Paul's perplexity.

"I don't get it," Jessica cried. "That just doesn't even seem possible. It sounds like you're saying that nothing exists until you think it exists. Which would mean that nothing exists! And that's just not possible. If you're going to ask us to present things like this to people who live in third dimension, you're asking us to do the impossible."

Slindah shook her head calmly, her eyes studying first Paul and then Jessica. "Nothing you present as a possibility to others will be impossible." She raised her small hand to stop their protest. "Let me explain why. Every person on Earth has a soul and every soul in existence knows the things you will uncover. You won't be presenting anything new to anyone at all. You will only be reminding them of things they already know. You'll be opening doors. That's all. And that's all that keeps one dimension from another. Doors. Your job will be to open doors and present possibilities."

170

"Doors?" Paul asked hesitantly.

"That's a symbolic word," Fedor explained. "A door can be open or closed. A mind can be open or closed. What lies behind a closed door, whether the door is open or closed, does not change. It is only the acceptance of what's behind the door that will make a difference. In other words, if there is an outraged lion behind a door, not opening the door does not mean that the lion no longer exists."

"And so," Jessica interrupted hesitantly, "the truths of existence remain the same whether they are acknowledged or not. Accepted or not."

"How could it be any other way?" Fedor asked with a smile in his eyes.

Jessica nodded, her lips pursed in thought. As the truth coalesced in her mind, a glorious smile of hope radiated across her face. "Absolutely," she whispered reverently. It was obvious that something deep within her had absorbed the truth and awakened her to something she had longed for.

But Paul closed his eyes in sudden weariness, his thoughts on the job ahead. It wasn't going to be an easy one. Though he knew for certain that everything he was learning and experiencing was real and true, presenting it to others in a way that would allow them to accept would be a huge challenge.

"What's next?" he heard Jessica ask enthusiastically.

171

Behind his closed eyelids he rolled his eyes. He hadn't had time to absorb the first truth and she was already racing on to the next. He opened his eyes and stared at Solomon with a challenge. "One second, ok? Before we go any further, let me ask you this." He waved his hand at their surroundings. "Why does this exist? Why am I seeing it? Why am I even seeing you if nothing exists until I think it exists? Did I think you into existence? Did I imagine you? Would you cease to exist if I stopped believing that you did?"

Solomon smiled serenely, apparently unaffected by Paul's obvious agitation. "Perhaps you're right. Perhaps it should be explained more completely." He exchanged a look of significance with Fedor before continuing. "Something or someone has to create something before it can exist." He touched Paul's arm in an attempt to reassure him. "Try to see it this way. Existence is what you might call a blank canvas. It is simply energy. That energy needs to be shaped in order to have an 'appearance.' Meaning that it is simply energy and nothing more until someone or something shapes it. Energy takes form when it is impacted by another energy. That energy can be as small as a thought form." He tilted his head and gazed into space for several seconds before continuing.

"If someone hands you a rock and dares you to prove that it does not exist, you wouldn't succeed in proving it because it does exist. But at one time it did not. It had to be formed. And, if you choose to change the shape of the rock by smashing it with a hammer, the energy that is the rock still exists. It only exists in a different form. The same is true of your life experience. It does not exist until

172

you live it, until you form it. You form it as you live it, as you think it, as you react to it. And you can change the shape of your experiences." He grinned. "But preferably not with a hammer."

His eyes met Paul's as he turned serious again. "How do you form your life experience?" he asked, fixing Paul with a penetrating gaze. "You form it by the beliefs that you hold." He glanced at Jessica. "Now, to address the issue you're so eager to address; detachment. When you can detach from the beliefs that you hold to be true, you can change the reality that you live."

He held up one finger as a caution. "I'm not saying that it is an easy thing to do. But I am saying that it can be done and that the human race is on the verge of understanding this truth. At least those who want to understand will have the open door to walk through if they choose," he added. His voice resonated with significance.

Paul felt a rush of energy run through him. It felt like he had walked through an invisible chapter in his life and was now on the precipice of living a life unlike anything he had imagined before. Eyes shining with possibility, he turned to Jessica.

She was obviously quivering with unexpressed excitement. Her trembling hand touched his arm. "Let's go do it," she whispered.

Solomon pushed open the great door and gestured them out. Expecting to see the pastoral scene that he'd seen when they had entered, Paul stopped and stared

173

with a slack jaw. Existence seemed to be a patchwork of threads, each shimmering with vitality and unseen activity. The threads crisscrossed each other and spread in all directions. Some seemed to be more solid than others. Some seemed to be filled with heavy significance. All of them captured and reflected crystalline light, shining with the possibilities of undreamed dreams.

"The grid of existence," Paul murmured, not knowing how he knew this was what he was seeing, but certain that he was right.

"Pretty much," Solomon confirmed. "At least this is a temporary visual that you're being given to make it simpler to understand. As you gain experience with grids, you'll see that they are much more intricate than what you're seeing."

"Intricate in what way?" Jessica asked.

Paul glanced at her. She was becoming more ethereal with each passing moment. Her inner being was shining through, making her appear to be edged with light. He wondered if the same was happening to him. He glanced quickly at his hands but could see no difference. Doing his best to focus his thoughts, he turned back to Solomon, waiting for his answer.

"Each shape in existence carries a different vibration of energy," Solomon was explaining. "We call them the sacred geometries of existence."

Jessica let out a soft breath. "I feel so blessed to be having this experience," she said reverently.

174

Solomon touched her arm in a gesture of affection. "It's a soul experience. Every soul has this experience at one time or another."

Paul searched his face. "What you just said hints at volumes and volumes of knowledge that we haven't tapped into yet. How can we live such a limited reality on Earth if, as souls, we know all of this exists outside that reality? How can we be so near-sighted and forgetful of who and what we truly are?"

Solomon allowed his eyes and attention to drift as he searched for the words that would convey the mysteries. "Every soul in existence will have a third dimensional experience, whether it be on Earth or elsewhere. When a soul immerses its focus into a particular dimension, it is for the purpose of learning and understanding that dimension in its entirety. Piece by piece, incarnation by incarnation." He glanced at them before continuing. "Think back to your school days when you needed to memorize a particular lesson. You had to focus all of your attention on that lesson. You immersed yourself in the knowledge until you understood it well enough to pass the test. Right?"

Paul nodded.

"Ok. The same is true of a dimensional experience. You won't be asked to pass a test on what you've learned but," he hesitated, "the ultimate test will be taken."

"And what's that?" Jessica asked quickly.

175

Solomon's expression was filled with compassion and mystery. "Once you understand all dimensions, you are qualified to become creators," he said quietly. "Actually, the truth is, that you always have been capable of being creators. You are creators. The integrity of the soul, however, insists that all things be experienced in order to embrace and understand all things within existence before committing to the responsibility of creating a reality that other souls experience."

Paul started to speak but Solomon held up a finger to stop him. "But there's another piece to this," Solomon continued. He waved his hand briefly through the air. "All worlds and realities that exist are co-creations of the souls who are experiencing them. In other words, all realities are consensual. The souls living the experience are, on some level, agreeing to have reality unfold and present itself in the way that it does."

The enormity of what Solomon had said sank into Paul and Jessica with a solidity that they knew would change their lives forever.

Jessica's eyes shone with purpose and excitement. She turned to Paul and grasped his arm tightly. "Do you see what he's saying?" she asked, barely breathing.

Paul nodded without answering her. His own thoughts were speeding through time and space, considering the possibilities. Long ago, when he was in his teens, he had experienced a dream that hinted at just such a possibility. Since that time he had been, in his quiet moments, wondering if the dream had been a Truth that was being revealed. Now he knew that it was.

Impulsively, he pulled Jessica into a hug filled with barely-suppressed excitement. His eyes met Solomon's over her head. The solemn nod of approval that Solomon gave him made his heart expand. It was time. This was a moment in his soul's history that he'd been waiting for. He released Jessica and turned to the thread-like grid. "Where do we begin?" he asked quietly.

The three of them wove their way through the grid, gliding through the soft atmosphere as though neither they nor the grid really existed. Solomon stopped them at a juncture where two threads of the grid joined. "Merge your thoughts, merge your existence, with this juncture, if you will," he suggested. "I'll be with you, but in another form."

Paul's hesitation lasted only a nanosecond. Since he had begun this dimensional learning experience, all fear that might have otherwise been within him had ceased to exist. He was, in truth, a multi-dimensional soul who was creating all of his experiences for the benefit of his soul. What was there to fear? He willingly merged his thoughts with the grid. He blinked in shock as he looked around at his surroundings.

The Jeep sat waiting beside the road. Jessica was emerging from the interior of a concrete outhouse that was set about one hundred feet off the road. Trees tangled with vines draped and shaded the exterior of the small, dirty-looking building. Jessica grimaced at him, slapping her hands against her jeans in disgust. "That place is filthy. I wish the human body didn't have to have this elimination process. Then I wouldn't have to endure places like this." She glanced back and shivered slightly.

177

Turning, she confronted him brightly. "You ready?"

Paul shook his head in stunned bewilderment. "Ready?" he mumbled.

She looked at him worriedly. "Are you all right? Is the heat getting to you? You look flushed."

Paul stuttered. "I'm ... I'm, uh, I'm all right." He stared at her in confusion. "Um, how long have we been here? I don't remember stopping." He brushed his hand through his hair in agitation. "Do you remember anything?"

"Remember what?" Forehead wrinkled, she studied him with concern. "Are you sure you're all right?"

Paul tilted his head back, studied the sky, tried to comprehend exactly what was going on. There was no way to prove that they had not been having the third dimensional experience they'd apparently been having. But there was no way to prove the one he thought they'd been having either. "You don't remember being taken to the eighth dimension? You don't remember Solomon appearing?" He glanced around. "How'd we get here anyway?" He pulled his fingers through his hair with exasperation again.

"We drove," she said worriedly, staring at him with concern. She laid her fingers lightly on his wrist as if she were taking his pulse. "Are you sure you're all right?" Before he could answer, she turned toward the Jeep. "I'm going to get you some water. And I'm going to drive," she stated flatly. "No arguments." She glanced at her watch.

178

"I think the plane leaves in a couple of hours. I want to make sure we get there in plenty of time to verify that we can use these tickets, even though the date on them is wrong." She paused to scan the skies, a look of concern on her face.

Following her gaze, Paul stared at the seemingly innocent sky. "What?" he asked wearily. He was suddenly exhausted. He drew a deep breath into his lungs. "What now? What are you looking for? Please don't tell me that we're being followed by alien spies or anything." He rubbed his fingers across his jaw line, his lips tight, his eyes narrowed by frustration.

Jessica pulled her gaze away from the sky and back to Paul, attempting a smile that would suggest she wasn't concerned. "Don't worry," she said, her voice ringing with a false tone of confidence. "Everything's fine. Here." She reached into the back seat, picked up a small bottle of water, and tossed it to him. "Drink this. And let's get going." She stared at him silently for several seconds. "And I know you have something to tell me," she added. "Tell me while we're driving, ok?"

Without protest, Paul took the passenger's seat. He was totally disoriented. He took a sip of the tepid water and watched her steer the Jeep confidently back onto the road. He was suddenly glad that she didn't recall their recent sojourn into the eighth dimension. The last thing they needed was for both of them to feel the way he did.

"We're only about ten minutes from the airport," Jessica told him. "At least as far as I know." She glanced at him.

179

"Are we being followed?" Paul asked. He turned to glance behind them but saw nothing but the dust that the Jeep was kicking up as it sped along. He tried to catch a glimpse of the speedometer but her arm was blocking his view. It felt like they were driving way above the speed limit.

"I haven't seen anyone following," she replied. Her hand automatically reached out to touch the bag of tiles that sat on the console between them. "But I sure feel like we're being watched." She pushed the bag toward him. "Why don't you put these in my backpack or under the seat?"

Paul did as she asked, tucking them into her backpack and then patting one of her sweaters into place on top of them. "Well, we are being watched," he said, zipping the backpack closed. "We have the tiles. Obviously we're being watched by the aliens who brought them here." He stared at her, wondering why she hadn't thought of something so simple.

Jessica tossed her hair in exasperation. "Well, I know that! I've been communicating with them all along! It's not them I'm worried about."

"Oh." The single word hung between them with significance. As did Paul's instant fear. Who ... or what ... was she worried about? He was afraid to ask.

"So tell me what happened," Jessica said, changing the subject abruptly. "What happened to you back there?"

Paul stared at his hands, flexing his fingers in a vain attempt to ease his tension. Staring out the window sightlessly, he briefed her on their eighth dimensional encounter. Finishing, he glanced sideways at her. "How do you account for the fact that I remember and you don't? I would think it would be the other way around since I was the one who was driving." He grimaced slightly. "Or at least I thought I was driving."

Jessica shrugged lightly. "I have no idea. But the whole experience makes sense to me."

"How so?" Paul asked. "It doesn't surprise you at all?"

Jessica shook her head, causing her hair to dance on her shoulders. "No. We're multi-dimensional beings. The focus of our spirit is on the third, making it seem like this is who and what we are and that's all there is to it. But that's as far from the truth as possible." She grinned at him. "If this was all there was, we'd all be in a deep world of trouble. I mean, look at the state this world is in, you know?"

Paul agreed with her. "But how do you account for the fact that I was able to drive and still be there at the same time?"

"You weren't driving. We pulled off so I could use that outhouse, remember? And then you shifted your focus, apparently. Or, I guess I should say Solomon shifted your focus for you. You were still here but your soul-focus, I guess we could call it, was there. So," she continued thoughtfully, "what can we figure from that?

181

We can be in various places at any given time. But that's kind of an accepted fact already, right?"

She didn't wait for his response. "So a soul needs to have a particular experience but we can momentarily shift our focus into another experience if there's something there that is imperative for us to know." She drummed her lips with her fingers, thinking hard. "Not only did you get the first insights into the information in the tiles, but I think what you learned, during the time your focus was shifted, is something that's imperative for your soul to use here at this time. Do you see what I mean?" She glanced at him, her face alight with the mysteries and intrigue of existence.

Paul thought about what she'd said before answering. "I think I see what you're saying. We're using this third dimensional experience as a tool, learning things that our soul wants to know. And if there's something on some other level that can make this experience more worthwhile, we'll receive that information and incorporate it into this reality we're currently living. And what I learned probably was a piece of what is inside these tiles. It's just that I needed, or wanted, the information right now. Which is why I had the experience now. Makes sense!"

Jessica tapped the steering wheel lightly for emphasis. "Exactly." She looked pleased. "Now tell me again. Exactly what did we say about creating a new reality?" She took her eyes off the road to stare at him eagerly.

Paul glanced at the road nervously. He didn't

182

particularly like being a passenger. "That was about all I was told. That it's possible. And that we're doing it right now."

"Exactly!" Jessica cried, startling him with the loudness of her agreement. "It's what I've always maintained was true. As a group of souls who are manifesting a third dimensional reality on Earth, everyone on Earth is agreeing to create what we see and what we experience. If everyone was to agree that things could and should change, they would change!" She beamed and slapped the steering wheel triumphantly.

Paul gave a small shrug. He wanted to believe ... and be as enthusiastic about it as she was ... but his view of reality and Earth's society told him it wouldn't be that simple. "Well," he said hesitantly, "it makes sense to me. But it's got to make sense to everyone in order to have it work."

"And so how do we, as a human-unit, so to speak, go about changing this reality?" Jessica asked zealously. She glanced at him. "How on Earth would you ever get millions of people to agree on anything?" She tapped her fingers on the wheel in agitation. "People rarely agree on even one thing. How would you get them to agree on millions of things?"

Paul stared at her in surprise. How could she not see the obvious? "But, Jessica. They already are in agreement. Everyone is already agreeing to create this third dimension as it is. Get it? You see?"

She looked at him, wide-eyed with the sudden but

183

obvious realization. "But of course!" She tossed her hand in the air excitedly. "You're right! And if we can create this reality then it has to be possible to re-create it. Or change it. However you want to look at it." She glanced at him again before turning back to the road. "I know. I know. I know all of this but sometimes things just get more concrete when they're said out loud. Like they become more possible."

"And," Paul continued slowly, "to re-state it in really simply terms ... if we're creating this reality then it's altogether possible that we can create another one."

Jessica turned her head slowly. Understanding and excitement began to slide into her gaze. Her eyes widened. "You're right," she breathed. She grinned at Solomon. "And isn't that the secret? Isn't that why we're really here? Doing what we're doing?" Her hand subconsciously touched the backpack. "And what do these tiles have to do with it all?" She glanced at him again. "This is no coincidence, Paul," she told him, her voice tight with suppressed excitement.

Before Paul could respond, she turned into the airport entryway. There would be time for universal speculation later on. Right now it was time to turn the Jeep in at the rental area, make sure their tickets were going to be accepted, and, most importantly, figure out how to get the tiles back to Phoenix safely.

Without thinking Paul swept the backpack off the console and set it on his lap. "What are we going to do with these? How can we get them through Customs?"

184

"I think I know," Jessica said mysteriously. She reached into the back of the Jeep and came back with a large, plastic, wide-mouthed water jug.

"What are you going to do with that?" Paul asked, puzzled.

"We're going to put the tiles in it."

"But it's clear plastic. You don't suppose they're going to see them, do you?" Paul's lips curled sarcastically. "And besides, they're made of some kind of clay. The water is going to melt that, I would think. Or, maybe not melt but somehow mess them up."

Jessica glared at him. "I wish you wouldn't treat me like I'm an idiot," she snapped. "We're going to alter their energy and make them invisible," she told him roughly, reaching for the bag on his lap.

"Yeah, right."

"Just give me the tiles, Paul." Jessica gave a small sigh of exasperation.

With a sigh of acceptance, Paul relinquished the bag and sat back to see what was going to happen next. He thanked the heavens for the fact that it was dark outside and no one appeared to be paying any attention to them at all. He was surprised to suddenly feel Solomon's presence behind him. Perhaps what she intended to do was possible after all and Solomon was here to help?

He didn't expect to see what he saw next. He even

185

went so far as to chastise himself for being a skeptic. How could he believe in some of the things he'd been experiencing and yet still have questions about the possibility of more?

One by one Jessica took the tiles from their resting place and dropped them into the plastic container of water. Solomon's hand moved above them and Paul watched in amazement as an almost tangible energy flowed from his hand and wrapped around the small tiles. A soft, angel-like light glowed around them now. Paul heard the air whisper beside him, as though it held a secret that it wanted to reveal. As he stared at the tiles, enraptured, they began to separate, becoming single cells swirling around each other in a clock-wise motion. Gently, and then more rapidly, they spun ... until they'd spun themselves into invisibility. They were now, apparently, water-like energy. A thought occurred to Paul. Who would re-materialize them when it was safe to do so? He shook his head at his own doubt. Obviously this wasn't going to be an issue. As he was seeing, anything was possible.

With a satisfied grin, Jessica shared what looked like a high-five with Solomon's energy form, and tucked the water jug into her carry-on. "You ready?" she asked Paul with an innocent grin.

Rolling his eyes with mock humor, Paul followed her into the terminal. They dropped the rental car keys at the kiosk next to the check-in area and turned toward the seating area, looking for a place to sit down and wait for their flight.

186

Movement on the far side of the terminal caught Paul's eye. His heart went into a wild, erratic heartbeat. He grabbed for Jessica's hand, intending to drag her back into the parking area. But it was too late. The two men in black were headed directly toward them. They looked like twins ... or clones. Dark, close-cropped hair through which their scalps could be seen. Square chins and dark glasses that Paul felt sure hid aggressive, dark eyes. Their black suits hung on them like they were still hanging on hangers, limp and unfitting.

Staring at Paul as if he'd suddenly lost his mind, Jessica failed to notice the men until they were almost on top of her. Paul heard her quick intake of breath and felt a current of electricity rush from her hand to his as her body transmitted her shock.

The two men in black, ramrod-thin and as stiff as boards, flanked them and, with nothing more than the promise of threat, tried to herd them like cattle toward a closed door on the right. Planting her feet, Jessica refused to move.

"Don't make this ugly, miss," one of the men snarled, his voice almost a hiss. He was the one closest to Paul. As he leaned across Paul to stare at Jessica, Paul caught a whiff of his breath. It smelled like hot tin. In front of them, two airport guards were rapidly approaching.

"What are you trying to do?" Paul demanded.

"Just come with us," the more vocal of the two ordered.

187

"Not without an explanation," Paul said, determined to stand his ground as long as he could.

By now the two airport guards had reached them. They looked from one to the other, apparently unclear as to what was going on and what they should do about it. A rapid-fire conversation between them left Paul with no more information than when they'd started. He suddenly realized how valuable it would have been to listen to his parents when they suggested that he study Spanish in school.

The older of the two guards turned to the man on Paul's right. From the staccato-like spurt of words, Paul assumed that the men in black were being asked for their identification. Reaching into his breast pocket, one of the men produced an ID of some kind. Paul wasn't able to catch more than a glimpse of it. All he saw was a black decal on the bottom right-hand side. Nodding as if satisfied, the two guards added themselves to the entourage around Paul and Jessica and helped the men in black drive them toward the closed door.

The room was bare except for a small table and two chairs. Paul and Jessica were informally pressed into them. The contents of their carry-ons were unceremoniously dumped onto the small table and searched. All of this commotion passed without words exchanged. The two guards stood silently watching, allowing the men in black to direct the search.

Finding nothing of interest, the more aggressive of the two leaders turned and pointed his chin at Paul. "Stand. Strip."

188

Paul blinked at him in shock. "No way," he said flatly. He could feel the burn of his emotions seeping onto his cheeks. Nothing made him more irritated with himself than allowing his emotions to be so easily seen. He concentrated on pushing the uncomfortable flush away and stared belligerently at the men.

The man pointed his chin at Jessica. "It's nothing she hasn't already seen, bud. Get up. Strip. Before I do it for you." He took a threatening step toward Paul.

Sensing Paul's rage building, Jessica set a calming hand on Paul's forearm. "Wait," she said coldly. "Just tell us what you want. We'll cooperate."

"Don't try to pull that innocent crap with us. You're well aware of what you have that doesn't belong to you."

At this the two guards grew more alert. Could it be that these two travelers were attempting to carry precious artifacts out of the country?

"We don't have anything you want," Jessica stated flatly.

For the first time the second man in black spoke up. The icy evenness of his voice sent chills down Paul's spine. "You can't possibly believe that you'll walk away freely from this."

"I have every intention of walking away freely," Jessica stated with confidence. "I have nothing you want and I'm no threat at all to you."

189

Now that he'd spoken, it was clear that this man was the one in charge. "I'm a reasonable man," he said. "I'll give you your privacy. You'll each have a room and a guard. A female one for you," he said, peering at Jessica. "You have what we're looking for hidden somewhere. We know this. But we're willing to let you attempt to prove to us that you don't."

He turned toward the two guards and spoke in a low voice that Paul couldn't hear. One of the guards stepped out, apparently to secure the help of a female guard. Paul exchanged a quick glance with Jessica. They were both looking for quick answers, but without success. With no way to avoid the authority of the people surrounding them, they were separated and strip-searched. When the embarrassment was over, they were brought back into the same room. Paul avoided Jessica's eyes. He believed, with all of his heart, that he should have thought of some way to prevent what she'd just endured.

But it appeared that the experience hadn't dampened her courage. She stood arrogantly next to the table, refusing to sit, as she'd been instructed to do. "Ok. You've had your fun. Now let us get back home." She paused significantly. "Or give me a phone so I can contact our embassy."

Paul's eyes carefully avoided the water bottle sitting on the table. Was someone from a higher dimension monitoring them and keeping them safe? How long could they maintain their invisibility?

The airport guards unexpectedly decided to leave

190

the room. As the door closed behind them, Paul and Jessica exchanged a nervous glance. They were now alone with the two men in black. Behind their glasses, the two men stared at them with open hostility.

"We can hold you here until hell freezes over," the one in charge stated flatly.

"You could. But what would that accomplish?" Paul asked. "There's obviously no point in holding us. That won't accomplish anything but trouble. A few minutes more of this and I'm going to be making a call to the American Embassy."

"The Embassy isn't going to help you a bit," the leader said flatly. "We have the power to haul you back to a base in the United States and hold you there. No one will ever hear from you again." The man's cold tone dropped a hint of frost into the warm room.

"But what's the point," Jessica asked serenely. "Like he said, you won't gain a thing."

The man in charge lifted one eyebrow and stared at her coldly. "You might be surprised to hear that I agree with you. I'm going to let you go on your way. But now you know that every move you make will be shadowed. There's no place you can go that you won't be watched." He stared at Jessica and then Paul. "I hope you're prepared to live with that."

As if they were sharing the same body, both Paul and Jessica shrugged simultaneously.

191

"What do you want us to say to that?" Paul asked, challenge in his voice. "What can we say? I guess you've gotta do what you've gotta do." He paused significantly. "And we've gotta do what we've gotta do."

The men stiffened with anger. But they'd already made their decision and Paul knew it. Locking them up or killing them would serve no purpose at all. The tiles would remain missing. Whoever these men were, whoever they represented, they knew that the tiles would be forever missing without Paul and Jessica.

With a look that spelled triumph, Jessica moved toward the door. "Gentlemen, if you'll excuse us, we have a plane to catch."

It wasn't until they were aboard, and both nursing a welcome glass of wine, that they were able to smile about the encounter. But the smiles were feeble. The threat was real. And, unless they thought of something quickly, another encounter with the men in black was certain. It was logical to assume that another meeting with them wouldn't end as cordially the next time.

The flight seemed much longer than it actually was. The cabin was dimly lit. Most of the passengers were dozing but neither Jessica nor Paul could rest.

"So explain to me, if you can, exactly how the dematerialization works," Paul said quietly.

"We just alter the vibration of the tiles to their

192

original energy and, voila', they no longer exist in third dimension."

Paul turned and studied her. "It's that easy?" he asked. Once again his mind filled with the vastness of what he didn't understand.

Jessica nodded. "The tiles are merely a physical representation of much higher dimensional thought forms and truths. Therefore, to return them to their original form is easy. The configuration of their original energy stays constant, no matter what dimension they are in, therefore making it easy to shift them from one dimension to the next. The original frequency, vibration, if you want to call it that, doesn't lower to a 3-D frequency. Only the appearance does."

Paul pursed his lips in thought. His eyes lit up with a sudden thought. "Well, that's exactly like a soul incarnating into a physical body then, right?"

Jessica beamed at him. "Exactly! People, souls actually, take on a 3-D frequency in order to incarnate and, by doing so, imagine that their original frequency is lost to them."

The realization was monumental and Paul knew it. But the tiles were foremost in his mind. "Ok. But going back to the tiles ... why are they here? Why do they have to be physically manifest? I mean, wouldn't it be easier if they weren't?" He glanced at Jessica. "At the very least, we would be safer. And we could retrieve the information through some other means - like dreams or something."

193

"What you're suggesting is logical. But an understanding of energy would tell you the answer. What you have is a form of alien, meaning off-planet, energy. What these tiles accomplish is the placement of energy from another planetary and dimensional energy into this one. It needs to be that way. The alien energy is impacting the energy that makes up this Earth-reality."

"Well, if it's the case that energies can be shifted and appear and re-appear as easily as these tiles just did, it should be that simple for us. For everybody, as a matter of fact. I mean, if we're merely representations of our souls, which are infinite and all-encompassing, then it must be that simple to return to our origins. I mean, isn't it true that our souls are one energy and remain constant? That they remain the original energy?"

Jessica nodded but stayed silent, allowing him to finish his thought.

"And if this is the truth and it's that simple, then there must be an extremely important reason why we don't just simply maintain our true energy. So, why do we continue to exist in places and situations that we don't like? Why do we create situations and realities that seem to be incompatible with the truth of our soul?"

Jessica shrugged lightly. "How better to learn all aspects of creation?" she asked.

Paul turned toward her more fully. "Earth is moving toward an evolutionary change, correct?"

She nodded agreeably, giving Paul her full attention.

"Let me ramble for a minute here," Paul requested. "Earth has served as a fantastic tool, a place for us to physically display our ability to manifest. And now, many if not all of us who live here, commonly agree that it is time to take it to the next level. To graduate, so to speak, into the next level of understanding about manifesting and creating. And," he continued, growing more excited as his thoughts flowed, "the dimensions above are preparing to receive us and help us on that next level." He leaned toward Jessica excitedly. "Am I right?" He waved his hand at the water jug, which sat nestled in the carry-on beneath Jessica's feet. "And they reveal this? And if the Mayan messengers had not been executed, this message would have come to Earth long ago? When the tiles were first brought?"

Jessica nodded her head once again, her eyes veiled with mysteries unrevealed.

Paul knew her well enough to read her expression. He wished they had a lifetime in which all of those unspoken thoughts and mysteries could be told.

"Humankind has interacted with those in other dimensions for most of the time that Earth has existed, though sporadically," Jessica advised him quietly. "It's rare to have an existence or a dimensional reality that is unaware or unconnected with other dimensions. The isolation of this particular aspect of existence stunned almost everyone who was not directly involved in the fracture that occurred in the Truth of this existence. Earth reality has, off and on through history, interacted

195

with other dimensional beings even to the degree of creating offspring." She stirred the air with her hand. "But then there has always come a division between realities. A struggle for power. A struggle for control. A lack of understanding between realities as those who interact lose sight of the fact that they are, in truth, interacting with brothers and sisters. It is not always the fault of the lower dimensional realities either," she added quietly. "On several occasions it has been the society within a higher dimension that seeks to control those in the lower dimensions."

"Wouldn't that be something like a third dimensional human attempting to control a second dimensional thing?" Paul asked. "I mean everything has a life and reality of its own." He shook his head, a puzzled expression on his face. "I don't get it. Why does one reality or person need to control another? What kind of power do they hope to gain?" He flipped his hands in agitation. "There is no real power except for the power of union with soul. Isn't that the ultimate truth?"

Jessica studied him before answering. "That's close to the ultimate truth. But there's more to it."

Paul blew a sigh out through his lips. "There's always more to it," he complained. "It seems like I'll never get to the bottom of the mysteries."

Jessica smiled at him. "But would you really want to? Wouldn't you be rather bored with your existence if you had total understanding of all things?"

Paul thought about it a minute, absentmindedly

196

scratching his arm. "I don't know," he said thoughtfully. "Perhaps." He looked past her at the night sky that sat outside the window. "Correct me if I'm wrong, ok, but my sense is that this reality was on the verge of making the change it's preparing for now when these tiles were first brought here. What happened? Why didn't things go as planned?"

Suddenly he was in another place and time, drawn into history as surely as if it were occurring in that moment.

197

CHAPTER SEVEN

THE NIGHT WAS JUNGLE-DARK. The moon feebly attempted to cast light through the overhang of the thick branches above. A slight mist rose from the river, causing the night to seem like a mystery. The smell of musty ferns crowded the air. There was no need for a fire to keep them warm as they waited on this night.

"It's late," Malik mentioned to Nevra, who sat silently next to him.

"Don't worry," she whispered, her murmur matching the esoteric silence that hung in the air. "They'll come. They said they would."

Malik nodded without speaking. She was right. They always came on the nights they said they would. He silently studied her under the dim light of the moon. Her long hair was rich black, as smooth as a raven's wing, and soft to the touch. Her nose tilted upward slightly, which charmed him for some reason. She was short and stout and strong. He often thought, though he never voiced it, that she might be stronger than he. He was shorter even than she and much thinner. His nose was hooked and his dark hair rough and coarse. He wondered, not for the first time, why she had chosen him to be her mate.

He thought again about the changes that had occurred in their lives since their small group had decided to leave the others of their village and live here in the jungles and in the caves. The changes had been wonderful, with visitations from the air-people who

198

shared all kinds of mysteries and wonders. And those who visited from the air had promised them that the changes would be far greater in the future. Another world, he murmured to himself, struggling to comprehend the vastness of the idea. They were going to assist the air-people in creating another world. It was beyond any dream he had ever had.

Nevra touched his arm urgently, transmitting to him through her touch a sense of excitement and urgency. He felt his heart react and immediately lifted his eyes to the skies above. They were here.

It was the mothership this time, not one of the much smaller scout crafts. The great craft slid silently into the atmosphere, its lights blinking hypnotically. It arrived without sound, parting the night and the world below with its presence. It was huge, blocking out the light of the moon and the stars above. The enormity of it, as well as the angles and curves, made it seem to Malik that it contained an entire world within its walls. They heard not a whisper of sound as a door opened in the craft, spilling intense light onto the ground below. Without realizing it, Nevra and Malik were now standing, waiting without breathing.

Six alien beings glided through the light beam, approaching Earth. Five of them held something in their hands. Nevra reached for Malik's hand, squeezing it with excitement. The time was now.

Five of the beings were ivory-skinned, five feet tall, and thin. They wore no clothing to disguise their taut skin. All of them had almond-shaped eyes that were as

199

black as night. They were hairless, with facial features that were so small they were difficult to notice. Their three-fingered hands held the gifts like they were treasures, which they were. The sixth member of their group was taller and even thinner. Her skin was pale-green and almost translucent. The set of her large head upon her long, thin neck suggested royalty. Her large oval eyes studied them silently as she stood before them. Malik felt Nevra's hand tremble in his as she reached for him, needing to calm or comfort herself. He didn't know which.

The tall being finally nodded. Malik bowed his head slightly in greeting, afraid to speak out loud. The being's long, thin hand moved the air around them as she gestured at the five smaller aliens who stood silently next to her, holding their treasures and studying the two Mayans who would receive them.

"This is an unprecedented event," the leader of the group said, speaking out loud. Her voice had an odd tone to it, sounding like it was coming from somewhere other than her throat. "You will receive our knowledge but it will be up to you to perform the work here in this reality." She moved her graceful hand toward the sky. "We will work from above." Her great eyes scanned the deep jungle around them. "I have been informed of your efforts to escape the life that the others have created. You are to be commended for your initiative. We believe you have the stamina and the soul-desire to unite with us in this effort to create a new world. We greatly look forward to working with you."

She extended her long arm and touched Malik on

200

the shoulder, as though she were knighting him. "If all goes well, we will meet again." Her gaze touched Nevra with kindness before she turned. She gestured again at the small crystalline forms in the hands of the five smaller beings. "Each of these is a geometric symbol that contains great truths. Each one contains knowledge of this Universe as well as the structure of existence and this earth's place within it." She turned back to them. "As you have told us, you agree with us that this world would benefit from a new reality that speaks to the truth of the original purpose of existence. As you know, we are in full agreement. As you also know, a new world cannot be created without the cooperation of at least a portion of those who are having the experience that is going to undergo the change. Your group is made up of those who will be responsible for providing the necessary balance.

"You must gather more people who believe as you do. Teach them what you know of Light and Truth. Work together to achieve the necessary balance of light here in the darkness of your world. When the balance is achieved to the degree that we are allowed to intervene, rest assured that we will be here to assist."

She touched one of the tiles with reverence. "The knowledge is within the crystalline threads which have been formed into sacred symbols. The symbols are revered throughout reality for they contain the knowledge of the foundation of this existence. Access your soul-knowledge and the sacred energetic grid of your soul and you will merge with these tools. At that time, the wisdom will be merged with you and you will carry it always."

201

Malik shivered as he was caught in a wave of energy that stirred every hair on his body. Was it his imagination or was it the touch of his soul that he was feeling? He glanced at Nevra, who seemed lost in thought as she studied the great being who stood before them. For perhaps the first time since he'd known her, he couldn't read her thoughts or emotions.

One by one the five small aliens set their treasures on the woven mat of ferns that the villagers had prepared for the occasion. When the visitors had gone, Malik and Nevra would carry this mat and its contents to the others.

The leader of the visitors once again set her hand on Malik's shoulder, causing him to lift his eyes to hers. For silent seconds he was held captive by her gaze. It spoke of worlds beyond his knowledge, power beyond his imagining, and compassion beyond his understanding. He felt fear clutch his heart in a vise-like grip. Was he worthy? Was he strong enough, smart enough, dedicated enough to follow through with this mission that would affect all of existence? He did his best to keep the fear from his eyes. But he was unsuccessful.

Without moving, it seemed that the great being withdrew from him. A cloud of doubt filled her eyes. The touch of her hand was slowly removed. Somehow she seemed to grow taller and more regal. Malik cowered within himself, ashamed and filled with a fear greater than his entire life.

Her voice was as soft as misty spring air and filled with compassion when she spoke to him. "You must be

202

aware that you are a victim only to your own doubts when you doubt the truth of your soul. I know your soul. I know your capabilities. I trust your heart and your intentions. And we entrust you with these sacred tools of creation."

She reached out her thin hand and touched Nevra's briefly. "You will serve humanity with the work that you do from this moment forward. Do it well for I know that you can. I know your soul." Her voice had faded to a whisper.

She gave both of them one last look before turning away. As she glided into the beam of light that still descended from the craft, she stopped. "We will meet again," she stated clearly. "And when we do, we will talk at great length about that which will follow this moment."

Nevra and Malik exchanged one quick glance of puzzlement before they turned back to watch the aliens and their craft ascend into the night as silently as they had come.

The others were waiting in the small clearing near the mouth of the cave. Malik and Nevra gently laid the fragile crystalline treasures before them as they told the story of the alien visit. The others listened breathlessly, some with their fingers hovering reverently in the air above the treasures, fearful of touching them. Malik and Nevra exchanged a look full of significance as they finished their story.

"I believe, with all my heart, that what we have been

called to do is possible," Nevra stated. The nearby jungle seemed to reverberate with the strength of her statement. "We left the others because we believed they were cruel and unfair. We were not treated as the great souls that we are. The others created the reality that they wanted and demanded that everyone else live it. As we all know, that's not the way it was meant to be." She pointed at the treasures. "These are the tools we need to create our own reality. They hold the knowledge." She tapped her chest for emphasis. "And we, in here, hold the key to opening and using that knowledge."

Her small, black eyes scanned each one in the small group. "The one thing that can stop us is fear. Fear will cause us doubt and doubt is the enemy of truth." She tapped her chest again, glaring at each one of them. "In here we know who and what we are. If we begin to doubt that truth, we will fail." She stared at them urgently. "And we cannot, absolutely cannot, fail. If we do, we are doomed."

Her strong words gripped the night and the hearts of those who listened. Malik, his heart trembling with the power of her words, looked away. He had fear. He hated it. He abhorred it. But he admitted it. But only to himself. He gave Nevra a swift, sideways glance. If she read his thoughts she would dismiss him from her life. He knew that for a certainty. He pushed his fear into his stomach and turned his attention back to the group, kneeling with them beside the treasures as they ooohed and aaahed over each one. And then, as they all agreed upon the safest method of preserving the crystals, he brought to them the pot of wet clay that they would use to cloak the small crystalline symbols.

204

With the task of cloaking the sacred symbols in clay, and having hidden them in the crevices of the cenote, the small group sat back and stared at each other silently.

"Now what?" one of them ventured to ask, vocalizing almost everyone's thoughts.

"Now we work with the energy of our souls and the sacred grids, as they taught us to do," Nevra stated firmly. "They'll stay in communication with us. They'll lead us through the process. When we're strong enough in our knowledge and our abilities, we'll leave here, travel to a distant place where it will be safe for the crystals to be displayed. And then we will begin the task of rebuilding our world, creating our new reality."

Malik spoke up. "We've been working on integrating our soul's energy into this experience for a long time. I think that the energy and knowledge that is in these tiles is the key we've been waiting for. With these tools now in our presence, it shouldn't take long."

Nevra smiled sadly at him and shook her head. "It's not about time, Malik. It's about doing it right." Her gaze took in the others. "If we want to create a reality that is the opposite of what we've seen happening here, it's going to take time and diligence. And secrecy," she added, staring at them. "If the others discover our plans, they will destroy us. A new world would strip their power from them. They're not going to like it." Her tone rang with the suggestion of doom.

205

Malik shivered with a sudden vision of his own death. Fear raced through him like wild fire. He tried, without success, to mask it. Nevra turned toward him aggressively. The look she gave him flamed his fear even more.

"Your thoughts are hanging in the air like lanterns," she snapped accusingly. She grabbed his arm and shook it. "Do you want to bring the others crashing down on us? If I can read your energy this clearly what makes you think they can't? Why," she cried, her voice rising, "why, are you so afraid? After all the training we've done and all the work we've done to access our souls. Why?"

"I don't know," Malik mumbled. He shook his head sadly, not meeting her eyes. "I don't know. I just can't stop thinking that something's going to happen to stop us."

"Well, something will happen if you let your fear send out messages like they are smoke signals!" She glared furiously at him. "I want this too much to let you ruin it for us." She waved her hand at the others who were watching them silently. "We all want this. This is an opportunity that probably comes once in a soul's life. And if you don't control your thoughts and energies, you're going to doom us to failure."

Malik knew she was right. He hung his head in shame, struggling to draw his energy into himself so that it could not be seen or felt by anyone outside himself. The tiny camp fell into silence. Several minutes passed before Nevra quietly suggested that they all retire to get

206

a good night of sleep. Perhaps, she speculated, their dreams would tell them more about the future that sat before them, like a book waiting to be written.

Malik's eyes flew open. His heart was thudding with fear. Had he actually heard something or had it been his imagination? The others were still sleeping. He could hear Nevra breathing softly beside him. He waited as his eyes adjusted to the shadows of the cave. He sat up cautiously. It had probably been his imagination or a dream. He had been successful in keeping his fear from the notice of the others for two days now. But it still plagued him. Perhaps it was his fear that had wakened him.

But there it was again. The gritty sound of a leaf being crushed beneath the weight of a person. Every cell in his body leapt into fear. His heart thundered in his ears, making it impossible to listen for more sounds. He shivered violently, hoping he wouldn't awaken Nevra. If they were to die he wanted her to be unaware of the moment. He started to turn, to search the night.

He felt the touch of the blade as it sliced through him. His spirit rose above him, watching as his blood spilled onto the ground. He watched in horror as the others were massacred. He was frozen in the moment, incapable of letting go of the screams caught in his throat, the tears caught in his heart, the terror caught in his mind. It felt like he had been sentenced by the judge of all time and space, his sentence one of immobility in the face of disaster. The judge of his soul wanted nothing more than to burden the rest of his days with the

207

vision of this slaughter. The slaughter and the screams of his loved ones would forever haunt him.

He watched as Nevra's spirit floated from her body and passed him without notice. He tried to whisper her name but nothing came out. He tried to pursue her but he was held captive in the moment, in the vision of death. Only when the deaths were final was he released. He floated away from the vision of blood and the smell of death and went in search of Nevra. Perhaps she would help him to understand.

Instead it was The Esartania that came fully into his vision. It looked no different to his spirit than it had to the eyes he had used to watch it descend to Earth just days earlier. It spread across the sky in front of him. Without hesitation, he passed through the walls of the great mothership and floated through the halls to the control room. It was as familiar as coming home.

Commander Korton turned as he sensed Malik's presence. His aura of authority filled the large room. His almond-shaped eyes scoured Malik silently. He had been the creator of this mission, the Esartania, and its subsequent entry into Earth's reality. His vast and far-reaching desire for healing universes knew no limits. He was known in all universes for his unwavering dedication. He had made it his soul-mission to involve himself in whatever reality fell out of alignment with the original Plan. He was unstoppable when he made up his mind to intervene on the behalf of the Supreme Creator.

Malik knew his reputation and presence well. Now he hesitated for only seconds before gliding the last few steps to stand before the Commander. They stood, eye to eye, and evaluated each other silently. With a relief that reached his soul, Malik suddenly knew that there was no judgment coming from the Commander. He felt himself sag with relief. The slaughter and the failure of the mission would not be placed on his shoulders. "What went wrong?" he asked quietly.

"The same thing that has continued to happen throughout time," Korton said quietly. "Power. Control. Fear." He sighed deeply, turning back to the control panel. The thoughts and emotions that he had about the catastrophe were his alone, cloaked by his stoic silence.

Malik watched in devastated silence as the great craft turned and glided silently through the black hole into the next universe, the next mission, the next attempt to set into motion the divine alignment of existence.

This time Jessica had gone on the mind-time-journey with him. Paul could see it in her eyes as his awareness came back to the crowded air of the plane they were on. Neither of them spoke as they looked at each other, Jessica with tears in her eyes and Paul with a stone in his heart. He wondered how he would deal with the overwhelming conflict of his emotions. He wanted to talk to her, but he couldn't find the words to even begin.

She sighed deeply and turned toward the window. The ocean beneath them passed by in utter silence. The

209

night ebbed away like a windless tide, ushering in a pink dawn.

A mood of gloom settled over Paul. He was anxious to reach the safety of Bill and Brenda's ranch again. He knew it wouldn't be possible to sleep for days, like he found himself wanting to, to heal his heart, his fears, his unanswered questions. But the need was there. The need to take the time to heal. But realistically, it didn't seem possible.

His thoughts wandered, struggling to understand the threads of the past, present, and future that he'd been shown in all of his visions. He recognized common links, experiences, and energies throughout everything. He wanted nothing more than to comprehend his lifetimes and mistakes. He wanted his pain to end.

Setting aside his self-examination, he went on high alert as they departed the plane in Miami. But after a sharp squeeze of his arm by Jessica, he realized that his nervousness could very well draw more attention to them. He forced himself to take a deep breath, glanced at the water jug to determine its safety, and followed Jessica through the long line waiting at the customs inspection station. It wasn't until the inspector pulled Jessica's bag toward him that Paul spotted a man in black watching carefully. Without any visible sign of recognition, the man stepped forward and watched intently as Jessica's items were pulled from her bag. It took all of Paul's reserves to stay calm and stifle his rage at the blatant threat.

The man never met his gaze, though there wasn't

any doubt that he felt Paul's glare. He watched impassively as Paul's belongings were piled haphazardly on the long table. When he was satisfied that everything in the bags had been sufficiently searched, he turned away without a word. Paul watched as the man met and spoke with yet another agent. The two turned back and watched without emotion as Jessica and Paul deliberately folded their clothes and arranged their items back into the bags.

It was with a great sigh of relief that they finally sank into their seats on the flight that would take them back to Phoenix. Paul wondered if he'd be able to resist his longing to kiss the Bronco with the relief of finally being back on familiar ground. He smiled slightly at the thought.

"What?" Jessica asked, glancing at him.

"Just thinking. I have to say I'm glad this is almost over."

Jessica shook her head slightly. "I wish I had your sense of relief. It doesn't feel like it's almost over at all. It feels to me as though it's just beginning."

Paul's lips twisted slightly as he admitted she was right. "I know what you're saying. But I guess I'm just saying that it will be good to be back on familiar ground to fight this fight."

"Familiar ground or not, it's not going to be easy. We're dealing with a whole new reality with these guys."

Paul knew she meant the men in black. He nodded. "But on the other hand, we have a lot of help from those above."

Jessica smiled. "Ah. You're finally admitting that we're not in this alone. Great! That will help enormously," she teased.

"Smart aleck," Paul growled. "I've always known we weren't in it alone. My question has been, how much help can they be? What miracles do they have up their sleeves? How much are they going to intervene?"

"Those are questions that remain to be answered. In the meantime, I think this is a matter of us living up to the strength of our souls. We chose this mission. Now we have to be strong enough and clever enough to do our part in the whole thing."

Paul sighed, a sudden exhaustion pouring through him. "Seems like we've done this several times throughout history. Hopefully we'll get it right this time."

"It's up to us. That's all I know." With that comment, Jessica sank back against the seat and promptly closed her eyes to rest.

As he'd suspected they would be, Paul's emotions were high when they finally spotted the Bronco in the airport parking lot in Phoenix. The air was hot and dry, the Bronco covered in a thick layer of dust. Smog blanketed the city, indicating that no wind had been through the city to blow it away. They hadn't spotted any agents but Paul had a sense that they were watching.

The thought sent a chill up his spine but he chose to ignore it. It was just good to slide behind the wheel of the Bronco and head toward Payson, a place he felt safe.

A couple of hours later, they pulled into Brenda and Bill's driveway. Both of them let out simultaneous sighs of relief. For Paul, he realized that having Bill and Brenda back in his daily life would not only help him to deflect his own spiral of thoughts but would probably lift Jessica out of the silence she'd fallen into.

She was stretching and reaching around to the back seat for the water jug when the front door of the house flew open.

Brenda was squealing with delight as she came flying out the door to greet them. Paul couldn't help but smile. She looked the same. Pert and smiling with a dishtowel in her hand and Fric and Frac at her heels. But why wouldn't she look the same? It had only been a matter of days since he'd seen her ... even though it felt like almost a year.

He grabbed her into a quick hug. Releasing her, he thought what it might have been like if he and his sister could have shared the quick camaraderie that he shared with Brenda. Pushing the thought aside, he watched as the two women exchanged a hug. He followed them into the house, grinning as the dogs frolicked in front, ears, tongues, and tails wiggling with excitement.

The house was as welcoming as ever. Pale ivory walls were off-set by lovingly polished, burnished oak furniture that stood out cleanly against the pale. The soft pastels

213

of the set of couches and chairs suggested a southwest atmosphere. Paul sank into the large stuffed chair near the door and gave another sigh of relief. It was good to feel safe again. He hadn't realized the full extent of the stress he'd been carrying.

Jessica and Brenda sank onto the long, low couch across from him.

"So tell me all about it," Brenda chirped, turning from one to the other. She clasped her hands in her lap impatiently. "Did you get them? Do you have them with you?" Her look turned nervous when no one answered. "You wouldn't have come back without them, would you?" she asked, her glance bouncing from one to the other.

Jessica's exhaustion showed as she reached for her carry-on and pulled the water jug from it. With a gesture of quiet ceremony, she set it gently on the coffee table.

Brenda peered at it quizzically. "And...," she prompted, looking over at Jessica.

"They're in there," Jessica told her.

Brenda raised one eyebrow comically and nodded. "I see...," she drawled. She grinned at Paul. "And of course you know all about this, right?" she asked, teasing.

"Actually I do," Paul replied. "But if I hadn't seen it for myself, I probably wouldn't believe it either."

214

"Are you trying to tell me that they're actually not tangible tiles? That you went all the way down there just to receive messages and information?" Now she raised both eyebrows in surprised speculation. "Or ... did you actually have an encounter and were given the information?"

"No," Jessica said. "They're actually physical." She nodded at the water jug. "And they're actually in there. They're just resonating at a higher vibration so they can't be seen."

Brenda opened her mouth with surprise and sudden understanding. "How clever," she cried. "And that's how you got them through customs and all!" She nodded with amusement. "Very clever, indeed. I'm impressed."

Paul interrupted. "Now the obvious question is, how do we get them back down to a resonance where we can actually see them again?" He paused. "I'm assuming that we need to in order to access the information."

Jessica twisted her lips thoughtfully. "I hadn't really thought of that because I just assumed that would happen naturally. But maybe they don't have to be tangible in order to learn from them."

Brenda was quick to protest. "I don't think that's right. After all, why would the ETs who brought them have made them physical in the first place if they didn't need to be? And why would they risk everything they're risking by asking you to retrieve the actual, physical tiles. There must be something more to the whole thing that we don't yet know."

215

Paul nodded. "I tend to agree with you. There must be a reason."

Jessica nodded as well. "Ok. You're right. Which leaves us with the question of how and when they're going to re-materialize."

"Who helped you de-materialize them in the first place?" Brenda asked.

"Solomon," Jessica responded.

"Well then it would seem to me that he'll be the one to help you get them back."

Paul stared at Brenda. Obviously she knew Solomon too. Was there anyone who didn't? "Then I guess we just wait for him to show up again. He'll know the right time and place, I imagine."

Brenda stared at him. "He's your guide. Why don't you just call him and ask him to show up now?"

Paul blinked. "It never occurred to me." He thought about it a second. "I guess there's no reason why he wouldn't show up if I asked him to."

Jessica smiled broadly. "That's what guides do best. At least that's what I've been told." She chuckled and Brenda joined her. Paul shook his head. Obviously it was some kind of private joke.

An air of respectful silence filled the room as, on

216

cue, Solomon's energy was sensed by all three of them. If there was such a thing as a white shadow, that's what Paul saw manifesting beside him. He watched in silence as Solomon merged his energy with the water. The water stirred slightly, as if someone had breathed on it. Before their eyes, the tiles began to re-materialize. Within seconds, the five small tiles laid at the bottom of the jug.

When Solomon had removed his energy completely, Brenda glanced his way and then leapt up to run to the kitchen to get a container to put the water in. Seconds later the tiles were gleaming wetly as they sat on a small woven mat on the table.

"I don't know what to say," Brenda murmured. "I feel like I'm staring at the secrets of creation."

"Well," Jessica said, "it might be interpreted that way actually." Her hand moved to touch the tiles but withdrew. "But now the real work begins." She looked at Paul significantly.

"Before you start talking about that, tell me what happened," Brenda demanded, smiling. "You can't get away with dismissing the whole trip as if it never happened."

"But I'd like to," Paul countered. "At least most of it," he added. He flexed his fingers, releasing more tension.

Jessica smiled at Brenda and touched her hand. "We have to humor her," she teased, turning to Paul. "She's our hostess."

217

Paul nodded with good humor and sat back to listen as Jessica told the story. She told it the way he remembered it ... except for his excursion into the eighth dimension. He allowed his thoughts to drift but yanked himself back to the present abruptly as he heard a sharp tone in his left ear. "What's that?" he asked, interrupting.

"What's what?" Jessica asked, looking at him curiously.

"That noise."

"There's no noise. Unless you're talking about me talking while you're not listening," she said with a teasing smile.

"No," Paul corrected, holding up an index finger. "I hear a tone, like a whistle or a hum. No. Like a signal. A signal of some kind."

Brenda's fingers flew to her lips. "Oh, Paul! That's fantastic! You know what that is, don't you?"

"Enlighten me."

"Those are actually tones being sent from other-dimensional beings."

Still hearing the tone, he rubbed his ear absentmindedly. The tone abated, as though his touch had chased it away. For a fleeting, possibly imaginary moment he envisioned Korton at the control panel, casually pressing a button to communicate with him through this tone. He blinked away the vision.

218

Brenda continued. "They're actually vibrational tones. You'll hear various tones at different times. What happens is the vibration of the tone enters your physical structure and touches your molecules at various angles. The tones resonate energy, of course, since everything is energy. And so the energy the tone brings impacts you. It stimulates change in your old cellular structure, which stimulates the transmutation of the old cells so you're more open to receive more light and higher energies into your body."

Paul was intrigued. "No kidding!"

Brenda nodded affirmatively. "Right. The tones heighten the vibrations of your physical body and allow more light to enter. The more light, the higher your vibration, and so on and so on." She moved her hands through the air, etching an invisible symbol. "And the process continues. As we allow more light to enter, we take on more of our Truth, and our Truth will take us into more Truth and higher dimensions. But the old vibrations have to heal and transmute. The tones help with that." She smiled softly. "Not to mention that it most definitely validates the fact that we're not alone, that someone, somewhere, is aware of us in this moment."

Paul had fixated on the implication of assimilating more Truth into his body. "And so your belief is that Humankind is actually evolving into a higher dimension?" Paul asked. "That we're going to alter our physical bodies enough to move out of third dimension? I know I've been of two minds about this. Is there another reality being created and we will transport to that reality or will this reality actually be altered." He stared at them thoughtfully. "Is it possible for a third dimensional reality to actually lift its vibration enough to become a higher dimensional reality?"

"As I understand it," Brenda said, "the grids of Earth, and the energy that generates from Earth, must be in alignment with the greater plan of existence, which means that nothing can be forced. At the soul level, we know all things change. As our internal world changes, the external world will change as well. So it's possible that this Earth will change and we'll stay." She paused, thinking. "I know for a fact that we as a species are changing. I believe Earth is changing too. But the question I have is whether, in the larger picture, a reality like Earth must exist in order to maintain a balance within the greater existence. If that's the case, perhaps Earth stays the same and the people evolve. Or, perhaps Earth evolves and there is another creation elsewhere that has the same vibration and purpose that Earth has now." She wrinkled her forehead. "I don't know for sure." She smiled at them. "I guess we'll find out though, won't we?"

As Paul and Jessica nodded, pondering the issues, she changed the subject abruptly. "Are you aware that the others who know about the tiles are still looking for you?" she asked. Her expression worried, she questioned both of them with her eyes. Her fingers rubbed the tile that sat in the palm of her hand.

Jessica exchanged a quick look of concern with Paul. "We had those encounters with the men in black, like I

220

told you. But I've been feeling someone else too. I can't identify them." She touched Brenda urgently on the arm. "They haven't approached you, have they?"

Brenda shook her head solemnly. "No. But I think I know who they are. I call them 'watchers.' They watch the energy of events in the universe and try to stop things from happening that they don't want to see happen. They let others know about what's going on and then the others interfere or challenge or downright attack."

"Why?" Paul asked instantly. "Why would anyone do that?"

"Control. Power." Brenda gazed unseeingly out the window. "It's the same story throughout time." She turned back to Paul. "You know that," she said flatly. "It's nothing new to you."

"Are these people on Earth? Or from elsewhere?"

"Both. Various governments employ watchers. But other dimensions watch us. And, unfortunately, have a lot of methods they can use to influence us. I mean the ones with ulterior motives, of course."

"What methods?" Paul asked flatly.

"Energy," Brenda responded instantly, looking at Paul with the obvious question in her mind of why he didn't already know the answer to the question he'd asked.

221

She continued. "And as far as people allowing themselves to be used, well, most of them aren't even aware of it."

"So what do we do?" Jessica asked, interrupting. "There's got to be a way to keep the tiles safe."

"Get the information out as quickly as possible," Brenda stated without hesitation. "If the information can reach enough people there won't be any way for anyone to stop it." Her fingers traced an invisible, repetitious pattern on the tile she was holding.

Her eyes were unseeing as they stared down at the history she held. Paul could feel her reluctance to voice her thoughts. He waited anxiously, knowing that if he spoke she might not say what she needed to say. His eyes met Jessica's. He read her thoughts as well. They waited.

Finally Brenda spoke again. Her voice sounded as if it was a thing that was being pulled from elsewhere and was now being brought to life. "You have to travel to the Pacific Coast. You have to help the ones from Beyond work on the Earth grid. You have to help them prepare the way for the new world."

She continued to stare at the tile in her hand. "The keys have been given to you. The keys to the divine alignment that is needed for this planet. The energetic vibration of these universal keys will affect this entire reality. But the resonance of them must begin there -- on the coastline of the Pacific. This is because there is a fleet of ships, with societies from many alien cultures and dimensions, working and waiting above those waters.

222

The work you do with them and with these tiles, these keys, will be felt across this world. And the world will become what it was always meant to be. It will not be easy and it will not be quick, but the change is inevitable."

She looked at them with unseeing eyes. "And the reason that it must begin on the Coast is that the next phase of energetic transition for Earth lies above the foundation of this ocean. The fleet of light-crafts and those who live there will be bringing the next level of higher dimensional vibrations that will stimulate the next vibrational shift for Earth." She stopped for a moment and stared at them intently. It was obvious that the trance-like state had passed. "Oh my gosh," she whispered excitedly, "this has everything to do with Lemuria! The energy of Lemuria being reborn!"

At the sound of tires crunching gravel they all jumped. Turning to look out the window, Brenda's face flooded with relief. "Oh, it's just Bill." She touched her chest quickly. "That scared me. I thought it was them." She grinned crookedly. "Funny how our imaginations can be, isn't it?" She rose from the couch and opened the door to welcome him.

After kissing his wife, Bill looked over her head at his visitors and grinned. "I thought I recognized that raggedy old thing parked in our driveway. How the heck are you?" He took a long stride to Paul's side and slapped him on the shoulder affectionately.

Rising, Paul shook his hand, pleased to see him.

223

As Bill gave Jessica a quick welcoming hug he looked back over his shoulder at Paul. "Actually, that old thing looks even worse than when you left. And what the heck are you two doing back already? We didn't expect you for another few days. That must mean things went well?" he suggested, curiosity all over his face.

"We wanted to get out of there as quickly as possible. We haven't even stopped long enough to shower or clean up." Paul looked down at himself with a small grimace. "You can probably tell. I look a little the worse for wear."

"Oh, my lord!" Brenda cried. "What a lousy hostess I am. I didn't even offer you anything to drink, much less a chance to relax and clean up." She smiled at Bill and wrapped her arm around his waist. "I was so anxious to hear what happened that I tackled them the minute I saw them."

Bill smiled down at her and touched her on the chin affectionately. "Well, why don't we give them some time to freshen up and then we'll have something to eat. I've got groceries in the car." He glanced from Paul to Jessica. "Okay with you two?"

Paul nodded. "That sounds like a good plan. I could use a shower." He started toward the patio door. He stopped and turned. "Why don't you wait a bit and I'll come back and help you cook."

Brenda waved at him with the back of her hand. "Go ahead. Relax. I can handle it. I'll give you a shout when we're ready if you're not back by then."

224

Paul shrugged with acceptance. "If you say so." As he headed for the small guesthouse he became aware of just how exhausted he was. First a shower and then sit mindlessly on the patio, he decided. Not polite but it sounded like something he really needed.

After a shower and a change of clothes he did exactly that. Sitting on the patio, staring sightlessly and mindlessly, he jumped when he heard a chair drag on the cement. He turned to see Jessica sitting down next to him. He blinked at her iridescent green blouse and smiled. "You certainly have a flair when it comes to clothes," he told her.

She patted her blouse. "You like it?"

Still blinking, Paul nodded with a grin. "Very eye-catching."

"Brenda and Bill threw me out." She smiled over at the patio door. "Seems they'd rather flirt without a witness."

"They make a great couple," Paul commented.

"Yep. If I ever take the plunge again I hope it can be into something as great as they have."

Paul glanced at her. "I used to think it was impossible to have a relationship like that. At least now I know it's within the realm of possibility."

Jessica nodded in agreement but didn't answer. Paul

225

guessed that she felt as numb as he did. The last few days had been exhausting. The responsibility that had been given to them had placed a weight that hadn't been there before. Simply allowing themselves to drift without thought or effort seemed the best way to recuperate. In silence they watched the slow painting of the sunset across the sky. The colors were glorious. Neither of them stirred again until they heard the patio door slide open. Jumping up, they helped Bill arrange the patio table and chairs. Minutes later they sat together at a burdened table with Fric and Frac eagerly keeping them company.

Paul groaned at the sight of all the offerings. "You went to too much trouble."

"Nonsense," Brenda said lightly. "It's not that much trouble. All easy stuff. Salad. Packaged rolls that I just had to stick in the oven. And this is not homemade gravy. The roast beef is left over from last night and the noodles cook in ten minutes." She waved her hand. "And ... voila' ... it's done. Now, stop fussing and enjoy it." She patted Paul's hand quickly and reached for a hot roll. Looking down at the two dogs who were staring at her avariciously, she grinned. "And I fed you two just a little bit ago. You can't possibly be hungry."

Frac's eyes followed her hand to her mouth as she took a bite of her roll.

"Okay," she told them softly. "I give up. I'll put some gravy on some more of your food when we're done. Maybe that will cheer you up."

Paul didn't think the two of them looked appeased at

226

all by her promise. He grinned and shook his head. "I don't think they're buying it."

Bill laughed. "Don't let Brenda fool you. She'll hide all the leftovers under a pile of their food and gravy and slide it to them. She thinks I don't notice."

Brenda looked properly offended. "Well," she defended herself, "I just think they must get awfully bored with the same food every day. I just give them a tiny hint of variety once in a while. It seems only fair."

Bill laughed and rolled his eyes. "You're just a softie, that's all. You can't resist those eyes. And they know it!"

Brenda joined in the laughter. "You're right. And, yes, they do know it." She smiled down at the two dogs that had lain down at her feet. "So," she said, looking at Jessica, "you two must be exhausted. A good night of sleep seems in order for you. Why don't you just relax and enjoy yourself? Head for bed whenever you feel like it, even if that's fifteen minutes from now."

"I slept most of the way here," Jessica admitted. "Paul did the driving. I imagine he'd like a nap but I think I'll just hang out by the pool with the pups." She rubbed Frac's ear affectionately.

Paul nodded in agreement. "I hate to mess up any plans you might have but I have to admit that sleep sounds like what I need. I can barely keep my eyes open."

"You won't be ruining any plans," Bill protested. "There's a good movie on that we were planning to

227

watch. You can join us or check out. Whichever works for you."

Paul studied him. It was good to see him again. It might have been a simple act of fate that they'd met but he was glad they had. "Okay. Hey, did you hear from Marlen while we were gone?"

Bill bobbed his head up and down, chewing and swallowing before he answered. "Yeah. He called last night as a matter of fact. He's doing pretty good. He went on up to Flagstaff. He's got a job up there for a couple of weeks. He sounded like he was doing all right."

"I'm glad to hear it," Paul said. "I was pretty worried about him." His gaze drifted, remembering the sight of Grandfather disappearing into the belly of the mothership. "I imagine it was a shock to see Grandfather disappear like that."

"I think that's an understatement but, yeah, you're right. I was concerned too but he's doing all right. At least he sounded like it to me."

"Maybe we'll see him when we go through there."

Bill looked confused. "Go through there? Are you heading out again?"

Paul nodded. "I think so. Brenda gave us the message that the tiles need to be taken to the Coast." He glanced at Brenda. "And I was feeling that too. Before she even gave us the message."

"I was too," Jessica inserted. "My instincts about it were getting stronger by the minute. It was like the tiles were telling me what they needed." She rubbed her forehead absently. "It was kind of strange. I've had a lot of messages throughout my years but the ones I'm receiving now seem to be coming to me through a different channel or something."

Paul studied her with concern but turned to Bill when he spoke.

Bill thoughtfully took a bite of salad. "You don't plan on heading out right away, do you? You just got here, number one. And number two, you both look like you could use some rest."

Paul exchanged a look with Jessica. "We haven't talked about it. I guess we can wait and see how tomorrow goes. I doubt we're going to wake up tomorrow morning and decide to go running off again."

"Oh, lord, I hope not," Brenda exclaimed. "I want some time with you two as well as some time with those tiles."

"Speaking of which, maybe we should try meditating with them before we all go our separate ways," Jessica suggested. "We might receive some pretty interesting information."

Brenda set her hand on top of Jessica's and gave it a gentle squeeze. "A great idea but I bet you'd fall asleep before you got even one message. You know how easy it is to get messages while you sleep. Why don't we just let it go and see what we wake up with tomorrow?"

Jessica nodded reluctantly. "You're probably right." She hid a yawn with her hand and chuckled. "As a matter of fact, you're obviously absolutely right." She yawned again. "I guess I'm more tired than I thought I was."

Later, with the table cleared and the dishes done, each of them went their separate ways. Paul sank gratefully into his bed in the guesthouse and was asleep within minutes.

Solomon waited on the other side of the veil. "Greetings."

Paul smiled at him. "Where are we going tonight?"

"Someone wants to meet with you," Solomon told him briefly.

With Solomon guiding the way, they drifted quickly through the atmosphere and within minutes were being sped through a vortex into the next dimension. Not stopping there, Solomon guided him through four more layers. Unlike the last time, Paul was totally aware of having entered the eighth dimension.

A building of crystalline light sat solidly on their left. Tall, with pillars of pure crystal leading into a rainbow-colored hallway, it sparkled with inner light. The outer light that was coming from an unidentifiable source touched it, casting rainbows into the air around them. Solomon entered without hesitating, motioning for Paul to follow.

Paul stood and stared with wonder at the huge area that greeted him. Apparently the large building had only one room for he saw no hallways or doorways or stairways leading away from the awesome room where he now stood. But unlike the angles of the exterior, the interior was the shape of a large, pale-blue dome.

Looking to his left, toward the back of the great room, he saw a figure sitting at a large desk that appeared to be carved from a crystalline-like material. As Solomon urged him forward, Paul saw that the man had a short, perfectly manicured, gray beard. His hair was gray as well. His facial features were strong and firm with eyes that were piercing and deep. Somehow they reached out and infused Paul with unspoken wisdom. In the recesses of his mind Paul recognized him but was unable to pull forward the memory of where he'd met this man before. Deftly arranging his pale-blue robe around him, the man stood as they approached.

Solomon touched Paul's arm, stopping him several feet from the desk. His voice, when he spoke, resonated with respect for the man. "Enoch, I would like to introduce you to Paul. I've brought him, as you requested."

Enoch bowed his head slowly, never taking his eyes from Paul. Paul found himself bowing as well. The two men stood tall, evaluating each other. Countless emotions flashed through Paul so quickly that he had no

231

time to identify them. In some way this man was reaching into his soul and awakening him. Paul's sense of awe at the moment and the unspoken honor overwhelmed him to the point of tears. He closed his eyes briefly, forcing back his unshed tears of emotion as he felt the love this man had for him, and opened them once again to meet and hold the great man's gaze.

Enoch's hand waved through the air. He nodded at the two crystalline chairs that materialized beside Solomon. "Please sit," he invited. His voice resonated with history, somehow seeming to cast into the air his personal experience on Earth. It felt as though his presence was infusing Paul with the invisible, energetic existence of Earth and the people who had walked upon it throughout time.

Paul couldn't help but think of the man's own history on Earth. Engulfed by the ancient, he struggled to keep his attention on the moment and the man who sat in front of him.

Enoch reached for and held an object that had inexplicably appeared on the desk. Smoothing the small object with his fingers, he spoke thoughtfully, drawing each word from his chest so that it resonated as it took form. "This is one of the tiles that you now have in your possession."

Paul stared at the object hypnotically, waiting.

"As you're aware," Enoch continued, "the Earth is undergoing an evolutionary shift. Though you've been, for the most part, unconscious of the fact, you've been assisting with the crystalline grid structure since your arrival there and so you know the sacredness of this grid. It is a structure of energy created by the Divine in order to provide a connection of light. The light realities that exist beyond the darkness send light along the crystalline threads of the grid, penetrating the darkness. It's critical, as you know. Now we've reached a point in Earth's evolution where this grid is being enhanced and directly connected to the two grids on either side of it. The sapphire star grid will be introduced, making the process complete. At least for this for this stage of the evolutionary progression. Evolution depends on the success of this part of the mission."

Paul found himself leaning forward, his spirit rigid with attention.

"This key that I hold will awaken a memory within many on Earth." He studied the tile silently for a minute before looking into Paul's eyes.

Paul felt the intensity of the look move into him and touch every fiber of his existence. The air above him stirred slightly, causing him to instantly become even more alert to the energy around him.

"In the pineal gland of the human body lies a pure cell of energy. Untouched by any reality outside of the reality and the Truth of God, the Creator of all that is, this cell harbors the physical body's ability to interact with Soul clearly and without interference. This key tells of the way that a crystalline thread is drawn down into this pure cell. The vibrations that lie in the soul are then transmitted through this thread of crystal, altering the

233

physical body so as to enable it to hold more light and Truth. This perpetuates and stimulates the evolvement of the individual and, in turn, affects the environment around the individual." He peered at Paul. "Due to the fact that energy affects energy, you understand?"

Paul nodded, indicating that he understood.

Enoch continued. "This single cell that I speak of acts as a conductor, if you will, that is in perfect alignment with the crystalline essence of soul. As the cell is purposely connected with the crystalline thread, several objectives are accomplished. One is that the individual who magnetizes a crystalline thread into his or her own experience draws his or her own soul-thread into the darkness of this area of third dimension. The more people who draw threads down, the stronger and denser the crystalline grid will become. The stronger it becomes, due to the recognition, acceptance, and interaction, the more influence it will have in the healing process of Earth. The second benefit is to the person. The crystalline thread brings a resonance and healing to the human body as it penetrates the pineal cell, assisting in clearing away the darkness that resides in the person's energy field. When the person consciously interacts with the properties of the thread, the vibrations resonate throughout the body. Similar to a tuning fork," he added.

Paul was listening intently. Beneath all of his other memories sat this knowledge. He understood that Enoch was not teaching him but was instead reminding him of something that he had forgotten. Accepting this fact, he knew he had taken yet another step toward his goal

234

which was to live the truth of himself on Earth.

Enoch had been watching Paul, monitoring his thoughts. He smiled with approval and continued. "This crystalline thread extends in both directions, both into the darkness and into the light that exists on the other side of the darkness. What this does for the person who is interacting with the thread is to enable them to more easily access their soul. The thread provides a clear path through the darkness and through the tangle of emotional energy that surrounds Earth. It's a clear channel, if you will." He studied Paul. "Do you have a clear vision of it?"

Paul nodded immediately. "Yes. It's absolutely clear to me. I can see the vision of what you're telling me clearly, as though it's physical."

Enoch's lips drew into a severe, thoughtful line. "Something does not have to be physical to be real," he admonished gently. "The physicality that lies within the entirety of existence takes up a minimal amount of space within the energetic space of this existence. The belief that something must be seen in order to be real is the cause of the greatest dichotomy and gap in clear thinking that Earth history has ever encountered."

It was absolutely clear that this issue was a sore point with the great man. Paul watched him silently as Enoch deliberately settled himself, obviously uncomfortable with his small outburst.

Enoch turned to Solomon with a small smile. "I don't know about you but the greatest hindrance that I have is the memory of emotions that I still retain from my Earth life." He shook his head. "The emotional energy of Earth is one of the most entangling. And yet it serves a clear purpose. In my opinion though, people would be better served by it if they worked with their emotions as a straight line of energy, or even better, a clock-wise spiral of energy rather than counter-clockwise or the more popular choice, which is a convoluted maze of thoughts and feelings." His lips curved in a small smile. "This would enable quicker learning and less pain and would prevent a continuous repeat of the circumstances that cause them distress and confusion."

"Ah, I concur, as you know," Solomon answered. "My memories of the emotional experience, as well as being so close to it through being Paul's guide, bring the dichotomy to my awareness in every moment." He turned to look at Paul. "We have among us a temporary earth-dweller who has the emotional energy of Earth-life around him. I hope it's not too uncomfortable for you?" he asked, directly.

Paul felt himself flush. He wanted to rise to his own defense, to explain away his emotional reactions, but he knew that Solomon was right. He felt himself resist the truth for a minute before settling down to accept it. As certain as he was that he was not truly from Earth and not truly a part of the reality in which he was living, he was even more certain that there was a reason for what he was experiencing on Earth. To resist the experience would be to resist the knowledge that he could gain from this Earth incarnation.

Enoch's eyes wandered over Paul, evaluating him.

Finally he smiled. "I am at peace with Paul." He gave Paul a direct and comforting smile. "You've taken on quite a task. You were totally in your element in the Questar region. The news of your plan to volunteer on Earth came to me shortly before you took on this assignment. I admit that I was surprised by the vast array of things that you planned to accomplish during your mission." He paused, dropping his eyes to the small tile he still held. "If I might interject a personal note to you, Paul?" His eyes questioned.

Paul nodded, giving him permission to continue.

"In other lives you have taken on missions that are similar but certainly not as arduous. Because you suffered greatly due to the efforts you made to change the realities you were experiencing, you have a great hesitation to place yourself in that position again. Like Commander Korton, who is your counterpart, you assign yourself to bring light and Divine Alignment to various regions. It's who and what you are. That will never change. If you can alter your thought process about your mission, you would greatly benefit."

"Alter in what way?" Paul asked curiously.

Enoch tilted his head thoughtfully. "I might suggest that you think of yourself as a vehicle of the Divine, rather than think of yourself as an individual who is away from home to do a job or accomplish a certain thing. Do you see?" He waved his hand slowly, thinking. "You are a soul of energy with a unique vibration within existence. As a soul you choose to issue your energy into a particular region of existence. Perhaps you can envision

237

it better if I state it another way. Think of yourself as a person with a flashlight. It is your job to shine the light into certain areas so that the way will be lighted for others to follow. And so you are not 'trapped' in the region where you have chosen to be but rather it is a choice. And this is your soul's task. This is what you were created to do. This is what you are choosing to do, not a punishment or situation that someone other than yourself is controlling."

Paul thought about what he'd said. Enoch's words de-personalized his life experience on Earth. The words seemed to be drawing him away from taking everything personally and putting him into a mind-set of detachment. It made sense. Especially if he was a counterpart of Korton's. Paul's thoughts halted abruptly. Did he actually say that I was a counterpart of Korton's? His eyes widened with surprise. He found himself turning slowly toward Solomon, looking for validation.

Solomon's eyes sparkled with mirth as he heard Paul's thoughts and felt his reaction. "Indeed," he said quietly.

CHAPTER EIGHT

DISORIENTED, PAUL OPENED his eyes. Where was he? What was going on? He blinked and rubbed his forearm across his forehead with agitation, trying to figure out what had awakened him. He turned his head to see a shadow standing near the door.

"Paul?"

Jessica's soft voice jolted him into in a sitting position. How long had he been sleeping?

"I'm sorry. I didn't mean to scare you. It's just me." Jessica stepped closer to the bed where the moonlight from the window touched the paleness of her robe.

As odd as it seemed, Paul's first thought was that her nightwear was much tamer than her day wear. It took him several seconds to assimilate the fact that she was in his room. When the awareness finally penetrated, he was alarmed. Had something happened?

She timidly took another step. "I'm sorry," she repeated. "I scared you half to death, didn't I? I thought you might be having trouble sleeping."

"What's wrong?" Paul asked, his voice hoarse with nerves. "Is anything wrong?"

"No," she assured him quickly. "Nothing's wrong. No. Don't worry. I just couldn't sleep, that's all."

239

Paul gathered his thoughts, sat up straighter, and pulled the blankets around himself. "Sit," he invited, drawing his legs up. He leaned back against the headboard and studied her as she perched nervously on the edge of the bed. The moonlight touched her face, making it seem like it was carved from ivory. Her high cheekbones emphasized her deep-set eyes. Her hair caressed her slim shoulders. The curve of her neck tempted him. What was she doing? Didn't she realize that if they were going to remain just friends she was going to have to play her role differently? He chastised himself silently. Obviously she needs a friend right now, pal, he told himself. Knock it off.

"I just had the greatest experience," he said, thinking that the story of his dream might distract both of them from their unspoken thoughts.

"Tell me," she said eagerly, scooting further onto the bed and tucking her legs beneath her.

To Paul she looked, just for the flash of a second, like an innocent child waiting for a bedtime story. Wanting to please her, he gave her the details of his time with Enoch, stopping short just before blurting out that it had ended abruptly when she jolted him with her presence in his room.

She listened attentively, her eyes glimmering as she drank in the information he'd received. "Oh, my lord!" she said when he finished. She leaned forward and gripped his blanketed knee urgently. "Do you get it? He gave you a lot of clues! Wow!" Leaning back, she placed her slim fingers over her lips and breathed deeply. "This

240

is wonderful. They're going to help us every step of the way with this mission. I just know it!"

"Clues? Obviously I'm going to need some time to think about it. What clues did you get from it? Other than the obvious?"

Jessica's eyes flashed in the dim light. "I think that, if we think about it long enough, we'll realize that he gave us one of the keys we need in order to begin building a new reality."

Paul was startled. "What do you mean? Where do you get that?"

"Well, it's right there," Jessica cried, raising her eyebrows at him. "Detachment. That's exactly what Fedor alluded to, remember?"

"Enoch didn't say anything about detachment."

"Yes, he did," she insisted. "When he told you to step back from your experience and see yourself as having made a choice to do this, that you're not being forced or punished. You see?"

Paul stared at her with a puzzled expression.

"What better way to detach from the illusion of this place and time than to step back and operate from your soul?" She slapped the bed lightly, triumphantly. "Do you get it? Well, it's not actually stepping back but more like stepping into the truth of being your soul and operating from that place of knowing."

Paul smiled as he realized what she was saying. "Fabulous," he whispered to himself. He grinned at Jessica. "You're right. He gave us the next key, didn't he?"

Jessica chuckled with delight. "Maybe this isn't going to be as difficult as I thought it would be."

"Don't be so certain."

The words were more of a sound that took the air out of the room than words that were spoken. Paul's heart leapt into his throat. His first impulse was to grab Jessica into the safety of his arms. But their enemy was invisible. How could he shield her? Or even himself? Without being aware of it his hands were groping for his robe. "Get the hell out," he said tensely, doing his best to keep terror out of his voice.

"Hell. An apt word, I would say." The words were an eerie laugh that snarled through the air, making the air feel thick with evil. The rank smell of malevolence seemed to literally shove the air from the room.

Jessica was standing now, holding her robe against her chest with a white-knuckled grip. Her face was pale and rigid with terror. "Who are you?" she demanded.

Finding his robe, Paul struggled into it, simultaneously untangling himself from the blankets. Shivering, he stood beside Jessica, facing their invisible enemy. He fought to keep himself from gagging at the rank odor and his own fear.

242

"It's naive to believe that you'll succeed." The voice was a soft, evil whisper of sound, seeming to come not from a person but from a vast source that knew no beginning and no end.

Paul was certain that the creator of hell was confronting them. Paralyzed with fear, he wondered ... how would it be possible to overcome a force that came from the depths of hell? Beside him he heard Jessica softly praying. Without hesitation, he immediately joined her.

Instinctively, he imagined the room filling with light. Together they called upon the presence of the Divine Creator. Murmuring ceaseless prayers, he and Jessica joined hands and stared into the face of darkness. They felt it begin to loosen its grip on the air in the room.

It occurred to him to imagine the crystalline thread that Enoch had told him about. He cast his imagination into the vastness of space, reaching for the essence of his own soul, drawing it down through his mind's image of the sturdy thread. He forced back his sense of triumph as he sensed the slow release of evil. It would be foolish to think it was that easy.

But he couldn't stop his foolhardy smile as he felt the last breath of defiance leave the room. With it went the stench of evil. Still imagining himself drawing light from beyond and pouring it into the room, he turned to Jessica. She nodded at him, her lips still forming soundless prayers.

243

"Is that it?" Paul whispered hopefully.

With eyes as sorrowful as the eyes of loss, she studied him. "Not by a long shot," she murmured.

Paul's eyes widened in surprise. He looked around quickly, wondering what she saw that he didn't. The air in the room had lightened. The smell was that of the innocent night air drifting calmly through the open window. He turned back to her, puzzled.

She shook her head with a grim smile. "We'd be fools to think they'd give up that easily."

"Who's 'they?'" Paul asked tensely. He could feel a muted rage building in his chest. He didn't want to have to deal with this. The power of the invisible force that had confronted them had made it appear invincible. She was right. It had left too easily. He heaved a sigh of exhaustion and frustration. How was it going to be possible to conquer such an enemy? He thought he detected the same question beneath Jessica's words when she answered him.

"'They' is a mixture of forces. Fear is the force that empowers them. Faith is the enemy. Every fiber of our being is going to have to believe in who we are and the success of the mission. Every atom of fear that has ever or will ever exist will probably try to tackle us. We're going to be confronted by people's fear of change. And there will be those who will say that we are the instruments of evil because we're threatening their beliefs by introducing new ones." She paused, studying him. "Don't think it will be a piece of cake just because we have all of the tools we have. Basically the message we're bringing is going to threaten the foundation of life that has been established here for centuries. People aren't going to want to give that up easily. Not to mention the fact that most people believe that all aliens are bad guys. There are probably millions of people who will resist the reality we're being asked to present."

Paul studied her face. It was obvious to him that she was infused with the agelessness of her soul and that her words were those of her Truth. Her eyes seemed to be the only source of light in the room. Filled with his own new-found sense of wisdom, Paul drew a conclusion that he shared with her. "We can't personalize this experience. If we start to take the resistance personally we might want to abandon the effort. We're going to have to keep in mind that we're only the messengers."

"Yeah. Don't kill the messenger?" She attempted a small laugh. "The atmosphere of Earth is filled with the invisible energy of emotions, both from those who are still on Earth and those who have passed over. There are disincarnates existing out there in limbo, caught up in the ceaseless, downward spiral of emotional energy and unable to disengage. There is the force of darkness that feeds the fear and plays on the emotional energy field of Humankind, the ones who placed and monitor and control the age-old grid that encapsulates Earth. And then there are all of the thought processes and beliefs that have been taught on Earth that alienate us from the Truth and from our own personal power, not to mention the mind-control grid that was placed a millennium or two ago.

245

"Not lastly, there are the malevolent alien beings that want us to stay where we are for their own personal reasons of power and influence over us. All in all, we're up against a huge force. We're going to have to be in control of our own emotional fields so we don't get lost. As Enoch put it, as you just said, we can't take things personally."

"How are we expected to succeed against all of this?" Paul asked, staring at her helplessly.

Jessica peered up at him, her eyes bright with determination. "Have you ever heard of light not being able to penetrate darkness?"

Paul tilted his head, thinking.

"Think about it," she urged, gripping his arm. "If you take a candle or a flashlight into a dark room, doesn't the room become light? Sure, the corners will still be dark until you take the light over there. But the area where you stand with the light will be lit up, right?"

Paul nodded, agreeing.

Gaining enthusiasm for her image, she continued. "Okay. Now think about someone else coming into the room with another light. The room gets lighter. And then another person comes in. And on and on. Pretty soon there's no more darkness, right?"

Paul couldn't help but smile. "Right."

"And we have not only people here on Earth

246

bringing in light but we have everyone who's working from above, from the higher dimensions. The way I see it, we can't fail." She gave a small, triumphant sigh and walked over to jump contentedly on the bed. She settled back against the headboard and stared at him. "So, it seems to me that we can be successful, right?"

Not feeling as confident as she, Paul joined her on the opposite side of the bed. He smiled as she touched her toes against his feet. Swallowing, he wished away the uncomfortable feeling in the pit of his stomach. This unseen enemy had easily and unexpectedly penetrated his safety. Obviously it could come again. It seemed foolish to relax. He even wondered if he would ever relax again.

Sensing his thoughts, Jessica sat up and began to rub his foot lightly. "Try not to worry. We'll deal with it as it comes."

"Obviously you've had more experience with this kind of thing than I have. This is huge," he complained.

Jessica shrugged. "Yes," she agreed, nodding. "But it's nothing we can't handle."

"I wish I had your confidence."

"Well, you're right. I've dealt with this kind of thing before so I'm probably a little better informed."

Paul waited for her to tell her story.

Instead she changed the subject abruptly. "We need

247

to talk about the massacre and the parts we played in it," she told him softly.

"You mean the part I played in it," Paul corrected. "I brought us down. It was my fear that led the others to our camp."

"It wasn't entirely that, Paul. We all played a part in it. Your fear didn't help, you're right about that. But all of us learned something from it. We all played a part," she repeated.

"You didn't create the fear-energy that alerted everyone. So it's easy for you to deal with." He knew that he sounded petulant. He did his best to rein his emotions in. He hated the thought of having played a major part in the failure of the tiles being brought to light. It was easy to mentally explain away. Everything happens for a reason. There are no accidents. The list could go on and on. But the bottom line was that it was his fault and it was a tough responsibility to shoulder.

"Did it ever occur to you that it was supposed to turn out the way it did?" She sounded like she was fed up with him, tired of his guilt.

Paul stared at her, his thoughts scrambling for a way to stop the argument he felt approaching. "How could that be? Look, I'm willing to bear the blame. You don't have to try to explain it away for me."

Jessica's eyes flared with anger in the dim light of the room. "I'm not going to dishonor myself by lying to you just to soothe you. I'm trying to give you a truth that you

248

haven't been willing to listen to for over a thousand years!"

Paul blinked. He was too surprised to say anything. He waited.

She leaned forward, her voice imploring him to listen. "I, and a hundred others at least, have been trying to tell you that everything happened the way it was planned. The tiles needed to be where they were. They needed to be in Belize. They weren't just sitting there. Their energy has been working all these years. That's why they were so deep in the ground. They worked with the internal grids of Earth. Now they're above ground. Now they can work on this level. And ...," she paused, "I believe that, when it's time, they'll be taken up one more level and they'll work from there."

Paul wrinkled his forehead, trying to follow her thoughts. Could it be possible that everything that had happened had been part of the master plan? And what was she saying now? "You mean you think these tiles going to be taken onto a craft?" His voice raised in disbelief.

Jessica nodded, choosing to ignore his tone. "I think so, yes. I don't know that for sure but ...."

Paul thought about it. It could be possible, he supposed. "Well, I guess that could make sense." Another thought occurred to him. "I wonder if this means that they need to physically be in various places across the planet before they're taken. Do you suppose we're supposed to travel with them?"

249

Jessica rubbed her forehead. "I don't know. All I know so far is that it's imperative for them to go to the Coast."

They sat in silence for several minutes, each with their own thoughts.

Paul broke the silence. "Jess? Why do you suppose that I couldn't hear this before? Why do you suppose I allowed myself to carry this guilt for so long?"

"I don't know, Paul." She touched his foot again, soothing him with her touch. "I've been trying to get through to you on all levels for a long, long time." She sniffed quietly.

Had she been crying? In the dim light Paul couldn't see her well enough to tell. "I don't know how to thank you for continuing to try to get through to me," he said softly. He leaned forward are and touched her hand as it lay on his foot.

She turned to him. Torn between his desire to let down his guard and his need to stay aware of possible danger, he stared into her eyes. "What?" he asked softly. Brushing a strand of hair away from her face, he confronted a heart full of conflicting emotions that stirred at her closeness.

"I want us to stand united in this mission this time," she whispered.

She was close enough to kiss. "We are united," he

told her, his voice as soft as the kiss of a distant memory. "You know that."

"I want to know it even more than I already do."

Her words were all he needed to persuade him to set aside any uncertainties he had. He placed his hand on the back of her neck and drew her toward him. Their kiss awakened memories and yearnings that threatened to overwhelm him. As she sank down next to him, he buried his face in her hair, not wanting her to see what most certainly was being revealed through his eyes. Too many years of searching, too many hours of wondering, and too many relationships that had led to disappointment made him want nothing more than to believe that the search was over. The woman beside him, he knew, had shared lifetimes with him. They had lived and loved and died together. The possibility that it could all happen again made him want to believe that she was offering him the dream he'd been chasing. But the fear that she was really only offering him a temporary respite threatened to consume him. He could feel himself drawing back into himself. He felt helpless to stop it.

She drew back, tracing his cheekbone with a tender touch. When he closed his eyes against her penetrating gaze, she leaned to kiss them. "I know," she whispered. "I know. It's the same for me. Why don't we both set aside our fear and let ourselves love?" She kissed his lips lightly, searchingly, waiting for his response.

Paul drew back slightly and studied her eyes, looking for the true emotion behind her words. Was she here for only this moment or did she honestly want to create

251

something they could both cherish for years?

As if she knew what he needed, she allowed the magnitude of her feelings to flow into her eyes. There, for a moment, their past, present, and future stood, a gift to them both from the heart of her soul.

Though she hadn't spoken aloud, Paul heard the words of her heart. Pulling her to him, he covered her with his kisses and his desire. For the first time in his life he allowed himself to display the hidden need that had been driving him. She received the secrets of his heart without judgment and, in turn, showed him hers. The morning light that came hours later revealed a new-found love and confidence that would combine their strength and carry them on the next steps of their mission.

Brenda set the frying pan in her hand onto the stove and pushed it to the back burner, her eyes moving from one to the other. The smile she gave them said it all. She knew they had found love. Without speaking she walked the few steps that separated her from them and grabbed Jessica into a hug. Her eyes sparkled with the joy she felt for them. Letting Jessica go, she touched Paul tenderly on his arm and turned back to the stove. Paul smiled as she attempted to discreetly dab tears from her eyes with the corner of a hand towel.

With her back still turned, she offered them breakfast. Not waiting for their response, she drew the frying pan onto the front burner and reached into the refrigerator for a carton of eggs. "Scrambled eggs and toast is the menu." She tossed them a quick smile over her shoulder, gestured at the table, and ordered them to sit.

"No," Jessica refused. "I'm going to help." She unwrapped the loaf of bread, dropping pieces into the toaster with a theatrical flourish.

Brenda gave her a quick glance before turning back to her eggs. "I'm going to venture a guess. You're going to leave for California, aren't you?"

Paul could feel her effort to keep her emotions in check. On an impulse, he walked to her and put his arms around her. "Don't worry," he said, dropping a kiss on the top of her head. "It's going to work out all right." He released her and leaned against the counter that led into the dining area.

She cracked several eggs into the pan and scrambled them quickly with the fork in her hand. Her smile was bright with unshed tears as she turned to him. "I'm not worried. I can see that the two of you have joined forces. I think this will give you both the strength and support that you need. But I'd be lying if I said I wasn't going to miss you." She turned and reached for a spatula. "And I'd be lying if I said every fiber of my being doesn't want to go with you," she added. Avoiding their eyes, she made a show of checking the progress of the eggs.

Paul and Jessica exchanged a significant glance, full of sympathy for their friend.

253

"You know you'd be welcome," Jessica said softly, tugging on Brenda's apron affectionately.

Still not looking up from her task, Brenda protested. "You know I couldn't do that. I can't leave everything here. And I won't leave Bill to go tripping across the country. Besides, it's not my mission. It's yours."

Bill chose that moment to come around the corner. "Mission?" He looked from one to the other. His eyes narrowed with sudden understanding. "You're leaving," he stated flatly.

Paul pursed his lips in distress. He felt terrible about leaving so soon but before they'd left the guesthouse, he and Jessica had discussed the urgency of revealing the tiles. There was no doubt in either of them that this had to be done on the Coast, as Brenda had told them. And they were both equally certain that the time for doing so was now. "I feel terrible," he said, voicing his thoughts. "But it feels like the right thing to do." He waved his hand anxiously. "Not the right thing to leave you two so quickly but the right thing to get the tiles to the Coast. I don't know exactly why," he added quickly, "but I assume the reason will reveal itself." He stared at Bill, hoping to see an understanding response from him.

"We understand," Brenda assured him. "We really do. It's just hard for us to see you leave so soon. But the tiles are a lot more important. We know that. You have a responsibility to them and to the mission. We're just the friends who are going to support you in doing it."

"Don't play down your part in it," Paul said quickly.

254

"Nothing would have played out the way it did if you hadn't been there for me all the way."

"And we're still here for you," Bill proclaimed, clapping Paul on the shoulder. "Who knows? You might get there, do whatever it is you're supposed to do, and end up back here. Come on. Sit down. Let's have some breakfast before I have to head off to work." He shook Paul by the shoulder lightly, like a puppy shaking a toy, released him, and shoved a handful of napkins into his hand. "You can help by putting the napkins on the table."

"Big job," Paul said. He pretended to buckle under the weight, trying to lighten the mood.

"So," Jessica interrupted in an obvious attempt to change the subject, "did either of you have any good dreams last night?" She leaned casually against the counter, waiting for the toast to pop.

Brenda was the first to answer. "Actually I had a terrible dream. I woke up terrified. It felt like someone was suffocating me. The whole property felt like it had been invaded by something evil which is weird because I always keep a protective shield of energy around it." She looked at Jessica inquiringly. "Did you sense it at all?"

"Yes." Jessica hesitated, glancing at Paul. "We actually were confronted by it." She paused, obviously deciding how to tell them. "You're right. It was an evil force of some kind. Its intention seemed to be to consume us with fear so that we wouldn't reveal the tiles."

255

Brenda nodded with understanding. "I get it. Been there, done that."

Paul raised his eyebrows in surprise. "You too? Why? What were you doing that 'they' wanted to stop you from doing?"

"I was trying to get a group together to create a unified light force. I figured where two or more are gathered, you know? I thought that the more people who got together to send light and prayers into the darkness the greater the counter-balance would be. It was my hope that we'd put together a group that would meet regularly and not only do light work but share experiences. Provide each other with validation, you know. When you share your experiences with others you often find that they aren't unique or as weird as you think they are. It helps you realize you're not nuts." She chuckled lightly.

"Amen to that," Jessica muttered, smiling. "I often think that if I told anyone about all of my experiences I'd be committed." She grinned. "I guess that's my fear and that's what keeps me quiet."

"You?" Brenda scoffed. "Quiet is the last word I'd use to describe you, my friend. You're more open about other-worldly events than anyone I've ever met."

"I haven't shared even half of it with you," Jessica said, waving her fork to make her point.

Brenda's eyes widened in surprise. "You're kidding?"

256

Jessica shook her head in denial. "Nope. As a matter of fact, you've probably heard only about one-eighth of my stories."

Brenda stared at her, one hand pressed against her chest in surprise. "You're kidding," she said again. "How the heck do you cope with it all then? What you've told me so far would fill three books! And you're telling me there's more?"

Jessica nodded again, smiling calmly. "Much more."

Bill was staring at her, holding his fork frozen in mid-air. "It's a good thing I didn't know this earlier."

Jessica laughed. "Why's that?"

"I couldn't have assimilated any more than I already have. What I've heard so far has stretched my mind past the breaking point." He grinned to show that he was joking.

Jessica wiggled her eyebrows up and down and pretended to stroke a long, non-existent mustache. "I could make your hair curl," she told him jokingly.

Brenda gave a quick burst of laughter. "Don't," she ordered. She reached over and tugged a lock of Bill's hair. "It's curly enough as it is."

Bill grabbed and kissed her hand. "So," he said, turning to Paul with a serious expression. "Are you seriously thinking of leaving today or could I talk you

257

into waiting until tomorrow? I had planned on picking up salmon steaks for dinner tonight. I don't suppose that would tempt you to stay?"

Paul rolled his eyes and groaned at the thought. "Ah, that sounds good."

"Don't tease them, Bill," Brenda chastised with a grin. She patted his shoulder. "We'll use that devise to get them to come back and visit later."

Bill laughed and pushed his chair back. "You're right. I'll buy the steaks and stick them in the freezer to wait for your next visit. But call and let me know when you're coming so I can defrost them, okay?" He stood. "Now, I hate to break this up but I've got to get ready for work." He dropped a kiss on Brenda's head. "Let me grab my jacket and briefcase and I'll be right back."

Paul watched him leave the room. He was going to miss him. It was a shame the four of them couldn't make this journey together.

As if she heard his thoughts, Brenda sighed. "It's too bad we can't all do this together."

Paul sighed silently inside himself as Jessica placed her hand over Brenda's. It was difficult, he decided, to place the importance of the long-term goals over the importance of the present moment.

Later on, after the dishes were washed and put away

258

and Jessica was in the guestroom packing, Paul found Brenda sitting alone on the patio. He slid quietly onto the chaise lounge next to her and softly laid his hand on her arm with genuine affection. He was going to miss her. "How you doing, sis?"

"That's it, isn't it, Paul?" she said quietly. "It feels like we're brother and sister."

"Maybe we were at some time." He looked away, not certain how to react to the tears he saw sliding down her cheek. "And, hey, if we once were, that means we still are. At least in my mind."

"And in my heart," she whispered.

"Bren. What's wrong?" Paul asked tenderly. "These tears are about more than just us leaving."

"I feel as though I'm never going to see you again."

Pushing his surprise away, he tried to answer calmly. "Why? What do you think is going to happen?"

"I feel as though you're heading into such dangerous territory." Brenda caught back a sob. "I feel as though, oh, I don't know! I'm just scared."

Paul pulled his chair closer to hers and set his hand on her shoulder. "Hey. Everything is going to be fine."

"I hope so." She sniffed, gathered herself, and gave him a tentative smile. "I wish I was going with you. I feel as though I could be of some help."

259

"I have no doubt that you could help," Paul said strongly. "But that's not what you're supposed to do. We all know that. You have your path. We have ours."

He turned to prop his feet up on the chaise and stared thoughtfully at the horizon.

"You and Jessica?" she asked quietly. Suddenly she was intent, studying him closely.

Paul shook his head without realizing he was doing it. 'I don't know. I don't know what's next." Paul blew out a soft sigh. "I honestly don't know how to feel. I know what I want in my life. I know what I don't want. What I don't know is whether or not I can create the life I want on this planet or not." He looked at her sadly. "I could love Jessica. Probably too much, actually, and that terrifies me. But I'm afraid this isn't going to last and that scares the hell out me."

Brenda caught her breath softly. "Oh, Paul," she said compassionately. "Why? I don't mean why are you afraid. I mean, why don't you feel it will last?"

"Just some sense I have. It could be my fear. But it feels more like it's something within her that is going to pull her away." He sighed again, taking a silent moment to study the stillness of the sky above them. "Bren, don't worry about this. It will all be exactly the way it's supposed to be. You know that as well as I do."

"But I want so much for you. I want you to be happy."

"My happiness is going to be found within me, Bren. And that's only going to happen by living every minute as the truth of who I am. No one else can make it happen for me."

"I know. But...."

Paul chuckled softly. "No 'buts.'"

Brenda touched his arm lightly. "Just don't forget that I care. Ok?"

Paul smiled into the night. "I know, sis. I know. And I care about you too." He turned his head to smile at her. "Try not to worry. It's all going to be ok."

Bill came home for lunch, wanting to see them before they left. The farewell between the four of them was more heartfelt than the one before. They all seemed to understand that it might be a long time before they saw each other again. Paul had cleared all of his belongings from the guesthouse, overriding Brenda's protests. He didn't know when, or if, he'd be back. With the Bronco loaded, they took their leave.

In his rear view mirror, Paul watched Brenda as she turned away from the vision of the Bronco driving away. Her emotions were easy for him to read. He glanced at Jessica in time to see her wipe a tear away. "It's not so easy to keep the emotions out of it, is it?" he asked quietly, reaching for her hand.

261

Her hand molded to his, like it belonged there until the end of time. "No," she gulped, sighing deeply. "We can talk about being detached all we want but when it actually comes to doing it, it's another matter." She scooted closer to him and leaned against his shoulder. "I just have this feeling that I might not see her again in this lifetime, that's all."

Paul felt a reverberation of shock run through him. "Why? Why would you think such a thing?" He stared down at her in surprise. "She's your best friend, isn't she? It would seem inevitable that you'd get together some time in the future."

Jessica shook her head slowly, ruffling her hair against his shirt. "I don't know. It's just a feeling I have."

Paul took his right hand off the steering wheel and put his arm around her, drawing her close. "Well, I don't have that feeling at all. Let's chalk it up to the fact that we had to leave so suddenly and let the other thought go, okay?" He smiled down at her tentatively. "You'll see her again. She's your best friend."

She attempted a smile and gave him a light kiss. "I hope so. I really do."

"Good. Now ... let's talk about us." Paul grinned at her.

Widening her eyes and raising her eyebrows, she did her best to look innocent. "What about us?" she asked.

With one eye on the road, Paul gave her a hard,

breathtaking kiss. Laughing, he grabbed the map off of the dashboard and shoved it into her hand. "Stop teasing me and read the map, my love."

CHAPTER NINE

THEY DECIDED TO HEAD north toward Flagstaff, head west when they hit there, and then drive north through Nevada into Lake Tahoe. It was the route Paul had first taken to Arizona. A trip that seemed like it had happened over a year ago, though it hadn't been anywhere near that long. But so much had happened in the weeks since he'd left Sacramento. He was returning as a different person. He was glad for the changes in himself, but at the same time daunted. But how, he asked himself, trying to answer the questions he kept asking himself, could I not live up to the standards of being who I truly am? It didn't seem possible that he couldn't achieve the task of being who he truly was. It seemed inevitable that he'd figure it out, that everything would work out just fine. He rolled his window down and breathed deeply. It had been quite a journey, he decided.

The tall pines that lined the road to Flagstaff looked the same. The air smelled fresh and full of promise. It hadn't changed. He toyed with the idea of stopping in Flagstaff to see if perhaps Marlen might be waiting in the same restaurant. When he mentioned the idea to Jessica she gave him a small, tired smile. He realized, with her unspoken thought, that it was a foolish idea and drove past the exit.

For a while they shared small stories of their separate pasts with each other but after a while the scenery became dry and monotonous and their conversation faded into silence. They each fell into their own

264

thoughts. Though they agreed that they were thrilled with the turn their relationship had taken, they both knew that any normalcy they had known in their lives was soon going to be only a memory. The task ahead would take them away from the reality that most of the world accepted as truth and lead them into another that was, at this time, nothing more than a whisper in the heart of the Creator and those who desired universal peace. The enormity of what lay ahead, they both agreed, was enough to silence the words of anyone. Too large to be spoken out loud, the mission had to be taken into the silence of the heart and soul in order to comprehend a successful conclusion. And both of them, without vocalizing it, worried about what the future pressures were going to do to their new-found love.

As Jessica fell into a light sleep, Paul's silence began to consume him. He felt his mind expanding, awakening, opening to possibilities. Flashes of pure light seemed to speed through him, entering through the top of his head, slipping down his spine. He sensed that the light was opening the way, permitting him to heal those parts of himself that remained in doubt of the Truth. His thoughts drifted through his past, the pain he'd endured and the damage it had done. He knew that, in order to move into the future in pure freedom, free from the past that had the power to damage the future, he had to heal himself. His pain had dictated his beliefs. His beliefs, he knew, were formed by his experiences, not by his soul. His soul had the wisdom to guide him but it needed him to believe in himself before it could.

He began to feel a tingle of energy in the frontal portion of his brain on his right side. It felt as though a door was opening. Light filled his mind and was replaced by a vision of a crystal pyramid. Symbols were laid upon the four sides. The symbols seemed to have been painted by a rainbow, pastel and hinting of fractured light.

As his soul stirred him with light he suddenly understood that Humankind had been repeating itself for centuries. Caught in the web of its own mistakes, people were spiraling in the midst of turmoil and chaos. He understood that humanity would live with the bio-consciousness of the old cycles until the keys would open within them the yearning to release the old reality and allow the new to be birthed. Only with mutual agreement and desire would the birth occur. And when it did, humanity would join the higher dimensions of the galactic community of wisdom and light.

He understood that light must penetrate each atom of the human body. Light is the key to re-programming the old energy that perpetuates the cycles of life that have been caught in the struggle of power and control, devastation and death. Light, he acknowledged to himself, does not die. Therefore life created with a base of light does not die. When one's life is filled with perpetual light, one does not die. The new world would have no death and would accommodate transition only.

In order to evolve, the consciousness of Man must be transformed, he thought. Light must fill the darkness. The mysteries will be revealed when light penetrates the human consciousness, exposing the untruths that lived there in the shadows. The tiles, the sacred geometrical symbols, were the keys to the bringing of light and the healing of darkness, the revelation of the truths behind the shadows. As his thoughts spun the wisdom, he knew with certainty that he was in the process of giving birth to his soul. His soul was pure light and by allowing that light to transform him, he would escape the limitations of the illusion of Earth reality and put himself in the position of living and sharing the Truth of his soul.

His next thoughts were of the common consensus of people on Earth to live the reality that they did. He knew that it would take a mass effort to release that reality in order to give birth to the new evolution. He realized that the aliens who had been interacting with him were participants in the healing. In his mind's eye he could see pinpoints of light around the planet. He became aware that the healing had been happening for quite some time. Individuals across the planet had been attuning themselves to Soul and allowing light to synchronize them with the higher dimensions.

The Light-gathers were, one by one, sharing their light and the higher vibrations of soul and higher thought-forms with Humankind. Perhaps, Paul thought, the balance of darkness and light had reached a point where the keys that were hidden within the tiles would have the opportunity to participate in the new evolution without being hidden or silenced again.

His next awareness came with the realization that some of the craft and some of the alien beings that he had seen were really beings of light. They had been presenting themselves to him in a way that he could understand and interact with. He knew, without doubt, that Solomon was one of those beings. As he accepted this truth, an endless thin stream of light appeared beside

267

him. It seemed extensive enough to reach from one end of existence to all others, without beginning and without end. He recognized the light as Solomon and smiled with a silent 'thank you' to him for sharing his time and experience. In his mind's eye he saw Solomon's face as he usually saw it.

"Indeed," Solomon's voice replied with a smile.

Paul felt a grin spread across his face. He was thrilled with himself and the knowledge. He began to sense the entire planet as an incredible globe of energy that had only to be filled with light in order to alter reality forever. The potential and possibilities filled him with an excruciating yearning to begin. He glanced at Jessica's backpack, mentally scanning the energy of the tiles that were hidden within it. He knew that he didn't yet comprehend the entire story -- but he was getting closer.

Beside him, Jessica snored softly. Paul wondered where, in her sleep, she had flown to. Wishing he were with her in spirit, he stared at the dull landscape and wished himself to the Coast. When his wish didn't happen, he resigned himself to the monotony and concentrated on the road.

The hours and the road seemed endless but eventually he saw the road sign for the Las Vegas exit. He touched Jessica's arm lightly. She woke up instantly, looking at him with concern.

"Is everything ok?" she asked, rubbing her hands over her eyes like a sleepy child. She tugged her melon-green T-shirt into place and smoothed her jeans over her thighs, yawning and looking around for signs of trouble.

A flash of regret tore through him that her first thought was of danger. "No, nothing's wrong. But I wondered if you wanted to stop off in Las Vegas." He smiled at her. "Maybe we could win enough to finance a trip to Hawaii," he offered jokingly.

She smiled. "I'd love to go to Hawaii. But I doubt that I'll get there by winning pots of gold in Las Vegas."

"You never know," Paul disagreed mildly. He pointed at the map that was back on the dashboard. "Anyway, we have to make a decision soon. We can turn toward Vegas and head north to Reno, like we talked about. Or keep going on to Barstow, which is going to have us driving across the Mojave Desert, or head down to Blythe and then across -- which will take us into Los Angeles."

Jessica shuddered playfully. "I don't want to get into Los Angeles traffic. It's notorious."

"No kidding," Paul agreed with a grimace. He glanced at her. "You want to head up to Las Vegas? We can stay there overnight and then head on first thing in the morning.

Jessica was scanning the map, her forehead crinkled in thought. With her finger she traced the lines that represented highways. "Hmm," she muttered. "No one really told us exactly where on the Coast we're supposed to be. I didn't think about that when we talked about this earlier. If we're supposed to be in the southern part,

269

we should head straight across." She clicked a fingernail against her teeth, thinking. "I wonder if it matters." With her fingernail she traced a line on the map. "But if it's north, like I think it is, we could head up through Las Vegas, go on through Lake Tahoe, and then go across through Sacramento, just like we talked about. I could take care of some business there and then we could go from there to San Francisco." She shrugged and tossed her hand. "We'd be on the coast and we could decide from there which way we're supposed to go -- north or south." She hesitated. "But my gut instinct tells me we're supposed to go north. Maybe up around Fort Bragg."

"I think so to." He kissed the back of her hand, which she had laid on his thigh, and grinned at her. "Las Vegas it is then." He dropped into the right hand lane and, when the exit appeared, they headed north.

The direction of north as opposed to west did nothing to change the monotony of the scenery. Paul's thoughts began to drift once again. "Why do you suppose we have to take the tiles to the Coast?" he asked thoughtfully.

Jessica gave him a surprised look. "I thought you knew already."

"Well, we talked a bit about it but it feels like there's something more to it than what we talked about."

She turned to him, settled on her hip, and proceeded to explain. "The energetic grid lines along the Coast have been worked on extensively due to the fear that's along there. Everyone fears and believes that the Coast will disappear in a horrific earthquake and so that entire area needs the most extensive work. Fear is the worst enemy, so to speak, of the Truth. And so it needs to be healed. The healing takes place through the exposure of light. And of course the energy grids support the light work that's being done. Not to mention that there is a fleet of alien crafts out there," she smiled.

Paul nodded, listening. "Tell me more," he suggested. He loved the sound of her voice, he realized. He could listen to her talk for hours.

Jessica smiled at him and tucked herself against his side. "You just like to hear my voice," she said playfully. "Well, anyway, let me see. What can I tell you to entertain you?" She grinned at him and kissed him softly, planting butterfly kisses on his cheek.

"You already know," she finally continued, "that everything is energy and all energy is contained within energetic grids. Well, the Earth grid has been in the process of being replaced for quite a while. Vortexes of energy have been established to usher in more light and energy from higher dimensions. Pyramidal zones of light have been established along the current Earth grid lines. And at these points, bi-pyramids and tri-pyramids of light intersect, coordinating and connecting the grids of Earth with higher dimensional energies. One of the greatest benefits of that is that healing energies and vibrations that are much higher in resonance are better able to penetrate and affect the density of the energies here on Earth."

271

She licked her lips, took a sip of water from her water bottle, and continued. "There's an elaborate system of intersecting energies above Earth. And there are certain places on and in Earth that are holding energy and information, such as crystals. At these points, the energies more easily interact. The Pacific Ocean has an intense amount of energy in and around it. It's known, by those outside of this reality, for its unique healing properties. That's where Lemuria was located, remember?" Her green eyes questioned him.

Paul nodded. "Yeah. We talked about that." A wisp of memory swept by him. It brought with it a hint of the interconnectedness of his lifetimes. He felt like he had been weaving a quilt of time and purpose throughout existence. A sudden yearning to remember everything swept upon him like an eagle spotting prey. His urgent need to understand unsettled him, making the day seem less peaceful.

Unaware of his thoughts, Jessica went on. "These keys, these tiles, are crystalline symbols underneath the clay. Remember? Crystal can be programmed with knowledge and energy. The energy of them on the Coast, interacting with the grid lines, will reinforce the work that's being done by those above." She rubbed the palms of her hands on her jeans, suddenly excited. "What I think is that these keys will not only make it possible for more people to transcend the energy of the old reality but will heal the energy grid to the point where it's possible for those above to descend, as well as for us to ascend." She shivered and gripped his arm with barely-suppressed nervousness. "Wouldn't that be the greatest thing you could imagine?"

Paul grinned at her. "This all makes sense," he told her, allowing himself to absorb some of her excitement. "That mass sighting that is supposed to happen along the coastline. Maybe the keys are the reason why. The reason it becomes possible for them to show themselves to us."

"Exactly!" Jessica crowed, shaking his arm excitedly. "Oh, my gosh! Think of it! Maybe, just maybe, they'll take us with them when they leave."

Paul looked at the glow of yearning that had spread across her face. He understood her desire. They both wanted to live a simpler, more spiritual life. The future of Earth and its reality was still in question. Could it be that the life they sought was only going to be possible on dimensions above? Or was it possible that Earth-reality could change enough to support the spiritual tranquility they craved?

Paul drove slowly along the Las Vegas Strip. People walked in front of them without even sparing them a glance, causing him to brake just short of hitting them. Neon lights glittered and men shouted. Casinos lined the sidewalks; doors wide open, inviting people inside. He could see slot machines pressed against each other, almost as though they were supporting each other against the assault of Humankind that demanded they give up the treasure hidden within. This was his first time in Las Vegas. It was frightening and exhilarating at the same time.

273

Beside him, he felt Jessica responding in much the same way. "What do you think?" he asked, not daring to take his eyes off the road.

"Why don't we stay in one of the casinos tonight. We can just park in their lot and get a room and then walk everywhere." Her eyes scoured the crowds nervously. "I don't imagine you're having much fun driving in this."

"Understatement," Paul muttered. He pulled into the parking lot of a large casino on his right and, with a sigh of relief, parked the Bronco. The casino towered next to them, glittering and steaming with gambler's dreams. Paul studied it doubtfully. "Will this do?"

"This is fine. It's only going to be one night." Opening her door, she dragged her carry-on bag out of the back seat. "Let's get a room and get settled. And then food. I'm starving!"

Paul gave her a contrite look. "I'm sorry. I got so caught up in driving and thinking that it didn't even cross my mind to stop for something to eat."

Jessica waved a forgiving hand. "Don't worry about it. If we'd done that we wouldn't be hungry now and I've heard they have fantastic food in these places." She had to lean back to scan the great heights of the casino. "Well, let's go." She hoisted the bag onto her shoulder and patted it, as if to assure herself that the tiles were still inside.

Paul hauled his own bag out of the back seat and

274

followed her inside. Fifteen minutes later they were standing on the red carpet outside the room they'd been assigned.

Paul pushed the door open to reveal a small hallway with a bathroom on the left. Built-in tables and two comfortable-looking chairs flanked a king-size bed. A small table with two more chairs sat before a wall of windows that were currently shielded from the outside light by heavy drapes. The wall across from the bed supported a low spread of shelves and drawers with a television anchored securely on top.

"This is pretty nice," Jessica said, dropping her bag on the bed as Paul closed the door behind them. She walked to the window, pulled the drapes, and stood looking down. "You can see the whole Strip from here," she told him. She held out her hand, mutely inviting him to join her.

Paul set his bag down and went to join her, wrapping her in his arms and resting his chin on the top of her head. "Hmm," he said noncommittally, staring down at the heads of those who scurried below.

She squirmed out of his tight embrace and touched his nose lightly. "Food? I'm going to perish right in front of you."

Paul fought against his impulse to draw her into his arms again. He was hungrier for her closeness than he was for food. Realizing his thoughts, she slipped past him with a grin. She transferred the small bag of tiles from her bag to her purse and stood expectantly waiting by the

275

door. With an exaggerated sigh, followed up by a grin, Paul joined her.

Stepping off the elevator, it seemed that the noise level had heightened during the few minutes they'd been upstairs. They walked through the crowd of slot machines and people and stopped at the first restaurant they spotted. Settling into a tall booth, they scoured the huge menus and, after much discussion, decided on an array of appetizers followed by a platter of fish they figured they'd share.

Jessica sipped her water, her gaze roaming the room like she was caged and looking for ways to escape. "See that man over there?" she whispered suddenly, jabbing Paul's arm to get his attention.

Paul turned to look at the man. "Yeah. What?" he asked curiously.

"He's a mind reader."

Paul turned back to stare at her. "How the heck do you know that?"

She smiled mysteriously. "You can tell by his aura. Besides, I can hear him."

"You can hear him?" Paul's eyebrows rose skeptically. "He's an absolute stranger. I know it's stupid of me to even ask but, how can you can hear the thoughts of strangers?" He waved his hand. "I mean, in this mass of confusion? I know you did that with Louis but the energy down there was totally different. This, this is just

276

mayhem," he added, grimacing slightly.

"Trust me," she said primly. "I can hear him." She looked down at the table quickly. "He just realized it too," she murmured.

Curious, Paul turned back just as the man turned to look at them. The man studied Jessica with hard eyes, not looking away, as most people would have done. Paul looked from one to the other.

With an angry glare, the man suddenly turned and walked away, fading into the crowd.

"What was that about?" Paul asked.

"He didn't like me knowing." Jessica watched him retreat into the sea of people before looking back at Paul. "I heard a rumor that the casinos watch out for mind readers. Maybe it's not just a rumor because he was trying to hide himself so they wouldn't throw him out. He didn't like the fact that I could read his energy so easily."

Paul found the fact interesting. It never would have occurred to him that there were people who were trained to spot psychics. "So, are they going to toss you out?" he asked, only half-joking.

Her laugh erupted and sparkled around them. "I hope not," she replied, eyes twinkling.

Before Paul could comment, the appetizers arrived. Jessica fell upon them like she hadn't eaten in days. Paul

277

followed suit. It wasn't until they'd finished the platter and were wiping their fingers with the hot, damp napkins that had been supplied that Paul noticed they weren't alone. An almost-invisible vapor of white hung over the empty chair at their table. Mentally he addressed it. "Solomon?"

"Indeed," came the reply. It resonated inside Paul's mind.

"What are you doing in a place like this?"

"I might ask you the same thing."

Paul nodded, understanding his meaning. "You're right. It's an odd choice considering the mission we're on."

"Maybe there's a good reason though."

"What would that be?"

"As long as you're here, why don't you try spreading some light around? There's a lot of darkness here."

All of a sudden Paul's mental vision cleared. He was able to see the pain and fear that hovered over most of the people around him. Like the freakish clamor of ghosts he began to hear the mental voices of the people. Voices of hope and speculation and fear. Planning on winning. Freaking out about losing. The emotional energy in the casino created a cacophony of mayhem in his mind. He wanted to clap his hands over his ears and run screaming into the street. But he knew that wouldn't

278

help. The chaos had invaded his energy field. A paralyzing fear seized him. He kept his eyes fastened on the vision of Solomon's vaporous energy. "Help me," he screamed silently. "Make this stop!"

Suddenly clued in to the fact that something highly unusual was going on, Jessica clapped her hand on his arm. The comforting warmth of it startled him. He turned to her, the panic in his eyes evident. He couldn't speak, his fear too high to override his need to connect with her. Searching his eyes, she knew. She rose quickly, found their waitress and paid for their meal, and returned to the table to pull him awkwardly from his chair. Holding his arm firmly, she guided him to the elevator.

Safely inside their room, she stared at him worriedly. "Is it better now? Quieter in here?"

Paul nodded without answering, running both hands through his hair in agitation. The voices were fading. Without thinking, he went to the bathroom sink, dashed water over his face, and returned to sink into one of the chairs. He stared up at Jessica with dull eyes. "What the hell was that about?" His voice was hoarse and tired.

Jessica shook her head in agitation. "What started it?"

Paul told her about Solomon's appearance.

She sighed and sat down on the edge of the bed next to him. "Something like this happened to me once. It was terrifying. When you experience a huge thrust of

279

awakening all at once a kind of crack happens in your psyche. It exposes the energetic world around you to the nth degree. You can't prepare for it. You don't know it's coming. And it's terrifying." She touched his face tenderly. "You were living a fairly secluded life as far as tuning into energies and thoughts go. You were mostly unaware of the energy around you. Now you've been kind of blasted open."

She studied his face worriedly. "You opened up your energy field to interact with Solomon and got impacted by all the other energies down there."

Paul stood and made his way back into the bathroom. He filled his hands with water again, splashed it on his face, and rubbed vigorously. Jessica followed him and stood leaning against the doorjamb.

"I don't ever want anything like that to happen again." He said it like he was giving a command to the universe. His heart still thundering from the unexpected terror, he walked past her to stand at the window, staring sightlessly at the pedestrians below. He barely felt her touch as she wrapped her arms around his waist and pressed against his back.

"It's going to be all right," she murmured. "I promise. I'm here to help. I'll work with you. I'll show you how to keep your own energy solid around you so that you won't get that kind of hit again."

"How can anything protect against that?" he snapped, suddenly furious. "This is what it's really like, Jessica!" He waved his hand in agitation, including the

280

entire planet with the wave. "This is real. This is what's going on. And this is what everyone is unaware of. Going blissfully along, creating absolute mayhem, making an absolute pile of crap out of the very air we breathe!"

Rather than retreat from his anger, Jessica stayed next to him, her soft touch trying to soothe. "You can only try, Paul. You can only do whatever you can to keep your energy field sealed. You do your best to protect yourself." She breathed a soft sigh. "You can't change anyone. You can't change all of this." She peered out the window at the masses of people below. "This is the reality of being in a human form with the ability to have thoughts and emotions. That's probably not going to change any time soon," she added reasonably. "But you can minimalize the impact it has on you. But first, you have to learn how. And," she added with a warning note, "you make sure you're totally engulfed in protection before you open up to communicate with Solomon or anyone else."

A thought puzzled Paul. "You talked to that man and nothing happened to you. How'd you manage that?"

Jessica dropped her arms and stepped away from him, seating herself in one of the bedside chairs. "Energy can be unpredictable. And there are forces out there that watch and wait for any opportunity to strike. They see a crack in someone's protective field and they rush forward to throw all the negative energy in there that they can." She studied him. "I've been in this field for years. It's taken a lot for me to learn how to protect myself from outside energies. I carry what I call an 'energy shield' around me at all times and I know how to work with it to

281

open up to any particular energy, such as that man. But even so, I sometimes get what I call 'hits.' Negative energy coming in. It takes time to learn, Paul. Everything doesn't come overnight."

"Why? Why would anyone deliberately throw negative energy at someone? What the hell do they hope to accomplish?"

"Think of it this way. Don't moths flock to lights in the darkness? Light attracts. You've been learning about light and trying to immerse yourself in it. It's going to attract the darkness. And for those who can see auras and such, the light you're sending out is going to attract notice. There's no way around it. And you need to know how to be so totally immersed in light that the darkness can't penetrate. Then you've become a Light-carrier. Wherever you go you spread light into the darkness. You become a kind of healer." She studied him with serious eyes. "You're lucky, really. Some people get swarmed by this sudden psychic surge of darkness and don't come out safely. Thank God I was with you."

Paul sank into one of the chairs at the small table, studying his hands as he laid them flat on the table. "Yes. Thank God," he murmured. He was still shaken. He thought about what could have happened if she hadn't been there to help him. The thought threw sudden terror into his chest again. He turned away from her, struggling against an unexpected urge to cry. He had seen the depths of the darkness. He had witnessed the fear and the absolute chaos of human emotions that sat upon the hearts of Humankind. How in the world could all of this be healed? How could this mission they'd begun ever see

282

even a glimmer of success? How could Humankind hope to find peace and harmony?

Jessica stood up and walked quickly to him, gripping his hands in hers. "Paul," she said urgently, "you have to hear me. This was no accident. We came here for a reason. All of this happened for a reason. You had to see. You had to understand how vast the need for healing is. You know that old phrase ... know thy enemy. You can't go blindly into this mission without first understanding what needs to be done. You see?"

Paul stared at her until his vision cleared. Her green eyes were urging him to listen, to hear and understand, and to heal beyond what had happened. She wanted him to see it as a chance for learning rather than allow it to damage him and give him fear. If he allowed himself to give birth to a new fear it would only be adding to the gargantuan pile that already existed on the planet. It would work against him in every way.

A flash of brilliant light slipped into his mind like a light being unexpectedly turned on in a dark room. The softest voice he'd ever heard whispered to him. The words and the energy-presence filled him with an incredible and unexpected joy and understanding.

The voice shared wisdom. "When you have fear, you are informing the Creator of Existence that you have no trust. You are not respecting the power of the Creator. You do not believe that the Creator loves you and wants for you all that is the best. You do not trust your soul to guide you wisely. You are looking at the face of creation and fearing that creation, that abundant force of

283

manifestation. You doubt yourself worthy of accepting the best, thus you are drawing to yourself that which is painful. And the pain creates even more fear. Fear is a closed door and does not allow either miracles or the power of creation to enter your life. This is the cycle in which Humankind has been immersed. This is the cycle that needs to be broken. The new evolution can begin with you if you will allow yourself to trust the Creator and your soul."

Paul spoke aloud, his voice trance-like and distant. "The Light is a living thing. We live within it. Existence is light. But one pocket of fear began and attracted to it another and then another and soon the light had a world of darkness in its center, like cancerous cells that taint the cells around them. And that world drew to it all of the souls who felt they needed to understand the darkness. But after many years that pocket of darkness began to spread its poison so far that the light became out-balanced by the darkness. Like a pendulum swinging, the time for Earth to swing back into the light has come. And now, slowly, the pendulum is swinging us back into the Light. And all that awaits us on the other side of darkness is light. And there is nothing to fear."

Jessica waited silently, her hands clasped tightly in front of her as she watched him, thrilled at the gigantic understanding that he was experiencing.

"Each person is a soul of light. As we draw upon the light of our soul, drawing it into our physical presence, we penetrate the darkness and accelerate the process of healing that needs to take place. As we draw upon the light, we lay open the wounds of fear and distrust, betrayal and pain. The light penetrates and, for a time, brings to the surface the pain, making it seem all-consuming. But, as poison must be drawn to the surface and then released from the body, so it is with the emotional poison of our world. As it draws to the surface it is revealed and it is more painful. Instinct causes us to push the pain back down beneath the surface, which stops the healing process. The opposite is also happening. The pain and fear are being brought to the surface and causing emotional eruptions. But the process must continue in order for the healing to happen."

Paul fell into silence, peering into the distant sky outside the window without seeing it. After a minute he turned to Jessica with glistening eyes.

"I get it," he murmured, joy flooding through his entire being. "I think I finally get it." He stroked his forehead thoughtfully. "Wow. What a revelation."

Jessica moved forward eagerly. "As you were speaking I could actually see what was going on with our planet." She was shivering with suppressed excitement. "I could see the light penetrating the darkness. I could see the resistance by the darkness. I could see all of these emotions boiling up in people, surfacing, and people didn't know how to deal with it all. Some were falling into depression. Some were breaking into rages. People who would never have thought of getting help before were looking for help. It was completely fascinating to actually see it and understand. I was actually witnessing light pouring in from the higher dimensions. As it poured in, it stirred up the darkness, caused more resistance and, seemingly, more pain. But all it was

285

doing was bringing to the surface the awareness of what needed to be healed." She brushed her hair back absently. "But I could see some problems too."

"Like what?" Paul asked.

"Well, as people are releasing these emotions, they aren't being transmuted into light immediately, the way it should be. The emotions are exploding into the energy around the planet but they're still in wounded form. Those above, and many people down here as well, are working like mad to keep up with the transmutation process. Now," she paused, thinking, "if more people could understand what's going on they could help in the process. That could make a major difference in how rapidly this transition for Earth happens."

"How do you transmute the emotional energy that needs to be healed?" Eagerness to learn was written all over his face.

"There's several ways. One is by using the vision of the violet flame, which is exactly what it sounds like. You envision a violet flame encompassing the energy you want to transmute. And that's a powerful tool. When I use it, I always follow up with a softening tool. So let's say you have an energy in the form of a thought or a memory. You imagine placing it in the violet flame and the flame transmutes it into pure energy. Then you envision that new energy being engulfed in a soft pink color, which is loving and soothing. Or, you can choose a different soft color if it feels more appropriate."

Paul watched her. Her face was aglow with the

passion of her subject. Obviously she was a teacher. Anyone who shows such joy and zeal when they speak is aligned with their truth, he thought. "You said there's other techniques?"

"There are other color rays and flames in addition to the violet flame. One of my favorites is the Divine Blue Flame. It's extremely pervasive, invading the long-concealed wounds in order to heal them. But it's soothing as well. It has an energy of unconditional acceptance so that you don't beat yourself up about any mistakes that you might have made. You simply release the energy without judgment. It's associated with the sapphire star grid that's one of the overlaying grids of this evolutionary process Earth is going through."

She continued, obviously enjoying the opportunity to talk about one of her favorite subjects. "And I've got another technique that I use constantly. When I prepare to meditate for personal healing reasons I imagine myself surrounded by a cleansing grid. Energy that I release has to pass through this grid before it can be emitted into the atmosphere. That way I'm not polluting the energy around me. And when I'm showering and washing away energies of the day I imagine a cleansing grid that runs through the drain. That way the water washes the energy from my aura, washes it down the drain, where it has to pass through this grid. You see? The grid transmutes the energy I'm releasing. That way it doesn't affect the planet adversely."

The images were clear to Paul. As a matter of fact, the more times grids were mentioned, the more clear his visions and knowing became. A suspicion was forming in his mind. Could it be that he knew more about grids than he remembered or had yet acknowledged?

But the sight of her next to him, radiant with joy, made him push aside the temptation of learning more. Rising, he took her hands and pulled her into his arms. With a murmur of contentment, she surrendered to his embrace. The feel of her in his arms caused everything but the moment to disappear. Tomorrow would begin the next leg of their journey for the good of others. Tonight was only for them.

CHAPTER TEN

IT WAS FOUR A.M. WHEN Paul was awakened by her gentle touch. Gathering her into his arms, he tasted her skin, breathing in the warmth of her heat. Without words they touched, searching each other for the secrets each of them held that would bring them to an intimate joy that would be theirs alone. For a blurred moment Paul was caught in the memory of another moment that had been the same. Lemuria. Golden beaches and sun-filled days when, tangled in each other's arms, they watched as the land gave birth to the sun. The passion they were sharing was almost the same as it had been then. But now it was deeper, as if their souls were connecting with the intention of uniting in ways that they perhaps hadn't back then.

Sated, holding her in his arms, Paul smoothed her hair as he felt her drift back into sleep, satisfied by the union they were both luxuriating in. For years he had wondered if his dreams and yearnings would reach fulfillment on Earth or whether he would have to wait until his life on Earth was complete to find the degree of love he craved. The woman who had shown herself to him in visions had held promises that seemed to be beyond that which could be attained on Earth. Though she looked different now than in the dreams, he now believed that the woman in his dreams was Jessica. As he drifted in her arms he couldn't help but wonder. Would this last? Had he been given the miracle he'd asked for?

The questions stirred an anxiety in his solar plexus. He found himself pushing his feet against the blanket,

289

wanting to escape the possibility of future pain.

"What?" Jessica murmured sleepily. "You're not getting up are you?"

Working to keep his irritation to himself, he kissed her gently. "Go back to sleep, my love," he urged.

Waking up more fully, Jessica watched him leave the bed. "Are you coming back to bed?"

Stopping at the door to the bathroom, he turned. "I thought I'd grab a quick shower and go down to see if I can win us enough to go to Hawaii."

"Not without me," she murmured groggily. Tossing aside the blankets with an unexpected vigor, she jumped from the bed, grabbed him around the waist and tugged him into the shower stall.

Paul had no idea how much time passed before he reached for a towel. Wrapping her tenderly in it, he reached for another to dry himself. Half an hour later she was dressed in a flamboyant green blouse and pale green corduroys and ready to go, her hair hanging damply on her shoulders.

Paul sat watching her as she picked up her purse and stood looking at him expectantly.

"What? Are you ready?" He waved his hand in the direction of the bathroom. "Don't you want to do the make-up thing and dry your hair and all?"

290

"Why?" she asked saucily. She giggled. "Don't I look ravishing as I am?"

Paul stood and grabbed her into a hug. "You always look ravishing to me. I just assumed ....."

She tapped him lightly on the nose. "Never assume anything with me, my love. You'll probably be wrong most of the time." She laughed happily and sauntered provocatively out of the room.

Shaking his head, Paul followed.

Even at this time of the morning an aura of excitement hung in the air of the casino. The huge chandeliers were fully lit, the slot machines sparkled with vivid colors and possibilities, and scrolling neon text messages tantalized the few early-morning gamblers with promises of jackpots. Liking the fact that there were only a few early-risers in the place, Jessica and Paul followed their instincts to a row of quarter machines.

Several minutes later Jessica was whooping with joy as bells rang and lights flashed.

Leaving his machine, Paul went to her side. "What'd you win?" he asked, peering over her shoulder.

"Six hundred," she said proudly.

Paul grinned at her and grabbed her into a hug. "Fantastic!" He kissed her soundly.

A bored and tired-looking attendant came around the corner to attend to Jessica's win.

"Keep it up," Paul said, kissing Jessica once more. "I'll go back and collect my winnings from my machine." He grinned.

"You do that," Jessica laughed. "I'll be waiting right here."

Confident, Paul sauntered away. He still hadn't won when he heard bells and whistles and Jessica's whoop of joy. Giving the uncooperative machine he was playing a wry, defeated smile, he joined her again. He watched as she collected several more times, grinning at her whoops of victory. When his largest win was $100.00 and hers was $2,400.00, he suggested they get on the road.

With a nod, she agreed. "Ten pulls in a row without a win. I think you're right. How about some breakfast first? My treat." She stood, pushed her stool toward the machine, and checked her purse to make certain it was secure. With a smile she tucked her arm in his and pulled him toward her for a quick kiss.

"I'll take you up on that offer." Paul dropped his arm around her shoulders as they headed toward the restaurant. He glanced at her purse. "I can't believe you won so much but even more unbelievable is the fact that we're here gambling with those under your arm." He nodded his chin at the bag where the tiles still sat securely.

Jessica patted her purse gently. "I don't think they mind. As a matter of fact, I think this was totally in order. What we won will probably cover most of the

292

expenses of our tour up the Coast. Motels are expensive and we'll be eating out. Expenses add up quickly."

Paul nodded, agreeing. "True," he said speculatively. He pointed at a booth. "Will this be all right?"

"Sure." She settled herself and smiled at him happily.

"I hadn't given much thought to this before now," Paul said thoughtfully, "but what do you think of making it a camping trip instead of a motel trip? It'd be a lot less expensive." He watched as the idea sank in, causing a dozen different reactions before she finally answered him.

"How about this as a compromise?" she suggested. "We take the stuff out of the Bronco and put it in my house and then we have room to take camping gear. Then we alternate. For a few days we camp and then we get a motel room. That way we can have hot showers and a soft bed." She grinned. "You should know that I have a propensity for small luxuries. Things like hot water and a clean body." She chuckled softly, obviously in a good mood.

"I guess I can live with that," Paul agreed. "But I think I'll put my boxes in my storage shed instead of your house. I don't want to clutter your place up and I already have some stuff in a shed there anyway." He chewed his bottom lip in thought. "I think I can fit everything into the one I have without having to rent a bigger one."

Her protest was mild but they finally both agreed that it was a good idea.

293

Paul studied her laughing green eyes and fought against his sudden need to fall hopelessly in love with her. It's too dangerous he chastised himself. "I have an idea," he said before he could stop himself. "We're in Las Vegas. Why not get married?"

He felt the blood drain away from his face as he realized he'd said the words out loud. Not registering her reaction, he reached across the table and grabbed her hand. "I'm sorry. That wasn't romantic at all. As a matter of fact, it's way too early for that. I don't know why I said that. Don't pay any attention to me." He forced himself to stop his panic-filled speech. Staring at her, not breathing, he waited for her to say something. Oh, God, he thought. What the hell have I done?

"Oh, Paul," she said softly. She stroked his hand tenderly, studying him with eyes full of love.

He found himself incapable of breathing. Here it is, he told himself. The shut-down. He could almost hear the door of her heart slamming in his face.

"I love you, you know," she said gently. She dropped her eyes. "But we can't get married. We just can't."

"Why?" The word was out before he could stop it. Who the heck was this idiot that kept talking, digging his own grave?

"This is going to sound terribly unromantic and I know that but it's the truth." She lifted her eyes to his. Her face was tight with intensity, wanting him to understand what she was going to say. "This may sound stupid but hear me out."

Paul simply stared at her, waiting.

Neither of them noticed the waitress who stopped nearby, a pencil hovering over her pad while she waited for a good moment to interrupt their conversation.

"The term 'marriage' has an energy all of its own," Jessica tried to explain. "The roles each person takes on, you know, 'husband,' 'wife,' have just about been set in concrete. The minute you get married both people fall right into that energy and into the roles and expectations." She studied him anxiously. It was imperative for him to understand. "The energy of the word, all by itself, sets into motion a huge subconscious reaction. I guess the energy of it is so strong because it's emotional and built on people's needs." She waved her hand in vague irritation at her own words. "Anyway, it takes a huge effort to be in a marriage and not fall into the energy of the expectations."

She stared at him, pleading with her eyes for his understanding. "That's what I believe anyway and I don't want that for myself. I don't want to fall into that pattern. I want to create something new. I want to create a partnership, a union. I'll even go so far as to call it a divine union," she rushed on. "I know that might sound like I'm asking for the world but I don't think it's unrealistic. If we're going to change our world for the better, we're going to have to change our relationships. And one of the things that needs a ton of work is the marriage relationship. Do you see?" She searched his face anxiously.

295

Paul nodded, his thoughts tumultuous. She had put into words, simply and completely, what he had been searching for most of his adult life. 'Divine union.' No other words could have explained it better.

Before he could respond, the waitress stepped forward, chewing thoughtfully on the tip of her pencil. "You're a smart lady," she said, staring at Jessica quizzically. "I don't know how you came up with those words, but I couldn't have put it better myself." She looked at Paul. "If we're going to be equal on this planet then it has to start somewhere." She tapped her pencil on the pad. "You ready to order?" she asked matter-of-factly.

Paul blinked several times, staring at her in a daze and trying to gather his thoughts. The abrupt change of subject had thrown him. "Um," he waved his hand at her, "can you give us a minute?" he said impatiently.

Not offended, she nodded and walked away, tapping her pencil thoughtfully on her lips.

Paul smiled at Jessica, pulling her hands into his. "You just defined what I've been looking for," he told her. "I couldn't put it into words but you just did. And, no, 'divine union' isn't too far-fetched an idea. I know what you mean by that and those are the perfect words for it." He reached across the table, tracing her face with his hand until his fingers touched her lips. His gaze held hers. "But," he said hesitantly, "do you think that's us? Do you think that's something we can manage?" He licked his lips nervously. His voice fell to a whisper. "Do you want that to be us?"

Not answering, Jessica pulled her hand from his. Startled, Paul stared at her. She rose and came to sit next to him on the bench, tucking herself against his side. Still without speaking, she drew his face close to hers with her fingers. Her breath was warm against his lips.

"I think it would be wonderful if that turns out to be us," she whispered. "But I have to be honest. I don't know yet. Can you give us some time? Will you be all right with that?"

Without volition, a vision of the dark-haired woman of his dreams flashed in front of Paul's eyes. The woman smiled calmly and nodded once, as if satisfied. The wind blew her hair across her face. The vision faded.

"You ready to order yet?" The waitress was back, tapping her pad impatiently.

After a hearty breakfast they tossed their bags into the Bronco and headed north. The few small towns they passed caught their interest but, for the most part, they were absorbed in learning more about each other. Paul shared the story of his past and listened carefully as Jessica talked about hers. The sister she had loved and looked up to had died when she was sixteen. The experience had changed Jessica irrevocably. As she talked of her sister's boyfriend and the subsequent abuse that she'd suffered by loving him too much to leave him,

Paul recognized the similarities of his parents' relationship. When she spoke of the way that her sister had died from her boyfriend's violence, he pulled the Bronco to the side of the road and held her as she wept. With her weeping in his arms he didn't bother to control his own tears. He wept for Jessica and her sister, for Stephanie, for his parents, and for the entire society of a world that had not yet learned to honor the magnificence of God within each person.

It was his clear understanding that nothing happened without a reason. He knew that he might never understand the pain that was such a prevalent factor of human life. But he could sense an awakening within himself, an understanding that he and Jessica had encountered similar experiences for a reason, though what that reason was he couldn't guess.

As he felt her tears lessening, he kissed her gently and released her. She wiped her tears as he put the Bronco into gear and headed north again.

Setting his hand on her leg, he patted her soothingly. "You okay?"

She nodded, sniffing quietly. "I'm all right. I guess I never completely got over her death."

"That's not something you ever get over completely."

"Probably not." She sniffed again and delicately wiped her nose.

"I was thinking," Paul said quietly. "Do you suppose

298

that, since we've both been so personally affected by abuse, that this issue has something to do with our mission?"

"I think it should be the mission of everyone on Earth," Jessica said flatly. "I think if it's not already, it should be. What are people thinking anyway? How can they justify harming each other when we're each representatives of God, or The Divine, or whatever term you might want to put to it? We are great and glorious souls who deserve honor and respect. If for no other reason than that is who we truly are. I don't understand. I never have. I never will," she stated.

Paul heard the stress in her voice. He knew it wasn't his to do but, nevertheless, he wished he could heal her pain. "I guess we can only do the best we can to make certain that we don't do anything to exacerbate the problem."

Jessica glanced at him. "There's not much chance of that," she said sharply. "I want to devote my life to stopping it, not making it worse."

"I know that," Paul said quickly. "Sorry. I was just thinking out loud. I didn't mean anything by it."

"I know that." Her voice held an unspoken apology for her reaction. She slid closer to his side and tucked her arm beneath his. Leaning her head on his shoulder, she asked, in an obvious effort to change the mood, "How long do you think we're going to be on the Coast? A week? A month?"

Paul smiled down at the top of her head as it leaned against him. "You know as well as I do that's impossible to predict. Actually, you probably know better than I do. I have a sneaking suspicion that when we 'volunteered' we forgot to put any time limits on our service." He smiled at her. "Seems to me that we're in this for the long haul." He glanced at her purse significantly.

Jessica touched it absentmindedly, her eyes unfocused and lost in her own thoughts. "I wonder..."

"Wonder what?"

"Just how much more there is to these tiles than what we've uncovered so far."

"I imagine there's a lot," Paul speculated. "They didn't go to all the trouble to bring them billions of miles just to reveal a little bit of information, as significant as it's been so far. I think that, maybe there are layers within layers and we've just touched into the first layers."

Jessica studied him silently for several seconds, her expression thoughtful. "I think you're right. I want to go to the next layer. I want to know all there is to know."

"I do too. But I wonder how we go about doing that."

"Well, if everything is energy and energy and dimensions exist in layers, it would seem that we simply peel the layers off."

Paul chuckled. "You make it sound easy."

300

"Well, it should be easy. It's only our own limitations and boundaries that would make it anything else. The only reason the human species can't access all of the knowledge of the soul is because we have thought-boundaries. That and the freakin' mind-control grids." She grimaced. "'Something's got to be done about those too. I don't know what ... but something."

"All right," Paul said with a slow drawl. "So ... how do we eliminate them? Seems like they're a major hindrance if the goal is for people to take back their power and think for themselves."

"I don't know. It's huge. A huge problem. But there's a reason for everything, as we know, and so we'll just have to see what we learn from the tiles. Maybe they hold an answer."

"And the question of people breaking through their own thought-boundaries, as you put it?"

"They access the soul's vibration, I imagine. By doing that, the vibratory energy of the soul helps to peel off the layers of false beliefs that keep us from knowing our soul."

Paul nodded but with skepticism. "Ok. You're still making it sound easy. But exactly how do you do that?" he repeated stubbornly.

"Well," Jessica said, thinking hard, "if we recognize that we are never separate from our soul and that we have only left the pure energy of soul in order to experience another energetic experience, we heal any

301

belief in separation with just that single thought. Right?"

Paul nodded slowly, following her thoughts.

"Ok. So if there is no separation then we can access our soul. The only thing in the way is the belief that we can't. Right?"

"You're still making it sound easy. And I don't think it is that easy. If it was, everyone would have done it by now."

"No," Jessica disagreed, shaking her head. "Not everyone is here for that experience. There are tons of people who just want to feel what it's like to have a physical incarnation. This is a school, a place where we come to study the aspects of existence that are available here." She pursed her lips in thought. "Let's think of it this way. If we, as souls, need to learn every single aspect of existence that is or could be possible, in order to be creators or even co-creators, then we must encounter every single experience. And if we're completely immersed in the soul vibration to the degree that we eliminate the human experience, we've defeated the purpose. We've left things unlearned. You see?"

Paul shook his head. "I disagree. I mean, I agree with you about everyone needing to experience everything. And that's for the purpose of learning the ins and outs of what can occur when you attempt to create a reality. At least as far as I understand it. The cause and effect, the impact, of one energy upon another. I get that part of it. But what I don't get is why anyone would operate within existence without understanding, without the connection to his or her own truth. What good does it do the soul experience to have a physical incarnation where you're totally oblivious to the soul? I mean, it would seem that the soul would provide solutions and understandings when the going gets really tough down here."

"Well, if you approached an experience with total understanding of it, would you still need to have the experience?" she suggested logically. "I mean, if you knew that you were going to create an experience that would include pain and suffering, would you willingly walk into it and learn from it?" Jessica shook her head. "I don't think most people would."

"And so maybe we're not supposed to have access to our soul." Paul felt himself fill with fear as his thought was spoken aloud. To believe that he was meant to continue living a life without understanding made him wish that he had never begun the journey. He shook off the emotions that tumbled through him like wind-driven tumbleweed and tried to focus on Jessica's words.

"My turn to disagree," she said. "If we don't aspire to greater heights and understandings, how will we evolve? How will we learn to live in enlightenment? How will we grow beyond the need to manifest lives filled with suffering and pain? I believe that the Earth-plane can become a place where we can learn through enlightenment instead of through pain."

"It sounds like a pipe-dream Wishful thinking," Paul said drearily.

303

Jessica pulled away abruptly and stared at him. "Why in God's name would you say a thing like that?"

Paul waved his hand impatiently. "Just look around you. Look at the crime. Look at the statistics. Look at the system, for Pete's sake! Do you honestly believe that everyone is just going to wake up one day and agree to stop killing each other, stop abusing each other, stop taking drugs and stealing and everything else? The entire reality of Earth is based upon a monetary system that is unequal and almost impossible to break away from. That very system, which we as a species have created, is the downfall of probably eighty-five percent of the population of the planet. Now how do you expect to fix that by becoming enlightened? People who are starving are not looking for enlightenment. They're looking for ways to survive."

"What the heck happened to you?" Jessica demanded. "One minute you were fine and the next you're yelling at me. I thought we were having a positive discussion that was leading us somewhere and you turned it around to be completely negative." She stared at him, demanding an explanation with her glare.

Paul didn't look at her. "I just think," he said, staring through the windshield with hard eyes, "that it's unrealistic to think we can change the world."

Jessica crossed her arms and turned to stare out the side window. "Well, I think it's unrealistic to give up without even trying. If every person accepts defeat and no one does anything, no one takes a chance, then you're right, nothing will change."

They rode in silence for several minutes. Suddenly Jessica shifted her position and leaned toward him urgently. Paul glanced at her without speaking.

"Look," she said, her words sounding rushed, "you agree that we're all limitless souls and have merely 'reduced' ourselves to this limited Earth experience, right?'

Paul nodded.

"Well, maybe there are those souls who have taken this experience in order to accelerate it, so to speak. To help it take another leap in evolution." She touched his arm. "I don't know what got us off track a minute ago but what I do know is that the problem started with a limited thought. Unlimited thoughts, ones that come from the soul, know beyond doubt that anything and everything is possible. Limited thoughts are what keep reality in the shape that it's in. It's going to take unlimited thought to get us out of it, to make a change in reality. And isn't that what a soul who is trying to learn how to become a Creator would do? Wouldn't a soul want to learn how to take pain and suffering and transform it into enlightenment and glory?" She pressed his arm imploringly, wanting him to understand.

Paul thought about what she'd said. It made perfect sense. As he allowed himself to believe in the possibility that all souls on Earth at this time were perhaps joined in a vast, limitless quest to change life on Earth, he felt his heart rise into his throat. Maybe, just maybe, he told himself silently, this is truth. He blinked away the tears

305

of hope that surprisingly blurred his vision. Maybe, just maybe, he repeated to himself.

He turned to Jessica, his eyes bright with possibility. "You might be right," he agreed. He squeezed her hand gently. "You just might be right. And I bet you anything that the tiles can help reveal how the impossible could be made possible."

The smile that she gave him warmed him down to his toes. She tucked herself against him once again. Within minutes she was sound asleep. Paul smiled down at the top of her head and drove on, thinking about their destination ... the Pacific Coast.

Solomon spoke quietly from the back seat. "She isn't really asleep, you know."

Paul smiled. "I kind of figured that." He glanced down at Jessica fondly. "Where is she?"

"Her guides are working on her energy field while her spirit is aboard a craft."

Paul laughed. "No wonder the car felt so crowded. How many of her guides are here?"

"Several of them."

"And the craft? You're talking about the Esartania?"

"No. I'm talking about the Dove."

306

"The Dove? What's that?"

"It's another Light Ship. Larger even than The Esartania."

"You're kidding! I know the Esartania can hold about 100,000 people. I can't imagine anything much larger than that."

Solomon laughed. "Sure you can," he insisted. "You can imagine universes if you drop your limited thinking. But even closer to your reality right now - you can imagine a craft that is as large as the United States."

"What?" Paul cried softly. He shook his head. Had he heard right?

Solomon chuckled lightly. "You heard me correctly. There is such a thing, you know."

"No. I didn't know." Paul scowled at him in the rear view mirror, waiting for an explanation.

Solomon nodded knowingly. "Indeed. Commander Wartauk. He's the Commander of it. There is a counterpart over Europe. Commander Wartauk's craft is stationed above the United States, hence the name. There are seventeen ambassadors from various universal societies aboard." His tone was conversational, as though this was an easy-to-accept fact. "I grant you that these crafts aren't directly above, hiding in the atmosphere. But they are there. Working along with everyone else to recalibrate the energetic grid around the planet."

307

Paul was disbelieving. He raised his eyebrows skeptically. "And this craft is as large as the U.S.?" He shook his head. "That's hard to believe."

"It will be for most people," Solomon said with good humor. He lifted one thin shoulder in a shrug. "But the facts are the facts. I certainly can't change them."

Paul glanced at the sky without consciously thinking about his action. "And you're telling me that it's up there right now?"

Solomon smiled slightly. "Indeed."

"And exactly what is it doing?"

Solomon shook his head, as though the question were a foolish one. "It has many functions and purposes. After all, by its very size you can assume that it is serving in many capacities."

"How long has it been there?"

"Since the beginning of the Earth-year 1998. But it increased its energetic presence following the event of nine-eleven."

Paul's heart filled with sadness at the reminder of one of the saddest days in Earth's history. "They tried to help?" he asked.

"They were not allowed to interfere. However, they were allowed to assist those who needed assistance. As long as the assistance was desired, that is."

Paul nodded. "I imagine that there were many from all over existence who came to help on that day."

"Indeed," Solomon agreed. His expression was as grave as Paul had ever seen it. "You have a lot to learn and to remember, my friend. But I am here to tell you that I'm proud of the progress you've made. I'm looking forward to walking with you through the rest of the journey." A sense of unrevealed mystery laced his words.

The words filled Paul with a strange sense of exhilaration. "What does that mean?"

"You're coming home to yourself. Your unlimited self. It's the only way that you can be the messenger that you're supposed to be."

"And what will this process entail?" Paul asked curiously.

"For starters, merging your physical cells with the vibration of your Soul. That vibration will then heal the energies of dis-connection."

Paul shook his head. "I don't get why any dis-connection had to happen in the first place. Why don't people just live the truth of their Soul, period? Why do we go wandering off into a reality that isn't the truth of the Soul? Why do we immerse ourselves in lies?"

"Why would you call this reality a lie?" Solomon asked quietly.

309

"Well, if you're not displaying the truth of your Soul then you're living a lie, correct?"

"It's not a lie, Paul. It's simply another place of being. It's another expression of life within existence. But you can choose how you express yourself within it. Within any of the various realities within existence, actually. When you complete one expression, you simply move into a new expression. That doesn't make the old one a lie."

"Ok," Paul said hesitantly, thinking hard. "So if it's not a lie, if the painful reality of Earth-life is true and appropriate, why then would we seek to move beyond it or change it?" He could sense Solomon's smile behind him. Paul knew he was enjoying the mental challenge of the conversation.

"Would you wear the same clothes for forty years? Or would you grow out of them?"

Paul shrugged. "I imagine you'd grow out of them."

"Exactly. And so you grow out of one reality and into another. When one reality has served you, you're free to move on to the next one. Many people who live in this Earth-reality call that 'death.' But it's not death. It's rebirth. Simply moving into a new reality. But there's another way of 'dying' to a reality. We call it transition. Or evolvement."

Paul thought about it for a minute. "Are you saying that the physical body doesn't have to die? Or are you

310

just talking about the spirit? And, if your physical body doesn't die, isn't it extremely difficult to move it into another reality? Let me see if I get what you're saying. You're saying a person can detach themselves from the reality that everyone else is living on Earth and create another reality that suits them better?"

"Exactly."

"Now that sounds impossible, I've got to admit. Maybe my thinking is limited but I can't imagine that at all." Paul waved his hand and then dropped it back to the steering wheel. "I could see someone emotionally separating. Or even physically, if you mean retreating into the hills or something. But that's not actually creating another reality."

"It isn't? Solomon asked. "Why would you say that? If someone decides that the reality around them is not compatible with the way they want to live, and they detach from it and create something that works for them, are they not creating another reality?"

"Well, yes, but I didn't think that's what you meant when you said 'create another reality.'"

"It's one way of doing it. But it's not the only way. Let me put it to you that way."

Paul still wanted more understanding. "Everything everyone does has to impact me in some way, right? Because all energy affects all energy. I'm a part of this energy exchange because I'm on the physical plane. So even if I remove myself, I'm still being affected. Right?"

311

"Does everything everyone else does have to impact you though? All energy throughout existence is interacting with all other energies. There are no boundaries. But that doesn't necessarily mean that you have to be impacted. Being affected and being impacted are two different things. And only you can control the outcome. Wouldn't it be more reasonable to assume that you can control your own environment?"

Paul knew he was being tested and that there was a universal answer that was understood by his soul. He did his best to think with his soul, but failed. "Ok. You've got me. I know you're trying to tell me something. But I don't get it."

"If you believe that you will be impacted by Earth-reality, you will be impacted by Earth-reality. If you believe that you will be impacted by God-reality, the reality that your soul and God intended before you immersed yourself in everyone else's beliefs, you will be impacted by God-reality."

Paul blinked. "It sounds like you're saying that all you have to do is change your beliefs and, voila', you're in another place and time. That's too fantastic to believe."

"Why?" Solomon asked simply.

Paul heard a genuine note of puzzlement in his voice. Before he could respond, Solomon went on. "As long as you believe it's impossible, it will be impossible. As long as you believe it will be difficult, it will be difficult. It will be what you believe it will be. But you are a great and powerful soul. Why would you limit yourself with limited thinking?"

"Well, I don't want to," Paul protested. "I just don't know how to get there from here."

In a tone that sounded like he was changing the subject completely, Solomon spoke. "What would it feel like to completely surrender all of your beliefs? Surrender who you think you are? Surrender all of your memories and understandings about your life experience. Surrender your reactions and your beliefs and even surrender the belief that you are walking in a physical body on a physical planet."

Bewildered, Paul shook his head. "I'm not following you."

"The only way to alter your reality is to stop believing that the reality you're creating is real and is the only one available to you. By holding the focus and the belief that this reality is the only thing that's real, you empower it to be the only thing that's real, the only thing that you have access to. In truth, it isn't real, in the true sense of the word. You're creating it and making it real by believing in it. But there's another reality on the other side of it. And another. And another. God lives in all of them. Soul lives in all of them. You're free to choose which one you want to live in."

Paul shook his head vehemently. "Oh no! I think you'd get an argument from anyone and everyone about that! That statement says ... the reality you're living, whether it be hunger, or poverty, or homelessness, or whatever, can be erased by the simple act of re-thinking it." He threw a hard glance over his shoulder. "Anyone would argue with you about that."

"Exactly!" Solomon proclaimed. He leaned back against the seat and folded his arms, tucking his hands into the sleeves of his robe, and smiling broadly, as if he'd just won the argument.

"What's that supposed to mean?" Paul howled. "You haven't explained a darn thing!"

Solomon untucked his hands and leaned forward urgently, laying his hand on Paul's shoulder. "What did you just do with the statement you made? You solidified your belief. You created a huge limitation and you gave it a massive solidity. You justified your right to create a reality that doesn't allow for miracles, as they are so loosely called. You created a solid wall of opposition that God couldn't drill through and won't drill through ... because you're free. You're free to make any choice you want to make. No one on the higher dimensions will interfere with your choices." He held up one finger as Paul opened his mouth to protest. "But God can and will drill through your limitations if you ask for help and honestly believe that you will receive it. Because God/Creator is unlimited. Soul is unlimited. And the union is unbeatable. Even if it takes a thousand lifetimes, you will get this lesson. Everyone will. But you don't make it easy when you throw up walls against the truth. You're only making it hard on yourself. The truth doesn't change just because you don't believe in it. The truth won't change. Which means that you have to."

He smiled gently. "I'm not throwing stones at you, Paul. I'm not telling you that you're wrong in any way. I'm pointing out the fact that you, as soul, know the truth of your own power to create reality. If you don't accept that fact, you're not living your own truth." He settled back against the seat and watched Paul attempt to assimilate his words.

"You're making this impossible to understand," Paul complained.

Solomon stared at him in the rear view mirror. "No, I'm not. I'm making it easy. All you really have to do is learn to surrender."

"And what does that mean?"

"Surrender to the truth of God." Solomon waved his hand at the scenery that was flying by. "The Creator of universes isn't limited. Nor is the presence and intervention of that Creator limited. That leaves only one person who is limited in this relationship between you and God. That's you. If you can teach yourself to surrender to the unlimited possibility of The Divine Union, you can heal the separation between the possible and the seemingly impossible." He smiled at Paul in the rear-view mirror. "Let me put it simply. Only one of those who are involved in the relationship between you and God is limited. It isn't God, is it?"

Paul opened his mouth to speak but got interrupted once again. "Now, mind you," Solomon said, "not everyone is ready to change realities. The reality people are living is serving them exactly. It's perfect. It's not

315

right or wrong. It is merely a vehicle through which the soul is learning. A reality that they are choosing in order to accomplish understanding. But ... when the Soul wants to move to a different reality in order to achieve a different purpose, it's possible to do so. That's all I'm saying."

"And are you saying that my soul is ready to do this? To move on?"

Solomon's voice was so soft that it almost wasn't there. "I'm saying that, when you were told, reminded, that you are from elsewhere, it was for the purpose of jolting you from the Earth-reality into the soul-reality. You came to this incarnation on a mission. If you stay locked into the Earth-reality and refuse to allow the greater truths to lead you, you won't open the doors that you are meant to open. You won't create a path that others will be able to walk along behind you. A path that will make it easier for people to move from one reality to the next. In other words, you won't complete the mission you came here to complete."

Paul had two immediate reactions. The first was a rush of dread that he might fail.

The second, he voiced. "Why me?" Paul asked softly.

"Why not?" Solomon responded just as softly.

316

CHAPTER ELEVEN

PAUL FOUND HIMSELF STANDING in a pillar of light. He was awareness, nothing more. The light pillar was cylindrical and seemed to stretch endlessly through infinity. There were other pillars of light. He and the others formed a circle. Though he could see nothing but pillars of light, he recognized each one as individuals that he knew. Together they formed a Brotherhood. Within existence they had a mission. They would move through existence separately but their mission would remain united. They were to take the energy of their light, their souls, and their unified purpose into the heart of existence, healing barriers between the Infinite and the finite worlds that had been created.

The objective was unity. Unity between worlds. Unity between universes. Unity between the finite and the Infinite.

They would travel along the grid lines of existence, healing the grids as they went. The matrix of energy that encompassed all that is lay before him. Threads of possibility that had the potential to bring the entirety of existence into one awareness, creating a unified body of Glory that would personify the original purpose of the Creator.

His group carried the resonance of Ka. As with each soul group, his had a unique resonance, an energy and tone that was theirs alone, identifying them throughout existence.

317

Paul blinked as Jessica stirred beside him. Oh my God, he whispered to himself. Worlds were merging within him. Truth was piercing his awareness like a blade.

"Indeed," Solomon whispered.

Paul's eyes flew to the rear-view mirror but the back seat was empty. He felt his blood tremble in his veins. The enormity of what he was being asked to believe in was beyond comprehension. But deep within the core of himself he knew that he wasn't dreaming. He was remembering. He stared unseeingly at the road, not feeling Jessica beside him, not hearing her words. Only when she touched his arm and pointed at a roadside sign was he able to bring himself into the awareness of the moment.

"Can we stop?" Jessica was asking.

Paul blinked again. "Sure," he said, rubbing his hand across his eyes in an effort to erase the confusion he was feeling. It was going to take time to heal the dichotomy between the world that he was seeing with his eyes and the one he was seeing in his mind.

Jessica studied him with concern. "Are you all right?"

"Yeah. Yeah. I'm fine. It's just been an interesting few minutes, that's all."

"Few minutes? I thought that sign said Lake Tahoe

was only fifteen miles."

Paul stared at her. "Did it? Are you sure it didn't say one hundred and fifteen?"

Jessica shook her head. "No. It said fifteen. I've driven this road before. I recognize it. We're not far from the Lake."

Paul rubbed his forehead tiredly. "Ok. If you say so. Let's stop and get something to eat. Take a restroom break. I could sure use it."

Jessica touched his sleeve lightly and kissed him sweetly on the cheek. "You sure you're all right? What happened while I was sleeping?"

Paul smiled. "It would take me an hour to tell you about it. And I'm not going to tell you in the restaurant. If people heard me talking about my weird experiences they'd lock me up."

"No, they wouldn't," Jessica responded. "You'd be surprised at how many people have metaphysical experiences and don't talk about them. Everyone thinks everyone else will think they're nuts. Bottom line, we're keeping secrets from other people who have the same secrets." She grinned at him.

Paul pulled into a roadside restaurant parking lot, turned off the engine, and pulled her into his arms for a quick kiss. Resting his cheek against her hair, he sighed deeply. There was so much to think about, not least of which was his growing need for her. "You're probably

319

right. But I don't want to take a chance. Let's just get something to eat and decide if we're going to keep driving or stay some place for the night."

"You're exhausted!" Jessica cried. "How selfish of me to sleep when I should have been helping you drive!"

"Don't worry about it." Paul grinned at her suddenly. "Now get the heck out of the car so I can lock the door," he said playfully. "I'm going to have an accident if I don't get into that restroom."

Jessica grabbed her purse and jumped from the car, laughing. "Me too."

"I'm right behind you." Paul slammed and locked the door and followed her hurriedly.

A few minutes later they were seated side by side at a window booth. Both of them grabbed their water glasses eagerly and downed them before the waitress had gotten back to the cash register. Smiling indulgently, she returned and filled their glasses again. "You must be thirsty. You ready to order?"

"I have a craving for fish," Paul said. "What kind do you have?"

They both chose baskets of fish and chips. When the waitress had gone, Paul closed his eyes wearily and rested his head on the back of the booth.

"Poor honey," Jessica murmured. "I'm sorry I made you drive all that way. I can drive from here."

"Do you want to stop in Tahoe for the night or keep going?" Paul murmured behind still-closed eyes. His hand reached for hers and she intertwined her fingers with his. Paul smiled at the comfortable feeling it gave him.

"Sacramento is only about two or three hours from here. I don't mind driving on. It would be nice to sleep in my own bed. What do you think? I drive, you rest, and we sleep at my place tonight?"

"That sounds ok," he agreed tiredly.

She paused, watching him. "So, tell me what happened while I was napping."

"Well, Solomon showed up. We got to talking."

Jessica chuckled. "And so you kind of slipped into another reality for a while. I understand that. It certainly makes time fly when that happens."

"He said that you took off into another one too," Paul told her, opening his eyes and studying her.

She nodded. "I sure feel like I did. I feel, I don't know, expansive might be the best word. It's like the space between my cells has somehow taken on a new energy."

Paul glanced around quickly. "People will think you're nuts," he warned her quietly. "Quite honestly, I don't think anyone in here could handle hearing that."

321

Jessica raised her eyebrows and wiggled them at him. "You'd be surprised," she teased. "And," she added, "I want to tell you about The Dove. I think I was aboard." Suddenly her eyes opened with shock. An inquiring expression crossed her face.

It took a second for Paul to register what her expression meant. It finally registered that she was shocked at something. He turned quickly to see what was going on behind him. With all that had happened recently, he was prepared for almost anything. It seemed that his beliefs were being shattered left and right. It wouldn't surprise him to find a man in long robes and sandals standing there.

But it wasn't a man in robes. It was a man in black, his sunglasses easily hiding the glare that Paul could feel but not see. Paul's heart leapt into his throat, almost strangling him with shock. He swung his hand to the back of the booth and started to push himself up. The man placed a hand inside his jacket, a clear and deliberate sign that he was prepared to deal with them with force, if need be. An ironic smile touched his lips, as though he believed he knew the level of their willingness to die or not die.

The man strolled deliberately to their table and stood looking down at them, his face expressionless. "I imagine you're surprised to see me," he said flatly. "You shouldn't be. You were told that we'd be back." He waved a thin hand at Paul, silently ordering him to stay put.

Paul caught a glimpse of the barrel of the gun in the

322

man's jacket as he slid into the booth and stared across the table at them. The gun seemed out of place. It didn't fit with the lean, business-like appearance of the man. His hair was trimmed, his face clean-shaven, his fingernails manicured. His suit was obviously expensive, though ill-fitting, and his shoes were shined to a mirror-like polish. But there was something different about this man that separated him from the others. Paul couldn't put his finger on exactly what it was but, for some reason, this man felt like an impostor. He wasn't as clone-like as the others, Paul thought to himself, if that makes any sense. He didn't know if that made him more, or less, treacherous than the others.

But the danger of the man was clearly obvious. Feeling trapped and vulnerable, gall rose in Paul's throat, bringing with it a rage so powerful that he was surprised that he could contain it, or even pretend to contain it. He opened his mouth but nothing came out.

"I'll talk," the man said quietly, his voice coming out as a sinister whisper.

The waitress chose that moment to reappear. She glanced at the man cheerfully. "Oh, will your friend be joining you?" she asked as she set the baskets of food on the table, totally unaware of the threat in front of her.

"What would you like, sir?" she asked brightly, not waiting for Paul or Jessica to answer.

"I could use a cup of coffee," the man said pleasantly, smiling up at her.

323

Paul blinked. The exchange seemed too normal to fit with what was really going on. The gun barrel was, he was pretty certain, pointed directly at him under the concealment of the table. The danger of the tiles being stolen was imminent. The possibility that he and Jessica were going to die in the process was more real than unreal. And yet the man was going to have a cup of coffee before any of these things occurred. He blinked, forcing himself to be calm, and risked a glance at Jessica.

Her eyes were calm and determined. Paul realized that she would die before she'd let go of the tiles. He felt an almost hysterical need to control the situation grip his throat. What could he say or do to eliminate the inevitable? His thoughts reached out to Solomon, demanding solutions.

The man pointed at him rudely. "Eat," he ordered. "People will wonder what's going on if you don't." His smile was pure but silent evil as he leered at Paul. "We wouldn't want that, would we? I don't like to be nervous. If people start wondering about us, I'm going to be nervous." He glared at Paul when he didn't immediately respond. "Eat," he commanded softly.

Paul and Jessica both lifted a fork of tasteless food to their mouths. Their eyes met as they struggled to communicate their thoughts ... without success.

The waitress looked at them curiously as she set a cup of coffee in front of the stranger. She didn't make any comment, turning away with a slightly puzzled look on her face. Paul noticed that when she reached the cash register she cast another curious look in their direction

324

but she disappeared into the kitchen without another glance. His hope that she might think something was terribly wrong and call the police faded abruptly.

He set his fork down deliberately and turned his gaze to the man. "Let's forget the pretense. We don't have whatever it is you want. And even if we did, we wouldn't give it to you."

"Oh, but you do have what we want and you will give it to us," the man insisted. A false smile was pasted on his face but behind his glasses Paul could sense that his hard, black eyes were saying a lot more than his lips.

"How do you figure that?" Paul asked, his voice tight with tension.

The man turned his icy eyes to Jessica. "You don't want to watch your girlfriend get hurt." He smiled coldly. "It works every time. I know. I've witnessed it more times than you can count. You'd be surprised at how easy it is to turn guys like you into whimpering sacks of nothing when they see their girlfriends squirming under a knife."

Paul's mouth went dry. The man was right. He'd turn over the tiles before he'd let any harm come to Jessica. His thoughts began to run wild, desperately fighting with reality as it was and reality as he wanted it to be. All of the things that he'd been hearing from Solomon, the ETs, and the Masters didn't ring true in the face of this present danger. How could he use the information he'd been given and apply it to the here-and-now? What use were all of the words if they couldn't re-shape events and save himself, Jessica, and the tiles? What kind of cruel

325

test was he facing? What kind of cruel god would allow them to be so close to a success that might help the world and yet stand by and watch it destroyed? A thought as quick and clear as a flash of light in the darkness came to him. He would have to force himself to see the situation from a different perspective in order for it to have even a remote possibility of changing. He heard Solomon's whisper and knew that he was being handed a key. Perhaps it would save the situation. Perhaps it would not.

"Will you allow your life experience to overpower your God experience?" Solomon's question rang in Paul's head like the toll of a bell.

Paul's thoughts raced. It was as though he were two people, with two minds. He clearly perceived the danger they were in. He clearly perceived that they were not in it alone, that there were unseen forces all around. How could that knowledge, that awareness, alter the course of events?

He turned and studied the man with an ice-cold glare. He shocked himself with the clarity of his thoughts.

This man is nothing more than cells separated by space. He is not solid. His gun is not solid. Everything is cells separated by space. He poses no threat. On another level he is Soul ... as I am Soul. He is a representation of God, as I am a representation of God. He has no power over me.

It was an unusual pattern of thought, and didn't

326

seem to accomplish anything other than to make him feel better because, within himself, he knew the thoughts were Truth. But he appreciated the internal insight. It changed his perspective. The understanding that the events going on around him were somehow necessary for his soul's learning came to rest in his thoughts, like a dove bringing a branch of peace. Paul felt himself relax, felt himself letting go of his internal fight, accepting without doubt that everything was going to happen the way it was supposed to happen.

The man was studying Jessica, his expression thoughtful and contemplative. Paul sensed that his hand was lax upon the gun, that his thoughts had distracted him. Paul thought about taking the opportunity to make some kind of heroic gesture that might save them but thought better of it. No. What he wanted was a miracle of another kind.

"Do you know what you're really looking for?" he asked suddenly.

The man turned to him, surprised. "What do you mean?"

"I mean, we all know that you're after something that was, and still is, in Belize. But do you know what that is?"

"What are you talking about?" the man growled, his irritation obvious.

"Do you know exactly what it is you're looking for?" Paul asked patiently.

327

"You have what I want. What I've been ordered to get from you. All I need to know is that you have something of value that we want. And all you need to know is that I'm going to succeed in getting it from you."

Paul's voice was slow and deliberate. "All right. But do you have the slightest curiosity about what it is that everyone thinks we have?"

"My instructions are to stop you from revealing what you have to anyone. And I'm prepared to do that in any way necessary. You will not be allowed to interfere with my society in any way. Trust me on that."

"Your society?" Jessica stuttered. Suddenly her eyes widened. She touched her lips in shocked silence, staring at him. "Oh my God!" she whispered.

Her eyes flew to Paul's. "They're disguised," she said in a stunned tone. "Paul! They're disguised."

Paul was totally confused, turning his gaze from one to the other. "Who are they?" he asked in a low tone, finally settling his stare on Jessica. He could feel the gun press coldly against his kneecap as the man moved it forward to reinforce his threat. Both of the men waited for her answer.

Jessica stared at him unseeingly. "The alien society that is trying to stop the evolution," she said softly, her lips barely moving.

To Paul she seemed almost hypnotized, caught in the web of her own interpretation of the man's presence. He

328

studied her for several seconds, puzzled by her behavior, before turning back to the man. There was no hint that the man was anything other than human. Even the slight five-o'clock shadow that he had suggested it. There was no hint of an alien origin.

The man turned to him calmly, surveying him as though he didn't even really exist. "Do you believe her?" he asked contemptuously.

Paul flicked his gaze to Jessica and back. Something deep in his solar plexus stirred, a shadow attempting to speak. "Yes," he said flatly.

The man raised one dark eyebrow in surprise. He smirked at Paul. "Oh, really? And why is that?"

The hair on the back of Paul's neck rose, stirring to the challenge of danger. "Does it matter?" he asked nonchalantly, camouflaging his reaction behind a small smile that he hoped didn't show his real thoughts.

The man shook his head. "No. It doesn't matter at all. You're right. The end result will be the same no matter what you believe."

The words set off a dozen fireworks in Paul's mind. Like bullets being fired from a Gatling gun, thoughts catapulted through his mind. No matter what I believe, Paul thought silently, I can change this whole experience by changing how I perceive it. Because life is a series of energetic exchanges, and energy is malleable, experiences can be changed.

329

The man's eyes still studied Paul. Apparently he read his thoughts. "Ah," he said softly, "a man determined to rise to the challenge, heh?"

Paul nodded slightly. "If you choose to see it that way, yes," he answered calmly.

The two men evaluated each other silently. It occurred to Paul that he had met this man before, or this challenge before, in another time and place. He had a feeling that he hadn't fared well in that exchange. He shoved away the thread of fear that attempted to curl around his stomach and smiled slightly.

"What makes you think you'll succeed this time when you failed so gloriously last time?" The question felt as tangible and threatening as a noose around Paul's neck.

"I'm not the same person I was then," Paul answered automatically.

One dark eyebrow wiggled in amusement. "Why would you assume that?"

"Let's just say that I know me better than you do."

The man shrugged dismissively.

Out of the corner of his eye, Paul caught the waitress staring at them curiously as she stood in the doorway that led to the kitchen. Catching his eye, she turned away. Paul glanced at his meal. He hadn't touched it. No wonder she was watching them.

It occurred to him that she could be his ally. Thoughts are energies, he told himself. Send her the message to call the police.

Almost as if she had heard the thoughts he intended to send to the waitress, Jessica turned quickly, staring at him with a look he couldn't interpret. She tilted her head, like she was listening. Paul smiled at her with confidence, thinking that she was asking him for reassurance. But then he heard what she was hearing; the sound of a siren approaching.

The man heard it too. His face betrayed no emotion as he glanced from one to the other. He looked toward the now-empty kitchen doorway. With a blank stare, he addressed them. "There are many more of us. You'll find us everywhere. One small victory won't win this war for you."

Paul shrugged. "Two victories. Or has it been three now? You're nothing more than a challenge to show people how powerful they really are," Paul told the man. His tone held a note of triumph. "We're reaching critical mass here. Light is going to outweigh the dark. I don't have any doubt of it."

"Don't bet on it," the man said, piercing Paul with a cold glare.

An instantaneous flooding of Paul's personal truth spread through him, as powerful as an unleashed storm. For several seconds his vulnerable humanity left him, leaving in its place the power of his soul and its many lifetimes. His chin thrust forward with challenge. "You've failed in your mission to control people time and time again. You would think you'd know when to give up."

The man gave him an evil smirk. "Why give up when your governments are foolish enough to believe in us?" A satanic laugh erupted from him.

The siren vibrated the air inside the small building, making Paul's ears ring uncomfortably. It faded abruptly. Two uniformed men were jumping from the vehicle. Paul glanced at them and turned back. With a shock he registered the fact that the man who had been sitting across from him had disappeared into thin air, taking his threat with him.

In the kitchen doorway, the waitress and chef stood, blinking rapidly, their mouths halfway open in stunned surprise. Jessica was staring at the emptiness, clutching her purse with one hand. The two cops burst through the door only to be met with total confusion as the waitress pounced upon them with her story. Looking doubtful, the men looked from her to Paul and Jessica and back.

Paul braced himself for the inevitable confrontation. How was he going to explain this? He sighed deeply as one of the officers headed toward the table.

Jessica shot Paul a significant glance. "This is one hell of a way to start a romance, don't you think?"

A laugh erupted from Paul like a burst of delight. Leave it to Jessica to erase the tension with a word.

332

Paul's story to the police was that the mysterious man had left while the waitress was in the kitchen. She just hadn't seen him. Since the man was clearly gone, the two officers had no choice but to believe the story. As soon as the story was told and accepted, Paul slid the payment for the meal under his plate and he and Jessica sidled out of the restaurant like thieves, anxious to put the episode behind them. As they backed out of the parking lot, the chef and the waitress were still gesturing wildly at each other. Paul felt regret. It would have been nice to let them know that they weren't imagining things. But the safety of the tiles was uppermost. To linger and explain would cost them time and energy he didn't feel they had.

Paul was rolling his shoulders, working on releasing the tension in his shoulders, when Jessica released a sharp laugh. "I'm still hungry. We never got a chance to eat."

Paul snorted softly, letting go of some of his irritation with the whole situation. "I imagine I will be too, as soon as I settle down. How are we going to manage to eat though? If we stop in another restaurant, we take a chance on them showing up again."

Jessica touched his arm lightly. "Paul," she said in a reasonable tone, "they can appear and disappear anywhere, it looks like. Unless that was a hologram and he wasn't really there. In which case, it was a damn good one! I believed it anyway. At any rate, we're being tracked and they can find us anywhere. We can't base

333

our actions on what they might or might not do."

"In other words, let's not starve ourselves and do their job for them," Paul quipped. He glanced at her when she didn't laugh at his small joke. "Ok. You're right." He rubbed her leg. "What do you think? Do you want to stop at another restaurant? Are you still in the mood for fish?"

"Why don't we just swing through a drive-through? There's bound to be a ton of them in Tahoe. I haven't been there for a few years but I'm sure we'll find something."

"Consider it done," Paul assured her. "Did we finish talking about plans? Do you still want to keep going? If we stop, we can gamble a little and maybe increase our pot."

"Or decrease it. I don't want to risk that. Why don't we stop and get something to eat. I'll take over the driving. And we'll just head on to Sacramento."

"I can deal with that," Paul agreed.

Within minutes they'd found a drive-through. Thrilled at the discovery that baked cod in a basket was on the menu, they sat in the car and ate in companionable silence. They were both wearied by the encounter, as much from the implications of future danger as from the stress of meeting the actual threat of the armed man. When Jessica slid behind the wheel, Paul retreated further into silence and then into a gentle sleep. He didn't wake until the Bronco stopped at a

334

traffic light.

He opened his eyes and looked around in surprise. "Where are we?"

"Sacramento." Jessica looked at him fondly. "You slept the whole way."

"I guess!" Paul sat up straighter and peered around. The darkness of the night was dim, lit by traffic lights and store lights bordering the street. "Wow. It seems like twenty years since I was here last."

"It hasn't changed," Jessica said. "You have though, since you left. That will probably make it seem totally different. That happens to me almost every time I leave for a while."

"Whew." Paul rubbed his forehead. "I'm still exhausted. How about you?" He peered at her through the darkness.

Jessica smiled. "I'm doing fine, actually. I like driving. And I'm happy to be home. I like my little place."

"How long have you lived there?"

"Almost five years. A friend of mine had it on a lease and wanted to move to Maui. So I sublet it, which led into my own lease."

"How long do you figure we should stay? Before we head to the Coast, I mean."

"Not long." Jessica's voice held a warning tone. "I think we need to move this as fast as we can. Any delay on our part will just give them more opportunities to try to stop us."

"Right," Paul agreed. "I'll unload my boxes into the shed tomorrow morning. Then I can come back and get you and we'll go get any camping supplies we need. We won't need much though. I think I've already got most of what we'll need." He glanced into the back of the Bronco, which still held most of the gear he and Marlen had bought in Flagstaff on that journey that now seemed like a year ago.

Jessica grinned. "I think you've got enough for us to camp in Alaska for a month! I doubt we need to buy a thing. You must have been a Scout. You've got that 'be prepared' motto down pat."

Paul laughed. "What can I say? Guilty as accused."

Jessica turned off the main street onto a small, darker street. "Almost home." She gave a gentle sigh. "Leaving always makes you appreciate home more, don't you think?"

The question hit Paul hard. For the first time the solid awareness hit him that he didn't have a home. He had pulled up roots when he'd left his job and apartment to go to Arizona. He hadn't established a home there, instead choosing to stay with Bill and Brenda. Now they were heading toward the Coast. He had no idea how long they'd be traveling. Where would he go when the journey was over?

He now understood that he was on a mission for worlds that existed beyond Earth boundaries. He understood that everything he was being asked to do was necessary to accomplish something that was for the greater good of all. But the human side of him wanted what Jessica had; a place to call home. A place of comfort. A place that he could rely on to offer him a sense of normality. Funny. A year ago he would have thought that the life of a nomad would suit him. He had always been restless, looking, seeking, wanting something that had no name or face. But when he finally accepted that he was from elsewhere, he knew that this had been what he was looking for: the knowledge, the memory of elsewhere. Now that he'd accepted this fact and all that it entailed, he needed to incorporate it with what might pass for a normal life on Earth. At least to the degree that he had a home base, a place that made him feel safe and welcome.

Jessica looked at him curiously. "Are you all right?"

Paul brushed the question off. "I was just thinking."

Jessica pulled the Bronco into her half of the driveway in front of her duplex. "Well, we're home!"

Were they? Was he? Paul gave her a small, tired smile and followed her into the duplex. He barely noticed the soft lighting, the calm pastels of the furniture, and the Renoir-like paintings that decorated the walls. His weariness consumed him, drawing him into an all-consuming need to sleep.

337

Dropping their bags on the living room floor, but taking Jessica's purse and the tiles with them, they crawled into her bed with half-closed eyes. Paul smiled softly as she nuzzled against him and promptly drifted into another world. As tired as he was, it was still quite a while before he followed her into sleep.

The crystal pyramid that he called home waited for him. For the first time he noticed four pillars of seemingly endless light vibrating at its corners. Questar glistened serenely outside the crystalline walls. The twin moons danced their light onto the stream that ran beyond the mauve meadow. The musical sounds of the night birds embraced the air. Paul breathed deeply, taking in the aura of peace like it was a tangible thing.

He sat cross-legged in the center of the pyramid. He was pure spirit, resting in the absolute vibration of his soul. There were no questions. There was no fear or doubt or danger. The history of his existence was his without mystery. It spanned time, taking him into soul-knowledge and experiences that went beyond definition.

An unexpected inclination rose to the surface of his thoughts. He closed his eyes and was instantly aware of the crystalline grids that ran throughout existence, sustaining matter and averting chaos. His spirit knew that these grids were sacred models of divinely ordered energy and light. Each thread within the grids vibrated with the energy of a universal color, many of them never seen on Earth. There were grids within grids, threads intersecting threads. Each grid was scientifically

338

calibrated to issue forth a distinct vibration and energy.

Here and there, throughout his vision, certain diamond-shaped grids glistened with magnificence, setting themselves apart from the other grids by their unique qualities. His focus narrowed until he was envisioning the grids that surrounded Earth-Universe.

He watched as energies that emanated from The Source merged with the grids. Colors were magnified as the new energy was assimilated. He understood, as he watched, that the hydrogen matrix of Earth-Universe was changing, elevating the third dimensional reality that had served Earth for thousands of years. The purpose was to enable an evolutionary shift for Humankind. The combination of the sacred geometrical grids, combined with the radiations of pulsating light and color, were in the process of healing the energy of the history of Earth. With the healing came the opportunity to move beyond limited thought.

He watched as various colored light beams, acting in a manner similar to laser light beams, infiltrated the genetic material of the human race. As the new spectrums of light intruded into the basic black and white spectrum of light, the planting of the universal knowledge of creation was issued into Earth's energy field. Humankind was being given, with the issuance of light, color, and energy from beyond Earth, the opportunity to move from the dense form of 3-D energy to the less dense form of matter-energy that exists in higher dimensions. Some people on Earth who were Masters, and who were assisting in the process by lending their physical presence to Earth, would accept the light

339

energies into their bodies and would then rise into spirit form without death when their missions were complete. The knowledge that this was most likely the future that awaited him filled Paul's spirit with elation.

His eyes remained closed as he accepted the facts that had been presented to him. He opened them when he heard a small voice beside him. He turned to see a tiny, wizened woman sitting only inches away. He studied her calmly. He knew who she was. A sense of deep honor at her presence held him in its grip. It had been his understanding that she never left her residence. To find her beside him told him that she had made an exception to her long-standing rule. "Greetings, Empress," he said, bowing his head slightly.

She nodded, gifting him with a small, benevolent smile.

Her hair was the color of a dove's wing and bound in a single braid that hung down her back. It reached to her waist. Her forehead was high and wide, her eyes deep-set and piercing. Their ruby color enhanced her ancient beauty, piercing through Paul's spirit like a hand of pure love. Her wisdom and power spoke through those eyes. She wore a smooth, suede-like gown that matched the deep claret of her eyes. She couldn't have weighed more than eighty pounds. Her hands were tiny and delicate.

Even though he was sitting quietly, observing her, Paul began to realize that she wasn't really there. He was looking at a hologram.

"You and the others set quite a task for yourselves,

340

didn't you?" she asked. Her voice resonated, each word forming a single, melodic tone.

"Indeed," Paul agreed with a smile.

"But it's going well," she assured him. "I understand that you successfully retrieved the tiles that the workers took to Earth."

"Yes."

"You've done well. And you encountered the 'others'?"

"Yes. More than once. They're as determined as they were over a millennium ago."

"I have no doubt." She smiled tolerantly, as if she were watching very young children squabbling over a toy. "I don't know why they persist. They have no chance of succeeding. Earth will move into its new evolution no matter how much they disapprove or attempt to interfere."

"I agree," Paul said solemnly. "But they will succeed in stopping the progress of some of the people. I imagine they believe their efforts are worth it."

The empress shrugged lightly. "They don't have the simple understanding that, even if they succeed in delaying some people, those people are actually making the choice to be delayed. Ultimately, no one soul has dominion over another. They can only attempt to cause an effect to the degree that the soul's choices vary slightly. Each soul will experience all things. Whether they do it now or later is of no consequence." She shrugged again. "In other words, this other society is accomplishing absolutely nothing."

Paul nodded thoughtfully.

"It's a simple shame that they don't use their talent and energy in a direction that will serve to accelerate evolution, rather than delay it," she offered, peering at him quizzically to see if he agreed.

Paul smiled widely. "I've gained some understanding, Empress, while I've been away. I can read behind your words. My response to you now, as opposed to the angry argument I would have given you before my time on Earth, is that they are serving by presenting obstacles to those who still need to believe in obstacles."

She laughed gaily. "I can see that you have grown wiser through the years. Congratulations."

Paul grinned and bowed his head in acknowledgment. "Thank you." He looked beyond the walls of the crystal pyramid and sighed contentedly. "I find myself anxious to create a home. I wish it were this one. I look forward to returning permanently."

"You have quite a bit of time before that will happen, other than the times when you return in this way." She gazed at him fondly. "I understand your need though. Perhaps you can create what you want down there? Something that will suffice?"

342

Paul tilted his head in thought. "Perhaps. I know I have some travel in my future right now though. I don't know when that phase of the mission will be complete. When it is, I'll see what I can do." He smiled down at her, enjoying the peaceful resonance of her company.

She studied him. "Mission first. That was always your way. But you might want to do yourself a favor. You might want to bring to memory the times when you neglected yourself, putting your mission first, to the degree that you lost both yourself and your mission."

Paul was surprised. "I don't remember that at all." He searched his spirit-energy, looking for the memory.

"You won't find it there," she told him quietly. "It was a huge event. Your soul took it into its heart and holds it there, so as not to forget the impact of that particular lesson."

Paul was even more surprised. "Really? Why don't I remember any of this?"

"Your connection to your soul, while in spirit form, becomes stronger and more evident all the time. And yet there is still more of that connection that needs to be revealed and nurtured." She glanced around before meeting his eyes. "Now would be as good a time as any. Don't you agree?"

Paul felt her words enter the energy of his spirit. He knew that he had just been issued an order. But it was an order that would give him a gift far beyond any he had ever received.

343

He was not surprised when he blinked and found that, once again, he was alone.

CHAPTER TWELVE

PAUL BREATHED THE ENERGY of the crystal pyramid into himself. Vibrant colors, followed by the softest pastels he'd ever seen, swept through him, flowing like rainwater into a stream. Slowly he felt himself losing even the effervescent sense of his spirit. He was merging with a vast, fathomless energy. An energy that contained both light and dark. It was all things. It was nothing. It was existence but it was the nothingness of the time before existence.

Forcing himself to not evaluate or seek to understand, he sought to simply accept the experience, merging with it in his quest for wisdom.

A violent flash of light, similar to the explosion of a nuclear plant, jolted through him. He seemed to be composed of only consciousness and so his response was mild, a simple interest and curiosity in what he was experiencing. His immediate thought was that he had somehow managed to blow himself up in some kind of catastrophe during one of his physical incarnations. Hearing again the Empress' words, and assuming that he had created the present experience in order to uncover the mystery of what she had said to him, he supposed that he had been on a mission when this explosion occurred.

His soul instantly radiated a message to him. No, his assumption was incorrect. That was not what had happened. Attempting to surrender to an even greater degree, he allowed the truth of events to suffuse him.

345

From the deepest knowing of his soul he began to understand.

His soul had issued forth a thread of itself. It was known as spirit and in spirit form he had manifested into a reality outside of his soul. With the thought of assisting this reality to heal beyond its universal pain, he had immersed himself in the full energetic experience of the suffering, absorbing the pain and chaos of that world, drawing it into himself. He understood why he did it. He was attempting to help, to heal. By drawing the pain into his spirit, literally absorbing this world's history into himself, he had hoped to give the people, the energy grid, the world, the opportunity to heal itself. In the process, he had gone too far.

He couldn't retrieve all of the details of what had occurred. Instead he re-encountered the horrendous flash of light. He watched in horror as his spirit form evaporated into nothingness. He had killed a piece of himself. The spirit form that had issued from his soul no longer existed, was not able to return to its origin, and had not been able to reunite with soul. He hadn't realized that such a thing was possible.

The ache within him, rising from his inability to honor his soul, lasted only seconds. Now in its place stood a deep conviction. Honor spirit and soul first. Do not put the illusions and energies of the external realities above your own. He vowed that he would never let that happen again. With that resolution standing firmly in his thoughts, he woke up to find Jessica smiling down at him.

He sighed deeply as he gathered her into his arms. She smelled like the sweetness of a flower garden bathed in morning dew. Burying his face into her hair, he held on to her. Was she the 'home' that would guide him to his soul safely? Would the love they shared be his beacon, his light, and his balance?

Whispering his love for her, he brought her to him gently. Receiving him, she brought him into the strength of her passion. Lost in her, it was daylight before he realized time had passed. He brushed her hair from her face tenderly, kissed her closed eyes tenderly.

Her fingers trailed lightly over his stomach. "You hungry?" she murmured.

"Famished," Paul said sleepily.

"Are you cooking?"

Paul could feel her smile against his chest. "Are there any places around here that deliver?"

She giggled. "Breakfast? I don't think so."

"Humph," he said lightly. "Well, we can do one of two things. We can get up and open a few cans of something since you haven't been home in a while and probably don't have a thing to eat around here. Or we can get dressed and go out. We could stop for breakfast and then drop my boxes in a shed. Then we can do whatever shopping we need to do. That should take us half a day, at least."

He leaned on one elbow and traced her arm with a light touch. "You're going to have to talk to your assistant too. To tell her you won't be able to take appointments for a while."

She opened her eyes and watched his hand dreamily. "How long do you think we'll be gone?"

"I have no idea." He yawned widely and sat up, wrapping his arms around his knees. "We talked about this, remember? It's going to depend upon where we end up going. If we're just going to San Francisco and around that area, I don't think it will be long."

"I don't think that's the plan," Jessica told him. "I'm almost positive that we're supposed to drive up the Coast. At least to the Oregon border."

Paul turned and looked over his shoulder at her. "How sure are you?"

"Almost positive," she repeated. "At least about the Oregon border part of the trip. We need to go at least that far, I think."

"And what's supposed to happen once we get there?" Paul asked, puzzled. "I mean, no one's told us anything except that we're supposed to take the tiles to the Coast."

"I know." She rubbed her arm absentmindedly. "Other than the fact that the energy of the tiles will be interacting with the grid lines along the Coast, I don't know. I guess I've just been assuming that we would be

348

told once we got there."

"I don't know about all of this," Paul said hesitantly. "I guess I'd like to have more of a plan than just driving until we run out of road."

Jessica sat up and rubbed his back gently. "You followed your instinct when it called you to Arizona and look what happened. You got to spend time with the others before they were picked up by the mothership. So that was the perfect instinct. You weren't being led astray by that. Can't you trust your instinct again?"

Paul tilted his head, contemplating her logic but thinking about his previous annihilation. His soul-memory of the night was fresh in his mind. His sense of regret about his previous action and subsequent death was a compelling argument against journeying too far and too long. Above all, he didn't want to get so caught up in his mission that he dishonored his spirit or soul.

He glanced at the bag of tiles that sat on the dresser. Here they were; tangible evidence that there were other worlds and other wisdoms that were available to the people of Earth. How could he question his part in this mission now, with the weight of the responsibility inside that bag? He felt the accountability for himself and the mission of the tiles creating a battle inside of him.

"You're right," he finally said, though his voice was hesitant. "Between us we have enough funds to keep us going for a couple of months. And if we camp, it will last even longer. I guess we have to do whatever it takes."

349

Jessica wrapped her arm strongly around his waist and pulled him to her. "You're not questioning this, are you?" she asked anxiously. "I mean, how can you?" She waved her hand at the bag. "There they are! Proof positive. How could you think of doing anything other than following through with this?"

Paul thought he heard disappointment in her voice. He wasn't a coward. He didn't want her to think he was. But he wasn't ready to share the memory that he'd acquired during the night. It was too fresh, too new, and there was much more that he needed to understand about it. His personal regret and pain sat just beneath the surface of his skin, too uncomfortable to be touched or comforted.

He forced himself to smile as he turned and put his arms around her. He used his legs to tumble them both back until they were lying down again. "I'm going. I'm going. But you have to promise me that I'll be able to get more sleep than I've had recently. Is it a deal?"

Jessica laughed. "If your only problem is lack of sleep, then we can fix that. You can sleep on the couch tonight. That way I won't keep you awake."

"Don't threaten me, woman," Paul growled in her ear. He kissed her lightly and released her. "Let's get showered and dressed. They're going to find nothing but hungry bones if I don't get something to eat pretty soon."

Later, Paul blinked at her as she exited the bathroom in a vibrant amethyst-colored blouse and deep purple pants. Her hair was swept up and held by a purple band that draped two sweeping peacock feathers that were long enough to brush her shoulders. On her, the outfit looked casual and fresh, not a statement of fashion but rather a statement of the joy in her heart. She would stand out in any crowd, Paul thought. She's fabulous, beautiful. With all my heart I hope this lasts.

She smiled at him gaily and spun around, her arms spread wide. "You like?"

"I love." Paul grabbed her and kissed her quickly. "Now let's go before I starve."

After a breakfast of bacon and avocado omelets , they took the things that they weren't taking on the journey out of the back of the Bronco and put them into Paul's storage unit. He had to fight back a clutching sense of loneliness as he slid the lock onto the door and pressed it closed. He was quiet as they drove to the camping supply store.

His unvoiced emotions made him tense. When he added the intensity of the crowds and nervous bustle, it got to him almost immediately. The difference between where he was and where he'd been for the last few weeks was gargantuan. The nervous energy reached Jessica as well. Dropping the few things they'd purchased into the Bronco, they agreed that the supplies they had were enough. One last stop at the grocery store and they would head home.

They pulled into the driveway with a combined sigh of relief. Jessica lifted the small bag of dinner and breakfast groceries from the back seat as Paul began to

351

rearrange the camping supplies and packages in the back of the Bronco.

"I'm going to go call my assistant," Jessica told him. "You want some help here?"

"Nope. I'm just going to give this a sense of order here. I'll be in shortly."

"Okay." She spun and headed for the door.

Paul watched her go with a smile. He realized suddenly that underneath his concerns and wonderings, he had been happy for days. He pushed back the tiny pinch of loneliness that he'd felt at the storage shed. Compared to the simple endurance of life that he used to carry around, his present state of mind was pure joy. He didn't want to let his human fear of homelessness ruin it. He'd turned a corner in his life. He took a moment to stand silently, appreciating the changes in his life, before turning back to his task.

The rest of the day they worked in harmony, cleaning the small duplex, weeding the front and back yard, and doing the basic things that needed to be done before closing it up for the time they figured they'd be gone. Jessica ran to the post office and put a temporary hold on her mail. Paul popped open a small bottle of wine and had two glasses ready when she returned.

"I think we can stop now," he told her, taking her hands and drawing her down to the couch next to him. "Dinner is simple. I can fix it while you relax. And then we'll just take the rest of the evening to ourselves. No more worrying and fussing over details. Everything here will be fine."

Jessica leaned against him with a smile of contentment. "All right. It's a deal. But I have one more thing to do. Why don't I do that while you fix dinner?"

Paul nodded and kissed her forehead gently. It was good to hold her in his arms. It had been wonderful to experience the normality that they'd experienced that day, working side by side to accomplish the closing-up of the house. It would be fantastic to have it last. He rested his chin on the top of her head as she leaned against his chest. He was happy. It was an emotion he liked.

Jessica stirred. "Well, I'm getting hungry. We didn't eat lunch, remember?"

Paul laughed. "Well, that breakfast was big enough to last us all day, that's why. They gave us enough food to last a week. If I'd eaten it all I would have exploded."

Jessica chuckled. "They do get a little carried away. But they're nice people. They want everyone to be happy when they leave the restaurant. I drop in there about once a month or so." Shaking her head and running her fingers through her hair to straighten it, she stood. "Let me write out the bills while you cook. That's the last job of the day, I promise."

Paul dropped onto a chair, wrapped his hands around her waist, lifted her blouse an inch, and leaned forward to land a soft kiss on her stomach. "It's a deal. It should take me about twenty minutes to fix dinner."

353

"The timing will be perfect." She stroked his hair gently before touching his chin and drawing his gaze up to meet hers. "I'm glad you came into my life," she told him softly.

Her eyes held the tenderness that Paul had needed for years. He pressed his face into her stomach and kissed her again. "I'm glad too," he murmured. "More than words can say." He stood and gathered her to him. They stood for several moments, holding each other without speaking, cherishing what they had found with each other.

With unspoken agreement, they moved apart. Paul smiled at the small, comfortable sounds of her moving around in the other room. This was, quite possibly, what he had been looking for over the last twelve years.

The sun was up early, almost as if it too was eager for them to get on the road. Both Jessica and Paul woke up with eagerness and excitement. Their high emotions took them through quick showers and a hasty breakfast. He washed the dishes while she dried and half an hour later they were dressed in shorts, T-shirts, and sandals and ready to go. Paul tossed their suitcases into the Bronco and slipped behind the wheel.

He took the route he'd taken so often before, heading west toward San Francisco and then taking the highway to Petaluma. They had agreed the night before to leave Highway 101 at Cloverdale and head toward

Albion. Having accepted their instinct that their journey was meant to take them up the coast to Oregon, they had decided to spend their first night in Fort Bragg. It had been a couple of years since Paul had driven through the rolling hills and orchards of the Napa Valley. Its beauty captivated him. The small towns were filled with charm. Stately mansions owned by vineyards graced the roadside. Jessica slipped a CD into the stereo. The enchantment of the music, combined with the magnificence of the countryside, lulled him into a deep sense of comfort.

He had no idea what to expect when they reached the Coast but he was at peace with whatever it might be. He was seeing the world with eyes that had always been clouded by a sense of unexplainable loss. He felt he was being healed on all levels. It wasn't only Jessica's presence in his life, he knew. It was also the fact that he had given himself permission to unite his personal truth with the life experience that he was currently having. The struggle to be somewhere that he wasn't was gone. The fight to mold himself into a person that he wasn't had ended. He understood that he hadn't completely assimilated all of his truth and his ET origins. But he was closer than he'd ever been before.

The sound of Jessica's singing began to weave a spell around him. He hadn't known she could sing. Her voice was soft and tender. It appeared to yield to the music, just as though she and the music had agreed to create a harmony that would enchant and hypnotize. He was unaware of the serene smile that graced his face. He drove quietly, willing the Bronco and the traffic to move with the flow of her voice so that she would continue singing. Like drifting on a dream, they made their way slowly toward the Coast.

Deciding not to stop for lunch but instead to snack on the nuts and fruit that Jessica had packed, they reached Ft. Bragg by late afternoon. The windswept trees that decorated the area gave it a beauty and wildness that drew Paul immediately into a deeper state of bliss. The motel they chose was simple but only steps away from the beach. Paul pushed the sliding glass door open to let the fresh, salt-saturated air inside. Taking turns, they freshened up and stepped out onto the small deck that faced the beach.

Without explanation, Jessica turned back into the room and returned a few seconds later with the bag of tiles. She held the bag on upturned palms, as though she was offering them to the heavens. For several seconds she merely stood, holding them, staring at the vast sea that crossed the world in front of them.

She turned to Paul. "Would you hold them?" She handed him the bag and went back inside. When she returned she was carrying five small crystals. She arranged them on the wooden banister of the deck and stood contemplating them. "Energy alignment," she explained when she felt him staring at her.

Paul nodded. "I get it." He sensed the subtle shift of energies around him as the energy of the crystals began to merge with the energy of their surroundings.

"We'll bring them inside when we're not here to watch them but I think this is the best place for them

356

right now."

Paul nodded in agreement. With the placement of the crystals and the weight of the tiles in his hands, he could feel his energy field shifting. He stepped backwards, perching carefully on the edge of one of the white plastic chairs that sat on the deck. He waited, staring out to sea without seeing it. His vision was internal, watching as the cells of his body absorbed the energy around him like a sponge.

Suddenly it was as though the veil between worlds had dissolved. Above, he could see the grids of the Earth glittering with crystalline energy. There was not one grid but many, all overlapping and all made up of geometric configurations. Small light ships moved slowly through the grids. Sporadic beams of various colored rays of light shot from the interiors of the crafts, touching, penetrating, and reflecting off of the crystalline threads. His internal vision was drawn to something beyond the grid maze. He gazed in awe at the large object. As he studied it, it became more distinct.

It was the shape of a long, double-terminated crystal. Within it were pyramids with strips of light between them. Each pyramid shape intersected with another, forming five diamond shapes. The lights were various pastels and were blinking intermittently.

As he watched, the long shape of the large crystal drew energy into one end of itself. He could sense the energy moving through the form, being drawn from one diamond-shape to the other. He knew instinctively that the energy was being transmuted as it moved. Watching

357

the process, he was surprised when more knowledge about it floated to the surface of his thoughts. He knew that the form was capable of transforming matter and that it, and others like it, were constructing portals between the physical and non-physical universes by using the light constant squared. This was done by converting light and energy by passing it through the internal workings of the form.

In addition, he sensed that the Light portals that were being placed were capable of neutralizing the impact of some of the Man-made devices that had come into being on the planet. He also knew that the portals were facilitating the transmutation of energetic thought forms that had been deliberately planted by several alien societies that did not want those who resided on Earth to gain their freedom and personal power. The thought forms that had been planted caused people who were susceptible to them to believe that they were victims on Earth. Strong enough to rob people of their memories of personal power and the fact that they were living in a reality of malleable energy, these thought forms had dominated thousands upon thousands of people. Paul fought back his instantaneous rage and desire to fight the invisible enemy who had placed the thought forms.

Who would be evil enough, and strong enough, to manipulate the energy of Earth reality this way? he thought.

His answer came immediately in the shape of a thought form that seemed to have been placed into his mind by Solomon.

"Everything that exists has a purpose. Conflict is necessary. It serves as a mirror to inspire a person to strive for something that lies buried deep within them. This isn't true of every dimensional reality, but it is true of this one. Yes, Earth has its opponents. Yes, the inevitable evolution of Humankind is being challenged. But this is a conflict easily overcome when people accept the truth of who and what they are. As people draw the Light of the soul into the physical expression of themselves, they will not only overcome the challenge but will create the foundation for a new reality. Throughout most of this world's history, as people co-created reality, the foundation for their creation has been fear. What we, those who are assisting Earth's evolution from higher dimensions, are encouraging is the acceptance that reality can be created with a base of Light, not fear and pain.

"It is true that a new reality is being born. It is being given birth by those people who accept the challenge of moving beyond what appears to be real. All of reality is an energetic experience created by common agreement. It is a reality made up entirely of energy. That energy can and will be transmuted. Energy is not stagnant. Because all energy is capable of change, it is suggested that it be changed by the power of Light, rather than the power of the human emotions. Each individual who chooses will draw into themselves the Light of soul, enabling them to understand how energy can be altered by Light and Truth.

"There are sacred geometric and crystalline qualities within the physical body. The vibrations and energies of the soul touch these configurations as a person strives to

359

integrate with the soul. As the soul vibration affects these configurations, they will be used for correlating genetic material. In some instances, the genetics of a lifetime spent elsewhere would be made compatible with this world, enabling a person to access the knowledge and energy of that other lifetime. In the earth-body, the carbon/oxygen/hydrogen/nitrogen aspect of the body has the capability of acting as a semiconductor for the energies that are being sent by higher intelligence beings."

Faces began to appear in front of Paul's closed eyes. They flashed so quickly that he only had one or two seconds to study one before it was replaced by the next.

"These are members of the Elohim Council," Solomon told him. "They are the keepers of the original blueprint of the Intention of God. They work with sacred geometric shapes and grids throughout existence. They influence existence by issuing specific energetic vibrations and intense vibratory tones of Light and color into areas of existence that are out of Divine Alignment or at a point in the evolutionary process of moving forward. They are currently interacting with Earth-reality, assisting the coming evolutionary shift. They have thousands upon thousands of others who are assisting them as well.

"The physical body cannot completely align with the total soul-Light until it is altered by certain reactions and energetic interactions that have to occur in order to assimilate the degree of Light sent by the soul. The Elohim, and millions of other higher-dimensional inhabitants, working by common agreement, are issuing into Earth's energy field the external energies that are necessary to heal the energetic patterns of thought that have haunted Earth for centuries. As individuals work independently to rise above the current consciousness level, they align themselves with these higher energies and thought forms. The physical body begins to heal and transmute the lower vibrations as it is touched by the higher thought forms and energies."

Paul's attention was drawn to his own body. He could envision it as cells separated by space. Even the solidity of his bones had dissolved. The vision intensified his attempt to understand and accept that he was creating a reality by causing himself to appear as a solid form, existing in a field of energy with millions of others doing exactly the same thing. Each person was made up of cells separated by space, a non-solid form that appeared to be solid. Each person had his or her own reason for creating such an appearance. Each reason was driven by the individual soul. The Divine Plan of the Creator drove each soul.

The thought brought with it a great burst of Light. The Light surged through the space that surrounded his cells. His body tingled as the Light flowed through his bloodstream. Small electrical charges flashed through his hands and up his arms. More charges shot from his ear canals into his throat where they appeared to shoot out of his body with tiny bursts of electrical light.

He found himself merging his thoughts with the space of his body, completing eliminating his cells from his awareness. Struck with wonder, he realized that, within the space, separate from everything else that he

361

had believed to be real for twenty-nine years, he was living another life. He lost himself to the experience, enthralled by the possibilities.

He was himself but he was soul. He was untainted by the thoughts and emotions of the life he'd led. He was pure knowledge and awareness, operating within Earth's energetic field as a body of Light and energy that emanated from elsewhere. It was as though he was leading two lives, one that was completely dictated by the reality of Earth and one that was completely dictated by the knowledge of soul.

He found himself falling in love with himself.

Pure love for who and what he was embraced him. He was pure joy. He was faith, and trust, and purity. He was capable of all things. He was a master of creation. He was awareness. He orchestrated every event and every experience that he lived. And while he was suffering he was also in joy. The semi-solid cells that he used to exhibit himself lived out the reality of pain while the space that embraced those cells lived in love and joy at the wonder of the reality that he was experiencing and the lessons he was learning as he created this wondrous external expression of himself.

The full impact of understanding stood like a sentinel within him. He knew that he would never be the same.

As unexpectedly as the experience had started, it was over. He opened his eyes to find Jessica sitting on the chair next to him, her feet propped on the railing, her eyes gazing peacefully at the rolling waves.

She smiled at him, her face bathed in serenity. "You're back," she commented. "You looked happier than I've ever seen you. I didn't want to disturb you."

His eyes were full of love as he studied her. "I'm glad you didn't. I wouldn't have wanted to miss the experience I just had." He picked up her hand and kissed it sweetly. Because he couldn't find words to fully explain the experience that he'd had within in his body, he told her about the grids he'd seen, the Elohim Council, and the double-pointed Light craft that he'd envisioned.

Jessica nodded slightly, staring at the ocean as he talked. When he finished, she turned to him. "You're validating things I've seen and heard for years." She smiled. "I love that. It helps me know that I'm not nuts." She chuckled lightly.

"I'm sorry to say that there are probably a lot of people who would say that we are," Paul responded. "Nuts, I mean."

Jessica shrugged. "I've been dealing with that ever since I made the choice to become a professional metaphysician. But I finally decided that I had to choose between one truth and the other before I drove myself crazy. It was making me nuts to walk the line between the two realities. You have to be all the way there, in full faith, to do what I do."

Paul agreed. "And I think the heat is going to get turned up even higher when we try to talk to people

363

about all of this."

Jessica pursued her lips in thought. "From some, I imagine. But with the amount of energy from higher dimensions that's now hitting the earth, I bet there are a lot more people who will believe than disbelieve. I mean, just look at all of the information and acceptance that's been happening in the last few years. It's like the floodgates have been opened. More and more people are opening their minds to the possibilities that are out there."

Paul grinned suddenly. "This is just fantastic. When you take time to really allow yourself to absorb what's going on, it's phenomenal."

"It's incredible to be taking part in it," Jessica agreed. "I bet that's why the population on Earth has increased so dramatically. Souls are desiring to incarnate so they can experience it all. I imagine it's not a common event. One reality evolving into another, I mean."

Paul shook his head. "Now that I don't know. I know all things have to change. Maybe it's more common than we realize."

"Maybe it's just uncommon for Earth," Jessica speculated.

Paul chuckled. "That I might agree with." He smiled at her. "You hungry? We haven't had much to eat today. We passed an Italian restaurant that looked pretty nice. It's close enough to walk to."

Jessica's mouth popped open. She covered it with her fingers. "I did it again! I let you drive all the way! I can't believe I keep doing that." She gripped his arm and shook it gently. "I'm sorry. I don't mean to do that." She stood, pulling her vibrant lime-green T-shirt over her hips. "Of course we'll walk. I don't want you driving anymore and I don't particularly want to drive either." She breathed deeply and stretched her arms over her head. "I want to just breathe in this air." She dropped her arms and tugged on her shirt again. "What do you think about sleeping with the sliding door open tonight?"

Paul glanced around. "I imagine it would be safe enough."

"Good!" She pivoted on one foot and headed into the room. "Let me make another pit stop and we'll go. Oh, would you bring the crystals in? I don't want to leave them out by themselves."

Paul gathered the crystals and carried them into the room. A few minutes later they were headed down the road with Jessica carrying her purse over her shoulder, the tiles tucked safely inside.

The ambiance of the restaurant welcomed them the minute they walked in. Dark cedar paneling dressed the bottom half of the walls. The tables were draped with the traditional red and white checked cloths. It was still fairly early in the day and they found themselves the only customers in the place.

They slid into a booth next to a window, sitting opposite each other so that they both had a view of the

365

ocean.

Jessica sighed peacefully. "This is just ideal, isn't it?"

"Extremely." Paul agreed. He took the menu that was offered by the waitress who had appeared from behind the kitchen shutter doors. Opening the menu, he failed to notice the puzzled look she gave them. His eyes opened wide with surprise when, a minute later, a man slid quietly into the booth next to Jessica.

Feeling the movement beside her, Jessica dropped the menu she had been absorbed in and grabbed her purse off the seat, clutching it to her protectively. A multitude of emotions flashed over her face as Paul attempted to stand up, slammed his thighs against the underside of the table. Grimacing in pain, he struggled to pull himself out of the booth, determined to drag the man away from her.

Studying the man's face, Jessica held up a calming hand. "Wait, Paul. Wait." She turned on one hip, pressed against the wall, still clutching her purse against her chest. The man waited silently, his eyes unmoving as he stared at her. A slow smile spread across her face. She looked up at Paul, who was now standing beside the table, waiting impatiently for her to explain.

"It's ok," she said quietly. "He's one of us."

Paul leaned toward her slightly. "What are you talking about?" he whispered hoarsely. The sudden stress and the memory of the gun pressed against his knee in the restaurant in Nevada had made his throat instantly

366

raw.

She bounced her hand in the air gently, urging him to sit. "It's ok. Sit. It will be all right. He's here to help us."

Paul hesitated for another few seconds before he slid back into the booth. He eyed both of them suspiciously. The man's expression was compassionate as he caught Paul's eye, as if he had walked in Paul's shoes in another lifetime and the memory of fear was still fresh.

Now that he'd gotten over his initial fright, Paul realized that the man seemed to radiate with tranquility. There was no sense of tension or threat. He allowed himself to relax. He must be a guide, he thought. Like Marlen was a guide in Arizona and Louis was in Belize. Having had these similar experiences, he was ready to believe that yet another person had stepped forward with directions from Beyond. "You don't mind if I ask who you are and where you're from?" Paul asked with a small smile.

"Not at all."

The man's voice was deep and slow, filled with the resonance of an inner stillness. Paul thought he detected an accent but he couldn't place it. He waited.

"My name is Matthew. I live nearby, along this Coast." He nodded his chin to the north.

"The Coast is a big place," Paul commented, waiting for further explanation.

367

"Indeed." The single word held a distinct ring of humor, edged with a challenge of its own.

Paul couldn't stop his short bark of laughter and surprise at the use of the single word; Solomon's favorite. He grinned at Matthew, understanding that he had offered the one word that would signal to Paul that he was one of the good guys. Something about the man, now that he had accepted his presence, seemed familiar.

He appeared to be about thirty-five years old. His hair was sparrow-brown, longish, and tucked behind his ears. The part in the center was so straight that it looked painted on. His complexion was light tan and he had amber-colored eyes. With a narrow chin, high cheekbones, and flawless, satin-like skin, he looked untouched by the human experience. As a matter of fact, everything about him made him look foreign. Or alien? Paul wondered silently.

Jessica, silent while the two men studied each other, reached for her water glass and took a long drink, eyeing them over the rim.

With long, thin fingers, Matthew traced a pattern onto the table with the moisture left by her glass. Paul leaned closer. It was a triangle enclosed in a circle.

"Unity between worlds," Matthew murmured.

Paul questioned Matthew with his eyes.

"Isn't that the ultimate mission?" Matthew asked,

368

turning from one to the other.

"Absolutely," Jessica asserted.

Paul only nodded, still waiting to hear what the stranger had to say. Every hair on his arms stood up when he heard Matthew's next words.

"Obviously you have the keys." He nodded at the purse that now sat in Jessica's lap.

"Some of them," Jessica responded.

Paul stared at her, slack jawed. "What do you mean, some of them?"

"There are more," she answered matter-of-factly.

"You never mentioned that before," he accused.

She grimaced, puzzled. "I thought I had. Well, anyway, I wasn't absolutely certain before. Now I am."

Paul glanced at Matthew. "Why are you certain now?"

Jessica's eyes darted from him to Matthew and back. "I don't know. I just am."

Something stirred in Paul's subconscious. She was right. He could sense more tiles and more information. It was as though there was an invisible line of energy extending from the tiles on her lap to others that existed elsewhere. He was surprised that he hadn't realized it

369

earlier. But there was something else nagging at him. Something that had been triggered by his quick search of the energy around the keys. He tried to grasp it but it evaded him.

"The other tiles won't be revealed yet," Matthew advised. "The union and harmony between civilizations needs to happen first. And that won't happen overnight. Of course the revelations will come in stages. As understanding and acceptance occurs, more will be shared." He looked from one to the other. "The two of you have received, through your recent experiences and messages, much of what these five tiles have to reveal."

Paul realized that Matthew's words and the tone of his voice sounded similar to many Masters that he'd heard. He looked at him point-blank and took a chance, voicing what he was thinking. "Are you from one of the crafts?"

Matthew smiled thinly. "You might say that."

"Which one?" Paul asked immediately, pouncing on the clue.

"The Dove."

Paul's thoughts leapt to his recent conversation with Solomon. Now he understood why Solomon had alerted him to the presence of The Dove. This meeting had been planned, which meant that their seemingly random choice of Ft. Bragg, the motel they'd chosen, and this restaurant were not really spur of the moment choices at all. Everything had been pre-arranged. His thoughts

370

attempted to absorb and understand the enormity of the implications this bit of information held. They were huge. The effort to comprehend the vast Plan made him suddenly weary. He closed his eyes and rubbed them.

"I made him drive all the way here," Jessica said softly, explaining him to Matthew. "He's tired."

Paul smiled behind his hand. "I imagine, Jessica, that you don't have to explain anything to him." He dropped his hand and looked at both of them. "I would guess that Matthew probably knows everything, including things we don't even know."

The smile Matthew gave him was genuine.

Having ordered a small salad, Matthew explained The Dove while Jessica and Paul ate their vegetable lasagna dinners.

"It's stationed over the Pacific Coast. It stayed in the Washington State area for quite a few years but it's now in the Northern California area. We're doing some work in the area. It houses representatives and workers from several civilizations and dimensions. It is, of course, a Light craft. It's unique in that it is capable of providing for a large number of societies and accomplishing a great number of tasks. Most of the other crafts are specialized, outfitted for a specific task or civilization.

"The Dove hovers in a pale blue energy field, which helps it operate unseen since its energy blends so well with the atmosphere. Of course, its higher dimensional energy makes it invisible to the third dimension, for the

371

most part. But the pale blue aura serves to camouflage the fluctuations of light and energy as various individuals and crafts come and go. Its purpose is to provide a way station, if you wish to call it that, for some who need to enter this atmosphere temporarily in order to accomplish a task. And, of course, there are those who reside with it permanently.

"It has quite a few instruments aboard that are used for various manipulations of energy. For instance, it has a photosynthesis area that has devices that work with radiant energy. It has a crystalline-based lab that contains communication devices that are capable of issuing communication into all dimensions and universes without interference. It's currently working directly in the path of the east-west grids that run through the Mt. Shasta area, which is one of the reasons we're down here in California."

"I've interacted with higher dimensional beings who have been aboard The Dove," Jessica advised Paul. "In my meditations during the years," she added.

Matthew nodded. "Indeed you have. We're quite familiar, you and I." He smiled at her.

Jessica flushed with pleasure, touching her hand to her chest briefly. "I thought I recognized you." She touched his sleeve lightly and grinned. "Should I say something like ... it's good to see you again?"

Matthew smiled. "Well, you could say that but it's only been a matter of hours since we saw each other."

372

Jessica laughed lightly. "Next you're going to tell me that I'm famous up there, right?"

Matthew grinned. "I can say that you're known up there. I don't know if famous would be the correct word. But you're known. Your efforts to work and communicate with those on the higher dimensions are known. The energy work that you've done in your home area is known as well. And, of course, you're known for who you are and the mission that you came to Earth to achieve. As you are, Paul," he added, glancing across the table.

Paul nodded without responding. His thoughts were reaching into the ethers above Earth, seeking the energy field of the crafts that hovered there. He knew there was more than one. The Esartania and The Dove were motherships, huge and capable of housing over 100,000 beings each. They were also capable of receiving the smaller ships; the scout crafts and the transporters. In his mind's eye he imagined that he was watching the activity of numerous crafts above the surface of the earth. As he watched, the activity grew until there were multitudes of ships coming and going through the atmosphere.

His instinct told him that the inhabitants were from other planets and other galaxies, as well as other universes and other dimensions. The enormity of the project that encompassed Earth's evolutionary shift was almost too much to comprehend.

He pulled his thoughts back to the moment. In all of his travels through dreams and visions he had yet to meet a more human-looking alien than Matthew. He commented on it, asking Matthew about his origins.

Matthew grinned at him and chuckled. "Paul, when was the last time you looked in a mirror?"

Paul stopped his fork in mid-air and stared at him, puzzled. "I beg your pardon?"

Matthew blinked at the question. "Well, you know who you are and where you're from, don't you?"

"I think I do, yes."

"Well, then I can say ... I've never met a more human-looking alien myself!"

Caught off guard by the comment, Paul burst into laughter. "I guess you're right," he acknowledged.

Jessica, who had joined in the laughter, tossed in her own comment. "It's something around the eyes, I think." She stared at each of them in turn. "Yes, definitely. Something about the eyes gives you both away."

The laughter had created camaraderie between them. The rest of the meal was light conversation and laughter as they traded wry comments about aliens enduring Earth ... and vice versa.

Wiping tears of laughter from her eyes with her napkin, Jessica summed it all up by making a comment. "I'm not sure who's more afraid of who."

Matthew hooted with good humor. "Indeed. I think

it's a toss-up. Folks here are worried about us dropping from the sky and taking over. And we're up there trying to help everyone heal and hoping that when they come to us, they won't take us over."

Laughing, Paul dropped his napkin on the table next to his plate. "That's a terrific way to put it." He leaned back and stretched. "Well, I don't know about the two of you but I need to walk this off. I ate too much. Why don't we head back to the motel?" He looked at Matthew inquiringly. "You're joining us, aren't you?"

"Indeed." He rose from the table and moved out of Jessica's way.

It was still too early for the darkness of night to have fallen when they stepped from the dim light of the restaurant. The sun was just easing its way toward the skyline. The sky was cloudless, the air fresh, and the scenery spectacular. They strolled in silent rapport, each deep in their own thoughts.

Paul breathed a deep sigh of contentment. Jessica's hand was tucked comfortably into his. The day, the future, seemed flawless. He felt as though the rest of his life was going to be orchestrated by a greater force. In his imagination he thought that he had walked through a doorway when he'd accepted that he was from elsewhere. Since going through the door, he had been walking down a hallway toward another reality. And now he had gone through a doorway at the end of that hallway. For some inexplicable reason, Matthew's arrival in his life had created a shift. Perhaps it was that his presence on Earth had subtly given Paul the permission that he had

375

subconsciously needed to walk on Earth as his true self. "It's still light enough," he said. "How about taking a walk on the beach?"

"Let's," Jessica agreed instantly. She glanced at Matthew. "You'll join us?"

"Certainly."

They passed through the motel room, taking a minute to drop their shoes in order to walk barefoot in the sand, and exited through the sliding glass door. Jessica hid her purse under the bed so she wouldn't have to carry it.

"So, Matthew," Paul began as they stepped onto the sand, "how do you manage to live on the craft and be here in 3-D as well?"

Matthew smiled at him. "You finally got around to asking the question you've been wanting to ask for the last hour or so." He glanced automatically in the direction of The Dove before answering. "Well, I have the ability to bi-locate, which means that I can put myself anywhere that I choose. The trick to that is to become absolutely detached from the illusion of the reality in which you reside. I guess that doesn't explain it very well. Basically, you have to become a master of energy and thought. You become the truth that all things, including realities, are energetic experiences and that, as pure energy, you are capable of placing your energy anywhere that you choose. You don't doubt. You don't hesitate or vacillate. You live it."

376

"You make it sound easy," Jessica told him.

"It is and it isn't. It's total control over the process of energy that you display throughout existence. You don't attach yourself to any reality or energy. Otherwise you lock yourself in. You create boundaries where there are none and once you do that, you've solidified your energy to the degree that you can no longer move easily."

Paul shook his head. "I wish I could get to that point."

"In one respect, you already have," Matthew assured him. "Think about all of the experiences you've been having over the last month or so. But you're going to go even further with it. My presence here proves to you that it can be done. Now that you have that proof, you'll begin breaking down the belief systems that lock you in. In other words, your subconscious has already started to argue with itself, convincing you that you can do what you used to believe was impossible. With your thoughts, you'll begin to break down your resistance to the idea and begin to detach from the appearance of the reality that surrounds you. You'll stop giving your power to the illusion, begin detaching yourself from it, and, by doing so, you'll eventually accomplish exactly what I have."

The words caused Paul's skin to crawl with goose bumps. He felt the solid truth of the words and knew that it was a truth he wanted to live. His acceptance of this filled him with elation. His heart reached out to the place that he called Questar. It would bring him joy unmatched to integrate his physical presence with the energy and reality of Questar. The joy he was feeling

377

peeled away, for the briefest of seconds, another thin layer of the veil that kept him from the full knowing of who he really was. For a millisecond he was pure alien, pencil-thin, tall, and looking through almond-shaped eyes that had the ability to see existence in its entirety.

He blinked in surprise, dropping away from the sensation, when Jessica dropped his hand. He stared at her unseeingly as she bent to pick up a cockleshell, examined it, and set it back down. Matthew was looking at him curiously. Paul raised his eyebrows in question.

"I was just thinking," Matthew murmured. He turned away and walked toward the shoreline, where he stood with his back to them, gazing at the Universe as it began to paint the first faint pastels of sunset.

Paul and Jessica walked slowly on, allowing him his quiet time.

Jessica broke the silence. "Can you sense the grids along here?" she asked quietly.

Paul could feel the aura of peace that surrounded her. It pleased him to be a part of the experience she was having. "Yes. Especially the north-south lines, for some reason."

"You'll feel the east-west ones stronger in certain areas. As you travel and cross certain east-west lines, you'll begin to feel the currents of energy as they get stronger. You get adept at identifying them. Each one stirs up a different energy in your personal energy field."

378

Paul nodded, understanding. Scientifically, it made sense. The electromagnetic fields of the Earth affect people, just as the tides and the moon do. Many of the grid lines are crystalline in nature and are obviously intersecting with the electromagnetic fields. His own energy field would be affected and would respond to the combined energy of the grids in union with the electromagnetic field.

It occurred to him that, in a way that was similar to static electricity, which can cause things to cling to each other, the electromagnetic fields of Earth were causing a coagulation of energy. The grids, he supposed, assisted in breaking up blocks of energy by interfusing their own energy and light. He also realized that the geometric shape of a grid, combined with the light and color of the grid, created a unique energetic combination of energy.

He began to understand the concept of Divine Alignment that had been mentioned in many of his visions and dreams. Pleased with how easily the understandings, or should he call them memories, were coming to him, he smiled to himself.

Walking silently on the sand, Matthew had come up behind them. Sensing his energy, Paul turned to him.

"There's more but you just got another nice chunk of the information," Matthew told him, smiling.

Paul nodded. "I like it. I like the fact that I can remember, or know, however you want to put it."

"The knowledge is universal. Everyone is aware of it

379

on some level, even if they don't think about it consciously." His gaze drifted up as a thoughtful expression came over his lean face. "Can you imagine what this world would be like if everyone began to interact with an awareness of energy? The energy their thoughts and words create, the energy of the past, the energy of healing and possibilities, and the energy of the spirit in each physical body?" He shook his head in amazement. "It would change this reality in a matter of days, I bet."

Paul agreed. He had thought the same thoughts off and on. The mere suggestion of the wide range of possibilities that could occur boggled his mind. It would be fantastic to see, to participate in. He grinned as a sudden thought occurred to him. "I imagine if everyone began to read the thought energies in the minds of everyone else, it wouldn't even take days to change. It might only take minutes!"

Jessica laughed out loud. Obviously the thought tickled her enormously. She dropped Paul's hand and skipped merrily to the shoreline, still laughing.

The music of her laughter carried on the wind. The two men, watching her, smiled at her joy.

"She's quite something, isn't she?" Matthew said quietly.

The tone of his voice caused Paul to turn toward him, slowly, deliberately. He studied him in silence. Something was nagging at him. Something that he didn't like at all. Would voicing it make it true? Or would

380

silence dissolve the thought, and the possible reality, as quickly as it had been born? "Yes, she is," he agreed softly.

Matthew turned to him when he heard the tone of his voice. The two of them stood facing each other, each silently evaluating the other. Neither of them spoke about the thought that now stood between them like a stoic armed guard.

Paul turned on his heel and headed back toward the motel without looking back.

Jessica caught up with him. She grabbed his sleeve urgently. "What's wrong? What happened?" She looked over her shoulder at Matthew who stood as still as a statue, his gaze fixed on the sea.

"Nothing," Paul said briskly. "I have to use the bathroom, that's all."

She was hurrying to keep up with him as he continued walking. She tugged on his sleeve. "Paul?" Her eyes were serious and concerned. It was obvious that she wasn't fooled by his excuse.

Paul forced himself to smile. He wrapped his arm around her shoulders and pulled her to him. "Come on. Hurry. I'll make you wash my jeans if I don't get there in time." He gave her another smile. Maybe if I smile enough I'll convince both of us that I mean it, he thought.

By the time he'd exited the bathroom, Matthew and Jessica were sitting on the deck, their chairs leaning back, their feet propped on the railing. Jessica had set the crystals on the railing again and the five tiles were interspersed between them. It was the first time Paul had seen the tiles so casually set in the open where anyone who passed by could see them. The sight of them jolted him. He stood in the doorway, deciding whether he wanted to vocalize his discomfort. He didn't have to.

"They're fine," Matthew said, glancing at Paul over his shoulder. "They're too small for anyone to notice. Besides, if someone does notice them you can rest assured that it's meant to be."

"Meaning?" Paul asked abruptly.

Choosing not to react to Paul's tone, Matthew explained. "There's a reason for everything. Nothing happens without the notice of the Universe and the soul. If something happens, it's meant to happen. There's nothing accidental in this Universe, believe me."

"Then you can explain rape and murder and incest and all those kind of things?" Paul's tone was challenging and slightly sarcastic.

Jessica opened her mouth to speak, her eyes surprised.

Before she could say anything, Matthew responded. "Of course," he said blandly. He glanced at Paul again and turned his gaze back to the sunset. "You know as well as I do that this is a region of existence that allows souls to experience all things. And that souls need to learn all things in order to understand God, the Creator, and existence. And you also know that before making a commitment to a life here, each soul plans carefully and knows what experiences it will have in order to learn what it chooses to learn."

"Then why are we all hell-bent on changing it?" Paul asked rudely. His jaw was set, his eyes hard and unseeing as he stared at the open sea.

"Paul!" Jessica said sharply. "What in the heck is wrong with you? Everything was fine and now look at you! You're behaving like a spoiled brat." She spun around to look at Matthew. "What happened between the two of you?" she demanded.

As if he hadn't heard her question, Matthew spoke. "One of the major issues that will need to be addressed during this transition and evolvement of Earth and its civilizations is the separation between personality and soul. Each soul, even when we choose to ignore its determined influence upon our lives, must dominate our earthly experience. Often it doesn't, losing the struggle between personality and ego, earth-based belief systems, and things such as that. If the soul loses the battle to dominate life experiences, it will have to create another lifetime and will have to endure the same or similar circumstances in order to learn. That's one of the reasons why we have multiple lifetimes. Of course, there are dozens of other reasons too," he added mildly. "Anyway, when the personality overrides the soul's needs and doesn't allow a person to have the necessary experiences,

383

the end result of the soul is not achieved. Ergo, the soul will issue itself into another lifetime."

"And what does that have to do with the price of beans?" Jessica demanded, staring at him. "Neither one of you are telling me what's going on."

Matthew glanced at Paul and dropped his gaze. "What that means is that when someone is confronted with a circumstance that is inevitable, they will suffer much less if they react with the soul, rather than with the personality."

Jessica fixed him with a hard stare. When he didn't react to her, she turned back to Paul. "Do you know what he's talking about?"

Paul shrugged heavily. "I think I do."

Jessica waited. When he didn't continue, she blew out a sigh of exasperation. "Well, are you going to be kind enough to enlighten me?"

With a clear eye, Paul saw the effect he and Matthew were having on her. An instant mourning dropped into his chest. She had been joyous only moments ago. He had robbed her of that joy by his behavior. Moments ago he had been reveling in the fact that he was sharing her peace and joy. Now he was responsible for stealing them from her.

Shaken by the revelation, he walked to her softly and sat on the chair next to her. Gently taking her hand, he lifted it to his lips and kissed it. With his free hand, he brushed her hair away from her face. "I apologize. I'm being a brat. I'm spoiling your day."

She shook her head. "No. I'm responsible for my own reactions. If I apply what Matthew just said to us, I'm choosing this experience and I'm choosing my reaction. But, quite honestly, I'm allowing my personality to choose, not my soul. I would bet you that my soul would understand all of this and would be peaceful no matter what the two of you said or did. It's my personality that's asking what the hell is going on." She attempted a smile and touched his cheek gently, brushing her finger across his skin as gently as a butterfly wing. "So," she asked tenderly, "are you going to enlighten me?"

Paul looked past her at Matthew, who was staring sightlessly at the shoreline. His face gave away none of his thoughts or emotions. Paul looked into Jessica's eyes. "I don't think Matthew is here by accident," he told her softly.

"Well, of course he isn't! He's here to help us with the tiles and the grids." She stared at him, puzzled, waiting for him to explain further.

"I think it may be more than that."

"Like what?" She swiveled to look at Matthew, who remained motionless. Perplexed, she turned back to Paul.

"What are you trying to tell me?"

Instead of giving her a direct answer, Paul asked her

385

a question. "Do you recognize him?"

Jessica turned to study Matthew's stoic profile. A stillness like sudden shock fell over her. She nodded so slightly that Paul would have missed it if he hadn't been looking at her closely.

"Where do you recognize him from?" Paul asked softly.

"I don't know," Jessica whispered.

"Do you think that maybe you're not ready to remember?" Paul whispered. "That you don't want to remember?"

The fading light reflected off her unshed tears. Paul sighed inwardly. A heaviness that couldn't be measured came to rest on his chest. Jessica continued to stare at Matthew's profile. Paul could sense her absence from him as though she had already left. He placed her hand gently on the arm of her chair and leaned back in his chair. It was possible that the inevitable was only a moment away.

CHAPTER THIRTEEN

THERE WERE SEVERAL MEMBERS of the Elohim Council at the table, including Abraham. Paul directed his comment to him. "It's inconceivable to me that I would choose to cause myself more pain than I've already endured. That would seem to indicate that I have no honor for myself, which is not true."

Abraham stroked his white beard as he thought about Paul's comment. "I'm not an argumentative man, as you know. However, I am going to have to argue with you on this point. Simply because you are misconstruing the definition of honor."

Paul's attention was distracted from the dream for a minute. He felt himself stir and felt the heat of Jessica's body next to him. He knew that they'd fallen asleep in each other's arms with whispered words of assurance and love. After she'd fallen into sleep, he'd laid awake for a long time, knowing that the words of love were true ... the words of assurance false. When he had finally fallen into a restless sleep, his spirit had flown to the Council as though it were fleeing from death, urgent and dissatisfied. In the bed next to him Jessica was stirring.

He assumed that she was moving with the rhythm of her own dream experience. He forced himself to remain where he was - in spirit -- with the Council members. It was imperative for him to gain a better understanding of his life.

"Perhaps a better word for the relationship that you

want to develop between all aspects of yourself, including God, would be reverence, rather than honor. It's less likely to be misunderstood." Abraham's fingers straightened the sleeves of his robe and he glanced at Solomon before turning back to Paul. "You can consider that at another time. At this moment, since we have so little time, it would be best to talk about your life choices. Do you understand why you drew Jessica into your life? Do you understand why you chose to lose yourself in the moment, rather than to remain detached enough to observe the life-path that she chose for herself long before she met you?"

Paul rubbed his hands together, staring thoughtfully at the table as he considered Abraham's words. "No," he said slowly, "I suppose that I don't."

"If you take the time to interact with your soul, you will enter into complete knowing about the path that you have chosen for this lifetime. The choices you've made were based upon your search for someone. Did it occur to you that the person you are looking for is yourself?"

Paul looked up at him with surprise.

Abraham fixed him with a stare. "Soul to soul, I ask you to take a moment to recognize what Jessica offered you. She has always known her soul-path. She's never varied in following that path. When she met you, she recognized you but she also recognized your pain. She offered herself to you as a mirror, to reflect your pain and misunderstanding back to you. In the process, she has caused herself pain for she will suffer for having been the

388

one to hurt you once again.

"She was prepared to take this journey with you, to retrieve the tiles, to take them where they needed to go. She was prepared to do this as a friend, not as a lover. Your need drew her in." He held up one hand. "Yes," he added quickly, "she had a lesson to learn in this as well. But do you see?" He stood abruptly, startling everyone at the table. He leaned on the table, palms down, and stared at Paul with eyes that compelled him to understand. "Do you see that one of the things that has to change in order for life to evolve is that each person must understand him or herself to the degree that no one draws another away from the individual path of each soul?

"Only by knowing and walking in union with soul will each person understand what it means to learn through enlightenment rather than through pain. Pain has been a primary tool for learning in the Earth-realm. But in its service it also causes delay. The personality gets trapped in the energy of the pain and, by doing so, perpetuates, re-lives, the pain over and over. The constant re-visiting of a situation that caused suffering delays the process that the power of the soul's intervention and subsequent understanding would have upon the experience. When there is an easier way, why would anyone choose not to take it?"

Abraham's intensity left Paul almost breathless. He studied the great man before turning to meet Solomon's eyes. Though Solomon didn't speak, Paul heard his message clearly. Several things happened at once. His spirit reached out to accept and embrace a brilliant flash

389

of royal purple light as it came into his vision. Abraham touched his forehead, leaving a searing, insistent pressure even after he lifted it. And Solomon smiled.

Paul accepted the next phase of his path. He would learn to live without pain. And if he could do this, he could teach others.

He was not surprised to find Jessica gone when he awakened. He knew without searching that the tiles were gone as well. What shocked him was the pile of cash that she'd left on the bathroom counter. It was the remainder of what she'd won in Las Vegas.

He went to stand in the light of dawn. Barefoot on the small deck, he looked toward the north, searching the skies for The Dove. Of course it wasn't visible. He didn't react as the air beside him stirred.

"I'm pleased with the degree of your acceptance and understanding," Solomon murmured.

Paul grimaced slightly. "Don't give me too much credit. I don't know if I've totally absorbed the shock yet. When I do I might not be so calm."

Solomon dropped his hand on Paul's shoulder. His touch transmitted a plethora of unspoken messages. They were communicating soul to soul. Until that moment Paul hadn't realized that all of their interactions had been teacher to student, father to son, Solomon's soul to his spirit. Now there was a balance, two souls

390

walking a path side by side, neither one leading.

"What happens now?" Paul asked. "Or should I already know that without asking?" He tried to smile into Solomon's eyes.

Solomon's dark eyes were filled with compassion. "You're still living in the third dimension. Keep that in mind. Until the veils between worlds are completely dissolved, you'll have things you can't see until they happen."

Paul fell into silence, his eyes still searching the skies. He finally spoke. "And so, am I right? Did she go to The Dove? Or did she just leave with him and they're both here on Earth?"

"She's aboard right now. But she's allowed herself to accept the fact that she can bi-locate. They'll be back and forth, as he has been for several years now."

"I guess I should be glad for her. She's doing what she needs to do." Paul rubbed his hand across his forehead as though it was an eraser capable of erasing his thoughts. "I thought maybe she'd leave a note or something." He glanced toward the empty room and then sat abruptly down on one of the deck chairs.

"She knew where you were when she left. With the Council. She knew you would understand completely by the time you returned. There really wasn't a need for a note, as you know." Solomon sat on the chair next to him and looked at him sympathetically. "Don't backslide on me now, Paul." He patted Paul's arm firmly.

391

"I'm trying," Paul muttered. He closed his eyes briefly and opened them to scan the beach. Sandpipers scurried by so fast that their legs were invisible. Two seagulls were having a standoff over a crab shell that had washed up on the shore. A couple walked, hand in hand, several yards away, absorbed in each other to the degree that they didn't even notice him. He looked away quickly. "So, where am I supposed to go from here? I guess I'm homeless. I gave up my apartment. Arizona's a long way away. Now what?"

Solomon smiled at him gently. "Everything happens for a reason. You're still a Universal Energy Master. You still work with the sacred grids. You brought yourself up here for a reason. It's no mistake. Look at it this way. You freed yourself up. You left behind the realities that didn't serve your soul. Now all you have to do is find the one that does."

Paul scoffed loudly. "Oh, yeah, right!" He snapped his fingers vigorously. "Voila'! We have a new reality. It's that simple."

"It can be," Solomon said softly.

When Paul turned to look at him, he was gone.

After finishing off the fruit and nuts that were left over from the day before, Paul spent the day examining the small town and himself. His thoughts and emotions ran the full gamut of emotions, assimilating the full impact of the path he'd been leading for the last several weeks. As he walked, enjoying the scenery but not enjoying the way he felt, he realized that he had to make some decisions. If, indeed, it was a simple task to change your reality, where did you begin? With myself, he decided.

He understood that he couldn't take Jessica's action personally. Her soul needed to have the experience she'd chosen. He fought back his instinctual questions of self-worth, blame, betrayal, and abandonment. Thinking over all of the things that he'd learned, he knew that he had to view his life, and her decision, from a perspective that went far beyond the third dimensional explanations and reactions.

The words of Abraham stayed in his memory. Everything he had said made sense. And so, Paul realized, based upon what I heard and what I know, the place to start would be to change my perspective. The first thing to accept is that I still have not completely integrated my personal truth. If I could completely immerse myself in the energy of my true self, which has alien origins, there's a good possibility that I would feel a lot differently about everything.

He played a game with himself, giving his mental, human boundaries a challenge. Start walking on the earth as an alien being. Start seeing yourself as that being when you look in the mirror. Do you walk the same? Do you talk the same? Do you feel the same? Are you analytical, scientific, unemotional? How do you interpret the world around you? If you use soul-vision instead of your eyes, do you see things differently? As an alien, what would you do next?

393

He forced himself to try to set aside the fears that tried to bite at him and drag him down. Thinking with limited thoughts, he realized that he could consider himself jobless and homeless. Though he could return to Payson and the job Bill had offered him, that choice didn't seem to fit. At least right now. But where would he go if he didn't return there? The limiting thoughts and fears didn't want to go away. He was at war with the dichotomy of his 3-D reality and what he knew to be his Truth.

He mentally heard his companions from other dimensions urge him on. He knew he was on the right path with his thinking. It felt as though he was trying to walk through quicksand. The effort was monumental. He returned to his motel room to sit on the deck, continuing to reach for an understanding that would enable him to change his way of being. He was lonely. He imagined that he smelled Jessica's perfume. He scanned the beach, straining his eyes, but, of course, she wasn't there. He called to memory the vision of the woman he'd been seeing in his mind's eye for years. Why had he thought it was Jessica? It was clear that it wasn't. But who was this woman? Where was she? Was she on Earth or would their meeting occur in another place and time?

As he stared at the vast expanse of ocean, he forced himself to concentrate on his soul rather than the emotions that clamored for his attention. He did his best to breath in the energy of peace. He called upon the essence of his soul to enter him and heal him. He reached into the place he called Questar and called upon his truth. Suddenly a sense of God surged through him.

394

His mind expanded, embracing the existence of the Creator and the enormity of the realities that lived beyond the boundaries of Earth. He knew they were real. He wanted to incorporate their truths and energies into his life. He wanted to walk with the other worlds in a way that made them as solid and real as the Earth-world.

He sat, willing the energies of the higher dimensions into himself, drawing them to him as though he were a magnet. With no one around to tell him that he couldn't, that what he was reaching for was not accessible, he became his soul.

His vision was unlimited. The veils between worlds were dissolved. The heavens opened to reveal a thousand worlds. Alien crafts soared through universal atmospheres like butterflies. The other planets in the galaxy seemed close enough to touch. Black holes became spirals of energy that led into other universes. The Earth itself became cells separated by space, making the healing energies from beyond its borders easy to accept and absorb.

At an urging from Solomon he turned his attention inward once again. He was cells separated by space. The cells had their unique energy, separate from the space that surrounded them. The space had a life of its own. Suddenly he was separate from both, existing in a neutral zone and watching from a distance as lights and colors from Beyond touched and molded him. He watched in fascination as pin-lights of ultra-violet rays were directed into his brain. He understood that the cells of his brain were being re-calibrated by the frequency of color and light. The mental blocks and veils were being disintegrated, making it possible for him to mentally absorb more of his personal truth.

As suddenly as the experience had started, it faded. He sat for a while, thinking about what had occurred, until he made a decision. Once the decision was made, he realized that he was hungry. As he walked to the take-out restaurant, intending to take his lunch to the beach, he realized that he was at peace.

Peaceful without Jessica. Happy with himself. He shook his head with good humor. Life was a pretty amazing thing.

His dream that night supported the decision he'd made. Once again he was sitting at the Council table with the members of the Elohim. Abraham and Solomon were, again, in attendance, as was Eia. He remembered her from the Esartania. His joy at seeing her again was evident in his heart's reaction as it fluttered in response to her smile.

Her almond-shaped eyes accented her elegance. Thin and ivory-skinned, she stood a little over five feet tall. Her severely-cut, royal blue uniform and bald head took nothing away from her beauty. She gently gripped both of his arms and touched her forehead to his with a feather-soft touch. "Greetings," she said softly. Her voice was as melodic as he remembered it.

His hand lingered on hers before releasing her and taking his seat beside Solomon. Looking around, he noticed that, for the first time, there was something in the room other than the Council table. It was a large screen, suspended in mid-air. Upon his notice, a scene began to play across it.

He recognized the Pacific Coastline immediately. He watched from above as his Bronco twisted along Highway 101 toward San Francisco. He watched himself exit the vehicle and enter a tall building. The walls of the building dissolved and he watched as he rode the elevator to the top floor. A man listened to his story, pressed an intercom button and, minutes later, he was ushered into another man's office. He wasn't able to hear the conversation but he watched as he and the man talked and then shook hands as if agreeing upon something.

They turned simultaneously to look through the large windows of the man's office. The Pacific Ocean glittered serenely. Their attention was drawn to the sky. A burst of light split the sky, revealing the world beyond. A glimmer of silver. A row of blinking lights. There was one craft. And then there were two. And then there were more. They entered the atmosphere and marched across the skyline. Visitors welcoming Earth to their world, offering gifts that went beyond the imagination.

Paul and the man turned to each other. Both of them smiled.

As the screen disappeared in the blink of an eye, Solomon touched Paul's arm lightly. When Paul turned he saw tears in his friend's eyes. It was the first time in two thousand years that he'd seen Solomon cry.

397

Abraham spoke. "We want to congratulate you for having the courage to accept your truth and change your reality. You have a pivotal position in the larger picture. Your decision takes us to the next step in the mission."

Paul looked at him with interest. "Really? I wouldn't have thought that the actions of just one person would make that much of a difference. I mean, I know that it's important for me to do what I need to do. But I wouldn't have assumed that it would have that much impact."

Behind him, he didn't see Solomon smile tolerantly.

Abraham answered him with a smile. "Every single person makes a difference when they shift their personal energy. Because no energy is separate, an energy healing for one is an energy healing for all."

Eia spoke up. "Something that you may not yet realize is this, Paul. There are some who have volunteered to enter the Earth-reality solely for the purpose of healing energies. Many of them don't even realize it. They absorb the energies that are out of alignment, taking the energies into their own bodies, and transmuting them. For example, a woman may choose to experience rape and in so doing, she gains an understanding of the energy that causes such events. As she works to heal her own reactions and emotions, she is working not only for herself but for all women.

"You see, each event has an energy of its own. When you work to heal a particular event through its energetic expression, bringing it into Divine Alignment, you work

398

on the entire event, not only your personal event."

Paul stared at her, a memory of his own trying to surface. It seemed that he had been told, or shown, a vision similar to what she was suggesting. Oh, yes! he thought. How could I have forgotten the experience so recently shown to me? The one in which I destroyed an aspect of my soul.

Eia nodded gravely. "Earth has experienced many events that captured the attention of people throughout this Universe and beyond. In many of these instances, the people who played the parts did so in order to bring international attention to the energy and emotion of the event. Subconsciously all people know what is and is not in Divine Alignment. Those talk shows that became popular overnight are a perfect vehicle to present Man's inhumanity to Man. Unfortunately, it's a double-sided sword. Some people react to them by finding the horror entertaining rather than appalling."

Paul nodded with pursed lips. He had noticed the same thing.

Eia continued. "Television has provided the perfect forum for exposing the atrocities that people inflict upon each other. It's brought abuse to the forefront of everyone's mind. When attention is focused on an issue that is clearly out of Divine Alignment, it brings the need for healing to everyone's attention. Light is shed on events that used to happen behind closed doors and people spring into action to do something about it. That's the point. A closed wound never heals. It just poisons the system without being addressed. And by then it's usually too late."

Paul studied her. She was passionate about her subject. He could feel her determination to help Earth's civilization. He knew there were thousands of others like her. He knew that he was one of them. It was a huge undertaking, but it wasn't an impossible one.

"Would you like to join me?" Eia asked suddenly, standing.

Paul stood without hesitation. "Certainly." He had no idea what to expect. When he found himself standing in the control room of the Esartania with Eia and Korton, he was thrilled. The huge craft, and the beings who lived there, were like home and family to him.

As Commander of the Esartania, Korton spent most of his time in the control room. Though his energy was powerful and distinct and could be traced no matter where he was, it was his belief that if he remained near his station it would make it easier for others to find him when they needed him. And so it was that Paul reacted with surprise when Korton suggested that they move to the conference room that sat directly behind the control room.

The room was a crescent-moon shape. Windowless, it sat in the center of the front half of the large craft. On the other side of it, opposite the control room, was the cafeteria. Paul remembered it with a small smile. He knew that he had recently been there in dream state and that he had engaged in a conversation with someone. The conversation had pleased him but, as hard as he

400

tried to recall the conversation, he couldn't bring the details to his mind.

Korton waved his thin, three-fingered hand at the conference table, indicating that he wanted Paul to sit. As Paul took his seat, several other beings stepped into the room. He recognized Zere immediately. He nodded with a smile.

Behind Zere was Thaline. Tall, translucent-green, with serious almond-shaped eyes, she resembled a praying mantis. Her appearance did nothing to deter Paul's instant recognition and rush of respect. Her race was known as the Antarians. Each of them were Universal Masters and adepts. They were capable of bi-locating, as well as the transmutation of their cells. They held great knowledge and mastery and were seldom seen in the internal workings of existence. Their energy fields were sensitive and it took a tremendous amount of energy for them to lower their vibration to the lower levels. They did so only to share information that would benefit the entirety of a society.

He was honored to be in her presence but what struck him even more was that he remembered her from elsewhere. A vision of himself, sitting next to her side, somewhere in the region of Questar came to the forefront of his mind. She had been his teacher. He stood, honoring her with a bow of his head.

Her features were unusual but Paul knew her well enough to recognize her smile. She nodded her head slightly and took a seat across from him.

401

When Zo entered, Paul felt a beam of pleasure cross his face. Zo was three feet tall, with ivory skin and a small paunch. More often than not, his almond-shaped eyes were brimming over with compassion and good humor. Now his small, three-fingered hand touched Paul on the arm as he passed by. His touch sent a small, electrical charge through Paul's arm. He knew that he and Zo had been friends for centuries, almost as long as he had walked with Solomon.

When everyone was seated, Korton pulled the small, silver device that had been sitting on the table toward him. He fingered it gently as he talked. "As you're aware, there will be a mass entrance of higher dimensional beings into Earth's atmosphere." He glanced at Paul, who nodded. Korton continued. "They will be coming in many different forms, many different vibrations, and with many different appearances. Some of them will never leave spirit form but instead will just use ectoplasm to give themselves a slightly more solid appearance. Many societies from beyond the third dimension will be represented." He waved his thin hand at the others. "Some of us are represented here. We're only the tiniest percentage, of course."

Paul studied the eyes of each being at the table. It was obvious that each of them was dedicated to the mission of accelerating Earth's evolution.

Thaline spoke up. "Greetings, Paul. I suppose my presence here surprises you somewhat. I requested the assistance of Korton in order to present myself to you. As a gesture from my society to Earth's, I want to inform you that the events in Earth's realm will be of a degree

402

sufficient to warrant my society's interaction. As you're aware, we rarely issue our energy into third dimensional realities. However, this time in history is an exception."

Paul smiled at her. "I was pleased to see you here. I'm even more pleased to know that your assistance is being offered. From my point of view, the view that I have from actually being on Earth during this time, I can see the monumental effort that will be needed to accelerate the vibrations. Your assistance will be invaluable, I'm certain."

Thaline bowed her head slightly, acknowledging his respect for her society.

Eia drew Paul's attention by speaking quietly. "As you're aware, the Ashtar Command has been interacting with many on Earth for quite some time. Recently, several years ago, the Haathors began to play a larger role. Of course, the Venutians, the Arcturians, and the others who live or work on some of the other planets in that galaxy have also been cooperating.

"The main reason that I brought you here from your meeting with Abraham is to alert you to the fact that two new communication portals will be activated soon. One of the portals will facilitate easier communication with Thaline's society, the Antarians. We've assigned a squad to oversee and contain the energies of that portal. As you're aware, it's critical that the communication exchange remain on a vibratory level that is compatible with the sensitivities of this society. If the vibrations are tainted, the portal will be closed." Her tone was firm. It was clear that there would be no debate or apology if the

403

time came that made it necessary to close the portal. The Antarians were a supreme race. No harm would be allowed to come to them.

Korton spoke again. "We wanted to thank you for the part you played in retrieving the tiles and transferring them to the next higher dimension. We are aware that circumstances caused you some difficulties with this assignment. Congratulations on coming through those circumstances unharmed."

Paul's eyes were solemn as he accepted Korton's compliment.

Korton continued. "The tiles, as you probably know, are now aboard The Dove. A group of assigned communication specialists have begun working with them to release the energies that have been encapsulated in them into the atmosphere of Earth. These energies will be released along the various crystalline grid lines, making them attainable by those on Earth who need to access them in order to take their next evolutionary step. We feel this method will be incredibly effective.

"For one, this will immediately make the energies accessible by anyone who chooses to learn from them. Secondly, the dispersing of these energies throughout the Earth grid will facilitate healing on all levels, personally as well as globally."

Solomon, who had been silent until now, set his hand on Paul's shoulder and left it there. Paul recognized the gesture as a message that their forces would be united. As Paul moved on to the next phase of his mission on Earth, Solomon would offer his support.

Eia touched Paul's hand lightly. "You know all of this on an intuitive level. And so you're not here to hear these things. These are only confirmations of what you already know. The critical thing that we need to say to you is this. We're going to ask you to take a more active part in working with these Earth grids. You've had the tiles in your hands, which means that you are now infused with their energy. A Universal Law is that like attracts like. And so it is that the energy of the tiles in your personal energy field will attract the energy of the tiles that are now in the higher dimensions. You have the capacity to act as a conduit, if you care to look at it like that."

"In addition," Korton interrupted, "you will be taking a more active communication role with each of us in the room. The combined energy of those of us here, as well as each individual energy, will assist you. You'll also be assisting the others aboard the Esartania, those who aren't here with us right now. With your permission, we can transmit energy to you and you can then consciously radiate that energy out to the Earth grids from below. We will be working with the exterior grid at the same time as you will be working with the interior grid."

Paul blinked, attempting to assimilate the information. What was being suggested seemed to be a huge task. He asked the first question that occurred to him. "I won't be the only one doing this, will I?"

Korton smiled. "No. Not at all. There are many volunteers working with the interior grid. Your

405

participation will only be unique in the aspect of having physically interacted with the tiles."

In his mind's eye Paul could easily visualize the grids that spanned Earth. He experimentally imagined a thread of energy and light being placed into the grid energy. The grid reacted almost as though it was an entity with a mind of its own. It instantly absorbed the energy he had sent, transmuted it into a pale orange-yellow color, and radiated the color through its threads.

Korton, who had been mentally observing Paul's experiment, commented. "The grids are strictly monitored. Any incompatible energy that attempts to interfere with the original purpose of the grid will be instantly rejected if it's not possible to transmute it the instant it is recognized. The incompatible energy is forced along a path until it reaches an energy field that has the capacity to transmute it."

Thaline caught Paul's eye before she moved her gaze to Solomon's. She smiled tenderly at him and spoke to the others in the room. "I have no doubt in Paul's ability to handle this job. I would, however, ask a special task of Solomon."

Paul felt Solomon nod slightly, urging her to continue.

"I would like you to establish a special circuit of energy that connects Paul to Questar. I would like to return there and interact with him from there, rather than stay here on the Esartania."

"That can be easily done," Solomon responded. He patted Paul's shoulder lightly. "I'll do that immediately upon his return."

Eia glanced up at him. "How much interaction does Paul have at this time with his other guides?"

"For the most part, his communication is with me."

Eia nodded thoughtfully, as though a question in her mind had been answered. "Now I understand." She turned back to Paul. "I met with Maritha a short time ago. Of course you know that she's another of your spirit guides." She continued without waiting for Paul's acknowledgment "She has a very different vibration and origin than Solomon's, which you're used to. But she was expressing a need to interact with you more directly." She eyed Paul seriously. "I would suggest that you spend some time fine-tuning your energy field in order to facilitate easier communication with the rest of your guidance. They have much they would like to share with you."

Paul pursed his lips and nodded in agreement. "I will definitely do that. I didn't realize I was neglecting anyone."

Solomon pressed his fingers into Paul's shoulders. "Each person on Earth has guides who walk with them through the years. Yes, we're used to being unacknowledged because we can't be seen and heard by the lower dimensions. By most people, that is. But, the energies are being cleansed and heightened on Earth. It's going to make it easier for everyone to interact with this

407

realm." He tapped Paul lightly on the cheek, a gentle reprimand. "Try it. You'll like it."

Whether it was the touch on his cheek or Solomon's joke, Paul woke up with a smile on his face. An hour later he had finished his breakfast and the Bronco was packed once again. The drive to San Francisco was lonely without Jessica. He missed the sound of her singing. But each of them had a part to play. He didn't know if he was going to walk through his life on Earth alone or not. But his priorities had shifted. His civilization was counting on him to carry out his part of the mission.

He checked into a small motel on the outskirts of the big city, bought himself a meal at the restaurant next door to it, and went back to his room to make some phone calls. An hour later he had succeeded in making an appointment for the next day.

The building looked exactly as it had on the large screen Abraham had shown him. Paul took the elevator up and found himself waiting in an area that also looked exactly the same as it had on-screen. He knew before he walked into the man's office what he would look like. Extending his hand, he shook the hand of destiny.

The man was tall and solid, neatly dressed in a dark gray suit and charcoal-colored tie. His salt-and-pepper hair was trimmed close to his head. Intelligence was clear in his eyes, which were bright with interest. It was obvious that he was a good listener. It was how he had reached the success that he had. He was clean-shaven and smelled slightly of peppermint. Paul noticed a small bowl of the cellophane-wrapped mints on the desk in front of him as he sat in the chair indicated. The chair faced a row of windows that overlooked San Francisco Bay.

As Paul told his story, Richard Hamilton listened carefully. He was fifty-three. He'd seen enough in his lifetime to believe in the possibility of just about anything. The story he was hearing was fantastic and almost unbelievable. But the man sitting across from him emanated with sincerity. His words had the ring of truth. When he talked about the appearance of a fleet of alien craft appearing over the Pacific Ocean, Richard couldn't stop an instinctual glance toward the window.

It was this involuntary reaction, this subconscious acknowledgment that what he was hearing could possibly be the truth, that caused him to listen more closely. If he couldn't resist believing in the possibilities that Paul was naming, it was certain that others would react the same way. Normally he made decisions only after weeks of mulling over facts and getting opinions from at least a dozen members of his staff. For the first time in his life he was inclined to throw caution to the wind and commit himself to a project without even a minute of thought.

His customary sense of caution wouldn't let him give Paul an absolute, though. He pressed his intercom, asked his assistant to call in Phil and Monique, his two assistant publishers. He sat back, his fingers bridged and his eyes surveying Paul carefully as they waited for the

409

arrival of the two.

A minute later the two executives appeared in the doorway. Trim and professional in an expensive-looking, tailored suit, Monique eyed Paul speculatively from behind small, gold-rimmed glasses. She was thin, business-like, and unsmiling as her cool hand shook his.

Phil, in a slightly rumpled suit, gave Paul a different impression. The tall, robust man stepped forward eagerly to shake his hand. It was rare for Richard to have them meet a client without first meeting with them alone to let them in on whatever was going on. Phillip could remember it happening only once during the eleven years that he'd worked for the firm. He was eager to meet the person who had been able to get Richard to bend the rules.

When everyone was seated, Paul sat back and listened as Richard outlined his story for the others.

Monique's cool blue eyes surveyed Paul as Richard fell into silence and waited for the reaction of the two executives. She was an intimidating woman. Direct in her assessment of him, she sat straight and tall, her legs and arms crossed firmly. Her jacket and skirt were black, her blouse a crisp white. Her eyes snapped with intelligence and an unspoken warning that she was not someone you'd want to tamper with. "This is a true story or one that you made up?" she asked coolly.

"It's true," Paul said quietly. He couldn't allow himself to be intimidated. The success of his personal mission would depend on his strength to confront and

410

deal with skepticism.

She studied him without reaction.

Phil's reaction was more palatable. His brown, spaniel eyes sparkled with enthusiasm. He shifted his weight, leaned forward with his forearms on his thighs, and confronted Paul. "If this is true, which I'm assuming it is because you couldn't make something like this up, this story needs to be told."

Paul nodded. "That's exactly why I'm here."

Phil looked over the desk at Richard. "What do you think? I know you," he said without waiting for an answer. "You wouldn't have called us here if you weren't inclined to make an offer."

Richard leaned back in his chair, tented his fingers over his chest, and nodded slightly. "I'm tempted," he said briefly.

Monique's eyes snapped to Paul. "Have you ever written anything?"

Paul shook his head no. He had expected the question. His response could end this meeting.

Monique turned her head quickly, staring at Richard. "I don't know. We're dealing with no experience whatsoever."

Richard nodded affirmatively. "That's true. But we're dealing with one hell of a story too. True or not, it's

411

compelling."

Phil spoke up. "What's wrong with hiring a ghostwriter?" He turned to Paul. "You can work with someone like that, can't you? Tell someone your story and help them with the writing of it?"

Paul's reply surprised everyone, including himself. "I'd like to take a shot at writing this myself. You might think I'm nuts when I say this but...." He paused, thinking carefully about his next words. "You've listened so far so, please, listen to this. I'm communicating with these beings. I believe they'll help me write it. After all, it's really their story, not mine." He glanced from one to the other. "I think I can do it because I know they'll be helping me."

The room fell into silence as each of them re-played his suggestion in their minds. Paul watched as Richard and Phil communicated silently with their eyes. He couldn't see Monique's expression, since she had turned away from all of them and was studying the view outside the window.

Richard broke the silence. "We'll make you this offer," he said strongly. The tone of his voice made his decision clear to everyone in the room. "You'll write the first one hundred pages. We'll review them. If we like it, we'll offer you an advance to finish the book. If we don't, we'll hire a ghostwriter of our own choosing and you'll split the advance with him or her. That is, if it's still compelling enough at that time. What do you say?"

Paul found himself nodding in agreement. He felt

pressure on both sides of his head, as though an invisible force was holding his head, causing him to nod. "That sounds fair," he responded robotically. His thoughts tried to race toward the obstacles that would confront him. He forced himself back into the moment. He nodded again. "More than fair," he added.

The meeting ended in a blur. Paul found himself back in the Bronco and headed toward the motel before he was even aware of having left the building.

CHAPTER FOURTEEN

HE SETTLED ON A SMALL COTTAGE rental that he found on the outskirts of Santa Cruz. It was furnished. All of the utilities were paid with one check to the landlord. It had all of the conveniences he needed without a lot of hassles. He drove into town, purchased a laptop and settled down to write his story. It took him less time than he thought it would to finish the one hundred pages that Richard had requested. He knew that it was because he had the help of the higher dimensions.

Falling asleep each night, he could feel the presence of Solomon beside him. Together they would float, side by side, toward the Esartania. Their relationship had grown into a partnership. Occasionally he could sense Maritha's presence, though he couldn't see her. He had mentally invited her to join him in his mission, opening his mind to welcome her communication but, as yet, he hadn't been able to hear her speak. He hoped that it was only due to the fact that he was totally consumed by his need to finish his manuscript.

During the nights, aboard the Esartania, Korton usually greeted him. Slender and pale skinned, his almond-shaped eyes scanned Paul each night, evaluating him as though he were looking for signs of illness. When he found nothing out of order, he would place his long fingers on Paul's shoulder and grip him gently. Paul took this as a sign of affection and approval, though Korton rarely vocalized his thoughts.

414

The majority of the time spent on board was spent in the crystal room. Zo and Godo glided smoothly around the room, arranging crystals, placing various ones beside him as he sat in the crystal chair. Solomon always hovered nearby, silent and watchful. Paul could sense that he was undergoing cellular healing and changes.

Most mornings he awakened refreshed though, on occasion, he awakened with a sense of pressure in various parts of his body.

During his morning walks along the beaches or the boardwalk or through the neighborhood, fresh bits of wisdom came to his mind easily. He developed the habit of carrying a pencil and notebook in his pocket so that he could jot notes as he walked.

As he stood at the counter in the local self-printing shop, waiting for the machine to spit out a copy of his manuscript pages, he was proud of himself. He'd done something he hadn't thought he could do. He was content. He had stopped searching and, in doing so, he had found himself.

Deciding to drive the papers to Richard, rather than mail them, he phoned for an appointment. The next morning he headed back to San Francisco.

This time only Richard and Phil were in attendance. Paul sat quietly in the waiting room while they reviewed his presentation. When he couldn't sit still any longer, he paced. He was standing in front of the waiting room window looking at the city below when the door behind him opened.

415

Phil was approaching him with an outstretched hand. "You're a natural," he said cheerfully. "It will have to be cleaned up, of course, but the story's there. That's what matters." He slapped Paul on the shoulder. "Come on in. Let's wrap this up with Richard and then get some lunch. You like Cajun shrimp? I know a place that will knock your socks off."

Totally full of shrimp, excitement, and victory, with a check large enough to sustain him for at least six months, Paul drove away from San Francisco, driving toward a future that he would never have imagined for himself. He wasn't startled at all when Solomon appeared in the seat beside him.

"Congratulations!"

"Thanks." Paul beamed at him. "Who would have thought it?" He shook his head in amazement.

"I would have. After all, it was the plan all along."

Paul stared at him so long that he almost drove off the road before he realized what he was doing. He corrected the wheel. "What do you mean? You mean I planned to be a writer all along?"

"Your soul did. It just took a while for your personality to catch up."

Paul thought about it. "All of this is a part of that pre-arranged lifetime that has been hinted about off and on then? I was never meant to be a high school coach?"

416

Solomon shook his head. "No. You were meant to do that. It was a piece of the puzzle. It was the step that took you to the next step."

"I would never have thought I'd choose this route. The thought of writing never entered my mind."

"When the personality allows the soul to lead, you can find yourself going in directions you would never imagine. Quite often, the personality has a tendency to want to protect, to guard against the unknown. On the other hand, the soul knows all things and so nothing is feared. There is no such thing as fear, or boundaries, hesitation or limitation at the Soul level. The ultimate goal that the Creator of this existence would like to see is for each soul to express its total and unique self without hesitation or limitation."

Solomon interrupted himself by reaching out and touching Paul's arm lightly. "I didn't come here to talk philosophy with you." He pointed toward the ocean. "Look."

Paul followed his finger. His mouth dropped open in shock. Carefully, as though he were dreaming, he pulled the Bronco to the shoulder of the road. Opening his door, he stepped out. Solomon did the same. They stood, shoulder to shoulder, staring toward the west as the sun's rays glinted off the edges of a large alien craft that hovered in the far distance.

Other cars were pulling over as well. People were stepping from their cars. Some were silent with awe.

417

Some tugged on each other's arms, overcome with excitement. One man, tall, silent, and familiar-looking, stood staring not at the craft but at Paul. Feeling his gaze, Paul turned. He knew instantly that the man was the same man who had held a gun on him in Nevada. He touched Solomon's arm and turned him gently toward the stranger.

Ignoring the fact that he was in ancient robes and sandals and that people were now staring at him, Solomon approached the man with a firm step. Paul followed.

"This is only the first," Solomon said, stopping a few feet from the man. "There are quite a few more coming. The people of Earth are not going to stand by and let you control them again. Once was enough. We're here to make sure they win this time."

The man gave him a grim smile. "You said the same thing last time."

TO BE CONTINUED in
"PEACE MISSION,"
3rd Volume of
OTHER WORLDS: The Series

WHAT THE FIRST READERS OF "TILES" HAD TO SAY

******

"I just bought from Amazon the paperback version of Called." I know I have to read it... Something really 'curious' happened to me a couple of days ago.

I saw a post you made here on FB from 'The Mayan Tiles' and, because of it, I went to Amazon to look for the book to see if I could 'sneak peek' a bit of it. I couldn't find it. But I did find 'Called' and I read the back-cover. Not even two minutes passed after I read it ... than an AVALANCHE, a THUNDERBOLT of information overwhelmed me as I haven't experienced in a while. I SAW all the answers I've been silently wondering about for the past few months. And that's not all.....

That day, I was going to do some commercial diving. The 'download' (this is the best way I can describe it) of insights, information, communication didn't stop. I felt I was literally listening to a broadcasting universal radio station in which the information didn't stop coming for the next several hours. I just KNEW IT. I just felt it all the way! Can't wait to read it! Much Love!"

Adrian A. Boniardi, Awakening Life Coach, Founder/CEO 'Mediitar, Underwater Meditation'

419

Fascination with every event... As I journeyed with the courageous characters in the story; I found myself contemplating the connections in my own life experiences as one with what Lauren has described. Paul with his quest for discovery, Jessica exhuberating with what can be, Solomon the wise unattatched guardian, so many hopeful visions which after reading this book evokes a feeling of greatness. Living from soul may seem out of reach, but ask yourself if living small is really serving a purpose. I look forward to future books by Lauren as limitless as time itself. Reading TILES was a wonderful reminder to me that living from a different perspective is not only possible but so necessary for all of mankind.

In appreciation,

Angela Johnston

Lauren, you are truly talented and I loved your 2nd book in the series even better than CALLED. I never believed I could as you are so "right there" answering my questions before they leave my mind in these books. Thank you for sharing The Mayan Tiles with me. I feel like I am in on a fantastic secret, one I do not want to be left out of. Thank you again.

Un-named reader, anonymous by request

MORE ENDORSEMENTS FOR "CALLED"

"CALLED incorporates many themes ... ufology and ufo crash recoveries, ET contact, and expanding human awareness ... Most unique is the fact that the author has articulated her personal interpretations of Truth, Soul, and Existence/Experiences, finding ways to express her knowledge of each by weaving specific insights and awakenings into her unusual, engrossing plotline."
Paul Davids, Executive Producer/Co-Writer, "Roswell" and Producer/Writer/Director, "Starry Night"

"CALLED ... appeals to both adults and young adults ... Many will enjoy it as a wonder-filled tale ... for some -- those often called 'wanderers' or 'starpeople' -- it will affirm their sense of identity and purpose here and 'elsewhere.'"
Jody Boyne, Librarian, University of Hawaii and Trans-human Counseling Psychologist

"Drama, suspense, humor and wisdom: CALLED has it all. Packed with profound spiritual truth, it's a 'must read' for metaphysicians and ET buffs alike."
Tony Stubbs, author of 'An Ascension Handbook'

".....CALLED, a fascinating metaphysical novel written by author, Lauren Zimmerman, described as 'mystic, author, artist' and creator of a series of books.....For those who loved 'Bringers of the Dawn,' enjoyed ET (the movie), and entertain the possibilities of other intelligence in the universe, this is for you! Well written and easy to read, this adventure tale touches upon many metaphysical subjects and spiritual truths."

Ocean Unity Book Club, Newport, Oregon

Official Apex Reviews Rating: 5 Stars

When vivid, detailed memories of another planet and family begin to surface, Paul is thrust in the midst of a daunting identity crisis. Finally deciding to embrace the truth of his unearthly origins, Paul soon finds himself reminded of the crucial mission that he accepted prior to visiting the earth: to reestablish a relationship between the people of earth and their universal friends and family. As the fulfillment of his mission leads him across the country, Paul soon becomes a hero to the imperiled occupants of a crashed alien space craft, ultimately learning secret truths about life, love, and the mystical workings of the world surrounding us.

Throughout the pages of Called, her imaginative, eye-opening new offering, author Lauren Zimmerman takes the reader on a mind-bending journey through the unfettered depths of time-tested, universal truths. As he progresses on his enlightening journey of exploration and self-discovery, Paul's spiritual metamorphosis will no doubt mirror a similar transformation in readers as they discover – in the same startling fashion – the deeper meaning behind life as we know it. Definitely not for the closed-minded, Called is a powerful invitation to challenge your own preconceived notions about the world in which you live, beckoning you to a level of higher thought from which the light of true understanding forever shines. A thoroughly engaging read.

~ APEX REVIEWS
www.apexreviews.net

WHAT READERS HAVE TO SAY ABOUT "CALLED"

"I loved this book. It filled me with hope and smiles. I am SO ready for the next one! (and the next and the one after that...)
Kris Billyeu, Portland, OR

"One of the best books I have ever read. Once I started it, I couldn't put it down. CALLED has changed my life dramatically and inspired me to find my 'spiritual path.' The story that I read never really leaves my thoughts daily. I think it will always be with me and this is an added plus. This is the first book that seemed to jump out and answer my questions before I finished thinking them. I was impressed and amazed."
Vickie Connell, Blaine, MN

"An exciting and insightful book that helped me to open to greater understanding of what I am here for. This book helped me to realize what I have been feeling about outer dimensions to be true."
Anna, Newport, OR

"I loved learning that what I always felt is true was written in this book as to be true!"
Sharon, Hawaii

"I had just finished a documented book about alien visitations and the military's perpetual cover-ups when CALLED was sent by a friend. Coincidence? I think not! I loved reading her 'novel,' and I suspect it will resonate with so many of us around the world who feel

424

that the 'shift is coming.' I simply cannot wait for the next in the series! I feel such hope and excitement!"

Nancy Leonard, Waldport, OR

"Serious but entertaining ... this book looks to be a future classic."

Bob Brennan, Waldport, OR

"I found CALLED to be thought-provoking, very well written, and suspenseful and most of all ... very validating."

Elaine Correia, Waldport, OR

"We need to hear what this book has to say NOW!"

Anja, Waldport, OR

"CALLED helps human beings become open to endless possibilities for themselves and Planet Earth."

Ruth, Waldport, OR

"As I read CALLED (chapter 18) I was surrounded by a brilliant rainbow. It provided me with the comfort I was seeking and I was overcome with joy and emotion."

An anonymous reader via e-mail

"CALLED will keep you in suspense, take you on a fantastic adventure, touch your emotions deeply, and offer new information as teachings with sincerity and gentle humor. If you enjoyed 'ET,' you'll love CALLED. It grabs your attention and curiosity on page one and doesn't let go until you've finished the book!"

Nancy Brennan, Waldport, OR

"This book represents one person's experiences and

425

journey toward spiritual enlightenment, during a time of great change in Man's development. The author has taken a topic of considerable controversy (i.e. 'are we alone and have we been visited') and woven an intriguing story of awakening, awareness, and hope for the future. Set in a time of one man's questioning his purpose and search for answers, the author crafts an enjoyable story that can be read as fantasy or fact-based. I found myself reading and re-reading each page as I searched for the deeper meanings hidden in the development of this story. It is a timeless and never-ending story that will make for a good read for adolescents and adults alike."

Jimmy Brown, Tigard, OR

The "Other Worlds" Series

Called
The Mayan Tiles
Peace Mission
Choosing Universes

by
Lauren Zimmerman

Proudly Published By
nLight Press
www.nlightpress.com

CALLED

"I awakened to the truth ... I am from elsewhere. Upon awakening, I was called to rescue a fallen craft. Some of my brothers lived, some did not. The opportunity to leave with them slipped through my fingers like rain. I remained to tell my story ... and the story of what is to come."

Vivid dreams of other worlds and other realities lead Paul to the realization that he has incarnated on Earth from another place and time with a specific mission-to awaken and inform humanity that reality as they know it is about to change. He sees how the human race has limited itself by defining its reality too narrowly. By breaking through the barriers of ignorance, he must clear the way for interaction with civilizations from beyond Earth's current reality.

His first mission, however, is to rescue the alien survivors of a downed spacecraft, an experience that convinces him that the reality he knows is but a miniscule fragment of a much larger picture, and that his "extraterrestrial" dreams are simply natural avenues of communication used by the inhabitants of his "home world." The goal, he is told, is to awaken mankind to the fact that they are not alone in the universe, and of the imminent arrival of ETs.

THE MAYAN TILES

Ancient tiles were brought to Earth many years ago. Given to the inhabitants of Earth by a species that lives beyond its borders, keys of wisdom for Earth's evolution were offered. But before the tiles could be revealed, those on Earth who were the custodians were slaughtered. Now the task to retrieve the tiles and once again attempt

428

to reveal them to Earth's society is given to Paul.

Still working to assimilate the image of Grandfather being lifted into the belly of a spacecraft, Paul and Jessica gather themselves for their journey into the jungles of Belize. But they're not alone. Many others know that the tiles exist. But only Paul and Jessica know where they have been hidden. The others watch and wait, stalking them like prey.

Wisdom from other worlds weaves through Paul's experience, urging him to remember who he is, urging him to live the truth of a reality far beyond Earth's current limitations. With the tiles in his possession, the veils between 'heaven' and Earth dissolve, leaving him with the task of accepting that the only thing standing between himself and the full awareness of existence is himself.

PEACE MISSION

"PEACE MISSION" is the ultimate voyage into the world of possibilities. Addressing the issue that we are not alone in our Universe, and that all things are made up of energy, and that energy has no boundaries, we must accept that the energy that we as a society are generating is impacting not only the world that we CAN see but the worlds that we CANNOT.

What if the day was to come when every society in our Universe banded together and arrived upon our shores to tell us that we are not alone? What if this fleet of other-world beings called upon us to explain? What if we were called upon to explain our history and our continuing wars? How would we begin to heal the rifts between our worlds? How would our world change if we were suddenly aware that there are thousands, possibly millions, of others watching us ... and waiting?

429

As dawn breaks over the Pacific Ocean, thousands watch and wait. Is that the sun touching the hull of a hovercraft? Is that the beginning vision of a mothership? Are they coming? What will they say? What will they do?

As thousands of crafts slowly descend from the sky, lining the shores of the Pacific Ocean from Mexico to Canada ... our world holds its breath and waits for its destiny to unfold.

CHOOSING UNIVERSES

"CHOOSING," as it is affectionately called by its author, was actually the first book given to her in the sequence of dreams that birthed this book series. The very title alone entices the subconscious and stimulates the human imagination. And not without delivering what it promises!

Having completed his mission on Earth, Paul is given the opportunity to travel aboard The Esartania, a mothership. Existence, as it was explained to the author during her life-after-death experience, is described to Paul as he watches universes pass by with Korton, the Commander, standing by his side. The freedom to choose his next reality is overwhelming. And behind every moment sits his yearning for the woman who is his destiny. But where is she? Will he choose the universe where she resides or will he postpone their union by choosing wrongly?

"But," advises Korton, "there is no such thing as a 'wrong' choice. There is only the path of your soul and its quest for understanding. All that remains is how you, Paul, the personality, choose to learn on behalf of your eternal soul."

OTHER BOOKS PUBLISHED BY
nLIGHT PRESS

MOMENTS OF MASTERY
By Lauren Zimmerman

LISTENING TO WISDOM: Volumes 1 though 5
By Lauren Zimmerman

WHERE IS MY FERNANDO?
By Lauren Zimmerman

Watch for future books by
nLight Press

Dedicated to the spiritual evolution of Humankind

www.nlightpress.com

Made in United States
Orlando, FL
23 March 2022